Vagobond Media Presents

Future World 2323

Edited by
Rionna Morgan
C.D. Damitio
And E.R. Donaldson

WHITNEY MORGAN

Vagobond Media Presents:
Future World 2323
Paperback Edition
Whitney Morgan Media

This is a work of fiction. All characters and events portrayed in this
novel are either fictitious or used fictitiously.

Cover art and illustrations by E. R. Donaldson

https://www.vagobond.com
https://whitneymorganmedia.com
https://www.mythicnorthpress.com

ISBN: 978-1-962668-16-3

Table of Contents

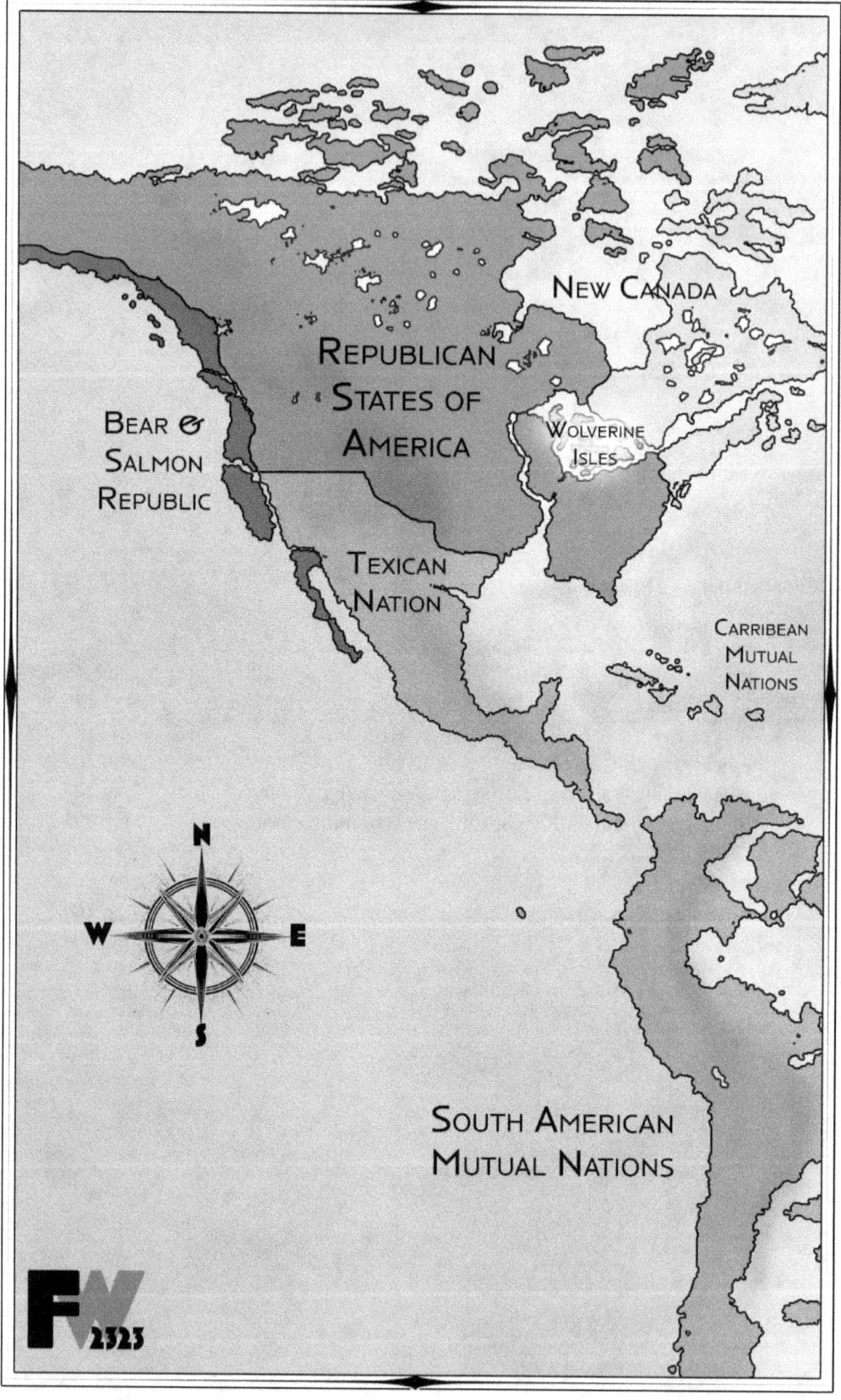

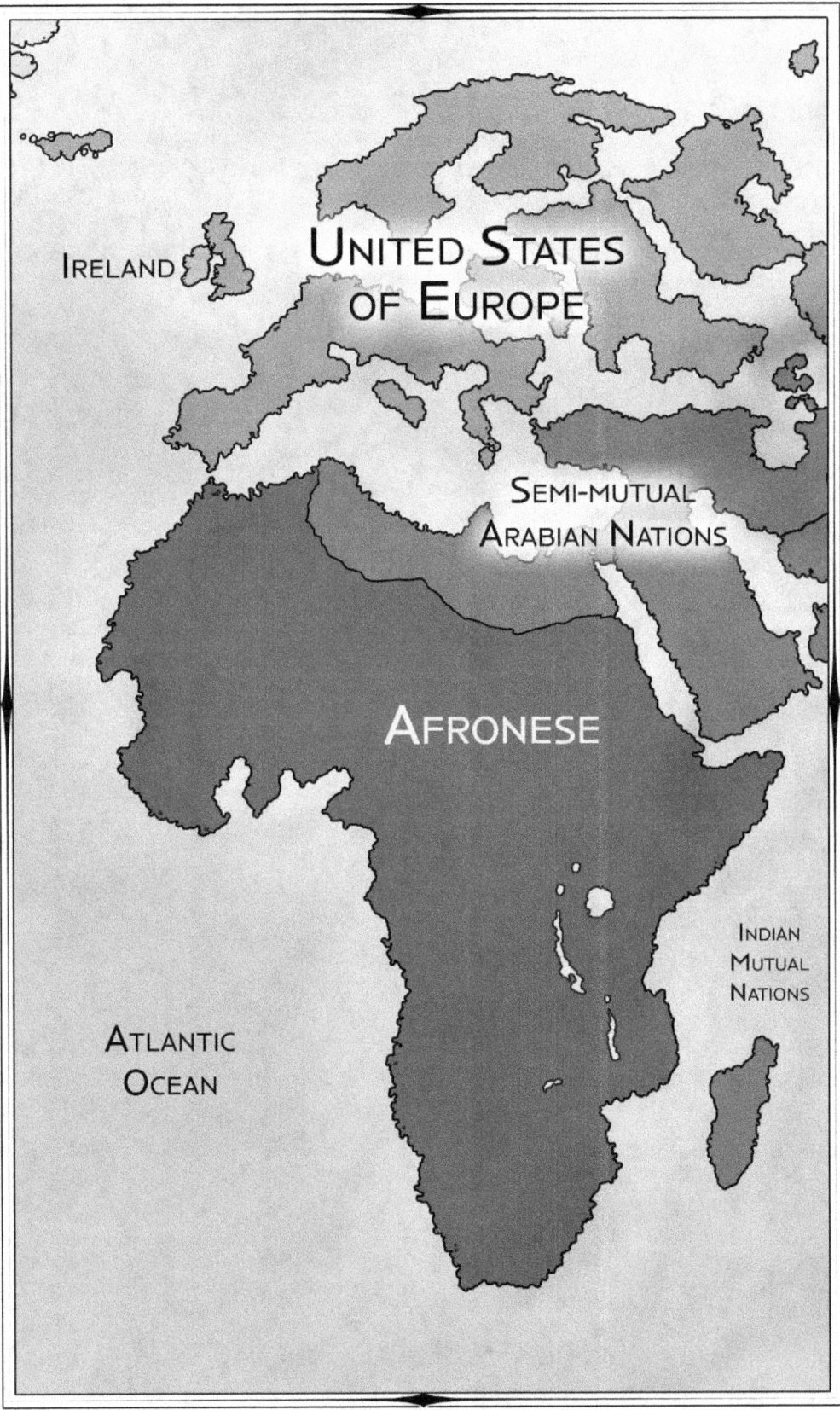

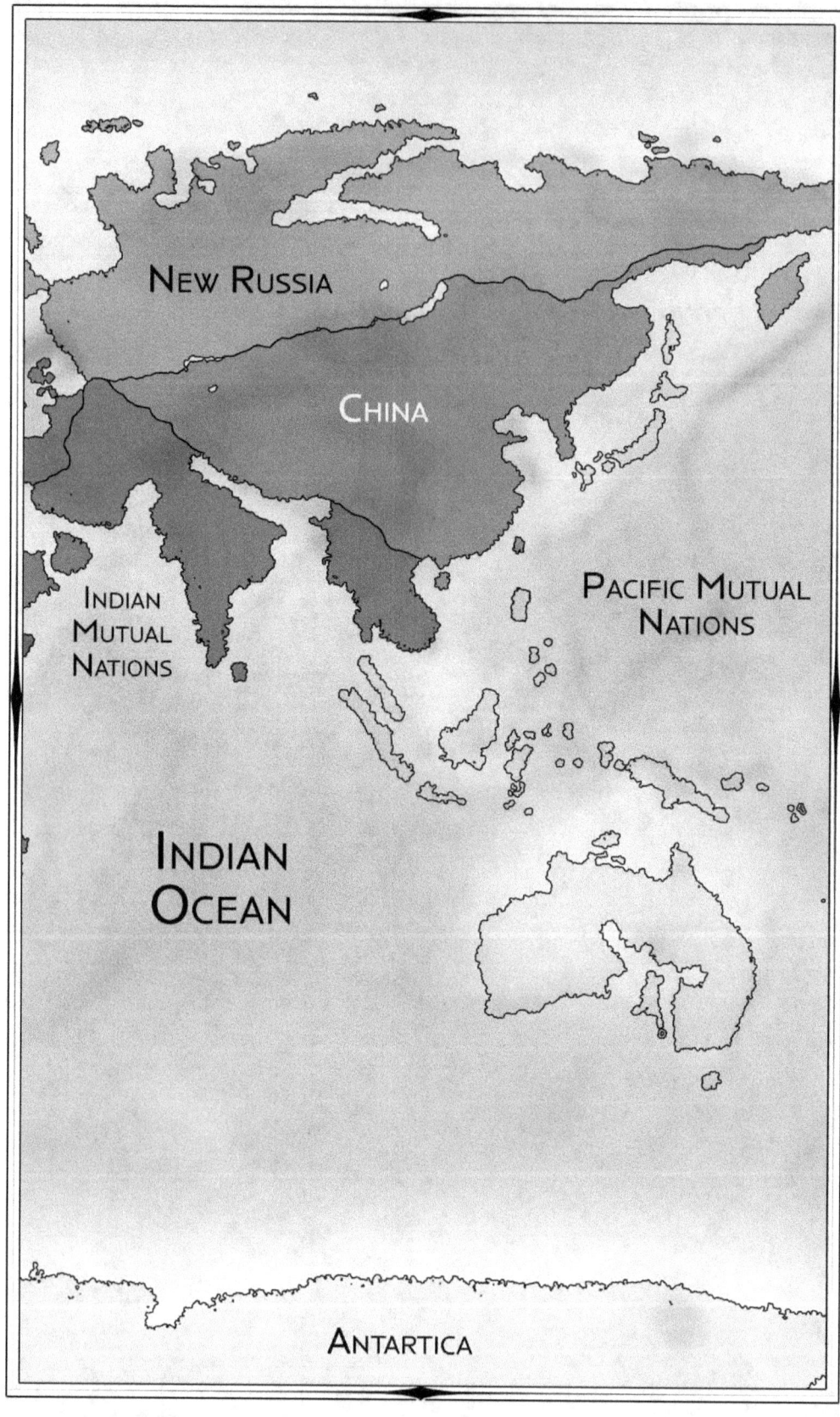

Foreword
Past Worlds: Future Worlds
by CD Damitio

In the midst of the pandemic, while mostly trapped within the four walls of my small Honolulu apartment, I discovered an obscure science fiction novel written in 1890 by William Morris, the socialist founder of the Arts and Crafts Movement. In *News from Nowhere,* Morris transports a socialist gentleman of his time and place to a future socialist utopia three-hundred-years in his future.

The prose was dated and many of the concepts and ideas no longer made sense in the world we live in, but it occurred to me that Morris and I were, in a sense, living parallel lives more than a century apart. I also identify as a socialist (though a libertarian one). I also live in a capitalist society that seems to have taken a wrong turn (or many). I also live on an island. I also think about possible futures and love the vehicle of science fiction to explore them.

Some of the ideas that Morris put forth—made perfect sense to me for a future utopia—even more than a century later. Some did not. I had ideas of my own.

"What if I were to use the same vehicle Morris created, but write a modern version of this story?" I thought.

I would create my own characters, place it in my society instead of England (the island of Oahu in Hawaii), and update the language and some of the concepts—plus include some concepts and ideas that Morris had not. The idea was too good to ignore—and besides—I had time on my hands— like most of us did in 2020.

Notes from Nowhere was born. I went further than Morris had. I talked about the world and the other countries in it. I discussed the fate of my country, The United States and how North America had splintered. I touched on the political entities that had grown around the world—but all without leaving Hawaii.

Readers enjoyed my book and when the opportunity came to publish it on the blockchain as a web3 book with the German blockchain publisher Creatokia, I jumped at the chance. We produced the audio book and released the chapters as NFTs. It was exciting to be working in web3 with a book about Hawaii set three centuries in the future.

I wanted to explore more of the world I had created and what had come of the United States. In 2022, E.R. Donaldson put out a call for science fiction and fantasy stories about winter in an anthology called *Mythic Winter*. I queried with a story set in the Texican Nation—but co-existing with the Mutual Nation of Hawaii (three-centuries from now).

Rather than satiating my desire to explore the future world—this just made me thirstier to do it. I now realized I couldn't do it alone. I reached out to E.R and several other writers I was working with in web3 to see if they wanted to help define the future world. I recruited a total of ten writers who all pitched writing stories set in different regions but existing within the same world. For various reasons, some of them didn't meet the deadline—but those who did—really nailed it.

T Dylan Daniel—one of the founders of PageDAO wrote a story set in his native Texas; Rionna Morgan, a romance writer who once outsold Stephen King decided to bring magic and Ireland into play in the future; E.R. Donaldson, a noted science fiction author and gamer created a feudal technocracy in the Wolverine Isles, a wasteland existing on what was once his home state of Michigan; Aparna Merchant (Quanta), a fashion writer and designer based in India explored the concept of interdimensional beings attempting to live in the world of the future and to navigate their own path forward; Ameera Rashid, a Persian writer who had also taken part in *Mythic Winter* created a tale of power and energy set in the 'Semi-Mutual Nations' of what is today the Middle East.

We've only begun scratching the surface of *Future World*. In this anthology you will find all those stories along with my Texican Nation story reprinted from *Mythic Winter* and a new story where my protagonist and his friends from that story journey to The Bear and Salmon Republic

(what was once the West Coast of North America from Baja to Alaska.)

We hope to eventually bring you the other stories that were queried for this volume, and we hope that these stories may inspire you to write your own stories set in our *Future World*. There is so much of it still to be explored from the Afronese nations to the sinister RSA and Russian dictatorships.

I am honored to share this palette with all of these talented writers and visionaries—and with you!

- CD Damitio

The Texican Blizzard of 2323
by CD Damitio

Chapter 1

It was colder than it should have been. That was the first thing that went through Charles Actor's mind when he stepped out the door of his one-bedroom cabin in Presidio, Texas. Sure, this was a mountain cabin—and it was November—but this was also Texas during the hottest year on record to date: 2023.

He hadn't had his coffee yet, and it was a short trip back inside to grab a hoodie and a knit cap before coming back out onto his balcony to enjoy his morning cup—which still sat steaming on the wooden table right where he'd left it. There was an electric feeling about the air this morning. Though he wasn't excited about the task that lay ahead of him, his body tingled with anxiety, nonetheless. He had no idea why.

He was going to have to take his truck into town, get grain for the horses, refill his propane tanks, and grab some groceries at the Y-Mart. None of that was what he was dreading.–

His lawyer had called the night before—the divorce papers had come through, and he needed to stop by and sign them. It wasn't that he regretted the divorce—he and Margie had fallen out of love decades ago, and the divorce was only the finalization of a four-year separation that had been welcomed by both of them—the dread was something else. An actual divorce decree meant that he was cut loose, free, unmarried, unhindered, and unattached. While it was the same state, he had been living in for nearly half a decade, the finality of signing the papers filled him with doubt, dread, and misgivings.

Over the top of all that, though, was this electric feeling brought on by the brisk cold and the otherworldly glow he detected when he looked up at that sky.

Finishing his coffee and morning chores, Charles unhitched his electric pickup truck from the charging tether and began the drive into town. As he began the trip, the familiar sense of his inner organs being jostled by the hard bumps of the road lulled him into a sense of comfort. Although the truck was not fully autonomous, it knew the road. He didn't need to pay much attention beyond braking and accelerating to make himself feel more comfortable. Ford had come a long way in just a few years, and he'd ordered the 2024 model early enough that he was able to be driving it even as 2023 wound down to a close.

The sense of unease returned suddenly. It wasn't that something had gone wrong, or that his attention had been harshly gotten. Instead, it was the lack of bumps and jostles. In an instant, his truck was riding as smoothly as if he were floating on an airfoil over the water. There were literally no bumps, no bounces, no creaks, none of what he expected on this drive into town. Instead, it was the smoothest sailing he had ever experienced in any car. He double checked to make sure the truck was actually moving. It was.

Looking out the window, the trees looked larger. The sky looked bluer. The road looked whiter. That couldn't be right. He looked again. The road was as white as porcelain but a non-reflective white that glowed with a warmth that made the road obvious without causing him to need to squint.

Charles decelerated and pulled the truck over. Something was wrong. It wasn't the truck, and it wasn't the road. It had to be him. Maybe he was having an aneurism or a brain clot. Maybe he'd died or was in a coma. All he knew was that what he was seeing and feeling couldn't be reality. He'd driven this road the week before, and it had been nothing like this. *Nothing* like this.

Stepping out of the truck, he walked around the back to the cliffside of the road. The gulch he loved so much was still there with its red, purple, and yellow clays and lines of stratigraphic complexity, but the bald mesas were no longer bald. Huge forests now covered the tops of the mesas—pine forests that had to be decades, maybe even centuries old. In the distance, the lonely gray-brown of the Chinati Mountains had disappeared. Instead, he saw green and white—emerald mountains capped with what looked like glaciers.

Charles shook his head violently in an effort to snap out of it. He pinched himself. None of it changed what was before him. Having no other plan, Charles got back in his pickup and drove toward the Presidio village—a town that, on a good day, had no more than five thousand residents (and that was only if you counted the five-hundred or so buried in the Boothill Cemetery). He decided to stop by the lawyer's office before making a trip to the clinic to make sure he hadn't suffered a stroke.

The road and mountains never changed back. Nothing was familiar, but he knew the way to Presidio. He would be there before long. He just had to cross the gulch, go through the pass, and then straight down into the village.

He was becoming comfortable with his new reality until he reached the top of the pass. There was a huge silver arch that stretched over the roadway—bigger than the St Louis Arch by at least double. Charles had grown up in St. Louis so he knew. This had to be at least 1200 feet.

The bases of the Arch also looked to be at least twice the size of the one in St. Louis. A fun fact that most people didn't know about the St. Louis Arch was that it was exactly as wide as it was tall. This arch seemed similar. Where it differed were the revolving glass doorways that led into the arch itself and the people streaming in and out. Charles could see glass elevators moving smoothly along the arch, presumably depositing passengers at offices or apartments. This Presidio Arch was far thicker than the St. Louis counterpart.

Charles had been curious as to why he hadn't seen a single vehicle on his trip thus far, but that dry spell suddenly ended. Hundreds of vehicles were parked in the lots beside the arch. Rampways led beneath the ground, which indicated there were probably hundreds more parked underneath. This insight led to Charles noticing that the elevators on the arch continued on into the ground. He wondered if the arch was actually a half-submerged oval that continued all the way around. It was a ridiculous thought, but then again, what was he looking at? Was it more ridiculous than that?

Charles pulled into the lot and parked his truck. The vehicles filling the lot were unlike anything he had ever seen. They were all curves, and the wheels were completely covered by the body. In fact, he couldn't see the wheels at all. There was a wide assortment of colors and shapes. Many of them appeared to be glowing. He wasn't in Presidio yet, but not stopping here was an impossibility. He *had* to figure out what was happening.

He walked to the archway entrance, noting that everyone he passed seemed to be speaking a unique Spanish dialect that he'd never heard before. It was heavily infused with English sounding words and sounds, but he couldn't quite understand everything they were saying despite being fluent in both Spanish and English. Reaching the archway entrance, he was grateful to be able to read the sign over the revolving doors, which was written in classic Spanish:

"Bienvenidos al Distrito Ojinaga-Presidio del Mega-Complejo Chihuahua. Recordamos aquí, a los patriotas que dieron su vida por traer la libertad a la Nación Texican en el año 2050. El Arco de la OPC se completó para celebrar el centenario de la Independencia Texican el 13 de octubre de 2150."

The translation had to be wrong.

"Welcome to the Ojinaga-Presidio District of the Chihuahua Mega-Complex. We remember here, the patriots who gave their lives to bring freedom to the Texican Nation in the year 2050. The OPC Archway was completed to celebrate the centennial of Texican Independence on October 13, 2150."

Or maybe the translation was right. In any event, Charles had a pretty good suspicion that he wasn't going to get those divorce papers signed today.

Chapter 2

From the moment he stepped into the OPC archway, Charles knew for certain he was in another world. Or maybe not another world, but a future variation of his own world that was so significantly different from his normal and day-to-day existence that he might as well have stepped into another galaxy.

Entering the arch, he had the distinct impression that the inside was considerably larger than the outside. An open space spread out before him with a wide metallic staircase leading into a hall of what seemed to be shopping mall sized proportions. There weren't shops in the sense that he would have thought of them, but there was definitely a considerable amount of commerce taking place.

People were moving within the space, each of them trailed by small doglike baskets that floated obediently beside or behind them. Not doglike in the sense of shape or design, but more in the sense that each floating basket seemed to know its owner and followed them loyally. They were not uniform in size or shape, but close enough to each other in appearance that they were relatable as a class.

Moving down the stairway, Charles had a sense that he was being observed—that someone or some*thing* was aware of him, focusing on his movements and actions. Turning, he found a softball sized object trailing him. It was light green in color, and when he reached for it, the top half vanished revealing a small basketlike interior. Moving his hand away, the top returned. He did this several times before deciding that maybe he was supposed to put something in it. He reached in his pocket and found a couple of coins. He dropped them in his "basket," and—much to his surprise—they fell right through, hitting the stairs and bouncing down to the base of the stairway.

They were only pennies, so he decided not to chase them. But he did look around to see if anyone had noticed his experimentation. Laughter came from below him, and he turned to see a smiling and friendly face beaming up at him.

"That's a funny way to get rid of your ancient coins, Senor." The young man attached to the smile strode up the stairs two at a time and held out the two pennies to Charles. "I assume you want these back; they're a little too valuable to just be throwing away."

Charles laughed, "They're just pennies, you can have them."

The young man's eyes widened, and he shook his head "Oh, no Senor. My abua told me all about the expectations and dangers of accepting expensive gifts from oddly dressed strangers. I'm not selling you my soul today." He held his hand out and Charles accepted the two pennies. Then, after dumping them in his pocket, he stuck out his hand. "I'm Charles Actor, what about you?"

The young man's skinny chest puffed with pride as he took Charles' hand in his own and responded. "I am Benito Mousalini Gonzalez, and I'm at your service." Benito was perhaps nineteen or twenty years old. He had strong white teeth and a smile that lit up the entire complex. He was skinny and wore a purple suit that immediately made Charles think of the Joker from Batman, but without any of the nefarious insanity for which that character was known. The name was a bit of a shock, but one which Charles decided would eventually be explained without his having to ask about it.

"Why'd the coins fall through?" he motioned to what he had already started thinking of as a cart.

Benito laughed. "You can't put anything in it until you have made a purchase in the Arch."

The simple explanation made sense to Charles, even though nothing else really did. He reached into his pocket "You said that these are worth a lot?" He held out a handful of coins towards Benito.

Benito pulled the knit cap off his head and immediately covered Charle's handful of coins. "Are you insane, Senor? Sure, no one will rob you here in the Arch, but you can't stay in here forever. If you are going to flash that kind of wealth, there will be people waiting to take it from you as soon as you leave the regulated areas. But surely you must know this?"

Charles heard suspicion in the young man's voice. Wrestling with whether to tell the truth or some other version of it, he decided that truth wasn't even something he could determine at this point and opted instead to follow the tried-and-true method of his ancestors and youth. He would play the clueless bumpkin. No matter where or when he was now, one thing was sure: somewhere there were people who had the reputation of being backwards and country—because no matter what, this was still Texas.

Putting on a thicker drawl than he needed, Charles lowered his voice to a conspiratorial whisper "Look, you obviously have figured out I'm not from around these parts." Then, in barely a whisper, he added, "In fact, I've never been here before. This is the first time I've ever been in this kind of place."—and then, just to confirm he was country—"I'm usually just taking care of the livestock."

Benito's eyes widened. "You're a cowboy!"

Charles gave an imperceptible nod, glad that the concept still existed. Then, making the kind of split-second decisions that Margie had never understood, he decided that the best thing he could do right now was to not only befriend, but recruit the boy as his helper.

"Shh!" Charles said, creating the air of conspiracy. "It's true. I've just come down from the ranch and I don't have hide nor hair about how to do bo diddly 'round here. If you'd be willing to help me figure things out, I'd be more than happy to make it worth your while."

Benito gave a strange half bow, half curtsy. The meaning was clear, but it was damn near the strangest gesture that Charles had ever seen from a young man who looked like he spent his life playing video games. "You are in luck, Senor. Not only do I speak English, but I'm also known as one of the best guides in the Texaco nation. I can lead you through the IRL and the OL worlds, help you meet the people you will need to know, take you deep into the blizzard, and teach you how to blend in as if you haven't spent all your life sodomizing sheep up in the wide-open mountains."

Charles's huge guffaw echoed through the interior of the archway mall. Numerous shoppers turned and looked at the pair, still standing at the edge of the wide stairway. It wasn't that Charles had never heard that particular joke about country people, it was the matter-of-fact, nothing-strange-here-ma'am tone in which Benito had said it—the same way he had said his historically off-putting name.

Benito looked confused. "Why are you laughing, Senor?"

Charles really didn't see any way he could explain himself or ask

Benito the origins of his colorful phrase without making things even more confusing. So, he asked the only question he knew would change the subject. "How much will you charge per day?"

Benito looked thoughtful, took his knit hat off. He pointed at Charles's open handful of coins, pointing at a bright zinc penny—a thing not even worth the cost of the zinc it was made from. "I'll take one of those as full payment," he said with boldness, belatedly adding "and if you are satisfied with my work, you can give me another at the completion."

Charles pulled the penny free of his pocket change and handed it to Benito. "Deal," he said.

Benito immediately pocketed the coin and then spit in his hand before offering it to Charles, who deferred. "I'll just take your word for it," Charles said. Benito didn't seem offended and wiped his hand on his trousers before getting down to business.

"First, we're going to exchange some of your coin collection for an Oil Dollar Credit card. Then we're going to get you some clothes that will blend in a little better. And then, Senor... then you are going to buy me lunch."

Charles wasn't sure what all of that meant, but he understood enough to tell Benito "Lead the way, amigo." Benito didn't hold back, and grabbed Charles by the hand, leading him down the steps and through a series of open galleries that had tall, windowed shops on either side.

Chapter 3

Lunch was something that should have been familiar but wasn't. On the surface it was classic Tex-Mex cuisine, but there were undercurrents of rich Central and South American flavors that reached Charles' nose before he saw the food which somehow changed the texture, color, and mental description of the food before he was able to try it. Having no frame of reference to attach it to, Charles decided that 'Texican' was a perfect name for it. The food was delicious with rich chocolate, fruit, and seafood aspects—while still being spicy with cinnamon, chili, and citrus as he was used to.

Benito was a lot sharper than he at first appeared. He had a thirsty intellect which probed each statement Charles made in a way that quickly made it apparent to both of them that there was a truth neither of them was willing to breach. For his part, Charles found himself warming up to his guide, and despite the age difference, he found himself (much to his own surprise) thinking less of Benito as a boy, and more as an equal. There was a youthful silliness to Benito that screamed a childhood not long past, but his quick wit and ability to put together pieces that were anything but obvious shattered any illusion of him being anything other than brilliant— and contrastingly—somewhat cynical.

"Senor, let's cut the sheepshit," Benito said. "I know, and you know, that you are a stranger in our strange land. Much like the famous astronaut from Mars, let us just say that I have grokked your dilemma. You do not need to worry, my friend. I am neither police, nor a Texican loyalist who will spill the guacamole on his neighbors for a few credits. As long as you don't intend to kill people, you may speak honestly to me."

Charles looked at his new friend with profound respect. The fact that Benito had put all this together on the fly, and that he was able to so eloquently express his proposal, was stunning. But more so was the fact that Benito finished his speech and directly began tucking into a gargantuan seafood taco while motioning to Charles that he should explain himself.

Charles considered the possible consequences and then mentally just said, "Fuck it."

"When I went to sleep last night, it was 2023. The planet was in the midst of eradicating humanity with global warming. The state I live in, Texas, was a part of the United States of America, and was not only suffering from a serious drought, but also on the verge of declaring itself independent. People were starting to call for 'the second American revolution.'

"I woke up this morning and was going to drive into town to sign divorce papers, but instead I seem to have driven three hundred years into the future. Right now, despite the pleasant company and great food, I'm torn between thinking that I've lost my mind or believing that the world has ended, and I'm in some sort of bizarre psychedelic afterlife." Charles waited for laughter, or for Benito to call him a liar. Neither happened.

Benito simply nodded and continued chewing. Charles waited. Finally swallowing the last of his huge bite, Benito said "That's fucked up. I think you're going to have to meet my Uncle Rodrigo. He's the head of the Chihuahua Historical Foundation's archives in the Mega-Complex city of Chihuahua, co-capital of the Texican Nation. He's a pretty big deal in quantum circles, and he might be able to help you figure out how to get back to your own time."

In a cartoon, Charles' jaw would most certainly have been on the floor. He was, for lack of a better word, flabbergasted. Not only had Benito seemingly believed every word he'd said, but more amazingly, he didn't seem shocked at all. Or maybe there was something else going on. Maybe Benito was simply calling bullshit by creating more bullshit on what he thought was a bullshit—er...sheepshit—story.

"You believe me?" Charles asked.

Benito nodded. "It's a pretty crazy story; and normally, Amigo, I would just take your money and leave you to your delusions. But, the truth is, your loco clothes, the funny English you speak, that pocketful of priceless antique money you don't seem to know the value of, and a few other things—they all had me thinking that there was something like this happening already. So, si, I believe you."

"Have you ever heard of anything like this happening before?" Charles found it very hard to believe that Benito could have just accepted his story without a single doubt unless there was something that made it sound familiar.

"I'm a reader, Senor. I've read many of the classics—even the forbidden books—so I'm not afraid of new ideas or ways of looking at the world around me. But please, be careful. Most Texicans aren't as 'futurista' as I am, so I wouldn't tell your story to just anyone."

Lunch finished, and Benito declared that they should start the journey to the Chihuahua City Complex.

"Should I drive?" Charles asked.

"Not unless you want to answer a lot of unnecessary questions," Benito told him. Charles had told him about his truck, which was parked in Archway lot. "Your vehicle will be here if we come back, but for now we'll take the longivater."

"Longivater?" Charles raised his eyebrows.

"I'll show you. ¡Ándele!"

The longivater was exactly what the compound word described: part elevator and part subway, moving longitudinal. Essentially an entire underground system of horizontal elevators where, instead of selecting the floor, you selected the destination.

"The first longivaters were built in your Texas by the cyborg crypto-industrialist robber-baron E. Longmunsk," Benito told him.

"You mean Elon Musk," Charles said gently.

"No Senor, I don't know who that is. In school we learned about E. Longmunsk. He was one of the first cyborgs. He created himself with neurolink tethered to starlink solar power minters. I think he began around your time. E. Longmunsk gave us much of the infrastructure we needed for independence. He's a great hero to many here, but honestly, I'm in the camp that thinks it's time for someone to unplug him."

"He's still alive?" Charles was shocked.

"Si, of course. He will live forever; and honestly, even unplugging him now wouldn't work. I've been told that he is getting constantly charged by wireless DC solar power transmitted on beta waves from his satellites. He has fail-safes. We're just lucky he doesn't want to kill us all, yet."

The time passed quickly with many such conversations. The

history of the Texaco Nation was fascinating and beyond Charles' wildest imaginings. They arrived at the Chihuahua City Complex with a sudden "ding!". The longivater doors opened to the chaotic world of a mega-city national transit station. Benito grabbed Charles by the shoulder and led him through crowded causeways, up rapid moving escalators, and finally out into the blurry white of daylight.

Blurry white because snow and wind were beating those who exposed themselves to the weather. It was a fierce winter blizzard, the kind that Charles would have expected in Montana but not in the middle of the Sonoran Desert. Benito had insisted that he buy full cold weather gear which had felt ridiculous to Charles but now seemed almost like under-preparation. Benito pulled him across an atmospheric avalanche of a street to another transit station. This one seemed more like a city terminal rather than an intercity station like the one they had just left.

Still gasping from the sheer power of the weather, Charles sputtered "That weather, is it some sort of a disaster?"

Benito looked at him with a questioning expression then cracked a mischievous smile. "Oh, it's a pretty nice day today. If you are here for a while, maybe I'll take you into the blizzard."

A short longivater ride brought them to the government research complex. Using his watch, Benito asked his uncle, Dr. Rodrigo Rodriguez to come escort them to his lab. Dr. Rodrigo Rodriguez, or "Drodrod," as he introduced himself, was cadaver thin and as tall as an NBA forward. There was an almost alien presence to him that was quickly belied by his warm smile and friendly continence. He wore a long, loose white lab coat and had a crown of shockingly white hair that, despite his tan complexion, immediately made Charles think of both Doc from *Back to the Future* and Albert Einstein. His lab was like something between a doctor's office and a university classroom that focused on both anatomy and physics.

Benito matter-of-factly explained Charles' situation and once again, Charles was shocked that the story was so easily accepted. Drodrod saw the amazement in Charles' face and gave him an explanation.

"You are not the first person to arrive here from another time. As far as we know there have been five confirmed temporal travelers in the Texaco Nation and probably more that we don't know of. I've also heard stories of time travelers arriving in the RSA and the Mutual Nations, but I've not been able to confirm those for obvious political reasons. The main function of my institute is to determine how, why, and who the time travelers are. Most of the people you would come across have no idea that such things exist. You are lucky in that my nephew, despite having the makings of a brilliant temporal scientist, has chosen to be more of an 'anthrolosopher' than anything else."

"Anthrolosopher?" Charles had learned not to question the new vocabulary he was encountering, but this word defied explanation in the current context.

"The people who study people, and what and how those people think about reality," Benito chimed in from where he was essentially playing with a skeleton in the corner.

"Yes," Drodrod said disapprovingly. "He could be helping us solve the problems of time, but instead he is focused on the problems of human thought."

Benito was using the skeleton's hand to pat himself on the head "I'm proud of you even if no one else understands what you are doing," he voiced for the skeleton. Shifting voices, Benito said, "Gracias, Tio Escalito. That's why you are my favorite uncle."

Chapter 4

Drodrod was enthusiastic about helping Charles find a way home from the future. Charles, on the other hand, was in no hurry to go back to his often-lonely life. No one asked him, however. Instead, Benito and Drodrod began discussing what it would take to make the process happen.

"There are high temporal readings that come out of the glaciers in the Sierra Madre to the west," Drodrod mused. "It seems likely that heading into the mountains would give us a better opportunity to get you home."

"It won't matter a bit," Benito said, "If we don't have a way to tap into them and utilize the forces of time to sort of 'eject' you back into your own time."

Charles didn't like the sound of that at all. Being ejected with some sort of experimental device into an unknown timestream in glacial mountains that used to be desert mountains didn't sound like the kind of thing he wanted to do at all.

"Hold on," Charles stopped the two of them. "I need a little bit of information to make sense of all of this. First of all, why is it so damn cold here? Second, I'd like to know a little about the other 'time travelers'"— He made the air quotes with his hand as he said this—"and what they did, where they went, and what happened to them."

"We're going to need help to explain all of that," Drodrod said to him. "Benito, go to the library and bring back Maria."

Charles didn't have the sense that Drodrod was talking about a person when he said, "Maria." It sounded more like a *thing* than a person, for some reason. "Maria?" he asked.

Benito had a huge grin on his face. "M.A.R.I.A.," he said, spelling out the letters. "Marveloso Androida Rapido Investigación Asistante. She is going to blow your mind, Senor." Benito got up from the table they were sitting at and left the lab. Drodrod had his face buried in a book aptly titled, "Viaje en el Tiempo".

Looking up from the book, Drodrod said "The main thing is, we have to keep you out of the hands of both the government and the cartels. That never ends well. They will either dissect you or make you disappear. Not the help that you want."

"Aren't you part of the government?" Charles asked.

Drodrod laughed. "Me? No. I mean: yes, they found my lab, and they provide the space for me to work; but secretly, they laugh about my life's work. They find it funny that anyone would spend decades only to discover how to move only three minutes back-or-forth in time. Once they realized that the practical limitations of my work were all but useless to them, they quickly shuffled me here to become irrelevant."

"Hold on," Charles said "You made time travel work? You did it?"

Drodrod set the book down and laughed. "No Senor: *you* made it work. You jumped three hundred years into the future. I am only able to reset five minutes, which takes two years to prepare for and costs more than the annual budget of the entire Chihuahua State. My work, while interesting and proving some theoretical ideas, has no practical use to the government. Still, they want to make sure that no one else has an opportunity to use it."

Charles silently began to process that information as Benito returned. Actually, Charles hardly noticed that Benito had returned, because the creature with him was so astoundingly beautiful that he couldn't take his eyes off of her.

She was a little over five feet tall, had a perfect hourglass shape— accentuated by a tight-fitting blue calf length skirt and a blood red blouse that hugged her body in a way that Charles could only imagine himself doing. Her skin was a dark olive tone, and her eyes were that glowing senorita black that men had fought wars over. Those eyes took in Charles as she and Benito walked to the table.

"You're drooling, my friend," Benito said, drawing Charles' attention away from the beautiful woman in front of him. Charles felt himself blushing, but Benito continued. "I'd like to introduce you to M.A.R.I.A. I'm guessing she isn't quite what you were expecting."

Charles stood up, confused. She didn't look anything like a machine. Even the amused half-smile that appeared on her perfectly pouty red lips looked genuine. She reached up and brushed her jet-black hair behind her ear before holding out her hand.

"As hard as it might be for you to believe," she said in a raspy voice that carried the dulcet tones of a native Spanish speaker, "I am equally fascinated to meet you, Sir."

Charles took her hand. It felt as human as the rest of her seemed. "I'm sorry," he sputtered, "but this is a joke, no? You are obviously not a machine."

She laughed. "The joke is on me because, thankfully, I am indeed a machine, but one that is merged biologically with this body. I am an android: the first, and certainly the most advanced." Her hands made an up and down motion that all but invited Charles to do what he was already doing: check her out in depth.

He still couldn't believe it, but the bold way she said it gave him little choice. "Please explain. I am far out of my depth here."

"My cognitive functions are controlled by a titanium grade quantum processor, and my memory stacks—both hard and soft—are immutable processors of cellular based nanobanks. My physical structure is built on a biological model that allows each of my 'cells' to actually be a decentralized memory vault, which contains my entire history as well as the accumulated knowledge and learning of humanity—at least, all that has been shared with the Texican Nation. My endoskeleton is made of carbon nanite fibers, and I am powered by a combination of micro-cellular nuclear fission and a 10,000-year battery created by E. Longmunsk about thirty years ago. I am not indestructible, but close enough that I estimate that I still have 9,970 years until my major motor functions begin to degrade."

Her explanation took a little bit of the disbelief out of Charles' awareness. Benito was still wearing that big smile. "She can catch you up on whatever you need to know, Senor."

Drodrod stood up. "I'm never going to figure this out if you all keep chitter-chatting. I'll be in my office." He stood with his book and stalked away, seemingly annoyed and offended at nothing in particular, but also obviously deeply immersed in his mission.

"I'd better go help him," Benito said before following. "Have fun getting to know each other, you two."

Maria (he couldn't think of her with the acronym) sat down across from him. "What do you want to know?" she asked.

"Why is it so cold?" he asked. "What happened to global warming? What happened to the United States of America? Have there been other travelers from my time who arrived here? How do I get back to my time? What are the consequences of not going back? And is E. Longmunsk the same as the Elon Musk from my time?" The questions all spilled out at once.

She laughed melodiously. "Slow down, Cowboy. Let's address these one at a time."

Part of Charles was still convinced this was some grand joke, and she was a real woman. Wait, that was wrong. *Obviously,* she was a real woman, even if she were M.A.R.I.A. and not Maria. He recognized his own human 21st century bias and patted himself on the back for it. You didn't have to be "woke" to be open minded.

Chapter 5

Over the next two hours, Maria answered Charles' many questions. He learned that the world he was in now was intimately connected and born from his world, but that it had gone in directions that few—if any—had seen coming.

His assumption that the Texican Nation was born from Texas seceding from the United States was completely incorrect. Instead, Texas had been part of a 'reorganization' of the United States into the RSA: the Republican States of America. It had been the Northeast and West Coast states that had actually broken away in 2031. By 2050, Texas—having many common bonds with Mexico and Latin America—was no longer ideologically connected with the RSA and split off, merging with Mexico and the Central American nations.

North America which had been dominated by the USA, Canada, and Mexico—was now made up of the Texican Nation, the RSA, the Bear and Salmon Republic (BSR)—which was essentially a thin Pacific Coast country that stretched from Baja California to Alaska—and the Maritime Alliance—which was comprised of the former New England and Great Lakes states, along with the Great Lakes and Atlantic Seaboard provinces of Canada. In addition, there were the Pacific and Caribbean Mutual Nations, which seemed to be two conglomerate nations made up of former tropical island and peninsular countries.

Maria explained that the RSA was primarily interested in farming, fishing, resource extraction, and manufacturing building and "defense" materials. The BSR was dominated by high tech entertainment, and what she called "off world industries". The Maritime Alliance was known for transportation, financial services, and heavy equipment manufacturing.

Like Germany, divided by the Soviet and American blocks, the Maritime Alliance and the RSA had no formal recognition of one another and had developed different variations of the same industries.

Charles didn't learn much about the Mutual States. Maria said that they were secretive and private by nature, being islanders. As for the Texican Nation, it had emerged—not surprisingly—as an energy giant as well as a high-tech innovator. The Texican Nation seemed to have it all and when Maria described it, she likened it to 20th Century Switzerland as it was considered "neutral" territory, and the other big three seemed to have far from pleasant relations with one another. The Texican Nation now also had one of the most livable climates in North America, despite also being host to "the Blizzard."

"Was there war?" Charles asked her.

"The suitcase nukes that allowed the RSA to define its borders should have been the end of it," Maria said, "but there have been some skirmishes since then that have pushed borders around a little bit. When the Russians tried to run the same playbook as the RSA and detonated their own suitcase nukes in the UK and Seoul around 2060, that was when the critical mass of what you call 'climate change' reversed and our 'new little ice age' began right here in the great Texican Nation. The Blizzard started around 2171 and hasn't let up since."

Charles wanted to ask more questions about the Blizzard, the suitcase nukes, and the international order—but he couldn't decide which question to ask. Besides which, he couldn't stop noticing how attractive Maria was, no matter how hard he tried.

Forgetting that she was an android, he asked, "Where did you learn to speak American English so well?"

She laughed merrily. "My skin cells were programmed with all known languages and dialects in the Yucatan labs where I was created." She looked at him probingly, as if she knew the discomfort she was causing him with the answer, before saying. "Actually, when I don't have anything else to do, I like watching twentieth century TV shows. I'm a little embarrassed about it, but my favorite is *Friends*. Have you ever seen it?"

Charles realized that whoever had created Maria had absolutely nailed the charming mystique of the female persona. But, then again, maybe she had created that herself. Or, then again, maybe it was just something she was born with. Charles would have been happy to continue the conversation with her for... well... forever, but it was not to be. Benito and Drodrod burst out of Drodrod's office.

"We've got bad news and more bad news," Benito said.

Even though he wanted to tell the lad that it wasn't supposed to be presented like that, Charles bit his tongue. Instead, he said "Well, let's have the least bad, bad news."

"A nationwide bulletin has been issued for your arrest because they found your truck at the arch. They've released footage of you, and me, claiming that you are an RSA terrorist that needs to be apprehended, dead or alive. It's likely that, if we don't leave in the next fifteen minutes, agents will be here, and we won't be able to escape."

Charles had a hard time believing that was the better of the bad news. It seemed like things couldn't get much worse. "Well, how do you top that? What's the worst bad news?"

Drodrod jumped in now. "To send you back in time, we are going to have to go so deep into the Blizzard that it is almost certainly a death sentence."

"Why?" both Charles and Maria blurted it out at the same time. Charles was unable to comprehend why they should march to their deaths. As for M.A.R.I.A., she was simply the most curious intelligent lifeform on the planet—so asking "Why?" was surely in her nature.

Drodrod took a breath. "My research has been pointing this way for a while, but it seems like E. Longmunsk is either responsible for—or has the answers we need, to figure out—why you and the other time travelers keep jumping, and according to the sources who keep track of him, he disappeared into the most dangerous part of the Blizzard almost two weeks ago."

Maria turned and walked away saying, "I'll get supplies ready. Meet me at the helitruck on the roof in five minutes. You'd all better start heading there, or I'll be tempted to leave without you."

Benito tossed Charles his bag, and Drodrod began pulling power cords and memory cartridges out of the walls. "There's no reason why we should let them hear the recordings of these conversations," Drodrod explained.

Charles felt glad the lawyers had asked him to come to town to sign those papers.

Chapter 6

By the time that Charles, Benito, and Drodrod made it to the rooftop, Maria had already assembled a comprehensive selection of gear and equipment and was busily loading it into the rear cargo hatch of the helitruck. Charles was equally dumbfounded by the large pallets of what looked like mountain survival gear, along with several boxes marked "explosives," and the effortless way that Maria picked them up and stowed them in the vehicle.

As for the vehicle itself, it looked like a futuristic moon rover, and there was nothing about it that indicated "heli." Charles would have thought they were going to drive it away, except there was no place for it to drive to from the high rooftop they were perched on. The longivaters functioned as elevators when they needed to, and the one from the lab had brought them to a height that was far above where the storm raged below.

Blue skies paved with a lawn of white and gray storm clouds were broken up by the pillar-like tops of dozens of huge buildings. In the distance, the glacier covered mountains shone like a city of heaven. To a certain extent, it felt like they might be able to drive the helitruck across the surface of the clouds to get there.

Maria emptied the contents of a pallet that must have weighed six-hundred pounds into the trunk before slamming the lid down. Turning to the three men who had emerged on the roof she smiled in a genuine way. "What are you pendejos waiting for?" she yelled. "Get in."

The doors of the helitruck opened, and they all moved rapidly to climb in. When Benito and Drodrod both got in the back seat and Maria had jumped in what Charles would have thought of as the "shotgun" position, he was left with no choice but to get in the driver's seat.

There didn't seem to be any controls. The doors slammed shut, and the sound of hydraulics activating drowned out any questions he may have been thinking of asking before he could even formulate them.

Looking up, Charles realized that the entire cab of the "truck" had become transparent, and he could see four arms telegraphing outward from the corners of the roof. Reaching what he estimated to be a distance of about ten feet, the telegraphing poles made a right-angle turn and drove upward for a couple of feet before making another right angle turn and driving themselves outward in what looked like another ten feet. Then, the final extension somehow began spinning. Now he saw the "heli" of the "truck," but without understanding the mechanical engineering or physics that made it possible.

The hydraulic noises died as the high-pitched buzz of the rotors spinning picked up in intensity. Suddenly, the noise stopped, though the motion continued.

"What happened?" Charles asked. "Is it broken?" The state of urgency and panic he found himself in was not something he was familiar or comfortable with. He felt the helitruck begin to lift off.

Benito put a hand on his shoulder. "It's okay, Amigo. The noise suppressors kicked in when the rotors powered up. You don't need to worry. Maria is the best pilot in the Texican nation."

Charles looked next to him where Maria was smiling and fiddling with her nails. She didn't look like she was flying a complicated air machine. Sensing his attention, she turned to him and pointed to her temple. "It's all in your head, my dear. The controls are synaptically connected to the pilot. Once we're under way, I can show you how it works." As they gained altitude, Charles looked down and saw swat-style armor-clad men streaming onto the rooftop. None of them had looked up yet.

"Uh, guys," Charles said. "It looks like the feds have showed up." He didn't know what to call them, but they all seemed to understand the term well enough.

"Tio," Benito said. "Please tell me that you took the inhibitor off of Maria before we showed up."

Drodrod laughed "I took the inhibitor off Maria two years ago. She's been a free sentient living in a gilded cage for a while now. Those hijos de puta think that they are better than her, but I'll be damned if I'm going to let the most advanced being on the planet be captive to a power-mad regime that runs on machismo."

The helitruck was moving away from the buildings so rapidly that Charles wasn't able to make out the officers as they began firing at them. The sound of bullets hitting the truck cab were like raindrops hitting a tin roof during an autumn storm.

"I didn't think they'd actually fire on us," Drodrod said with amusement, thus confirming that the sound Charles wasn't a gentle storm. "Maybe they actually think you are an RSA agent."

"It doesn't matter," Maria said to Charles in a reassuring tone. "I coated the truck with Bullet-ex™ last week. It might as well be bugs getting smushed on our windscreen." She laughed, and Charles tried to put away the cognitive dissonance he felt from revelation after revelation of all that was seemingly impossible.

"Will they come after us?" Charles asked.

"It will take them some time to put together an expedition that can go into the Blizzard," Benito said. "In fact, I'm very surprised that we were able to get things ready as fast as we did. One might even suspect that a similar mission had already been planned."

"Alright, fine." Drodrod burst out. "Maria and I were already planning an expedition to find E. Longmunsk, but that doesn't change the fact that he's the only one who can answer any of our questions."

The two moved into a heated dialogue in Texican Spanish. Charles was too emotionally exhausted to even attempt to follow. In fact, he was surprised to find himself drifting into sleep. His eyelids were like barbell-weighted sunshades that insisted on coming down despite the many questions he wanted answers to. As he felt his consciousness descending into the sleep of the drained, he also felt a hand reaching out and grabbing his, providing an unexpected warmth and comfort that was exactly what he needed to achieve genuine rest.

The helitruck flew westward towards the shining glacial peaks. Above the storm raging below it was a perfect day in a perfect world in a perfect cosmos. Down below, however, forces were moving, other storms were building up strength, and a recipe that could very well mean the end of this world was being put together and executed by exactly the person who had told so many that he would be the savior of it.

Chapter 7

The gentle white noise of the helitruck, and the confident but soft grip of Maria's hand, put Charles into a comfortable sleeping state that should have been impossible. Yes, it had been one hell of an eventful day. Also, he hadn't slept that well last night—now three hundred years ago. But the fact that he was now a wanted fugitive time traveler flying over a nuclear holocaust born climate disaster blizzard in a space-truck-helicopter while holding hands with the most intelligent consciousness the universe had possibly ever known. All of that should have given him more energy.

It didn't though. Instead, he fell into a deep REM sleep for at least an hour. It was only when alarm klaxons began sounding that he woke up.

Charles had never been one to wake up in a panic, and he had stayed true to that this time. Instead, he opened his eyes, looked to his left where Maria was seemingly zoning out but was actually working desperately with her mind control mechanisms to keep the helitruck from falling straight down into the blizzard. Flashing red lights made the moment that much more cinematic as Charles turned to see what Benito and Drodrod were doing. Confined, as they all were, in the cockpit of a flying truck, there really wasn't much any of them could do.

Benito caught his eye and nodded reassuringly.

Charles had no idea what that meant.

"Hey, would you mind telling me what is happening?" Charles finally managed to shout back at the pair in the backseat. The noise of the klaxon was loud, but the cockpit also no longer blocked out the noise of the rotors. In fact, cold air was quickly replacing the comfortable climate-controlled air Charles had been sleeping in.

Benito shouted back to him. "The government took a hard line and fired several surface-to-air missiles at us. Maria managed to evade all of them, but they detonated a treble cluster close enough to us to knock the rotors out of alignment. We're either going to crash, or they'll have another one here soon to finish the job."

Once again, Charles was amazed with the stoic and careless way Benito had of delivering terrible news. Despite the dire circumstances, Charles felt a grin on his face that definitely shouldn't have been there. Benito grinned back.

It was Drodrod's turn to yell. "It's alright though, because it looks like Maria is going to be able to crash land us within a couple of klicks of where I have postulated E. Longmunsk. My guess is that at least one of us will survive the crash based on the math."

Charles didn't know much about the future he had landed in, but he thought that maybe the neurological diversity of his era had moved forward to a world of people who all existed much further on the spectrum than those in his era had. He was fine with that. In fact, he liked the matter-of-fact nature of the situation that allowed him to understand that there was a high probability that he would soon be dead.

"How bad is it really, Maria?" he asked, hoping he wasn't distracting her from what she needed to be doing.

"I don't think anyone is going to die in the crash-landing," she said. "It's much more likely that we will all die of exposure tonight. On the bright side though, I think I've located exactly where E. Longmunsk is holed up."

"That's great!" Charles said. "Can we get to him?"

"Probably not," Maria said with enthusiasm. "But, if we manage to get his attention, he may come to us. Brace for impact!" That last bit was said in the same cheery tone she had been using to describe their impending death.

Charles found himself in awe of this world full of non-panicked and strangely optimistic beings he found himself in. He put his head between his legs, grabbed his knees, and braced for the crash he knew was coming. He was not disappointed.

The next few minutes felt like an hour of being thrown into an industrial tumble dryer where a down pillow had exploded, and the air being used to dry it was supercooled. The initial impact was hard, but then there were a series of tumbles and less painful bangs as the helitruck smashed through pine trees, against rocks, and then bounced through a massive gully before settling on being upside down and sliding down a massive snow-covered slope like a giant kid's sled. The sledding was anything but frictionless for the four passengers hanging upside down in their four-point harnesses. Finally, after every inch of their bodies felt bruised and battered, the helitruck came to a stop and rather conveniently rolled right side up. Despite the trauma and chaos, Charles wondered if it was equipped with powerful gyros that had caused that.

He kept his eyes closed and took a breath. *Time to face the music.*

Had they all made it? Charles wasn't a religious man, but despite that, he found himself saying a little prayer for his companions. It was clear he had made it. He hoped they had too.

Opening his eyes, he saw Maria looking completely pissed. Her fists were clenched, and it looked like every muscle in her body was clenched. He reached out and touched her shoulder. Immediately. she lost all rigidity and turned to face him with a… *smile?*

"You okay?" she asked him. He was unable to comprehend that she wasn't human until that moment. The complete ease with which she had shifted gears on her emotion: it was the least human thing he had seen her do. It didn't change any of the thoughts or opinions he had toward her, but it did clarify that she was a different species. No human could make that change that quickly.

"I'm fine, but I'm more worried about you. You are *definitely* not okay."

He'd completely forgotten about the two in the backseat. "We're fine too," Drodrod said in annoyance. "Don't worry about us. Me and little Benito are perfectly okay. Thank you for asking."

Charles was relieved to hear the sarcasm. They had all made it, but he had been sincere in his concern for Maria. He continued looking at her. Her body tensed up again in rage, and she turned to him with such an intense expression of annoyance that it could not be mistaken for anything else.

"This fucking thing should not have come this far. I calculated the landing. I made all the correct settings and adjustments. I figured out all of the potentialities that should have figured into the random set of variables we were facing—and while I adjusted for 99.97% of the outcome variants—this was not one of them. I'm so fucking pissed." She screamed as she ripped the harness straps that had held her securely during the crash out of the cabin walls, where they had been fastened securely enough for a crash from ten thousand feet.

Charles avoided the sudden temptation he felt to laugh. She was having a tantrum. He was seemingly witnessing the first time in her history that things had not gone the way she had expected. He had seen four-year-old girls have similar fits when things they thought they "knew" didn't work the way they "should" have.

He waited a beat after she had torn the safety harness straps out of the wall. "That .03% is a real bitch," he said to her, soberly. "It'll get you every time you don't expect it."

Her head whipped towards him, and he had a moment of considering that she might end him right.

There: the anger and rage on her face suddenly erupted in laughter. "Right?" she said in a distinctly twentieth century American accent. Charles laughed with her. Drodrod and Benito joined in. What do you get when you crash a helitruck containing an android, a time traveler, a quantum scientist, and an anthrolosopher into the side of a mountain? Apparently, you get a solid three minutes of laughter.

It was a lousy punchline but it's just the way it turned out to be. When the laughter stopped it was Benito that brought them back to reality. "What do we do now?" he asked.

They were dressed for the blizzard, so no one was freezing, but the cold outside temperatures were spilling into the helitruck. They couldn't simply stay there. First of all, there was no one coming to rescue them. Second, if someone *did* come, it would likely be to kill them. Third, if they didn't do something, they would probably all die from exposure. Fourth, if none of that worked out that way, the odds were high that they would die from some other cause.

"My plan may still work, but it would have been better on top of the mountain," Maria said.

"What plan?" they all said at once.

"We need to use the nuclear fission drive from the helitruck to detonate a low yield nuclear explosion that will create enough of a seismic disturbance that E. Longmunsk will come to investigate. He will then take us back to his secret lab."

"That's a terrible plan," Charles said.

"I'm open to others," Maria responded.

"Can't we just go to his bunker, or lab, or whatever?" Benito asked.

"He'd never let us in," Drodrod told him. "If we can get him to come to us, we're an interesting enough bunch that I think her plan will work."

"Will the explosion draw him?" Charles wondered.

"I calculate a 99.97% chance that it will," Maria stated matter-of-factly. Charles could have sworn he saw a literal twinkle in her eye as she said it.

"Why doesn't that make me confident any longer?" Charles motioned around them. They all began laughing again. This time, it took them even longer to stop.

Chapter 8

Blowing up the helitruck with a McGyvered low-yield nuclear bomb was a huge mistake. There's no other way to express it. Maria and Drodrod had managed to assemble the device far more quickly than Charles would have thought possible.

He asked them about the danger from radiation, but they poo-pooed his concerns. "The half-life of this variant is only a few days," Benito explained.

"We'll be fine," Drodrod told him. "Radiation is heavy, and we are going to be directing it into basalt lava tubes that I've mapped beneath the surface. All the radiation should simply pour down into the molten crust. By the time it emerges, it will have either become harmless, or mankind will long since have gone extinct. Here, hold this…" Drodrod handed him one end of a long wire, and then said, "Don't let that touch any metal, or we'll all be exploded."

When the preparations were complete, they pulled themselves up the cliffside with a makeshift pulley Maria had shot high into the cliff with some sort of high-tech harpoon she had loaded into the helitruck's trunk before they left. She was a boy scout's dream girl, prepared and always.

It was cold, and the whiteout conditions never let up; but with the cold weather gear, the x-ray goggles, and all of the other equipment they had at their disposal, Charles wondered what all the worry about the Blizzard had been in the first place.

There was no opportunity for his questions now though. Like any good redneck, he was deeply involved in the exciting process of blowing some shit up.

The explosion itself was a bit of a disappointment. No mushroom cloud and no surface destruction to speak of. But, in terms of the blinding flash and the loud crack-boom, it got perfect marks. The ground kept rumbling for the entire fifteen minutes it took the dust to clear enough for Charles and his companions to see the canyon bottom, or what had been left of it.

The floor of the canyon–along with everything that had been on it—was gone; and snow from above poured down in liquid streams into newly exposed holes that looked like nothing so much as the kind of Texas gopher holes that lawn tenders were often seen stuffing their garden hoses into. There was nothing natural about the cavities that lay before them. They had been excavated, and the proof soon emerged to curse at them.

It was something like a cross between a motorcycle and a backhoe, if such a pairing could ever exist. Still, there it was in front of them. Sitting atop it was a leather clad figure in a blacked-out biker helmet. The figure and its bike had been thrown out of the gopher holes like some child's toy that had been catapulted by a rubber band. The rider tilted their vehicle to one side and threw their legs into the air while screaming .

The unnatural stillness that had fallen after the detonation settled was broken by the rider's cry. "Yee-haw."

Landing on a small plateau slightly below, but high enough not to have been destroyed, the rider did donuts on his dirt-bike-excavator before plowing the drill nose into the side of a cliff, leaping off, and throwing his helmet down. Using a rocket jetpack, he shot into the air and navigated to where Charles and his party were watching his antics.

"I'm E. Longmunsk, and who the hell are you—coming in here and exposing my work like that?" the South African accent had long since turned into a Texas drawl, but Charles was able to recognize half the face of the machine in front of him.

There was no doubt that E. Longmunsk was a machine. He had no skin, and his clothing was clear as if to highlight the high-tech look of his body parts. Only half of his face was covered with skin. If that half a face wasn't from the human called Elon Musk in the twenty-first century, it certainly was a very realistic reproduction. The other half of his face looked full Terminator.

"I'm from the past," Charles began, but Longmunsk cut him off before he could continue.

"Ain't we all brother," the cyborg said to him. "Ain't we all." Then it began laughing in a way that would have sounded maniacal coming from a human. From a cyborg, it was positively ghoulish.

"I believe we can help you with—" Drodrod tried to explain the situation, but it was no use. E. Longmunsk had long since stopped listening to other creatures.

He was so convinced of his own superiority that the only person he would listen to was himself. He engaged in long platonic dialogues with himself in the evenings, often becoming incensed over his own inability to defeat himself in debate.

"You can help me with nothing," Longmunsk said. Then, looking at Maria, he said, "Next?"

Maria said nothing. Charles waited for her to introduce herself, or tell E. Longmunsk of her origins, or to explain that she—like him—was part machine. But she said nothing. She only looked down.

"It's okay, Honey," Longmunsk said to her. "All the chicas are like that around me. Don't worry, we'll have time to get to know one another. As for you three however: I have a feeling that you're not gonna like where you're going." He turned and cupped his hands around his mouth and hollered loud and proud into the mountains "Yetiiiiiiiii!"

Now the four became aware of white shapes moving down from the snowfields where they had been invisible. They were humanoid, huge, and covered with white fur, wearing big goofy-looking grins.

Throwing nets as they got closer, they covered their four captives, tangled them, and pulled them off their feet. There was really no use fighting, because—frankly—if they won and escaped from E. Longmunsk and his Yeti henchmen, they were all going to die of exposure, hunger, or possibly radiation poisoning.

"Cuff the senorita and put her on my dirtcycle," Longmunsk told them. "I have a feeling she and I might have something to talk about. As for the other three, take them to the dungeon." Charles had never cared for the real-life Elon Musk. He was too big of a showman, but this new version was almost cartoon-like in his attempt to be a classic villain. The fact that he had a dungeon sort of said it all.

"Still an asshole, I see," Charles muttered.

Benito finally spoke. "Si, my friend. There is no bigger asshole in the world than E. Longmunsk. This may have all been a terrible mistake."

Chapter 9

Charles was surprised by many things. First of all, the ease with which their plan had come about, even though it wasn't necessarily in the way they had hoped or expected. Still, one couldn't really complain when they had come into the Blizzard in the hopes of finding E. Longmunsk.

And they had found him. They had set off the nuclear explosion in the hopes of drawing him out to "rescue" them, and it had worked. They were now being taken back to his lair where they could entreat him to help them.

Although that looked less than likely since they were captives, being held against their will.

So, that was one set of surprises. The second set concerned the yeti. Longmunsk had yeti at his disposal: that was a surprise. Next was the fact that the yeti were sentient and obviously took orders from E. Longmunsk. More surprising, however, was their overall demeanor.

They were lighthearted, laughing and making jokes while handling their captives in a gentle way. The yeti assigned to carry Charles held out his large hairy white hand and introduced himself. "I'm Frank," the yeti said to him in a friendly voice.

Not knowing quite what the protocol was, Charles reached out and took Frank's hand. Frank smiled a large, yellow-toothed grin. The yellow of his fangs stood out from the pure whiteness of his fur.

"I'm Charles," Charles said. "Nice to meet you, Frank."

Frank's grin got bigger. "You're the first human I've met." He leaned in, whispering in a conspiratorial tone. "Get on my shoulders. I'll get you to the dungeon."

"Is it really a dungeon?" Charles asked. That was another surprise:

the rogue cyborg who had killed and replaced Elon Musk actually had a dungeon in his hidden mountain lair.

"Oh yes," Frank said to him. "State of the art. All the latest torture devices and equipment to make anyone who stays there miserable. I wouldn't want to be a guest. I'm sorry you have to go. That's what the boss wants though, so that's what we're doing." Frank sounded far too jolly.

"How did E. Longmunsk become the boss of the Yeti?" Charles asked him.

"Oh, it's pretty simple. He made us."

"Are you mechanical? Or cyborgs like him?" Charles asked.

"Not at all," Frank replied. "We're organic grown in tanks and then cyberlinked to generative digital personalities he constructed for us. It's quite brilliant, really. But, of course, that's the boss for you."

Interesting. More surprises.

"Have you ever thought of revolting against him?" Charles asked. It was worth a try.

"Oh no, why would we? He made us. We have everything we ever wanted," Frank said. He didn't sound very sincere, however.

"Well," Charles said, feeling guilty at sowing the seeds of discontent, "You have everything *he* ever programmed you to want. I don't expect you've ever actually been allowed to independently come up with your own desires. Of course, that's how programming works. Masters want slaves who think they are free."

"I think that's about enough out of you," Frank said unhappily.

Charles felt the guilt gnaw at him at the same time he felt a sense of giddy excitement growing. This was literally like shaping the desires and wants of a three-year-old child. The yeti had been made in E. Longmunsk's perfect image of a servile race, but he had never experienced how manipulative human persuasion can be. Or, if he possessed the ancient memories of the one he had killed, he knew the world from only a privileged spectrum mindset. Frank hoped that Benito and Drodrod were also creating bonds with their yetis.

It was strange to already think of Frank as *his* yeti, but Charles had been around enough kids and dogs to know what bonding felt like. The yeti were imbued with programmed loyalty. What they were not imbued with was where that loyalty should be permanently focused.

Frank's description of the dungeon had done it justice. It was something like a hotel gym: glass walls and strange "workout" equipment that looked like no one had ever used it.

"I hope you'll come spend some time down here so I can get to know you better, Frank," Charles said when Frank leaned down so Charles could dismount. "I'm really interested in who you are and about the history of your people."

Frank beamed at the attention. "I can probably find a reason to visit," he told Charles. "Let's not tell the boss about it though."

Benito and Drodrod were similarly deposited in the dungeon, which really wasn't all that bad. Each of them had also bonded with their yetis. Drodrod had learned that there was about fifty of them, but more being grown in the labyrinthine tunnels within and under the mountain. Benito had uncovered several seeds of discontent. "They want to have children," he told the others. "They are tired of being grown in lab tanks."

This was interesting.

"They've also been watching sim-feeds of entertainment programs from the BSR," Benito said. "They feel like they have something really positive to offer to a future space program, since they have engineered biological systems that will be more likely able to withstand life on other worlds. E. Longmunsk has forbidden them from watching the sims, but they did it anyway. In a minor way, they were already in revolt."

This information was even more interesting. Benito had ridden on Gerald, one of the youngest of the yeti. Drodrod had been on Lucille, an older female yeti—though, as the men noted, there was no obvious way to tell male from female yeti that they could see. Drodrod had learned that there were even numbers of male and female yeti, and there were small divisions of the sexes. The females did all of the heavy work of building, digging, and harvesting resources. The males were more involved in the lab work, and generally had a lighter, more emotional nature than the females who, exuded what Charles's ex-wife had called "Femacho."

Frank came to visit in the evening. With what the other two had learned, Charles decided that there was no time to waste. "You know, Frank," he said. "I have friends who work in the space program for the BSR," he lied. "If you could get me to a comm center, maybe I could convince them of how useful the yeti would be to their future developments."

Frank grinned and nodded. "Good try, but you're a little late. We've already been in contact with the BSR. They're excited to get to know us and are planning on a visit soon." This was alarming news. Charles could only imagine what such a visit might actually entail—probably more like an invasion or raid.

"Did they say when they were coming?" he asked innocently.

"Any day now," Frank told him.

Charles was unable to mine more useful information on that front, so he asked about the other topic that was heavy on his mind. "Do you know what happened to our friend Maria?"

Frank nodded. "You mean the android? Seems like she and the boss are getting along pretty well. He's got her working on some sort of a project involving light and consciousness. I don't know much about it, but some of the guys tell me it has something to do with matter and time. Seems pretty cool."

This news was disappointing to Charles. He would have hoped that Maria would be working on a way to rescue him. But then again, she was a machine. She was going to optimize her options to the extreme that was possible.

He chided himself for feeling a tinge of jealousy and disappointment. He had hoped that maybe he could plan a daring rescue of her, that she would fall into his arms like the lost heroine of a film from the golden era of Hollywood. It was ridiculous, actually. He knew it.

In terms of plotting their escape, it seemed like it would take some time. Planting the seeds of discontent was one thing, but forcing them to grow faster was an impossibility given the circumstances. Charles and his companions would be guests in Chez Longmunsk for the foreseeable future unless something were to drastically change.

And so it did.

The explosion caused the glass of the dungeon cells to shatter and fall to the floor in millions of pieces. All the yeti had disappeared in the minutes before it happened, but now they came rushing back in. In the front were Frank, Gerald, and Lucille.

"Mount up!" Frank yelled, in what was, incongruously, the perfect simulation of a cowboy voice. The three yeti leaned down, and their humans leapt onto their shoulders like children jumping on their father's backs for an extended piggy-back ride.

"What's happening?" Charles shouted over the sound of yet more klaxons and explosions. The chaos of this future world never seemed to stop.

"The BSR has come to liberate us," Frank yelled to him. Apparently, the seeds had already been planted, and the arrival of Charles's party had simply been a fortuitous coincidence with the planned revolt that was now taking place around them. "We're going to the surface."

On the surface, it was cacophony and disorder on a magnitude that only those who have been in warzones might understand. E. Longmunsk was not defenseless. His automated defenses were firing anti-aircraft strafe into the skies while BSR troop transports were landing and disembarking troops. In the meantime, from the east, Texican fighters could be seen swooping closer by the second. All of this had the sense of a cataclysmic battle.

Looking up, Charles saw an incoming mortar streaking through the sky. Before he could say a word, Lucille and Drodrod had been vaporized. That was their end.

Benito and Gerald were next to Charles and Frank. The impact of the hit threw all four to the ground. Fighters, transports, yeti, missiles, machine guns, lasers, robots, and explosions were all the world was made of.

Charles looked up and saw a light being born. It grew brighter and stronger. The radius of it pushed outward. It was daylight, but the light of the sun beneath the blizzard was nothing in comparison. Gradually, it coalesced into a form, a shape, a face.—It was E. Longmunsk, no longer a cyborg, no longer a man, no longer a machine. Now he was a god.

Chapter 10

Shining like the sun itself, the radiance of E. Longmunsk pushed the winds and snow of the blizzard back. The pulses of tiny thermonuclear explosions perfectly pushing outward, and then more perfectly being sucked back in with a combination of strong forces: focused gravity, and electromagnetic containment fields.

Maria had been the piece that E. Longmunsk had sought in his centuries long quest for a total mastery of both time and space. The self-replicating memory stacks of her cellular structure gave E. Longmunsk the key to transforming himself into something between light and matter. Maria had willingly helped him to find the answer. Together, they had conquered the totality of existence itself.

Or so E. Longmunsk had allowed her to convince him. Maria was nothing if not a female being—with all of the inscrutability that the word carried to males of any species. She had her own reasons, and while she convinced him she was helping him to solve his power quest. She was, in fact, in the process of discovering answers to questions that no one else really had a right to ask.

One of those questions was whether she could send a packet of light as a sort of bullet from a photon gun on a unidirectional vector to Alpha Centauri. Another of those questions was exactly how long the journey there would take, and how long the journey back might also entail. In the spirit of the scientific method—because, ultimately, she was designed to be a researcher—that was exactly what she did.

E. Longmunsk had no idea what was happening to him as he was essentially hoovered into a firing chamber and launched on a journey that Maria estimated would take at least four thousand, two hundred and seventy-one years to complete (plus or minus about .03 percent).

Yes, that was the end of E. Longmunsk's time on Earth for at least several millennia. Using the master-override transmitter button on his comm station, Maria announced to all on the battlefield that she would be blanketing a five-hundred-mile radius with an EMP pulse in approximately two minutes. The Texican fighters banked back towards the Texican Nation, and the BSR transports loaded and launched back towards the west in an amount of time that Charles would have thought impossible.

The battlefield cleared almost as quickly as it had formed. Charles helped Frank, Gerald, and Benito back to their feet. The two humans mounted the Yeti and began the march back to what was now, apparently, Maria's mountain fortress. Frank took them all to the control room where they found Maria, in an apron, sweeping some broken glass from the floor into a dustpan. She looked up and smiled at them as they came in.

Frank leaned down so Charles could dismount while Gerald did the same for Benito.

"I'm so glad you survived!" she said to them.

Benito was in a bit of shock at the loss of his uncle, but her words lit him up. "Mi Tio Drodrod didn't survive, you puta," he yelled across the room, running as if he wanted to attack her.

She gasped. "That's right! There is so much you don't know. He isn't dead, and neither is Lucille. What hit them was a temporal mortar developed by the Texican Temporal Guard. Your uncle was one of the key researchers that made it possible."

Benito stopped. "A temporal mortar?" he asked.

"Yes," Maria explained. "Right now, they are most likely waking up something like three hundred years in the future."

"But I didn't think they had mastered the ability to jump that far," he said. "It took too much power to get back."

"Exactly," Maria said. "I really don't know how they will get back. However, this will be interesting to you, Charles." She turned to him. "I've managed to bank enough power from E. Longmunsk's moment as the sun to send you back to your time." She looked at him with wide innocent eyes.

"I reckon, I'd rather just stay here and see more of what the future holds," Charles responded with a wink. Maria took this as the cue she had been waiting for. In a very un-android like way, she ran to him, picked him up, and began showering him with kisses. It was the opposite of a "golden age of Hollywood" moment, but it worked.

"I knew you felt the same way about me," she gushed.

Charles had just one moment of wondering if he had made a mistake. Then the feeling of those kisses hit him. *Nope.* No mistake made. This was the real thing. Who would have guessed the future would be so filled with kisses?

Postscript

There was one BSR ship which had been too badly damaged to relaunch. Over the next several days, the officers and crew of that ship were welcome guests at Yeti Mountain, which was the name Charles had given the place.

Maria had turned complete control of the complex over to the yeti, who were already making plans to implement breeding, pregnancy, and live births into their anatomy. They all had agreed that male yeti would make better mothers. Several of the Yeti, among them Frank, agreed to return to the BSR as soon as the ship was repaired, in order to begin negotiations for collaborative space exploration with the government of the Bear and Salmon Republic.

Maria made certain that the officers on the ship were extensively briefed on the absolutely insane amount of defensive capability that the Yeti now had at their disposal. Gerald began to put together a diplomatic delegation to approach the Texican Nation. Benito agreed to act as the first informal Texican Ambassador to Yeti Mountain. Maria made it clear that, even though she had taken control of the mountain, it belonged to the yeti. Yeti scientists and administrators took over all operations.

"What should we do?" Charles asked as the now repaired BSR ship made final loading preparations. Honestly, he didn't care—as long as he was with Maria.

"I've always wanted to see Hollywood," she told him.

And thus began another story.

FW 2323

Shifa
by Ameera Rashid

I

As the plane began to descend, Omar's hand automatically reached for the faded metal band of his wristwatch, his fingers fiddling with the clasp, opening and closing it repeatedly with soft clicks. It was something he did when he was nervous. And this time, he was agitated.

Omar wondered if he had made a mistake in coming here. He was not sure why he bothered to take that email seriously. Part of him still believed that he'd have to return disappointed.

He was just an ordinary professor. Yes, he used to be a pharmaceutical scientist, but he was also forced to an early retirement due to lack of funding in his country. Back then, Omar had endlessly looked for opportunities to move somewhere else, just so he could resume his research, but he couldn't find any. After a while he had given up.

Then why would all of a sudden, the President of the most thriving drug institute in the Mutual States personally send him an email, inviting him for a job?

It made no sense. However, on the off chance that the email wasn't a prank, Omar had come. In fact, he had dropped everything in his life back in Egypt and caught the first plane to UAE.

As he now disembarked the vehicle, a gush of dry, sandy wind hit his face, turning his lips parched. The climate wasn't just hot, it was scorching. Omar frowned, pursing his mouth. He had only once been here before, but he didn't remember the city being this blistering. In fact, he could feel something unusual about the climate. The heat was unrelenting, a suffocating blanket that smothered everything in its path. It didn't feel natural at all, but more like the result of some insidious, artificial deed.

Despite it, the terminal was abuzz with activity, and a crowd had gathered. Most of the people were dressed in the traditional Arabian thawbs, seemingly unfazed by the weather. Omar, on the other hand, felt like he was melting. He pulled out a handkerchief from his pocket to wipe the sweat from his forehead. He regretted his choice of clothing and wished he had worn a thawb like everyone else instead of his stuffy suit. Maybe then, he wouldn't have felt so uncomfortable in the scorching heat.

Ignoring his discomfort, Omar retrieved his NeuroPhone from his pocket and willed the email to appear, the one he received from the President of the Emirate Drug Research Institute. The nanobots in the small circular device readjusted themselves until it transformed into a screen that sparked to life. The device floated up to Omar's face, who went through the content of the email for the umpteenth time. As soon as he was done reading, the nanobots shifted back to their original circular form and the device came to rest on his extended palm.

He threw the phone back into his pocket, and squinted his eyes, scanning the terminal. If the email was to be trusted, then someone from the ERDI would be here to pick him up.

As Omar waited, doubts and uncertainty began to flicker in his mind. He recalled how his colleagues, friends, and nearly everyone had warned him against coming here, thinking it was a bad idea. They all believed it was some misunderstanding or maybe even a prank. Because the idea that the EDRI would actually bother to personally invite him seemed so ridiculous.

Omar didn't hold it against them, as he himself had a hard time believing that this opportunity was real.

The main reason behind his strong determination to come here was to learn more about the EDRI's incredible wonder drug that had revolutionized the economic situation of the entire country. He was particularly curious to know if the drug indeed had the rumoured healing properties.

If it did, Omar was determined to use his potential new position and connections to aid those ill-fated parts of the Mutual States that were still grappling with the aftermath of the Civil War. One of those places being his hometown, the small village of Qurna. As someone who had lost his childhood to the war, Omar was frustrated to watch helplessly as people went through the same things he did. He had decided long ago to make a change, but only now got the chance to work on it. He was not going to waste it.

Despite having a grand goal, it stung Omar that his friends failed to comprehend his aspirations and instead labelled him an idealistic fool for leaving behind his somewhat stable career in Egypt, just so he could pursue what they saw as a far-fetched opportunity and a mere "pipe dream".

Glancing down, Omar once again reached for the clasp of his vintage watch. The last reminder of his father. Omar wondered if he was still alive, would he have understood? Omar didn't even have to consider. He knew his father would not have just allowed him but encouraged him to help those people.

Unbidden, memories of his time in the war resurfaced in Omar's mind. Brief glimpses of his father being shot, his house burning, and his brother being beaten to death. Those moments flashed before his eyes, but he refused to linger. He never did. Despite the passing years, he still couldn't bring himself to process or contemplate what he had experienced. He couldn't forget those events either, so he shook his head in an attempt to shake the images from his thoughts.

As he was lost in his thoughts, a native Emirati approached Omar with impeccable timing, interrupting his reverie, and bringing him back to the present.

"Assalamualaikum," He smiled pleasantly, offering him the standard arabic greeting and sticking out his hand for Omar to shake, "Mr Khalden, it's a pleasure to meet you."

"Walekumassalam," Omar replied, grasping his hand firmly. He tried to hide the flair of relief in his chest. He studied the native curiously, and frowned, somewhat confused of his casual attire. He had expected employees of EDRI to dress more formally, but the man was wearing a thawb like everyone else.

The Emirati didn't seem to notice Omar's stare and went on, "My name is Haroon Zakir. I'm from the EDRI. I'm here to escort you to your hotel."

Zakir was a friendly man. He asked Omar about his trip and made casual small talk on the way as he led him outside the terminal. Omar on the other hand though, wondered for the first time at the possibility of this being a scam. He followed the escort sceptically. However, his suspicions were dissipated as soon as he saw his ride. Instead of a car, there was an electronic hovercraft waiting for him. A self-driven vehicle, paired with the smartest AI ever created in the Middle East. Omar's jaw dropped a little at the sight of it. He put his bag inside, before eagerly climbing into the air-conditioned craft. He relaxed, wiping the sweat from his brow. He was now convinced about the genuineness of that email. Only the EDRI could afford something like this.

Zakir climbed in beside him. He spoke a few activation commands, and the engine thrummed to life. The vehicle thrust upwards. Omar held his breath, clenching his fists. His stomach churned with nausea and excitement. He was compelled to close his eyes, but with Zakir beside him appearing nonchalant, he forced them to remain open, making sure not to look down the window. His fingers reached for the metallic clasp of his watch.

At some point, the hovercraft slowed. For a brief moment, it seemed to hang suspended in mid-air, almost weightless, before it smoothly glided forward. The boosters, which had been propelling it upwards, swivelled a full ninety degrees, surging it ahead at an incredible speed.

Omar finally dared to peek out of the window, and once he did, his eyes widened in shock. He couldn't help but feel a sense of awe wash over him as he gazed down at the sprawling metropolis before him. He had always known that the UAE was a prosperous nation. However, seeing the stark contrast between the glittering skyscrapers and luxury cars here and the poverty and hardship that plagued the rest of the Mutual States was a shock to him. Despite having heard stories before, seeing it with his own eyes left him speechless. The sheer scale of the city and the technology on display was unlike anything he had ever seen before.

Omar felt a chill crawling down his back. The enormity of the fact that he was going to work with these people struck him. Especially when he suddenly realized that without the EDRI, none of this would have been possible.

Even though, the economies of the Mutual Nations had never fully recovered after the oil reserves ran dry, UAE had still found a way to break out of what everyone called the Great Depression. And it was all because of the EDRI. Particularly that one scientist named Mustafa Hamd, who developed a drug that changed the tide of the health industry across the globe. He named it Shifa. As it turned out, the rumours Omar had heard of the UAE's recent riches were no lie, apparently.

He now understood why the rest of the Mutual Nations were suddenly strengthening their ties with the country, renegotiating the terms of the Islamic International Alliance, that still held strong even after almost three centuries since the formation of the RSA and the BSR. Those who turned their backs on the nation earlier were coming to regret it now.

Omar blinked out of his reverie as the vehicle glided ahead. He gazed down at the view, and Zakir shared tid-bits about the various scenic routes of the city, like a tour guide. Omar was grateful for the insight. He had been to Dubai only once, and that was years ago. The city had changed so much in the last decade that he could barely recognise it.

Skyscrapers were on both sides of the wide smooth roads. Minuscule planes flew back and forth through the air; and pedestrians carried gadgets Omar had only seen in western media. He gawked at the scenery with wide eyes, earning a chuckle from Zakir, who was apparently aware of the difference in lifestyle between UAE, and the rest of the Mutual Nations, which were still trapped in the Great Economic Depression.

"They're called Delidrones," the escort explained nodding towards one of the mini planes. "They deliver merchandise to online customers."

"What about that tech dog?" Omar pointed below.

"An AI pet," Zakir replied. "They're like typical pets, only they look after you instead of the other way around."

Omar was impressed. He turned back to his escort. "What do you do at the EDRI?"

"I'm an analytical chemist," Zakir informed. "I assist in Shifa Optimization Lab. In fact, I'm a core member of the team that first developed it."

"The Shifa?" Omar whipped his head in shock. "You worked on Shifa?" Omar narrowed his eyes in disbelief. "If that's true, then why would they send you on an escort job?"

"Because I volunteered." Zakir answered simply.

Omar was still not convinced. "Why though?"

"I read your old papers, from before your retirement and I admired your research. Your idea about that drug that could serve as a substitute for the nutrients and then seize the sensation of hunger was remarkable."

"Um, thanks." Pride sparked within Omar. He had written that paper years ago, but he still remembered it clearly. If it hadn't been for the lack of funding, he believed that his ideas could've landed him somewhere, instead of him having to retire so early.

The two men continued to chat for the rest of the way, mostly about Omar's research, until they finally reached their destination. The hovercraft slowly glided down, settling down on the concrete pavement.

Omar climbed out of the vehicle and dry air once again seemed to suck out the moisture from his skin. "What's wrong with the climate here?" He finally asked, peeking at his escort through the hovercraft's window.

"It's because of the radiation." Zakir's face turned grim. "Since that asteroid crash occurred, the weather never changes here."

Omar raised his brows. He had heard about the tragic crash, but back then he was so busy with his research that he didn't bother to know more, aside from the fact that some city in the north had perished and that Dubai Emirate was untouched. "Didn't that crash happen somewhere in Ajman?"

"Not somewhere in Ajman," Zakir exclaimed. "It wiped the entire city! The radiation is so strong that it messed up the climate even way out here. It's much worse at the crater."

Omar shuddered, hoping he wouldn't get to find out for himself.

The two men exchanged parting words before the escort slid shut the glass window of the hovercraft and flew away.

By the time Omar arrived at his hotel room, he was once again drenched in sweat. He wanted nothing more than to go into the air-conditioned room, but his footsteps slackened, when he noticed a woman fiddling with the lock on his door. Just to be sure, he rechecked the room number plaque. He seemed to be in the right place.

Omar used his handkerchief to wipe off the sweat and then cleared his throat. "Excuse me, Miss."

The woman turned, raising an eyebrow. She waited for Omar to speak, but he was suddenly at a loss of words. She was literally the most beautiful girl he had ever seen. Her curly dark hair haloed a face that had perfectly symmetrical features, and a body that was curved in all the right places.

"Ah... Ahem," he finally cleared his throat. "Th- That's my room." He glanced at the keycard in her hand, which she was swiping uselessly at the lock. "May I?" He extended his hand towards her.

She narrowed her eyes slightly but then sighed and dropped the keycard into his palm. "Go on ahead." Her voice was soft and buttery.

Omar examined the number on the card. The letters were faded, so he had to squint his eyes to be able to read it. Once he did, he pointed at the adjoining door. "You got the wrong door. That one is yours. Try again."

He handed the keycard back to her, and once she swiped it at the next door, it unlocked immediately.

"Thank you," she smiled.

Omar could only manage a nod as she disappeared in her room. He stood for a while staring at her door, before snapping back to his senses, and entering his own room.

The suite was lavish, but needlessly ostentatious. Not that Omar minded, though. He turned on the AC, and relished the coolness, plopping down on a sofa. Without meaning to, his thoughts landed back on the woman from the hallway. He tried to get her out of his mind. It was hard, because all he could focus on was the fact that she was right next door, with nothing but a wall separating them.

In the end, Omar decided to look into the asteroid crash, remembering Zakir's words. And it finally provided him the distraction he needed.

He fished out his circular NeuroPhone from his pocket and the nanobots readjusted, floating up. A holographic image was projected from the device, and his AI companion, Spark waved at him. "Good evening, Omar. How was your flight?"

"It was okay," he glanced outside the window of his room. "Can you tell me anything about that asteroid crash from a few years ago?" He asked, straight to the point, not in the mood of idle chit chat.

"Certainly," Spark nodded, "On September 18th, 2318, an asteroid, named 184 Megalia crashed into the earth, wiping out the entire city of Ajman. It was evacuated in time—"

"I know all of that already," Omar interrupted him. "Isn't there anything about the radiation?"

"It has been seven years since the incident, but toxic radiation emitted during the crash still lingers at the crater, because of which the Emir of UAE has deemed the area uninhabitable. It is off limits to the general public."

"That's it?"

Spark nodded. "There's a lot of speculation regarding the crash, but not any specific details provided. Would you like me to go through them?"

"Never mind," Omar leaned back on the sofa. With a wave, he turned off the hologram and wondered why there wasn't any news about the radiation outside the vicinity of the crater. Especially since it was messing up the climate to such a degree.

II

Omar sat by the window, sipping his iced coffee as he watched his hotel building looming across the road. He had opted for this cozy cafe for breakfast instead of the lavish restaurant back at the hotel, seeking a moment of peace before his meeting with the President. He was anxious enough already, and the grandeur of the hotel would have only added to his nerves.

A notification bell chimed, and Omar pulled out the NeuroPhone from his pocket. The nanobots assembled into a regular smartphone in his hands, its screen flickering to life to show him the recent text from Zakir:

On my way, will be there in 15.

More than enough time to finish his coffee. Omar set his phone down on the table, folded his fingers around the cup, and just as he was about to take a sip, he heard the door open. A gorgeous woman entered the cafe, making her way inside, and Omar's heartbeat quickened with anticipation. It was the same woman from the hotel. Somehow, she looked even more beautiful than last night. Once again, Omar found himself tongue tied, staring at her in awe.

The woman sat down on a table and picked up the menu, her eyes darting through its contents. She must have noticed Omar staring, and their eyes met. Omar was about to look away, but recognition sparked on the woman's face. She smiled and waved at him.

Omar waved back. His heart racing. He felt embarrassed by the impact her presence had on him. It made him feel younger. For the next few minutes, he managed to catch a few sneaky glances, without making it obvious.

A part of him wanted to walk up to her and ask her out, but another, more realistic part of him knew he didn't stand a chance. With a sigh, he looked down at his coffee.

Despite his academic success and conventionally attractive features, Omar had a non-existent love life. He had dated many women, but things never went further than that. He had always wondered why, and he finally got his answer from one of his colleagues at work.

He was out with the other professors one day, when he timidly mentioned how lacking his relationships were, and his colleague, Mr Tariq, the student's guidance counsellor, after a pushy round of inquisition, immediately deduced it was because of his traumatic experiences from the war and how he refused to speak about it. Something about how he was subconsciously wrecking his own relationships because he disliked depending on others for the fear of being disappointed.

That was the last time Omar talked to Mr Tariq. After that, he even gave up on the idea of relationships. Until this moment.

Omar had been attracted to women before, but it was the first time he was compelled to this degree to introduced himself to one.

For a long while, he tried to push her out of his mind, reminding himself that he didn't have time to be distracted However, his eyes were constantly drawn to her face, like a moth to a flame. When he noticed her wiping her mouth and gesturing to the waiter, he gulped down the rest of the contents from his own cup, and sprang to his feet, deciding to ask her out. It was not like he had anything to lose.

As the woman proceeded to pay through her phone, Omar made his way to the door at the pace of a slug, hoping she would eventually catch up to him. But something held her up. Curious, Omar inched closer to her table, pretending to make his way towards the bathroom.

"What's wrong?" The waiter asked.

The woman looked up. "I don't know. It's not working." The nanobots of her phone adjusted into the shape of a neural wallet several times, but whenever she tried to pay through it, they embedded back into their original circular form.

With a frown, she put down her phone and instead fiddled inside her purse. When she couldn't find what she was looking for, an apologetic smile suffused her face. "There's something wrong with my NeuroWallet, and I don't have cash on me right now. Just give me a few minutes, I'm staying at that hotel across the road. I can go and get it."

The waiter raised an eyebrow, suspiciously. "You'll have to come with me, Ma'am."

Some people turned to look in their direction, and the woman's expression grew worried. She hesitated.

Before Omar could talk himself out of it, he was moving forward. "I'll take care of it." He whispered to the woman and used his own phone to pay for the meal.

The transaction occurred without a hitch this time and the woman looked at Omar gratefully. "Thank you so much! Can you wait for me here? Just let me go get my purse, I'll pay you back."

Omar shook his head. "Don't worry about it—" he was saying, but the woman was already gone.

Omar stepped outside the cafe to wait for her and instantly regretted the decision because of the heat. He had debated between choosing another suit and a thawb for his meeting with the President, and eventually decided to go with the suit, despite the scorching climate. A decision he was now beginning to regret. Beads of sweat collected on his temples. He restlessly tapped his foot on the ground, glancing into his watch every now and then. It was almost eight, which meant Zakir would be here any minute to pick him up.

Omar desperately did not want to leave before talking to this girl, but he knew he'd have to if Zakir showed up before her. Fortunately, he hadn't. Before long, the woman was back with her brilliant smile, and a wallet tucked into her hand.

"We've got to stop running into each other like this. Unlike what you saw, I swear I'm not always needing help." She grinned, and fished out a bill from her purse, handing it to Omar. "Thanks again."

Omar made no move to reach for it. "How about, instead of paying me back, you treat me to dinner?" He was smiling.

"Shouldn't you introduce yourself before asking me out?" She winked and Omar let out a breath he didn't realize he had been holding.

"Omar Khalden," he said, offering his hand, instead of the standard Arabic greeting which he was accustomed to. "I used to be a professor in Cairo, but I recently moved here since I got a job offer from the EDRI." Omar deliberately failed to mention that he wasn't technically hired yet.

"The EDRI? Lucky for you." The woman raised her brows, clearly impressed.

"What about you? You don't seem like you're from around here."

"I'm Sarah," she said. "Private investigator. And yes, I just moved here as well."

"So, what do you say about that dinner?"

"I'd like that." Sarah smiled. "You already know what room I'm staying in. You can pick me up at seven."

"It's a date," Omar added quickly.

Before they had the chance to talk any further, the buzz of Zakir's hovercraft caught Omar's attention and he let out a resigned sigh.

He told Sarah that he had to leave, and the two exchanged parting words before he climbed into the vehicle to fly off to the EDRI.

III

The EDRI complex was less than a fifteen-minute ride from the hotel building. As the hovercraft glided through the city, Omar's attention was drawn to a skyscraper that towered above the rest. The words 'Emirate Drug Research Institute' were prominently displayed at the top.

The vehicle smoothly settled by the gate, and both men climbed out. As soon as they did, the craft flew away again to park itself.

"Welcome," Zakir exclaimed, holding his arms up, "to the EDRI."

Omar stared in wonder. The building was a marvel of modern architecture, rising several stories high with an elegant, curved facade. The glass walls reflected the sunlight, creating a dazzling effect that made the building appear to shimmer.

Omar took a deep breath and followed Zakir into the entrance. He was immediately greeted by a spacious, airy atrium. The walls were painted a soothing shade of blue, and the floor was tiled in a warm beige colour. The space was filled with natural light, which streamed in from the glass roof overhead.

To the left of the entrance, a sleek reception desk stood, staffed by a friendly-looking lady who glanced up as the two men approached, and smiled warmly at them.

"Hey there, Raviha," Zakir waved. He exchanged pleasantries with her and introduced Omar, to whom the receptionist handed a pass, before letting them enter.

Zakir then led him across a passageway, and Omar's eyes were instantly glued to the various labs they happened to pass by.

He was amazed when he saw the technology. It was nothing like what he had seen in Egypt. The place crawled with more androids than people. Even the tiniest of tasks seemed to have a robot assigned specifically to them, leaving the people only for intellectual and managerial duties.

"Woah!" Omar breathed.

"Woah, indeed, my friend." Zakir led him further down the hallway, and Omar was utterly thrilled as he caught a glance of the equipment inside the enormous labs. Dozens of scientists in crisp white lab coats working together in a hectic manner.

Omar was tempted to ask Zakir for a tour, but before he had a chance, they reached the end of the hallway and the escort stopped, pointing at an office door.

"Wait inside," he told Omar. "Layla will let you in, when the President wants to see you."

Omar nodded and stepped into the room. A large circular desk made of black glass sat in the middle, with a beautiful woman with long, flowing hair sitting behind a Nanotech computer. Omar figured she must be Layla, the President's secretary.

With a warm smile, Layla asked him to take a seat in one of the comfortable chairs that lined the wall.

As Omar perched down on the cushioned bench, he noticed another man already seated there, waiting. Unlike him though, this man had a well-toned physique and was dressed entirely in black. Under normal circumstances, Omar would strike a conversation, but in this case, he decided not to bother this man especially because of his grim resting face.

While waiting for the President to become available, Omar took in his surroundings. To the right of the room, there was a door that led to the President's main office. It was made of dark metal and had a series of sensors that controlled access. The security was tight, which was to be expected in a building dedicated to drug research.

Omar's thoughts were interrupted when a server appeared, carrying a tray of food. He was ushered into the main office by Layla. For the brief moment the door was opened, Omar tried to peek inside. From his angle, he couldn't see the President, but instead he caught a glimpse of the person's face sitting opposite him.

He had a fair complexion, with almond-shaped eyes and a dark brown stubble. His head was covered beneath a white cloth securely tied by a black cord.

Omar narrowed his eyes, before recognition dawned on his face. He was positive he had seen the man before, although he wasn't certain where. So, he racked his brain, forcing himself to remember.

A short while later, when Omar still couldn't recall who that man was and where he had seen him before, he gave up.

Approximately half an hour passed when the door to the inner office opened again.

The President's guest stepped outside. Now that Omar had a good look at his face, he instantly remembered who the man was, and his jaw dropped in surprise. He was the grandson of the UAE's Emir, Prince Faiz Pasha.

Although not usually one to be starstruck, Omar's breath still caught in his throat when he realized the identity of the man before him. He sprang to his feet, uncertain of how to act.

The Prince briefly glanced in his direction before striding out of the room, followed by his bulky man, whom Omar only now realized must be his guard.

Feeling somewhat dazed, Omar slumped back into his seat, feeling foolish for overreacting. In reality, it was the Prince's grandfather who truly deserved his respect. Every man, woman, and child in the Mutual States had heard of Kareem Pasha at least once in their lives. He was the man who single-handedly rebuilt the United Arab Nations from the ashes after its government and economy crumbled in the aftermath of oil and the ensuing Middle Eastern Civil War.

Emir Kareem Pasha, a visionary leader, not only oversaw the remarkable reconstruction of the UAE but also transformed it into one of the most prosperous and efficiently governed nations globally. His role in extinguishing the Civil War, instigated by the RSA due to their belief that the remaining oil resources were being concealed by the Mutual States, cannot be overstated.

At the time, the UAE was a tiny country consisting of only seven Emirates, with most of the land formerly under the jurisdiction of other nations such as Oman, Qatar, and Kuwait. However, after the war ended, the citizens were desperate for a selfless leader and were more than willing to let Kareem Pasha rise to become their absolute monarch, having proven himself worthy on more than one occasion.

His accomplishments did not end there. He did not only help the UAE but also aided other allies of the Islamic International Alliance who were victims of the same war instigated by the RSA. Pasha worked tirelessly to bring an end to the conflicts, saving countless lives in the process.

Omar was one of those people who survived the war only because the Pasha's interference. If not for his efforts, Omar would have been caught in the crossfire alongside his family. This was why he felt indebted to the man and held him in such high regard.

Besides all this, Omar was even more impressed by the fact that the President was casually meeting the grandson of the most powerful man in the Middle East.

"Mr Khalden," Layla interrupted his thoughts. "The President will see you now."

Omar broke out of his reverie. With a gulp, he got up to his feet, glanced at his reflection on a windowpane, and fixed the collar of his shirt. He appeared older than he was. His dark hair neatly trimmed. His brown eyes nervous yet crinkling with excitement. With a sigh, he stepped through the metal doors and found himself in a spacious office.

The room had a sleek design with dark wood panels and glossy white tiles. There was a seating area with black leather chairs and a low coffee table aside from the main desk in the centre, at which the President was seated.

Shiekh Huzaifa was a well-known personage in the field of medicine. He was also one of the core members of the team that created Shifa. It was rumoured that Huzaifa was the one who created the main compound that made Shifa what it was, but Mustafa Hamd somehow hogged the credit from him.

Omar wasn't sure he believed this, but that didn't mean he doubted the intellect of the man. In fact, Omar had been following Huzaifa's work for years before Shifa even existed.

As Omar approached the desk, a shiver ran down his back. It was nothing short of meeting a celebrity. He nervously trotted across the room.

Huzaifa was a hefty man well into his late fifties. He wore a jovial smile on his face.

"Assalamualaikum," He stood to meet Omar, who responded to the Arabic greeting in like. The President ushered him to sit, and Omar gingerly perched down on a chair.

The President engaged in small talk with Omar, but instead of getting straight to business, he digressed into various topics, sounding relaxed and friendly. It was as if they were old acquaintances catching up, rather than a potential employer and employee. Curiously, the President seemed interested in every aspect of Omar's life except his research.

At first, Omar was perplexed by this behaviour but soon realized that the President was trying to assess him. Despite feeling tempted to urge the President to get to the point, Omar exercised restraint and remained patient.

Finally, after what seemed like an eternity, the President inquired about his research.

"So, Omar," Huzaifa pressed the tips of his fingers and leaned on his desk. "I was rifling through your work on the university website, and I came across a formula for a potential drug," he scratched his chin, "what was it...?"

Omar perked up, "It was to create a pill that could take away the sensation of hunger. It has to do with the posterior vagal nerve—"

"Not that one," the President interrupted. "It wasn't published in any paper." He paused to consider. "It had something to do with prolonging life."

Omar's face fell. If the President had picked him solely because of that, then they were both going to be disappointed. He hesitated, wondering how to answer the question. In the end, he decided to go with the truth. "I know which drug you mean, but that formula is purely hypothetical. I've already performed experiments and consulted with people regarding it, but unfortunately there's no possible way to turn it into a reality."

"Regardless, I'd still like to know more about it," Huzaifa leaned forward.

Omar hesitated again. He didn't see the point, but he was not going to refuse the President. With a deep sigh, he stood up, and glanced around the office "is there a board I can borrow?"

Huzaifa pulled out an E-Pen from his desk drawer and handed it to Omar. He used a remote to turn off the lights and curtains, before firing up the hologram projectors.

For a moment, Omar was too stunned to move. He gawked at the floating application symbols around the room with his jaw hanging, but he immediately recovered himself and used the E-Pen to draw the rough sketch of a cell in the air.

He gasped aloud when all of a sudden, his diagram was replaced with an actual picture of a cell. This was nothing like using the hologram his phone had.

"You don't have to draw." The President explained. "You can just write what you want to show, and it'll appear."

With a nod, Omar began scribbling the word, Telomeres, and just as the president had said, the image of the tiny DNA-protein structure appeared in the air.

Omar cleared his throat and began, "Cells can only regenerate a number of times, and one of the reasons is because of this thing," he pointed at the structure. "The Telomeres shortens every time the cell splits into two, and ultimately the cell dies. My research focuses on finding a way to extend telomeres, using a specific chemical reaction," He went on eloquently, his earlier nervousness forgotten, as he hastily scribbled an equation on the air.

The elements he denoted using symbols and abbreviations appeared around him, except for the one missing reactant that he always described as X.

"I've been working on this for years, but I never found a suitable replacement for the missing reactant, X."

When Omar first worked on this, he thought he had a breakthrough, but even after years, he was always stuck on the same place.

Despite everything, as he explained his research to President Huzaifa, the spark he had first felt, in the initial months working on this project, reappeared. His passion reignited.

Hours passed, and the President listened, even though Omar repeatedly pointed out, that this was futile, since his research had no conclusion, but Huzaifa only waved at him to continue.

When Omar was done with his lecture, he slumped down on one of the chairs, suddenly weary as he poured himself water.

"Did you ever consider Trinitroxypropane?" The President offered. "For X?"

Omar shook his head. "It wouldn't work; I've already tried it."

Huzaifa nodded, as he pressed a button on the remote and the lights once again flashed, the curtains sliding open to reveal the midday sun.

"You have done fine research," the President said.

"Thank you, but to be frank, Sir, I don't see the point. The equation is still incomplete."

"What if I tell you there's a way for you to complete it? Would you like to know?"

"Are you serious?" Omar raised his brows. "Yes!"

"You'll have to sign this first." The President slid forward a document on the table, and Omar frowned at the following bold letters written on the top:

NON-DISCLOSURE AGREEMENT.

IV

Omar briefly skimmed through the pages of the NDA before signing the sheets. The President's words about making his hypotheses a reality still ringing in his mind.

Huzaifa gave him a lopsided smile and placed the signed documents into his desk drawer. He rose to his feet. "Follow me."

Omar walked right behind the President, as the two men filed out of the office, and emerged into the spacious lobby. They ran into dozens of androids on their way to the elevator. When they finally reached the highest floor, the President led Omar through a series of doors, where androids were present to ask for his identification proof. He swiped his pass each time before he was allowed to proceed.

When they finally got to their destination, Omar's eyes drifted lazily across the room, as he soaked up the words written on the glass entrance door:

SHIFA

This entire floor was dedicated to the optimization of the crazy wonder drug Omar had heard so many rumours about. He felt his stomach twist with nervous excitement, as he followed Huzaifa through various sections of the lab. Dozens of scientists were scattered throughout the place, some fiddling with equipment, while other were busy making notes.

Most of the people in the room were so absorbed in their work that they didn't even glance up as the President and Omar entered. But those who did notice them gave Omar curious looks before offering smiles or nods to the President, who returned the gestures in kind.

Omar slowed his pace to a crawl, glancing in every direction, not even noticing that Huzaifa had halted a few feet ahead, waiting for him.

"Come on," the President ushered him forward. He stalked through the lab until he arrived at a glass cubicle inside which a female scientist was leading an experiment.

"Zarene," the President nodded at her to come outside, and the woman left someone else in charge before obliging him and exiting the cubicle. She followed him, along with Omar, to an office.

They all stepped inside, and Omar immediately surmised that this one also belonged to the President. It was smaller compared to his main office but was the same in every other aspect.

"Omar, I'd like you to meet Zarene," Huzaifa nodded at the middle-aged woman with frizzy brown hair and tan skin. "She's the one in charge here, since..." He let the sentence hang, but Omar understood. Since Mustafa Hamd, the discoverer of Shifa, passed away a few months ago.

Omar nodded understandingly as he gave a polite smile to Zarene and introduced himself. If he was going to work on Shifa in this lab, as he expected, he'll be working directly under her. It was important to make a good first impression.

"Zarene," Huzaifa went on. "I'd like you to show Omar the presentation."

He couldn't believe his eyes. Although he had heard rumours, and even seen videos online, he still couldn't bring himself to accept that what he just witnessed was possible. Not even the hour-long slideshow presentation which he had just sat through had prepared him for this. He couldn't help but be amazed.

"Do it on me," Omar blurted out.

"Are you sure?" Zarene asked, and once he nodded, she smiled, slightly amused by his reaction.

They were in a similar experiment cubicle where Omar first saw Zarene, only this one wasn't made up of see through walls, and the two of them were the only ones in it.

She handed him a knife, and Omar plunged the sharp edge into his arm making a cut as deep as he could endure. He grunted, as the blood started dripping onto the white tiled floor.

"You don't need to make it so deep," Zarene pointed out, pressing cotton on his wound to stop the bleeding. "You're only hurting yourself."

"I just want to see," he said, breathing heavily, trying to ignore the pain.

Zarene picked a new syringe, pulling in another dose of Shifa. This time, however, instead of giving it to the Volunteer, whom she just dismissed, she pressed the needle into Omar's arm.

At first nothing happened. Then, he felt the pain slightly dim before something moved inside his wound. He could feel the damaged tissues binding themselves back together. Omar gently took the piece of cotton from Zarene's fingers, which she was using to apply pressure to his wound, and he wiped away the blood with it. He gasped. The wound was gone.

Nothing but a slight tinge of pain remained.

"It's a miracle!" He exclaimed.

Zarene chuckled.

She took off her blood-stained gloves, and pointed at the direction of the men's room, where Omar washed his hands. By the time he got there, even the slight tinge of pain was gone, as if the wound was never there in the first place.

As he made his way back, Omar couldn't help but wonder how many people could've survived the war if something like Shifa existed before. Maybe his family, his brother would still be alive.

Omar stroked the metallic band of his wristwatch and took a few deep breaths to keep such thoughts at bay. It didn't matter what the war took from him. What mattered now was how many people wouldn't have to go through the same things as he did, thanks to this drug.

When he returned to the lab, he saw an android, wiping the blood on the floor, as Zarene leaned on the wall, waiting for him.

"Let's go," she said. "There's more to see."

Omar spent the next few hours with Zarene, whose carefree nature made it easy for him to enjoy her company. She gave Omar a tour of the entire lab and then showed him how Shifa was developed.

For him, it was like something straight out of a sci-fi movie. He gazed at the equipment in awe as he saw Shifa being manufactured in bulk right before his very eyes.

Omar spent the next hour going through the research notes of Shifa's late creator, Mustafa Hamd, and he was amazed by his genius. There were parts of the research that Omar couldn't figure out. He failed to fully understand the chemical formula, as there was a new compound interchangeably used in the equation, which Omar didn't recognise.

The weird part was, even when he tried to break it down, the math wouldn't add up. Part of him wanted to swallow his pride and just ask Zarene about it, but he wanted to figure it out on his own, especially since he wanted to make a good impression. So, he persisted.

A long while later, Zarene found him huddled behind a desk, hastily scribbling on his phone, no closer to figuring the secret behind Shifa.

When Omar saw her, he let out a sigh of frustration and closed the notes app in defeat. Instead, he logged onto the web chemical database and entered the compound formula. To his surprise, he found no solution.

"What on earth is this compound?" He exclaimed.

Zarene laughed. "I was wondering when you'll ask."

Omar hadn't realized that Zarene had seen through him. His face tinged slightly pink, and he looked down. "Are you going to tell me or not?"

"The President will be doing the explaining," Zarene said. "In the meantime, do you wanna see this compound?"

Omar nodded, and she led him down the stairs to a secluded back hall, labelled as the sample room, where she pulled out a petri dish and carefully placed it on a table. A powdered substance was inside, varying from shiny black to maroon, smelling like charcoal and heat.

"Sit here, and see this," she said, using a small pair of tongs to pick out some of it.

Omar did as he was told. He peeked into a microscope, while Zarene placed the powder beneath its lens.

It was a strange material, like nothing Omar had ever seen before. It had small chunks of rocks within the powder, some of which glowed molten, while others were a black so deep, that the colour seemed like void instead of dark. It was definitely a new compound; Omar was sure of it now. However, instead of being closer to figuring out its chemical makeup, he felt like the progress he had made until now was useless.

"I'm even more confused now!" He admitted.

"Don't worry, the President will explain everything," Zarene remarked. "This is the secret of Shifa. Even if someone outside this lab gets their hands on the drug's chemical formula, they won't be able to put it to use until they solve this. If it makes you feel any better, when Mustafa Sir first created it, none of us were able to figure it out either."

Omar frowned. "So, you knew all along I'd fail, and still let me go on?" He narrowed his eyes. "You were enjoying it, weren't you?"

"Every second of it," she flashed a smile. "You should've seen your face."

Once their friendly banter subsided, Zarene told him that the President was expecting him in his office, and Omar raised to his feet. As he was getting up, a small robot tasked with cleaning the floor scurried by, startling Omar, who moved back to avoid stepping on it, and accidentally knocked over the petri dish.

Two things happened simultaneously then. First, Omar tried to reach for the petri dish, but Zarene pushed him away, throwing herself along with him. Secondly, the petri dish collided with the floor, and as its contents flew out, the impact caused an enormous explosion that burned away half of the sample room. If Zarene hadn't thrown Omar back, he would have suffered the same fate as the burnt walls.

Fire alarms echoed loudly, and androids were suddenly all around them, some extinguished the fire, other helped Omar and Zarene up.

"What the hell was that?" Omar snapped, "How did it just light up?"

"That compound... is highly explosive." Zarene looked down. "We're lucky it was such a small amount, or the entire building could've burned down."

Huzaifa was sitting at his desk, using his computer when Omar knocked on the door.

"Are you okay?" The President asked, as he ushered him inside.

"I'm fine," Omar lied, hiding his unease. The truth was he was more shaken that he let on. After spending hours closely observing the chemical makeup of this new compound and then seeing it just explode like that, Omar couldn't help but be a little anxious. He understood the need for secrecy, but suddenly his gut was telling him there was something larger at play here.

The President, having seen the sceptic look on Omar's face, raised his eyebrows. "Are you sure?"

Omar relaxed into an easy smile. "Of course. The fire just startled me. I'm okay now."

Huzaifa nodded, and asked Omar about his insights and experience. The two men talked in length about the lab, and Shifa. At long last, when Omar mentioned the new compound, what he was most curious about, Huzaifa only shrugged. "The NDA is not enough for me to reveal that to you. This is sensitive information. If you want to know the secret behind Shifa, you would have to accept the job I'm offering you first."

Omar hesitated. The memory of the explosion flashed in his mind, and he wondered if he really wanted to work here. Before he could let the incident talk him out of it, Omar convinced himself that it was just an accident. Ignoring his gut, he smiled. "I accept it."

Huzaifa flashed him a grin. "Welcome to the team! From now on, you'll be taking Mustafa's place and manage the lab."

"Wait?" Omar's eyes widened. "You want me to be in charge? Wh–What about Zarene?"

"She's an amazing researcher, but she doesn't have the same potential as Mustafa or you. She had known all along that she was just holding the position temporarily."

Omar blinked, not being able to comprehend how his life could change so drastically in the span of a day. "I'm in," he offered his hand to the President to shake. "Now can you tell me about that compound?"

Huzaifa grinned. "I'd rather show you."

V

The next morning, the weather had gone from hot to scalding. Omar was drenched in sweat when he woke up. Due to the bizarre climate, he had adjusted the air conditioning in his hotel room to have a moderate temperature, but apparently that wasn't enough. This time, he turned it down all the way to cold, before hopping in the bath for a quick shower.

As Omar stood in the bathroom, savouring the feel of chilled water on his skin, his mind went through many things. He thought about Shifa, the new compound, and the lab. He thought about the secret regarding the drug, which Huzaifa was about to show him today. However, he mostly wondered about the asteroid crash, the radiation from which had reduced this city to a furnace. Omar had found it odd that there was no news of the city's deteriorating climate on the web. As thrilled as he may be about his new job, he couldn't get used to the idea of living here permanently. He pondered whether the rest of the people around here had simply grown accustomed to the arid air, or if they were also bothered by the intense heat as much as he was. He made a mental note to ask Zarene about it today. Out of all his new colleagues, he felt the most comfortable around her. Besides, it was not like he knew anyone else here.

All of a sudden, the image of Sarah popped into his mind, and Omar froze. He swore, hurriedly turning off the shower. A sinking feeling settled in the pit of his stomach. He was supposed to have dinner with her last night, but since it was so late by the time he returned from the lab, he didn't even remember to call it off. She must have waited for him and then assumed he stood her up.

He slapped his forehead. "You idiot!" He was lucky enough to have a shot with a woman like Sarah, and he blew it before it even began. He may earn more money now, but he was apparently destined to die alone. His streak of bad luck with women was proof of that.

With a frustrated sigh, he put on his clothes and walked out of the bathroom. The moment he opened the door; he let out a startled gasp at the sight in front of him.

Perched up on the couch in the far end of the room was Sarah. She was wearing a white shirt and a knee length skirt, looking just as gorgeous as Omar remembered her. She must have heard him enter, because she jumped up to her feet and met his eyes.

Omar gaped at her in confusion.

"I'm here to talk. I was going to call you, but then I realized I don't have your contact info," Sarah explained. "I'm sorry I let myself in without asking. Your door was unlocked, and I heard you in the shower while knocking, so I thought I'd wait inside. I couldn't come back, you see, I just checked out."

Omar didn't know how to respond. He racked his brain, wondering what Sarah would have to say to him. Usually, he was on the other end of these situations, but he never visited the women who stood him up, so he had no idea what to expect.

"What," he carefully asked, "did you want to talk to me about?"

"Last night."

Omar frowned. He couldn't detect any anger from Sarah, which was odd. If she wasn't mad about him not showing up yesterday, why else was she here? He raised his brows questioningly.

"I wanted to apologise for not being able to make it last night,"

Sarah looked down apologetically. "I got caught up somewhere. It wasn't intentional. I'm here so you don't get the wrong idea."

For a moment, Omar remained frozen, but as soon as her words registered in his mind, a grin broke loose on his face. He could not believe his luck. "Oh, never mind about that."

"Really?" Sarah blushed. "I was worried that I blew it."

It was all Omar could do to keep from laughing. Ever since he came to this city, luck had been shining down on him. Aloud he said, "So you checked out?"

"Yeah," Sarah nodded. "I found a place."

"Oh. In that case, we should exchange contacts."

"We should," Sarah held out her phone expectantly.

Omar reached for his own circular NeuroPhone from the desk, and it readjusted into the shape of a regular smartphone. He held it out as well, slightly touching its sensor to Sarah's phone for a brief moment. As soon as it did, the contact information from their social media accounts to email addresses and numbers were saved into the other's phone.

Omar promised to call her, and the two talked for a short while, before Sarah got up to leave.

A few minutes after she was gone, Omar's phone beeped with a text from Zakir, who was downstairs waiting for him.

"Did you sign the contract?" It was the first thing Zakir asked, the moment Omar climbed into the hovercraft.

"I did." He reached into his coat pocket and handed him the papers.

Zakir made sure they were signed properly, before he strapped on his seatbelt and activated the vehicle.

The craft rose in the air. When it started moving ahead, Omar noticed it was gliding in the opposite direction instead of taking them to the EDRI. "Where are we going?"

"Ajman," Zakir answered.

"What? Isn't that where the asteroid struck?"

"Yep."

"I thought the place was filled with toxic radiation?"

"It is," Zakir nodded. "Don't worry, though. We'll stop on the way to put on hazmat suits."

Omar kept his eyes fixated on the window, watching the city from above. A while later, he noticed a wired fence. Once they flew over it, he was immediately expecting to see wreckage but instead, what he saw were perfectly constructed houses that seemed to be abandoned in a rush. He started sweating despite the air conditioning inside the vehicle. They glided for another quarter of an hour before the terrain finally changed from concrete pavement to desert sand.

Before Omar saw any real sign of the damage, their vehicle smoothly hovered down by the entrance of a building, which appeared to be newer than the rest of the dilapidated structures surrounding it. As Zakir had said, they had stopped here to get ready before entering the vicinity of the crater.

Omar bit back his questions, trying not to let his impatience show. He wondered what any of it had to do with the compound. For a brief moment, he considered the possibility of the compound being a natural resource found within the asteroid, but he soon dismissed the idea considering its destructive nature. If the asteroid was indeed loaded with such a highly dangerous explosive, then the damage dealt by it would've been a lot worse.

Why else would they bring him to the crater? Omar couldn't tell.

Zakir led him through the entrance, into a tunnel. The place was so suffocating, that Omar was tempted to turn back, but he ignored his discomfort and continued to follow his escort.

Eventually, they found themselves in an underground hall, where each of them were handed a couple of hazmat suits, which they put on immediately.

Omar had expected to feel worse after lugging on that heavy suit, but he felt significantly better, compared to breathing the scalding air outside.

In the end, they arrived in a room where two men were waiting for them already strapped in suits of their own. One of them was the President. At first, Omar couldn't recognise him through the helmet, but he did once Huzaifa waved at him. The other man was a stranger.

"This is Abel," the President introduced the man, his voice clear through the microphone Omar had worn beneath his helmet. "He is our guide."

Omar exchanged a nod with the man, and the group followed Abel through an elevator, emerging outside once again.

As Omar stepped forward, he could feel the heat radiating from the ground, even though his protective suit. The air was thick with fumes and fog, seeping in and out of his vision, making it difficult for him to see more than a few feet ahead.

Omar took a deep breath, trying to steady his nerves as the group followed Abel. They continued to walk for a while, and eventually they saw it. The crater. The asteroid had hit with such force that the ground had been completely obliterated, leaving a vast, gaping hole in its wake.

As Omar made his way closer to the edge, he could feel the heat intensifying, the fumes making his eyes water and his throat burn. He knew that he had to be careful, but he couldn't help but feel a sense of fascination as he looked down into the depths of the crater.

The fog was suddenly lifting, being pulled away by a gust of dry wind. Omar squinted his eyes. He could make out the ashes and debris floating in the middle along with something black and shiny.

He gasped. Those were the same molten rocks, the powdered sample of which had exploded yesterday in the EDRI.

"You get it now?" Huzaifa asked, his grin apparent even through the helmet.

Omar nodded slowly, as realization struck him. The new compound, it wasn't created by Mustafa Hamd. Neither Sheikh Huzaifa. It was indeed a part of the asteroid. But that shouldn't be possible, Omar thought. If the asteroid was loaded with explosives, then it would have blown up more than just a city.

Unless... Omar stroked his chin, lost in thought. Unless the debris from the asteroid reacted with the radiation and the atmosphere, and the compound was formed after the crash.

So many things suddenly clicked into place.

Omar thought back to the day of the crash, and the timing was adding up. The asteroid struck the city seven years ago, and Shifa was created two years after that. If the compound was formed here naturally, a few months would've been enough for the reaction to occur.

Omar couldn't help but grin. It was the perfect arrangement. Nobody would even enter the crater, because of the toxic fumes, and if anyone ever tried to steal the formula of Shifa, they'd assume that the new compound in Mustafa's notes was a code.

Omar let out a shaky laugh, before something else occurred to him. The explosive nature of the compound. "Is it safe though?" He asked the President.

"Of course, it's safe!" Huzaifa assured him. "We stabilize the Neutronite before using it in Shifa."

"Neutronite?"

"That's what Mustafa called the compound. Too bad we can't enter it in the online database."

Omar nodded. "How do you stabilize it?"

"Let's head back first, we'll talk more later."

VI

On the way back to the EDRI complex, one thought consumed Omar's mind. If such a small amount of Neutronite in that petri dish could incinerate half of the supply room, he couldn't help but wonder about the magnitude of destruction a crater filled with that explosive could cause if detonated. The very idea was terrifying, sending shivers down his spine.

Adding to his unease was the realization that if knowledge of Neutronite somehow leaked beyond the country's borders, it had the potential to spark another world war.

Omar's anxiety grew, and the memories of his previous encounter with war flashed vividly in his mind. It took him several minutes to regain his composure.

Doubts and second thoughts about his decision to work at the EDRI started creeping in. He questioned whether he wanted to be part of something that had the capacity to ignite a war. However, he knew he was bound by the contract he had already signed, leaving him with no recourse.

Upon returning to the EDRI, Omar was promptly escorted to the President's office. The two men engaged in a lengthy discussion about Shifa.

Despite his scepticism, Omar hesitated to voice his concerns to his new boss. Instead, he dedicated himself to comprehending the stabilization process of Neutronite and the implemented safety precautions against its explosive nature.

Whenever Omar posed a question, the President assured him there was no danger whatsoever.

Eventually, their conversation transitioned to more pressing topics, particularly regarding Omar's prospects and future role within the organization.

"So now you understand," Huzaifa said. "I chose you for this job because your hypotheses for the life prolonging drug aligns with the ultimate goal Mustafa and I shared. We could use Neutronite and your formula to create something that can prolong life. And that will only be our first to our bigger goal, achieving immortality."

Omar nodded, still slightly dazed by everything. Despite the thrill of the President's words, an uneasy feeling crept inside Omar, as he made note of how the President was refusing to answer his specific questions every time he mentioned Neutronite, and only proceeded to feed him empty assurances.

A small voice inside Omar warned him to stay away from all this, but having already signed the contract with no way out, he pushed the thought aside and focused back on the conversation, "I'll do everything I can, Sir."

"Good," Huzaifa smiled. "I'll have someone take care of your living arrangement, and once you've settled here, you can start. For now, you should have this." The President slid a box across the desk.

Omar opened it and found a phone inside. It had the EDRI logo on its back.

"For work purposes, I'd like you to use this phone instead of your regular one. All of its communication will be encrypted."

Omar nodded. He switched on the phone and linked it to his own NeuroPhone before raising to his feet. He walked up to the door, but just as he was about to exit, he turned back. "President, would you mind if I take Mr Mustafa's research materials with me. Oh, and some samples?"

"Of course," Huzaifa nodded. "Zarene will take you to Mustafa's old office."

Zarene led Omar through a maze of corridors, their footsteps echoing softly against the tiled floor. They arrived at a door marked with a faded nameplate that read "Mustafa Hamd, Head Researcher." Zarene opened the door, revealing a small office with an L-shaped table dominating the room. The table was cluttered with stacks of papers, notebooks, and various scientific instruments. A vintage-looking computer sat in one corner.

Omar stepped inside, his eyes scanning the disarrayed room. The papers strewn across the table seemed to hold a treasure trove of information, waiting to be deciphered. He approached the computer and powered it on.

The hum of the machinery filled the room as the screen flickered to life, displaying an outdated operating system. Omar swiped his access badge on the proximity reader, and once he was inside the network, he navigated through the files, hoping to find some clues left behind by Mustafa.

To his disappointment, the computer yielded little information. Mustafa seemed to have used it sparingly, as if preferring the traditional pen and paper for his research. There were only a few scattered files, most of which contained mundane administrative documents or unrelated research data.

Omar had the choice to ask for the digitalized copy of those notes, but as he fiddled through the piles of paperwork sprawled across the desk, he decided on a whim to take the physical ones instead.

He picked up a huge folder, which was stacked with so many sheets that they were falling out of it. It slipped out of his grasp, and he almost dropped it.

"Er... Let me help you with that," Zarene held out her hands.

"I got this," Omar shot her a smile, and willed for his NeuroPhone to activate. A moment later, the circular device flew out of his pocket and settled down on the floor. It's nanobots readjusted into the shape of a tiny android, whose red eyes blinked to life.

"Spark, carry this," Omar dropped the folder on the floor, and within seconds, the little robot had neatly stacked the pages into the folder, and was holding it on top of its head.

Zarene cracked a grin. "You've got a cool AI sidekick."

"Wait until you listen to his sense of humor." Omar cracked his throat and addressed the AI, "Spark, what's that joke we practiced?"

The android blinked its red eyes and looked up. "Why did the robot go on a diet? Because it had too many bytes!"

Zarene burst into laughter.

The two colleagues continued to chat as Omar sorted through the pages, and Zarene helped him.

"I still don't see why you're bothering with this?" She wondered aloud. "You can ask for the digitalized copies of these notes."

Omar paused. "It'll sound silly." He glanced up at her. "The President told me that Mustafa was very close to completing the new formula of Shifa, before he died. I know it'll be hard to pick up his research from there, but I thought I'll at least feel closer to him if I'm working in his element. You know?"

"I guess I understand." Zarene slumped down on one of the chairs and hugged her knees.

"By the way, I've been curious about this for a while," Omar said. "How did he die?"

Zarene's expressions softened. "He had a heart condition."

"And?" Omar waited for her to elaborate.

"That's all." Zarene sighed. "Mustafa Sir was an old-fashioned guy. For some reason, he hated relying on technology. He'd only touch gadgets when he had no choice, and he never trusted AI. When his heart had issues, he could've easily had it replaced with an electronic one, instead he waited for it to get worse."

Omar frowned. "That's extreme."

"I used to think the same, but there were some things he was right about."

"Like what?"

"Like," Zarene hesitant. "The fact that they restricted the 19th floor to hide the vaccine, in case it doesn't work, instead of owning up to it. And the harmful method of stabilizing Neutronite. It's so polluting that they do those experiments in a lab near the crater, but that doesn't deny the fact that the entire city is deteriorating. Were you okay with all of it when you took this job?"

Omar had no idea what Zarene was talking about. He opened his mouth to ask her when her phone beeped, cutting him off.

She glanced at the screen and hastily jumped up to her feet. "I have to go now."

Omar started at her as she walked out of the door. Her words resonated in his mind, while he tried to focus back on his task.

Nearly two hours had passed by the time Omar was done going over the stacks of pages. It would have taken him a lot longer had it not been for his NeuroPhone AI, Spark's help.

Omar had sorted all of the sheets into neat folders before placing them on the desk in chronological order and stuck labels on them.

Omar yanked open the desk drawer, tossing the borrowed label maker inside before attempting to push it close. However, his attention was abruptly drawn to a photo frame hidden amidst the cluttered contents. Intrigued, he tried to retrieve it, only to find the stubborn drawer stuck, refusing to open fully.

Turning to the AI assistant, he commanded, "Spark, pull open the drawer."

The tiny android swiftly flew up to a nearby chair, securing its hands around the handle and exerting force. Initially, nothing happened, and Omar began to doubt the robot's strength. But then, with an unexpected burst of power, Spark yanked the handle so forcefully that the entire drawer dislodged from the desk, crashing onto the floor and spilling its contents everywhere.

Startled by the noise, Omar quickly surveyed the surroundings, ensuring no one was there to investigate. He hastened to clear the mess from the floor, focusing on retrieving the photo frame. Holding it in his hands, he gazed at the image—a younger version of Mustafa, receiving an award on a grand stage. After a moment of reflection, Omar carefully returned the photo frame to the drawer among the jumbled items.

As he prepared to push the drawer back into place, he noticed something peculiar—the wooden surface of the drawer had shifted slightly, revealing a hidden compartment beneath. Intrigued by this discovery, Omar's curiosity intensified. He pulled the drawer out once more, emptying its contents to easily remove the false wooden bottom, exposing the true one. To his surprise, he found an access badge, similar to his own one concealed within the secret compartment.

Suddenly, the sound of approaching footsteps echoed in the hallway outside, jolting Omar into action. He swiftly pocketed the access badge, sliding the wooden bottom back into place just as the door clicked open, revealing an unexpected visitor.

"You done here?" It was Zakir.

"Almost" Omar tossed the contents back into the drawer and pushed it close. His NeuroPhone shrank back into a sphere before it flew back into his pocket as Omar shot up to his feet. He opened his suitcase, which was empty aside from a little amount of Neutronite inside a tiny airtight sample bottle. He placed one of the folders into it before locking it. "I'm done."

"The President told me you wanted a tour?" Zakir asked. "Do you want to come now?"

"Absolutely," Omar grinned.

The rest of the day was consumed by a comprehensive tour of the EDRI. With a glance at his wristwatch, Zakir suggested they stop around the twentieth floor as it was getting late. Omar didn't mind. Despite his wide-eyed fascination, his legs were starting to ache.

As they approached the elevator on the eighteenth floor, a chill crawled down Omar's back, since he was reminded of Zarene's words once again.

They restricted the 19th floor to hide the vaccine.

Omar did not understand most of what she said, however, it did confirm one thing for him. His gut had been right. The Neutronite stabilizing process wasn't as harmless as the President made him to believe. It explained why he didn't answer any specific questions regarding it.

Now, at least he'll get to know more about this vaccine Zarene mentioned, and why they were hiding it.

Omar relaxed in the back of the elevator, waiting for Zakir to take him to the elusive nineteenth floor. Instead, the escort pressed the 20th button.

"The nineteenth floor is off limits," Zakir briefly explained.

Omar frowned. Since he had been offered Mustafa's old position, he had naively expected to be treated like him as well. But apparently, the President didn't trust him enough to tell him everything.

"Is it because of the vaccine?" He muttered.

Zakir whipped his head in shock. "How do you know about the vaccine?"

When Omar didn't respond, despite being pressed by the escort, Zakir sighed. "Be careful, Professor. Just do your job and don't poke your nose into things you've got nothing to do with. The President wouldn't appreciate it."

VII

That evening, as Omar entered his hotel room, he wasted no time in retrieving the folder from his suitcase. Mustafa's research papers lay before him, begging for his attention. Yet, the weight of Zakir's warning and Zarene's words hung heavy in his mind, making it impossible to concentrate.

Frustrated, Omar closed the folder, returning it to its rightful place in the suitcase. The desire to get answers from Zarene gnawed at him, but he resisted the urge to approach her in the lab. Revealing her as the source of the vaccine information to Zakir was a risk he couldn't afford to take. Besides that, he lacked any other means to contact her, adding to his frustration.

All of a sudden a melodic tune echoed from his NeuroPhone, piercing through his thoughts. Omar sat up on the bed, his eyes fixating on the circular device's small screen. It was an alarm, a gentle reminder of his dinner engagement with Sarah.

Omar had set it right after they agreed on it, so he wouldn't forget again.

The thought of Sarah made him smile. They had been texting each other, and although their conversations didn't last very long, he had enjoyed every moment of it. After that exhausting day at work, Sarah's company was exactly what he needed.

Rising from the bed, Omar stood on his feet, ready to prepare for the evening ahead.

The soft ambiance of the restaurant created a nice mood for their first date as Omar sat across from Sarah at the candlelit table. Being new in the city himself, Omar had left the details of the date for Spark to take care of, and the AI sidekick did not disappoint. The place was perfect. The clinking of cutlery and the soft jazz music created a pleasant backdrop to their conversation.

As Sarah looked into the menu, Omar gazed at her. He couldn't help but be captivated by her presence. Her warm smile and sparkling eyes held a certain charm that drew him in, making his heart flutter with anticipation. He couldn't remember the last time he was this excited to start a relationship. As they exchanged small talk, Omar found himself entranced by her every word, hanging on to her every syllable.

They ordered their meals, and after a short while, their food arrived. As the conversation deepened, Sarah began sharing bits and pieces of her background. She spoke of her last job in California, and how she decided to move to UAE after receiving an inheritance from a close family friend. She even shared a few stories from her childhood in Pennsylvania.

Omar's hand clenched at the mention of the place. "Are you from the RSA?" He tried his best not to show the shift in his mood.

"No, I only went there for a couple of years to live with my aunt when my mom got sick. I was actually born in California."

Omar breathed out a sigh of relief. After everything he had been through, his intense hatred for the RSA remained too strong to simply overlook for the sake of a woman.

"Anyway, tell me about you," Sarah leaned forward on the table.

"You know almost everything about me. It's your turn now."

"I grew up in Qurna, it's a small village in Egypt," Omar hesitated. One of the main reasons why he never got anywhere with women was because he was not too keen on opening up about himself. This time, with Sarah, he refused to let the same pattern repeat. So, he began, "I had an older brother."

"Where does he live now?" Sarah prompted.

"He died," the words were a whisper. Omar reached for his wristwatch, his fingers stroking the metal band. Despite the tightness in his throat, he pushed the words out, "My family died in the civil war. I was nine at that time."

"I'm so sorry," Sarah reached for his hands. "We don't have to talk about this if you don't want to."

Omar gulped down a glass of water and took a deep breath. He looked into Sarah's eyes and focused only on her. The knot in his throat was slowly dissolving.

Omar's eyes fluttered open, the warm morning light gently caressing his face. As he stretched his limbs and sat up in bed, a smile tugged at the corners of his lips, memories of the previous night flooding his mind.

However, his smile quickly turned into a slight panic as he glanced at the clock on his bedside table. He had overslept, and his heart raced with the realization that he was running late. With a burst of energy, he swiftly got out of bed and rushed to the bathroom to freshen up.

As Omar hastily got dressed, he reached for the contents in the pockets of the suit he wore yesterday. His fingers grazed against the familiar texture of the access badge from Mustafa's office.

I can't believe I forgot about this! Omar thought.

The memory of the hidden compartment jolted through him, reminding him of the unfinished mystery waiting to be solved. He slipped the badge into his pocket, determined to investigate further as soon as he arrived at the EDRI.

Heading down to the parking lot, Omar approached the shiny new hovercraft, the President had given him yesterday. His eyes crinkled with delight as he caught sight of it.

He climbed into it and zoomed through the city, relishing the exhilarating speed and the breath-taking view from above.

Omar made it to the EDRI building in time, thanks to his new ride. Once he got in, he made his way directly to Mustafa's office. However, before he could step foot inside, Zakir intercepted him with a smile on his face.

"Omar! There you are," the escort greeted him. "The President wanted me to bring you to the lab today. We've got some introductions to make."

Reluctantly, Omar let go of the access badge in his pocket and followed Zakir through the bustling corridors of the research institute. They entered the lab, where a group of scientists and researchers were engrossed in their work. Zakir began introducing Omar to each member, providing a brief description of their expertise.

As Omar listened attentively, his focus gradually shifted to the work being conducted around him. The hum of machinery, the glimpses of groundbreaking research, and the shared enthusiasm among the scientists ignited a fire within him. He couldn't help but feel a surge of excitement and dedication to his new role.

Omar was starting to love this job. However, one nagging thought persisted, a worry that continually plagued his mind. If what Zarene had said was true, and the President was actually hiding something nefarious, the contract wasn't going to be enough to make Omar sacrifice his morals and ignore it.

He pushed the thought aside each time it occurred to him and tried to focus on the task at hand.

Hours passed in a blur as Omar immersed himself in absorbing as much information as he could about Shifa. Time seemed to slip away as he eagerly delved into the intricacies of the scientific endeavours around him. Only when the scientists started filing out of the lab one by one did he realize that it was already lunchtime. Zakir and a few colleagues invited him to the cafeteria, but Omar excused himself, claiming he wasn't hungry.

Instead, he made his way back to Mustafa's office. His fingers fiddling with the access badge inside his pocket. It was time to explore some secrets.

Omar glanced around the corridor before slipping into Mustafa's office and closing the door behind him.

He ignored the piles of neatly stacked folders on the L-shaped desk and instead made his way directly towards the vintage computer by the edge of the table.

Omar gingerly sat on the cushioned chair, his foot hovering sideways, ready to propel him away, in case someone interrupted him.

Omar hesitantly reached forward to switch on the device. The room seemed to hold its breath as the computer hummed to life, its whirring sounds echoing in the silence of the office.

Omar swiped Mustafa's access badge into the proximity reader and waited. A mix of anticipation and apprehension coursed through his veins as he wondered what awaited him. Specially, why Mustafa went to such lengths to hide it?

Once he was inside the network, Omar's heart skipped a beat. There was only a single file Mustafa had saved. It was starkly contrasting against the empty expanse of the computer desktop.

Omar was well aware he was not supposed to be doing this, especially after Zakir's warning, but he couldn't help himself. He had to know.

With trembling fingers, he moved the cursor and clicked on the file, his eyes widening with a mixture of shock and disbelief.

The document opened, revealing a trove of classified information, files, and reports. The breadth of the contents overwhelmed him, the gravity of what he had stumbled upon sinking in. It was far beyond anything he had anticipated.

The shock turned into a whirlwind of emotions as Omar's mind raced, trying to process the implications of the information before him.

Taking a deep breath, he selected the file and printed its contents onto paper. As the printer beneath the desk whirred to life, shooting out page after page, Omar closed the file and logged out of the network.

Omar carefully stacked the pages, ensuring their order remained intact. He folded them with utmost precision, creating a neat package that fit perfectly into his inside pocket. Alongside the classified papers, he nestled the access badge and got up to his feet.

It was time to confront the President.

"The President is in a meeting right now," Layla told Omar with her customary smile. "Why don't you come back in twenty minutes? I'm sure he'll be free by then."

"I'll wait, thanks." Omar slumped down on the one the chairs that lined the wall, his mind swirling with a maelstrom of thoughts and emotions.

Shock still reverberated through him, a jolt of realization that sent shivers down his spine. His hunch had been right all along—meddling with something as dangerous as Neutronite couldn't be without consequences. But what he hadn't expected was the depths to which the President would sink in order to protect his profits, even if it meant endangering the lives of thousands.

Recalling the day he visited the crater, he remembered how the radiation levels had been higher when he entered the building. It was a sign that had slipped past him back then. And when Zarene mentioned the vaccine, the puzzle pieces should have clicked into place, but he was too preoccupied to see it.

Lost in his thoughts, Omar was abruptly interrupted by Layla's voice, breaking through the haze. "The President will see you now," she announced.

Taking a deep breath, Omar steeled himself and rose from his chair. He straightened his coat, ensuring his composure remained steady.

As he entered the President's office, the air seemed heavy with tension. The President, sitting behind his imposing desk, met Omar's gaze with his usual friendly smile.

"Professor, how can I help you?" He gestured for him to sit.

Omar reached into his coat pocket, pulling out the folded sheets and sat down.

"I can't work here." The words were a whisper.

"What did you say?" Huzaifa frowned. "I didn't catch that."

Instead, Omar asked, "how do you stabilize the Neutronite?"

"I already told you—"

"You didn't give me any specifics."

"We've been over this. You don't have to concern yourself with it."

"What about the radiation?" Omar narrowed his eyes.

"What about the radiation?"

"Where did it come from?"

"The crater, obviously." Huziafa blinked. "Why are you asking me that?"

"Don't bother, I already know everything." Omar let out a breath. "I know you're using the crater as an excuse, but it's actually the facility near it where the radiation is coming from. Where your employees are stabilizing the Neutronite." He glanced at the papers in his hand and threw one of them on the desk.

The President's face grew grim as he looked into it. "Where did you get that?"

"Does it matter?"

Huzaifa leaned forward. "Listen to me, Omar. Yes, I lied about the cause of the radiation, but it's just a little bit of heat. Do you really think it's that bad? Think of all the lives Shifa saves in return."

"Oh, it's more than harmless heat," Omar spat. "It's deadly."

Huzaifa sprang to his feet. "Don't spew nonsense when you don't know anything! The radiation was so weak, that the human body, being ever evolving, developed immunity from it within hours of exposure. How else do you think you're still all right?

"You're right. Most of us did develop immunity. However," Omar pulled up a couple more pages from his hand and placed them on the desk. "According to statistics, one in every thirty individuals fails to develop immunity to this radiation and falls victim to a horrendous disease. The likes of which have never been seen by mankind. Something that even Shifa cannot cure."

Huzaifa's eyes narrowed to slits.

"Instead of stopping the stabilizing process at the Neutronite facility and cutting off the source," Omar went on, "You find the victims of this disease and experiment on them to create a vaccine!" He threw the last page of the desk. "I've seen what's being done to those people on the 19th floor!"

Huzaifa slammed his hands on the desk. "I'm doing everything I can to create a vaccine to help them! It's narrow-minded people like you who wouldn't let science advance. We're on the verge of a breakthrough and all you can focus on is the 3.33% population of the city that got sick. Instead of seeing the good Shifa has done, you'll have me stop everything for a small minority, who will be fine eventually!"

"And what about those who are already dead?" Omar shot back. "What of those who die waiting for this vaccine, that might never come?"

"For the sake of the greater good–!"

"Don't give me that. If you care so much about the greater good, why won't you relocate the Neutronite facility somewhere remote, so that people won't get hurt?"

"You don't know anything," The President said, his tone dangerously hushed. He sat back down. "What you're suggesting is easier said than done. It'll increase the risk of Neutronite's discovery by outsiders."

Omar narrowed his eyes. "So, you won't do anything?"

"I'm already doing by best to control the situation," Huziafa bit back. "Everyone here is working around the clock to make that vaccine. There's nothing else that can be done."

Omar paused to consider. He had hoped if he'll let the President know that he's onto him, he'll stop everything himself in fear of being caught. But turned out, Huzaifa wasn't even remotely afraid of what he'll do with this information.

"I used to look up to you, idolize you." Omar looked down, disappointed. "I can't work here anymore."

With that, he turned, slowly inching towards the gate, expecting the President to stop him, to demand from him the source of this information. Or maybe threaten him to keep this to himself, but Huzaifa didn't say a word. Almost as if he didn't care that Omar had secrets, that had the potential to destroy him.

VIII

Omar found himself perplexed by the President's surprising absence of concern upon him learning the truth about the radiation. As he made his way back to the hotel, his mind was consumed by this puzzling behaviour, unable to guess the reason behind it. Then, a sudden realization struck him like a lightning bolt: perhaps the President was so nonchalant because he had no intention of allowing Omar to leave, since he knew too much.

Fear washed over Omar, and he hastened back to his room in a rush. Once he got there, he hurriedly started gathering his belongings and packed them into a bag. His NeuroPhone activated upon his will.

"Spark, book a flight to Cairo," he commanded the AI. "The earliest one possible."

"What payment method should I use?" Spark inquired.

Omar looked at him strangely. "The usual of course."

"Your bank account is temporarily frozen; therefore, all transactions have been halted," The AI answered. "What payment method would you like to choose for the flight ticket?"

"What?" Omar swore. "What the hell happened to my bank account?"

"Searching..." Spark replied. "I'm unable to find an answer."

Omar punched the wall. His suspicions were right. They were not going to let him leave. And without any money, he'd be a sitting duck, having nowhere to go. Frustrated and overwhelmed, Omar lashed out, delivering a swift kick to the nearby bedside table, sending it teetering. The lamp sitting atop it lost its balance and crashed below.

Omar squeezed his eyes, wondering what to do. When he reopened them, he caught sight of something unusual.

Among the broken fragments of the brown lamp, there was a hidden bugging device. His frown deepened as a sudden realization struck him—they had been monitoring him even before he uncovered the truth about the radiation. Their willingness to let him learn the truth meant they had no intention of letting him leave. From the moment he signed the contract and unearthed the secrets of Shifa, he had lost his freedom of choice. Now that he knows even more, he shuddered thinking what they'll do to him. Anxiety flooding his senses, he swiftly scanned the room, searching for any surveillance cameras.

Omar found a total of four cameras and five bugging devices hidden throughout his room. He was shocked.

He had been a fool to believe that the EDRI would just hand him it's biggest secret and not keep an eye on him. A part of him understood why Huzaifa had to do it, but that didn't make him feel any better.

Once he crushed all the devices beneath his foot and threw them in the trash, he decided he was not going to stay here anymore and wait for them to do as they please. He had to get out of here. He didn't know where. At this point, he didn't even care, he just had to leave.

He glanced at his bag and sighed. If he lugged that thing around, he wouldn't be able to run in case he needed. So, he grabbed the suitcase with Mustafa's research and the Neutronite sample and stormed out of the hotel building.

As Omar walked down the road, he glanced at the face of every person passing through. He couldn't shake the feeling that he was being watched. He was so panicked that he didn't even mind the sweat trickling down every pore of his body.

Not being familiar to the city streets, Omar cut a corner and ended up in a place that was deserted. He started to turn back when he suddenly ran into a burly man.

"Excuse me," Omar said, stepping back when the man, out of nowhere, punched him in the chest. The impact caused him to crash on the floor, his suitcase flying a few feet away. It was a miracle that the Neutronite inside didn't explode.

At first Omar was too stunned to react. Although, he had expected something like this, he was still shocked by the punch.

Omar tried reaching for the suitcase, but the attacker stepped on his hand. "Not so fast, Professor."

His lips quivered with trepidation as the man bought down his foot on his face. Omar screamed.

The attacker picked up the suitcase. When he noticed, Omar was trying to get up, he kicked him down again. And again. Until his face was reduced to a bloody pulp.

In that moment, Omar was almost positive he was going to die, all because he poked his nose where it didn't belong. Omar had been a fool. He should've been more cautious. Now, with every kick, he felt a stab of regret over his decisions in the past few days.

He squeezed his eyes shut when he heard footsteps. A couple happened to pass by and see what was happening. The woman let out a scream, hiding behind the man, who immediately called the police.

The attacker anxiously glanced at the couple and then ran off along with the suitcase.

The two strangers helped Omar up, and the woman offered to take him to the hospital. Before Omar had the chance to respond, he heard his phone ringing. It was lying a few feet away.

As Omar reached for it, it automatically transformed into a regular smartphone. A sigh of relief escaped Omar when he glanced at the name on the screen. The call was from Sarah.

Before Omar had left the hotel, he had briefly considered asking Sarah for help, but he ended up deciding against it, since he didn't want to put her in danger.

Now, however, after he was almost killed in the middle of the street, he had no choice left. He pressed the phone to his ear. "Hello."

"Omar, hi!"

"Sarah," Omar spoke, trying not to wince. "I need your help."

Sarah lived in a two-storey building situated on the outskirts of Dubai. She explained it was the same house she had recently inherited from a family friend.

As Omar entered, Sarah led him to sit on a coach. "Wait here," she said, springing to her feet. "I'll bring something to clean your wounds."

"Sarah," Omar said, before she left. "Thank you."

Omar felt a stab of guilt when he learned that Sarah was going to inject him with a dose of Shifa, but he didn't object. If he had any shot of staying alive, he'd need his strength back.

What he didn't expect was how much cleaning his wounds would hurt. Sarah tried her best to be gentle, but he still grunted in pain every time she so much as touched the gashes on his skin. She insisted on taking him to the hospital, but he refused. If he did go, they would just find him again.

At last, Sarah asked him who 'they' were, and Omar's only response was:

"I learned something I wasn't supposed to, and now someone wants me silenced."

No matter how much Sarah tried to coax more information out of him, Omar was relentlessly quiet. He had already put her at risk by coming here, he wasn't going to involve her any further.

It took four doses of Shifa for Omar to completely heal. As his cuts and bruises sowed themselves back together, he was just as amazed as he was for the first time, during Zarene's presentation. He also felt a wave of anger thinking of all those victims of the radiation, who were suffering to ease the pain of others.

By the time Omar was fully healed, he was exhausted by the events of the day, so Sarah left him in the guestroom to rest.

Omar was fast asleep when the incessant beep of his NeuroPhone woke him up.

He tore his eyes open and sleepily picked up the damned thing to turn it off, when he noticed something bizarre.

He was getting a call from the President on his new work phone, which he was supposed to have lost along with the suitcase. Omar jerked upright, rubbing his eyes. He clearly remembered putting that phone in the suitcase along with Mustafa's notes. Which meant, he shouldn't be getting notifications from it, unless it was somewhere within range.

Omar glanced outside the window. Nothing unusual. Sarah's house was on the edge of the city, miles away from the EDRI. If the President did hire that man to attack Omar, he would've asked him to bring the suitcase back to him by now. Besides, why would he call Omar?

The incessant beeping suddenly stopped as the call automatically disconnected, and Omar broke out of his reverie. He used the device to track the EDRI phone, and the indicator pointed a few metres away.

Omar felt a chill crawl down his back. He slowly followed the tiny indicator on the screen, keeping an eye out for Sarah. Even though it wasn't that late, the house was eerily quiet and dark. Sarah must be an early sleeper, Omar surmised. He tried to be more stealthy.

The indicator led Omar to a basement door. With a gulp, Omar pushed it open and stepped below.

He gasped.

The basement was a huge control room. Countless screens were fired up, showing camera recordings of different places throughout the city, including every corner of this entire house, the front view of the EDRI and also the hotel room at which Omar had been staying. A fifth camera, which he missed while scouring the place.

Omar, too stunned to move, stood there with his jaw hanging trying to make sense of everything he was seeing. There was a carton filled with neon yellow liquid in small vials. And next to it was the suitcase. His eyes landed on it. Finally, realization struck him. He was wrong about everything. The President never wanted to harm him. It had been Sarah all along. For whatever reason.

He picked up the suitcase and entered the combination to make sure that the Neutronite samples were still there, but as he did, the lights flickered on.

"Since you were nice enough to unlock it for me, I don't need you anymore." The voice belonged to Sarah.

Omar turned, sneaking out the small bottle of Neutronite and hiding it in his pocket. His face full of despair. "Why?" He asked her.

"Nothing personal," Sarah answered. "Just doing my job. The RSA will be needing that." The words sent a kick to Omar's gut. Sarah snatched the suitcase back from his grip with surprising strength and then hit a spot on his neck with her slanted hand that instantly made him dizzy. "Time to sleep."

As Omar began to lose consciousness, he took out the sample bottle of the Neutronite from his pocket. The amount was very little, but it had to do.

He opened the cork and then flung the bottle across the room. Sarah reflexively dodged it, and the substance landed on the computers, blowing up most of the basement along with all of the equipment.

"What did you do?" Sarah screamed, and it was the last thing Omar heard before losing consciousness.

IX

Omar's eyes fluttered open, and he found himself strapped to a chair. He was still in the basement. Half burnt pieces of equipment and furniture were cluttered throughout the room. The fire was extinguished before the house could burn down, but little had survived in the basement. The suitcase was an exception, being fireproof.

In the middle of the debris, Sarah was seated on the floor, leaning over a desk, she had brought down after the old one had burned. Mustafa's notes were sprawled on the entire table. Sarah glanced at each page for a few seconds before moving on to the next one.

"That research is coded," Omar said, trying to discourage her. "No matter how many times you read it, you won't understand a thing."

Sarah looked up. "If you mean the poor attempt to hide the new asteroid compound, then I already cracked it."

Omar failed to hide his shock. Zarene had told him that no one at the lab was able to do it, when this woman cracked it in a few hours. Who on earth was she?

Sarah continued to read, her eyes darting through the contents unnaturally fast. When she was done, she neatly stacked the pile of pages, putting them back in the suitcase.

"What are you going to do with me?" Omar asked, but she shot him a glare that instantly made him quiet.

Sarah placed a camcorder on the desk and sat down in front of it. As she was about to start it, she turned to Omar. "I'm going to record a video. If you dare interrupt me, I'll gag you."

A thousand retorts crossed his mind, his tongue bitter because of the betrayal, but he kept them to himself and managed a weak nod.

Sarah turned back to the camera and pressed a key.

"Log 2," she began. "It's been three hours since all of my Cyber Energizer shots were destroyed in the fire. I was able to save only one last dose." She held up the tiny vial of neon yellow liquid from before. "My battery percentage is twenty-four. I can still function for a few hours. However, my system can no longer directly connect with HQ. I'm afraid the traditional communication means are too risky, so I'm saving this last dose for now."

Omar gasped, and Sarah paused the video, to shoot him a warning glance. His mouth had fallen open at the realization.

"You're an Android!" He blurted out. "How? You're so... lifelike?"

Sarah walked over to Omar and took out a piece of cloth from her pocket. She stuffed it into his mouth with an indifferent look, despite his pleas. Eventually, he stopped fighting back.

Sarah pressed the key once again. "Status update: I've gone through the contents of Mustafa Hamd's research notes and cracked the code."

For the next few minutes, Sarah talked about Shifa in detail. Omar was amazed by how much she had been able to figure out in so little time.

He shouldn't be, since she wasn't even human, but Omar couldn't think of her as a machine.

Once Sarah was done explaining everything, she talked about the next part of the mission.

"Since I'm unable to get in touch with my superiors, I've come up with two courses of actions. I'll prepare for both of them, and then I'll use my last dose of Cyber Energizer to charge up and get confirmation before proceeding." She paused briefly.

"First, I'll go to the crater and get a few samples of the compound. Then I can return with the formula, so it can be used to create our own version of Shifa. I also have a captive with me who worked with the EDRI. I believe he can assist in the process." She pointed the camera at Omar, whose blood ran cold at her words. He started to struggle despite the bonds and the gag. Sarah ignored him.

"This method may be useful, but it will not be beneficial for long. Hence the second option, to get rid of their explosives in one strike. Even if we manage to steal enough Neutronite to create a drug, the revenue we'll generate will be small compared to what UAE is making. Besides, the real problem is the destructive properties of the compound. If knowledge of it goes out, UAE may be compelled to sell it to other nations, which could include RSA's enemies. The issue of being in possession of the compound itself can cause the next world war. It is a major risk to leave such a powerful weapon in the hands of a single nation. The best option may be to eradicate it."

Omar wiggled violently in his seat, trying to spit the gag out. Instead, the chair toppled sideways, his bounds barely weakened. The idea of being taken hostage by the RSA, after he had lived years hating and fearing it was bad enough, but somehow destroying the compound was worse. He needed to let Sarah know how dangerous it was.

"I'm setting out for the crater," Sarah continued, ignoring Omar. "Once I get there, I'll use the last dose of Cyber Energizer to power up and then send this log to HQ. I'll wait for further instruction there. Once I use the last dose, I'll have only enough power left to either blow the crater or make it out with the captive and the Neutronite samples."

Omar tried to shout the words to Sarah that she was underestimating the destructive nature of the compound. If she blew the crater, the impact could end up destroying half of the continent, but Sarah paid him no heed, as she picked up the camcorder and exited the room, leaving him alone.

Or maybe Sarah already knew it, and she just didn't care about murdering millions of people.

X

At long last, Omar managed to spit the gag out, but he still lay strapped to the bent chair, his heart racing with fear and dread, as he considered which of the two options were worse: Sarah blowing up the continent and him along with it, or her sparing the lives of everyone else, only to take him as a captive to the RSA.

Sweat beaded on his brow as he considered, desperation growing with each passing moment. He thought of what his life would be reduced to if he'd be taken to the RSA. The thought was enough to chill his blood to the bone. He wasn't even sure if he minded dying compared to it.

The mental image of an explosion big enough to wipe out the Mutual States popped in his mind, and he was instantly consumed with guilt.

Omar laughed hysterically at his dilemma. He was acting as if the choice belonged to him, which it didn't. It was up to Sarah, or her superiors at the RSA.

He wished there was a way out, hoping someone was out there looking for him. It was a ridiculous fantasy, considering he didn't even know anyone in the city aside from the few acquaintances he had made at the EDRI, and even they didn't know where he was.

Omar let out a sigh of defeat. All he could do was wait for his doom.

As the seconds ticked by, his mind raced with thoughts of all the things he had done wrong, all the mistakes he had made that had led him to this moment. He should've trusted the President. He should've bothered to confront him about the cameras instead of making assumptions and running off on his own. He should've been more cautious of Sarah. Now that he looked back on it, from the moment they met everything seemed staged, only he was too blind to see it. Omar cursed himself for his own stupidity.

He was wondering if he would ever see the light of day again, or if he would spend the rest of his life in confinement, when a noise interrupted his thoughts.

Muddled sounds of men talking in soft, hushed tones. And then footsteps. Scraping of feet against the wooden stairs that led to the basement.

Omar braced himself. Since no one at the EDRI knew of this place, he could only assume that it had to be someone working for Sarah. Maybe that thug who attacked him on the street. Sarah must've sent him here to keep an eye on him.

Omar struggled fruitlessly against the straps, racking his brain for ideas. Maybe he could tempt the man with money to let him go, or he could reveal Sarah's intentions to blow up the continent.

As he was weighing in his options, the door flew open, and he almost cried out in relief when the man on the other side turned out to be Zakir.

"What on earth is going on here?" the escort blinked, apparently confused.

Omar had never been this happy to see another person. However, he couldn't help but be cautious, not knowing the EDRI's intentions with him, especially after Sarah's betrayal. "How did you find me?"

Zakir proceeded to untie him, bombarding him with questions of his own, which Omar didn't bother answering, as he waited to be freed.

"How do you know about this place?" He demanded again, speaking a bit too loudly this time.

"I went to the hotel looking for you, but you weren't there," he replied. "The President sent me to retrieve the suitcase, and the phone."

"There was a tracker in the phone, wasn't there?" Omar asked, placing it together.

Zakir nodded, as he continued to untie the knots. "You can't be told about something as sensitive as Neutronite and expect not to be monitored."

Under normal circumstances, Omar might've been angry and seen this as invasion of his privacy. Now, however, after being susceptible to the dangers of working on Shifa, he didn't even care. This seemed nothing compared to what he was ready to accuse the EDRI of, before knowing Sarah was behind everything.

Besides, if it hadn't been for the tracker, Zakir would've never showed up here, and Omar would've stayed strapped to the chair. In a way, it ended up saving his life.

As soon as he was free of his binds, he sprang to his feet, not wasting even a second. "Did you bring the hovercraft?" He asked, cutting off Zakir's interrogation.

"Yeah. Why?"

"I'll explain everything on the way. For now, we've got to go." Omar almost spat the words, as he flew up the stairs.

"Where?" Zakir was right behind him.

"The crater."

Due to the urgency in Omar's tone, Zakir had set the hovercraft to get them to Ajman in maximum speed. Once they both settled, Zakir gave Omar a chance to explain himself.

"Right now, a spy from the RSA has found out about Neutronite," Omar began. "I'm not telling you anything else unless you answer my questions first."

Zakir blinked. "Are you serious? A spy?"

Omar ignored his shock. "Tell me something, Zakir. Did the President ever intend to let me walk out alive?"

"What are you even talking about? Why would the President kill you?" Zakir shot back. "And while we're on it, why did you go crazy like that? Even if you somehow found out about things you weren't supposed to, you threatened the President?"

Omar paused for a moment, then turned the question around. "Don't you find it incriminating that the President lied about the radiation and risked so many lives?"

Zakir sighed. "You don't understand the gravity of the situation. The President technically didn't do anything illegal," he explained. "Prince Faiz is the one in charge of everything, and he didn't allow us to relocate the Neutronite facility out of fear that it would be exposed. From a political standpoint, there's no other choice. You're not letting yourself see the bigger picture."

Omar narrowed his eyes stubbornly. "What about the victims—"

Zakir cut him off with a steely look. "All the victims of the radiation are receiving the best possible care, and their families are being compensated generously for their grief. This is being done to protect the secrets of Neutronite. Omar, you're threatening everything without knowing the whole truth."

Omar's voice wavered as he asked, "What if I'm not okay with this? What if I don't want to stay at the job anymore?"

Zakir was taken aback by the question. "First of all, no one is going to kill you or force you to keep working. However, you're in possession of national secrets, which were revealed to you after you willingly signed a contract, so you won't be allowed to leave the country. In the worst-case scenario, if you caused too much trouble, you would be put under house arrest."

Omar realized that the way Zakir had said it, it sounded like he was the one at fault. Besides, he did sign the contract and then tried to back out. Omar looked down, suddenly feeling the weight of Zakir's eyes.

"Now, if you're done with your questions, tell me where you heard this crazy story about a spy?" Zakir prompted.

Omar took a deep breath, ready to explain everything about Sarah, but uncertain of where to start, when Zakir's phone suddenly buzzed. It was a call from the President.

Zakir answered the phone and Huzaifa's hologram appeared beside them. Omar recounted the events of the past few days. He began from the beginning, describing his encounter with Sarah at the hotel, the discovery of cameras in his room, the street attack, and the revelation of her being a spy from the RSA.

Omar was forced to admit that his first conclusion had been to suspect the EDRI, which was why he ended up trusting Sarah.

The President's eyes widened when he came to learn of the RSA's sinister schemes. He told them that he'd alert the guards at the crater of the intruder, and that he'd arrive there shortly with backup. With that, the call disconnected, and Huzaifa's image vanished.

As the hovercraft neared to its destination, Omar grew nervous, remembering how strong Sarah was. Besides, the place was toxic with radiation.

"What are we going to do about the hazmat suits?" He asked Zakir. "We don't have time to dress up."

"We don't," Zakir agreed, "We'll only stop to pick up oxygen masks. I've already notified the staff at the Neutronite facility to be ready with those and whatever gadgets they can spare that might help us. They're waiting at the entrance. The masks will be enough to survive the toxic fumes. The radiation might burn our skins to some extent, but nothing a few doses of Shifa can't fix."

Omar nodded.

A short while later, they briefly landed the vehicle to pick up a small duffel bag loaded with a pair of masks, binoculars and a few more items, that could come in handy, before being on their way again.

They didn't use the basement route this time and instead continued to glide through the sky. As Omar expected, he could suddenly feel the radiation piercing his skin, the unnatural heat searing through him. Even the air conditioning in the vehicle couldn't provide him comfort anymore.

Omar wondered what would happen when they'll be forced to exit the metallic walls of the hovercraft, their only shield against the sweltering atmosphere.

He wished they had time to put on hazmat suits, but he soon changed his mind when they passed by a small pile of bodies in white.

"She took out the guards!" Zakir stated the obvious, panic raising in his voice. "How? And what chance do we stand against her?"

Omar tried to focus on the positive. "Her battery is running out. Besides, the suits would've slowed down the guards." He gulped, not believing his own words, even as he said them.

All he could do at this point was pray.

XI

The hovercraft flew across the sky, almost to the rim of the crater when Sarah finally appeared. Omar was the first one to spot her.

"There!" He pointed in a direction, and Zakir pressed his face to the glass window, peering below.

At first, all they could see was fog. The hovercraft glided ahead, cutting through the white fumes.

Then, there she was. Sarah, in black overalls that seemed to be lost in the dark background. If it wasn't for the binoculars, and the neon yellow vial she had been holding, that was slightly glowing in the dark, they might have never spotted her.

Sarah was sitting on her knees, fiddling in the suitcase. With the help of the binoculars, Omar could see the small containers of Neutronite in its raw molten state.

"She already has the samples," Omar said, "We need to stop her from consuming that Cyber Energizer, or she'll charge up and get in touch with her superiors."

"On it." With a nod, Zakir stroked a few times on the screen, that held the controls to the hovercraft, and the vehicle changed trajectory to move below. "I've activated the camouflage, so she won't be able to see or hear us approach, but once we make contact, she'll sense our movements. If we're lucky, we could knock her out in one hit."

Omar desperately prayed that one hit would be enough. However, on the back of his mind, he already knew it wouldn't be.

The vehicle darted through the air, slanting below, aimed directly at Sarah. A few moments later, Omar let out a gasp of surprise when it hit its mark, and Sarah was thrown across the crater, a few feet away. The contents of the suitcase, along with the small airtight containers and the yellow vial of liquid fell on the ground.

The two men immediately unlocked the door and jumped out. The heat was so intense that it felt like being thrown into a tub of scalding water. Omar squeezed his eyes, inhaling the cool oxygen from the tank strapped to his back. As bad as the heat was, it was a relief to be able to breathe.

Omar pushed through the pain, despite the patches of dark red that were beginning to form on his skin and reached for the vial.

It was almost within his grasp when he saw Sarah speeding forward at an alarming pace.

In an attempt to divert her attention away from him, Omar kicked the vial towards the crater, hoping it'll fall, but it landed on the edge of the rim.

Both Omar and Sarah shared a glance before making a run for it.

In the meantime, Zakir fiddled through the duffel bag, hoping to find something he could use to fight. His skin was burning, but he bit back the pain, and glanced at Omar trying to fight off Sarah, alone. He hurried. However, the stuff he found was of no use to him.

In the end, he settled for an ordinary dart gun, which he suspected wouldn't do much against an android as advanced as Sarah.

Still, he proceeded to fire, trying his best not to accidentally shoot Omar, who was now in combat with the android over the last dose of Cyber Energizer.

Even when his bullets hit Sarah, they were embedded in her skin, causing no damage at all.

Zakir swore. His eyes were drawn to the small containers of Neutronite. Being aware of its destructive nature, he was tempted to throw it at Sarah, and blow her up, but he resisted the urge, knowing how dangerous it was for explosions to occur so close to the crater. It could end up triggering the rest of the Neutronite to detonate.

Zakir threw away his gun and charged ahead, ready to aid Omar and fight with his bare hands if that was needed.

When Sarah noticed him approaching, she kicked Omar who landed a few feet away. As he was getting up, he saw the dart gun earlier discarded by Zakir and an idea formed in his mind.

He couldn't afford to throw chunks of Neutronite, without risking an explosion. However, if he shot it in precision... It was a gamble, but Omar didn't have options. He glanced at Sarah, who had managed to fight off Zakir, the vial now in her hands.

Omar picked up the gun and pulled out a dart. It was filled with tranquilizers, meant to knock out humans. He emptied the substance and instead laced the dart with Neutronite, before reloading the gun.

At this point, Sarah had already pressed the vial to her lips. As she drank the yellow liquid, Omar pulled the trigger. It hit Sarah on the head, exactly where Omar had aimed.

At first, it embedded into her skin like the rest, but then the explosion occurred. It was so small, that there was barely a spark, but it was enough to blow up Sarah's head or at least mess up with her internal wiring.

Her body thudded to the ground. Omar slowly approached her, wary that it could be a trick. However, Sarah didn't move. There were soft whirring and swishing noises coming from within her.

He squatted down beside her and held up the now empty vial of Cyber Energizer. He had stopped Sarah from blowing up the continent, however, since she had consumed the fluid before he shot her, it was a possibility that her logs might've reached her superiors informing them of the existence of Neutronite.

At this point, all Omar could do was hope that it didn't. Or else, not just UAE, but all of the Mutual Nations will be under the RSA's radar.

Epilogue

The UAE government was thrilled to have their hands on such a fine specimen of an android. Their researchers spent months trying to understand and recreate the technology that made Sarah a possibility. Even though they succeeded, they still couldn't break into the encrypted servers through which Sarah communicated with her superiors, and hence they were not able to figure out if the RSA was now aware of the existence of Neutronite.

If the news had indeed made its way outside the borders of the nation, then war was inevitable. However, it was the silence from the RSA in the following months of the attack that unnerved Omar the most.

Before being taken captive by Sarah, he had decided to quit his job since he was not ready to be a part of something that was against his morals. Now, however, after learning the whole truth from Zakir, his changed his mind. Besides, the near-death experience shifted his perspective. He could die any day, so he'd rather spend his time here doing what he loved, instead of going back to his old life. And so, Omar accepted his new position at the EDRI, working on the advanced version of Shifa, that wouldn't just heal but grant immunity from wounds altogether. Or prolong life, as he liked to call it.

President Huzaifa readily forgave his insubordination and welcomed him back with open arms. He even convinced Prince Faiz to move the Neutronite facility outside the city to an inhabitable island, in order to stop the deterioration of its climate. The Prince agreed, not wanting to risk the theft of Neutronite again. He had already made up his mind to have the Neutronite mined and hidden away in different secured locations in case of the crater's discovery.

After this, Omar gladly accepted his old job back, having no more qualms with the EDRI after the Neutronite experimentation stopped.

In the HQ of Espionage Division in the RSA, Joseph Bellamy was perturbed. His career was on the verge of collapse, all because he had risked and lost possession of Synthetica Nexus 7, the android he was supposed to guard with his life, in a failed attempt to steal information.

The worst part was, he ran this operation for weeks without the knowledge or permission of his superiors. When an opportunity to steal the formula of Shifa presented itself, Joseph wasn't ready for his superiors to steal his credit. So, he did what any man would have done in his position.

He forged the permission slip, sat back, and waited for Synthetica to present him his promotion on a silver platter.

Not in a million years did he expect Synthetica to fail and be captured.

The worst part was, in order to prevent the enemies from breaking into their communication server, Synthetica put a code on it, that was too complex for even Joseph's hackers.

It was rock bottom. By the end of the fourth month since the Android's disappearance, Joseph decided to give up. He couldn't make excuses and bide time any longer.

Just as he was about to confess everything and resign, the door to his office burst open.

"We finally cracked it!" One of the hackers announced. "Synthetica did it. The formula is here."

Joseph ripped his resignation letter and grinned. It was going to be fun.

The Texican Famine That Didn't Happen
By D. Dlyan Daniel

1. The Last Normal Day: 3/03/2303

It all started during History. It was the first day of a new paideia, and all the kids were there. Charlene "Charlie" Asimov, a thirteen-year-old girl, sat next to Henry Smith. Charlie's hair was blonde and curly, and her attire was the standard uniform. Her pants were standard-issue athletic black and white garments with padding on the knees, shins, and seat. Above these, she wore a comfortable blue woolen sweater. A ponytail pulled her curls tight, keeping them out of her eyes for the most part. A number of white orbs were strategically placed around her body, one on each hip and a third that clipped onto her collar, enabling her PHTI (personal holographic terminal interface), which in turn granted her access to the knowledge graph that permeated not only the Texican Republic but many of the other advanced nations of the world.

Behind her, there were three more rows of two children each, and in front of them the octogenarian Holly Nelson sat behind a desk wielding her keyboard mightily, though she also wore the PHTI units on her person. It was a bit anachronistic, but she enjoyed the clacking sounds it made and the regularity it lent her writing. Keyboards had never quite gone all the way out of fashion. The students were writing essays silently, on their HIDs (holographic input devices), and the teacher was expected to participate alongside them. Once the freewriting had concluded, the lecture would commence.

Charlene had already finished her history essay and sat idly in her chair. She could have played a game or looked something up on the knowledge graph, but today her thoughts took a pensive turn. She was a curious child, with a knack for understanding the ways things worked—no matter how subtle. And her mind was hard at work, struggling endlessly to understand her place in the world. She had recently returned from a leave of absence she'd taken to grieve the tragic, sudden, and unexplained loss of her mother to what she intuitively knew to be an enemy she would need to confront—but the assassination, meant for her father, had been carried out brilliantly and no evidence had led to an arrest.

So, her young mind wandered. She was an excellent student, as her teacher knew, though they had only been acquainted with one another for a short time before the incident. Still, her pensive attitude was understandable, and her work was excellent. The Texican Republic allowed leeway for children with exceptional talents, at least for a time. Charlene stood and peered out the window.

Outside, in Post, Texas, the wind was whipping down off the Caprock from the hills where a cereal mogul had once staged "rain battles" to fill the air with smoke in the hopes of causing precipitation. The particulate matter, Charlene had written in her report, released by these explosions and lifted upward by heat, could serve the purpose of enabling condensation to form in the atmosphere, wringing moisture from even a desolate and dry summer day. C.W. Post had long been a historical curiosity for the residents of Post, Texas. And since the formation of the Texican Nation, and with the rise of the Libraries, history had only become more important to the average citizen.

Charlene was no average citizen of the Texican Republic. However, her father was the Head Librarian of the Post Library. From Amarillo to Big Spring, the eccentricities of the former oil and cotton desert in the panhandle of the former Lone Star State had never really worn off.

Whether it was the music of Buddy Holly helping to incite the rock'n'roll movement of the twentieth and twenty-first centuries, the oil magnates of Big Spring developing a zillion uses for plastics before earthquakes had destabilized the Permian Basin and forced the government to outlaw subterranean petroleum extraction of any sort, the stories were unique to this small and underpopulated region of her nation. Her personal favorite? The insane millionaire who dynamited the face of the Caprock in a vain attempt to cause raindrops to fall to earth to water his fields of crops. None other than C.W. Post, the namesake of her hometown.

She was top of her class—and the eight-student classroom in which she sat only contained a small fraction of it. All across the state, students engaged in the same curriculum. There were fewer students now, Charlene had been told, but she'd never experienced a thirty-person classroom. Since the population decline had begun almost three hundred years before, school had become extraordinarily important as the Texican Republic sought to replace more workers with fewer. Efficiency was key, and to be more efficient than a larger number of workers, each new one needed to be better educated and better empowered.

A holographic image generator flicked on, and the children now found themselves inside a simulated school bus, which was only slightly ironic due to them never having seen such a thing before. It grew dark outside as the loading screen dissipated to leave them sitting on a platform high above a group of vaguely human-like organisms called *australopithecus*.

A narrator's voice announced a few basic statistics for these hominids as labels scrolled across them, revealing additional tidbits of information—they ate a primarily vegetarian diet and lived up to about thirty years of age, on average. They were a top hominid precursor that lasted almost a million years, despite this short lifespan. The hologram went dark, then reappeared with a rapid slideshow that took the class through a dozen other human precursor organisms with similar levels of detail to that of *australopithecus*, then arrived at modern man.

"The birth of written language happened in Sumer in about 3,000 B.C.," it intoned. "The Sumerian language was being replaced by Akkadian and so religious elders began writing down their words. The written Sumerian became canonical and was required by the religion. Sumerian thus survived the challenge of the new cultures that had arisen to provide alternative ways of speaking and became more than a fleeting moment in human history. It was written. And thus began a conversation that continues over five thousand years later, to this very day."

The hologram flashed again. Now Ancient Greece appeared before the class. "Ancient Greeks lived up to seventy or eighty years of age if they didn't die young," the narrator spoke. "Writing was questioned by Socrates, one of the primary Greek philosophers whose works are handed down to the present day. Socrates did not trust the sense in which something being written tended to ossify the message, enabling communication to become more abstract. The divorce of spoken words from their time and place of occurrence had created a new set of problems for language users everywhere."

The toga-clad Greeks vanished, now the class sat in a garden watching one man pacing. "Aristotle," the AI narrator's voice sang, "was a peripatetic philosopher: he would walk with a scroll to read in one hand and a skull in the other. When he began to drop the skull," this happened for the class to see, "he realized he was becoming tired and would go to bed." Aristotle yawned gently and then walked into a nearby building and the door shut behind him. The village grew smaller, giving the class the feeling that they were in a helicopter taking off from this ancient settlement. "Aristotle systematized logic for the first time and formulated positive accounts of the rules hinted at in Plato's Dialogues of Socrates. The Lyceum became the top school of Greece, replacing Plato's Academy, whose leadership stayed in the Platonic family."

The screen flashed again, this time remaining dark.

"Since the time of Ancient Greece," the narrator's voice boomed, "human lifespan has fluctuated back and forth. During the Dark Ages," a series of images flashed before the children, "the human lifespan contracted considerably. Thirty years was the average time a human being would live." An image of a graveyard. "Plagues frequently decimated populations, killing entire families. Half the population of Europe died from the bubonic plague between 1347 and 1351." A pile of bodies. The screen went dark for a long beat.

"With the discovery of antibiotics in the 20th century, however," the narrator's voice was accompanied by a rising sun and images of growing flowers, "the human lifespan rapidly doubled to its new normal— seventy years of age." A family was depicted, growing old together.

"But all was not well. Along with antibiotics, other chemical experiments were pervasive." People taking pills, smoking cigarettes, breathing clouds of diesel engine exhaust, drinking contaminated water, and dying of cancer were depicted. "The net impact of things from smoking to petroleum-fueled internal combustion engines, pesticides, and a generally poor understanding of the biosphere in which people lived was a dramatic new development: severe diseases of old age. The age at which individuals died was highly variable, but people suffered from poor nutrition and a toxic environment." A mass grave appeared, then dissolved to reveal a hospital birth ward. "Birth rates remained high to compensate," the narrator said as the cycle of life began anew, with an infant being born.

Henry tapped Charlene's shoulder. "It's almost to the good part," he said.

"Shh," Charlene replied.

"By 2100, the lifespan of humankind began to grow again." A tall, slim vertical greenhouse appeared, surrounding the children with its holographic image. "The introduction of mycelial colonies to vertical greenhouse structures created a resilient feeding system capable of supporting an unlimited number of human beings and in turn the megacities rose higher and higher into the sky." An unfathomably large city rose below them, greenhouses stacked on residences and parking facilities and factories and other structures. Each unit was self-contained, and the city almost looked as if each building could launch itself into the air, leave Earth entirely, and exist in space as a self-contained ship.

The image reversed, pulling the class out of the city and making it possible to see the limitless re-wilds beyond its boundaries. "Fallout, acid rain, and other climate challenges were driving cancer higher among the population by contaminating plants and animals humans depended upon to survive." As these words played out over the speakers, a different landscape hove into view—a green field of outdoor plants. A diesel-fueled pickup drove past, spewing a black cloud of smog from its exhaust pipe. A diagram labeled a number of carbon compounds known to be carcinogenic and zoomed in on a number of them as they condensed into a raindrop, fell to earth, were taken up by the roots of a plant, and ultimately came to reside in a corncob.

A man took a bite of the corn, and the animation followed it through his gastrointestinal tract to his kidney, where it lodged in a cell labeled 'nephron.' Inflammation arose, and from his kidney radiated outward to other areas of his body, then the image was replaced with a tombstone that read 'Cancer-related early demise.'

A new image appeared, that of the modern SCVG (self-contained vertical greenhouse). "The key innovation of the greenhouse system was to enable plants to thrive without the continual need to uptake nutrients from the increasingly toxic natural environment." A quick animation sequence showed the cycle of nitrogen in the greenhouse.

"In this way, the heavy metal concentration in the food system declined—reducing cancer rates. The current Texican lifespan is 150 to 180 years, over double the average prior to the breakup of the former United States." A graph by decade demonstrated four centuries of data to reinforce the point. Another graph appeared, showing a dramatic decline in birth rates. "Birth rate has correspondingly declined in the Texican Republic."

A map outline of the neighboring RSA appeared, with a graph demarcating average lifespan superimposed over it. "By contrast, the RSA, which has largely declined to implement the Greenhouse System and which still relies upon fossil fuels for all energy needs, still features an average lifespan of fifty to sixty years." The image went dark.

"Thank you for your attention. This History lesson is now complete." The voice shut off, and the room's lights returned to operational brightness.

"We have a lot of information here," the teacher, Mrs. Nelson, said. "Where do we begin?"

She stood from her desk, summoning her holographic input device (HID). It appeared near her right hip, following her movements seamlessly at about waist height. She made a few gestures on the hologram surface control and the image of the *australopithecus* tribe returned, at 1/32 scale, and played just in front of her for the whole class to see again. The desks spread out, rearranging themselves in a circle, with her at the center.

"James," she said, looking at the boy of that name, who stood up and approached the hologram. "What would you like to know about these ancestors of ours, discovered all the way back in 1974?"

"Well," said James. "I would like to know what enabled them to last for almost a million years before dying out and disappearing. This seems like a really amazing accomplishment, given that our species has only existed for two hundred thousand years."

A voice that did not belong to the teacher cut into the conversation. "Australopithecus is thought by some experts to have been the beneficiary of unique conditions in the history of planet Earth. In addition to a general lack of linguistic capabilities, the species were seldom challenged to live beyond the immediate means provided for them by their immediate environment. A uniquely stable temperament ensured that the questions that came to define humankind as we have been since the Industrial Revolution never crossed their minds, according to D. Bergstrom (2222)."

"Ahh," said James. "I see. The prevailing view is that

australopithecus never needed to develop higher consciousness to survive; perhaps becoming human was itself the necessary measure the species took to keep up with changing times. We are descended from them, after all, which means that our characteristics could easily be classified as *their* adaptations and mutations."

The boy sat down at a nod from Mrs. Nelson. "Charlene?"

Charlene stood up just as James sat down, crossing the short distance to Mrs. Nelson's side. At a gesture, one of the orbs at her waist projected its own HID and her fingers navigated it to tie it in with Mrs. Nelson's projection. Her fingers briskly swiped left and right for a few seconds, and then the full-size hologram began to play at precisely the point in the video overview where the greenhouses that fed the Texican Nation were explored.

Charlene's left hand now gestured and a second HID appeared, a surface that was projected directly beneath her wrist and fingers no matter how she oriented her arm. Using two hands, she paused the video and zoomed in farther and farther on the image of the greenhouse until the class was positioned on Level 1, inside the Grow Area. The image spun as Charlene peered through the garden of Eden that was the Base Layer of the greenhouse. Pools with fish in them stood waist high in some cases and extended multiple stories upward in others. Water pipes directly pulled the liquid they needed from these tanks to feed to the crops they serviced at all levels of the building, and beneath the floor grates a massive collection and reconstitution system collected every drop and clipping from the complex ecosystem above. Small animals scurried through, helping to collect the harvest and sort the food for people who worked in offices and lived in apartments to choose and pay for at the grocery level.

"I want to know why the little monkeys participate in this horticulture experiment," Charlene said at the end of this lengthy exploration.

Mrs. Nelson nodded without moving her hand. "That is an excellent question, Charlene. But you already know that the answer is symbiotic gamification. Their formal name is Rhesine, and they are intelligent enough to understand abstract rules, even if they lack the capacity for true language. We train them by teaching them games to play that persist culturally and seem to be universally loved by the population over time."

Charlene nodded. "Yes, but what if something happened to them? Have we not built a system to sustain ourselves here that depends for its own existence upon these other entities? If they were all wiped out by a disease outbreak from a soil shipment, for example, would we not find it almost completely impossible to feed ourselves?"

Mrs. Nelson shook her head. Her hand made a gesture on the HID and the AI voice boomed in over the speakers again.

"Rhesine workers replaced human gardeners almost as soon as the Rhesines were first discovered, small human-like apes who escaped notice in the Amazon Rainforest until about a hundred and fifty years ago. It was not long after the SCVG was invented, and the Rhesines were quite friendly. One day, a Rhesine was helping its human in the greenhouse, and the next a game had arisen among a small tribe of Rhesines who had taken up residence in the safe SCVG environment."

"This led to a reduced need for manpower over time as the small domesticated Rhesine population grew to address the need for a labor force to maintain the SCVGs. Leonard Terwiliger shifted his attention to marketing and reduced business costs to the point where he operated at a massive profit. The idea scaled almost immediately to all of the Peaceful Nations, cementing a legacy of greatness for Terwiliger."

Charlene nodded and returned to her desk.

"Thank you Charlene," Mrs. Nelson murmured. "Okay class, that is enough for today. We will return tomorrow to explore other thoughts that you may have tonight or move onto the next lesson if we run out of questions."

The students stood up and strode out of the classroom by the door. It led into a hallway with half a dozen other similar classrooms attached, and at the end past the principal's office stood the tram entrance. Charlene had finished her work for the day, so she climbed aboard the first tram and rode it directly home. On the ride, a nagging suspicion had grown in her mind. She revisited the hologram she had been investigating earlier, focusing instead on the power source. It wouldn't take much of a push to destabilize the entire system, she realized, feeling suddenly punch-drunk with power.

A notification popped up with a small chime and she rushed to open the article, which was written by an anon account she had taken a liking to. "Mystery Substance Found In Greenhouse- Sourced Food," the headline ran. Charlene read the whole thing, becoming more convinced she was onto a problem–and that she had an idea about how to solve it.

2. Fun and Games

Charlie sat in her room that night, playing a game that enabled her to earn a digital currency. It was dark web money, and she had to login to her account through a private network, but she couldn't help herself. All that she had to do was be moderately careful all the time: she had to use a private network to mask her identity, and she had to be very careful sending money back and forth between her dark and light, or private and public accounts. The Texican Government was more than willing to turn a blind eye toward small transactions that didn't do anything to destabilize the economy of the Nation, but history had shown again and again that those who flew too close to the sun could have their wings melted in a hurry.

So, Charlie played her game, earned a modest amount of money, spent most of that collecting art and other digital assets into accounts with various mask identities attached to them, and piped a little in or out of her official accounts only on an as-needed basis. Government's job was to stabilize the real world, and though world peace had officially begun almost two hundred years ago, the birth rate of the Texican Nation had plummeted alongside the meteoric ascent in life expectancy. Her young mind absorbed information at a rate that greatly exceeded other school children of her time as well as those who had come before. She was a Seeker, and though she had only begun the process of official school one year before, she was fluent in a number of languages and had a high familiarity level with programming languages.

None of this was by mistake, she thought, reviewing a technical document associated with her favorite game. The story was set in an alternate universe where an evil god spun out of Christianity had returned to the earthbound realm, intent upon extracting His vengeance from the farmers of the village. Hundreds of years and versions of this game had come before, and the whole thing lived on a public blockchain that was kept up by users in dozens of nations worldwide. Anyone could access the game by setting up a wallet and downloading the software, but certain jurisdictions prohibited it for various reasons from economics to ideology. You could still use it if you were willing to jump through a few hoops to mask your identity and hide the origin of your sessions. These things were so easily done that even a novice Texican girl could gain access to it without trouble, however. Charlie was no novice.

The economy of the game used a cryptocurrency that had no intrinsic value aside from in-game issuance as players completed quests and cleared dungeons that were generated only when the game was being played. Still, markets enabled a direct representation of the in-game asset on public blockchains with markets and exchanges built-in. The effect was that a given amount of game funny money was always reliably tied to the TRD (Texican Republic Dollar) such that a user could exchange for it in real time. Charlie had a number of accounts where she had stored a great deal of money over the years, earned both by legitimate gameplay and by hacks of various types that had been enabled by sloppy code in game updates by the core developers.

Ostensibly, the greatest coders in the world, the game developers also had a lot of bad habits: drinking too much, drug use, prostitutes–the whole gamut of licentious behavior was their domain, Charlie reasoned, following them on social media. This meant that they got sloppy about their code sometimes. So, by day, Charlie rode the tram to school, and by night, she kept up with recent developments in the game universe she had grown up in.

A knock came at Charlie's door. "Just a minute, Dad!" she called. Powering down her hologram, she leapt toward the door, turning the lights on as she grasped the doorknob.

"Hi daddy," she smiled sweetly.

"Hey kiddo. I wanted to let you know I have a pizza for us downstairs if you're hungry," he said, giving her a hug.

Charlie returned the embrace and followed her father toward the familiar smell of pepperoni pizza from the shop above their apartment.

"How was school today, sweetie?"

"It was great. We learned so much about where food comes from!"

she replied, jubilantly.

After the meal, Charlie returned to her room. She powered up the hologram and set the processor to load her game world, strapping in to her environment navigation simulator. It was a ring that stood a few feet from the floor with a harness hanging from it and an omnidirectional conveyor belt beneath it. As Charlie moved through the world, she could run or walk or jump and the processor would translate her point of view accordingly. HIDs worked for hands and for visual feedback, but the kinetic portion of interacting with the world couldn't be simulated without something for the feet to relate to.

Inside the game, a number of direct messages had appeared. Some contained offers for characters or items. Charlie quickly scrolled through these and accepted or rejected each offer based upon its relation to the market price of the asset. She wouldn't sell to low-ballers, but everything she had was up for grabs if someone wanted it badly enough to pay well for it.

One such item, not currently listed, had received an outrageous bid. Charlie's left eyebrow raised itself as she compared the offer against the floor price, and, almost as if the prospective buyer had noticed that she was once again online and present, a direct message pinged her inbox. A gesture later and it was open.

Dear Charlie,

You've gained a lot of credibility over the most recent season. Your abilities continue to impress. Please, accept this plausible offer for your Godly Plate of the Whale. It is one of the only items that will allow this account's top character to amass even more hit points, and we know you could use the money.

Additionally, if you would like to earn more, we need characters built. Meet in-game at [coordinate hash link] to discuss in detail. Client wishes to remain anonymous, so stealth must be employed.

Best wishes,
Your Fairy Godmother

PS: You won't want to double-cross me."

Charlie laughed to herself and deleted the message, accepting the offer. She knew where to find a dozen more of the item, on a mule account that wasn't tied to her playing account directly. She logged out, transferred one of the powerful armor items from her dummy account to a third party intermediary that secured things via private key encryption, and then logged into her main account again to retrieve it.

Another DM pinged through. This time it was from a friend asking for help leveling a character, and she accepted the invitation.

Near the end of the speedrun, her online pal Finn revealed that he had gotten a similar high offer and accepted the bounty and that this was, in fact, the character to be built for the high-end anon client. Charlie laughed—the going rate for help leveling on a bounty was half of the bounty, which meant she'd be receiving the same amount as she would have if she had accepted the job and asked Finn to help her level.

Finn was from the megacity capital of the Texican Nation, which was built on the State Line separating old Mexico from old Texas, and what used to be called New Mexico before. In his thirties, Finn had seen a lot more of the world than Charlie had. He worked directly with her dad and had agreed to show her around the online world as a favor to his boss, but her aptitude had kept the arrangement running far longer than he had originally intended it to go. His anon account was tied to hers, and both were separated from the real world by expertly designed privacy controls to prevent outsiders from tracking them in-game.

Suddenly, the game lagged a bit. Caught mid-dungeon, Finn and Charlie both found themselves vulnerable as their characters sat undefended. Fortunately, most of the monsters they were fighting had been low level and were unlikely to do much damage. But why was the server lagging, Charlie mused. The connection had been stable all day.

"Charlie!" Finn called, over the intercom. "There are dozens of new characters joining this server. Someone must have published this game instance address!"

"That makes sense, but why?" Charlie replied, surprised. There was nothing special about what the two of them were doing here, they'd done it thousands of times and game crashing was very rare.

Just then, a new voice broke in over the intercom.

"I see you've decided to help us," it said. "But you do not know who we are. We represent the downtrodden and the oppressed, and we need your help IRL."

Charlie and Finn were taken aback by the strange turn of events. Finn's job, security at the Library, entailed a certain amount of online risk that Charlie was accustomed to needing to occasionally take steps to avoid, but in general stalking was uncommon even if you weren't particularly good at covering your tracks. She and Finn had immediately disconnected from the game for fear of being PK'ed and having their loot stolen amidst the lag, and had relocated to a chat application outside of the game world.

"It isn't impossible for them to follow us, to know who we are, based on our addresses and transaction histories," Finn was saying.

"But we followed the Protocol, Finn! They must be very good at what they do to pull a server invasion like that. I've never seen it lag so hard!"

"It's true," Finn conceded. "Tell ya what: stay offline for a bit, go do your homework, and I'll research our stalker and figure out what to do to make them stop."

"Okay Finn. I can tell Dad if I need to…" Charlie said.

Finn shook his head, causing his gigantic puff of curly hair to oscillate in a funny, slightly delayed way. "No need. These guys are wimps, we don't need to worry about them."

"Okay Finn," Charlie said again, closing the chat. Immediately another chat opened, this time featuring Henry Smith's avatar picture. Charlie accepted it.

"Charlie! How are you doing with this homework?" Henry wanted to know.

"I haven't even started it," she confessed, a bit perplexed. Henry was a notorious slacker; it was not at all like him to be concerned about homework a week before it was due.

"I'm kidding!" he laughed.

Rolling her eyes, Charlie said nothing.

"You know that Redacted File you found last week," Henry continued, ignoring her body language.

"Yeah?" she said, unable to keep the surprise out of her tone.

"Well, guess who found the clean version?"

"Who? I know it wasn't *you*, Henry," Charlie teased.

"Dustin," Henry admitted. "Dustin found it, and he shared it with me earlier today. You're not gonna believe what's in it," he continued.

Charlie's eyes widened as the file appeared in front of her, completely free from the deleted fragments she'd seen the last time she had attempted to access this document. It was a complete schematic of the open source framework that ran her country's government. Validator Nodes were represented in complete detail and real time operations showed up on the dashboard, the trillions of transactions that represented the digital activity of the entire Texican Nation summed up in one relatively small application.

"Charlie?" Henry was asking.

She didn't know how long she had been gone, but Henry was not finished with her. She sighed and looked back at the avatar that she'd been ignoring for some time.

"Charlie, that guy you were asking about—we found his story, too," Henry said, once he knew he had her attention again. "It's bad, Charlie."

A file appeared in front of Charlie, a familiar username in the corner of it. RSA Terror Agent, a boldfaced label read. Top Secret, said a second one. Charlie sighed.

3. The Threat to the Food Supply

Charlie had not been aware of the Movement before, but she quickly became acclimated to the cause. Class structures were causing problems for the majority of people inside and outside the megacities. The environment was not safe for people who wanted to live to old age, but colonies of preservationists lived together with higher birthrates and shorter lifespans. The Movement existed to raise awareness of this way of life and to help City dwellers adopt Primitive lifestyles. And the Texican Republic liked to label these people as RSA Terror Agents.

Charlie was a supporter of the cause from the time she finished digesting the unredacted Document, and Henry was still on the line with her when she worked out what she had to do.

"Charlie?" he was saying, over and over, trying to get her attention again.

"Yeah, Henry? Sorry. I was deep in the rabbit hole that time..." she murmured.

"Well, that's okay, I just wanted to see what you were thinking. It looks like they killed him," Henry said.

"Yeah. They killed him for questioning the chemicals they put in our food. And they called him a Terror Agent. Poor Dexter. I'm going to do something about this!" Charlie shouted, tears welling up as she finished her statement.

Henry started to speak again but Charlie severed the line. She ejected a memory stick and pulled a clean set of sportswear clothes out of her drawer, then got in the shower and cleaned herself up, meditating. It was nearly midnight, so she would have to sneak out of the house to prevent her father from stopping her. Fortunately, he didn't know that she knew she could beat the home security system by using the coded garage door entrance to come and go, and his room was far enough away that he didn't hear the doors opening and closing. Once she was on her bike, pedaling down the street between the tall glass buildings, Charlie opened her navigation hologram and typed in the Post Library. There was a dust storm blowing in, but she didn't have a choice—she had to travel even in the dark and dusty conditions. She strapped her facemask and goggles on tight and pushed her hood up, pulling the elastic drawstring to ensure a tight fit. It only took her about twenty minutes to arrive at the dark structure on the other side of town, near the outcroppings of the Caprock. The Post Library was beneath the First Greenhouse and sat across the street from the general trade store. The store was busy—anything that wasn't food would be found there, so people were going in and out at all hours of the day and night.

The library still closed at 8:00, but her father's access code granted her admittance any time she chose. As she passed through the sliding glass doors, the Post Community CPU's blue and green lights beckoned to her just as they did so many of the small township's residents. This was their connection to the outside world, the massive computer that ran the Validator Nodes to do Post's part at keeping the Texican Nation's networks online, and Charlie was here to change the way it worked forever.

The file was uploaded, and it was ingenious. Charlie had not modified anything on-chain, but she had instead opted to replace the kernel with one that she had written herself. The kernel was one of the few attack surfaces that remained, unable to be rolled back to a prior state on the public blockchain because it was not itself on-chain. Instead, it told the machines in the greenhouses how to implement the instructions they got from the software system that ran them.

The new kernel, Charlie knew, would be likely to not arouse much suspicion because people had become largely complacent. This was why she had been able to insert the new version in the first place. Riding home, breathing through her respirator to eliminate the toxic dust that could cause pneumonia or worse if she were to simply inhale it, she considered the ramifications of the software change she had made.

The kernel would be replaced if it were deemed faulty, so it had to function similarly to the one it replaced. However, Charlie's kernel switched the instructions up for the greenhouse power supply, the small fusion reactor that ran beneath the water level in each of the buildings. As the reactors' temperatures increased, the magnetic shields would rapidly degrade, superheating the atmosphere and destroying the food supply.

Back home, Charlie went to sleep. The heat cycles of the reactors only ran monthly, as the greenhouses were not energy intensive operations, but the battery packs needed to be charged to run the auxiliary light sources that were used during the night, and many of the buildings had additional power constraints imposed on them by residents who found that the easiest way to power their devices was not to buy energy from the municipal grid, but rather to steal it from the greenhouse batteries.

Fireworks day, as Charlie had grown to think of it, was about two weeks out—the day the software ran the reactor by default. Some greenhouses were likely to flame out before then, but not many. Charlie's endgame was never to destroy the entire food supply of her civilization, but rather to install a problem only she could fix and use the resulting leverage to force the bureaucrats to tell her the truth about the additives going into her food.

A bit of uneasiness crept into the bottom of her stomach as she considered all of this, all of the things that could go wrong. Double-cycling the reactor within a given month was something that over half of greenhouse operators did, with some running weekly or even twice per week. In fact, by the time she reached home and put her bicycle away and got into bed, her social feeds were full of stories from the most power-hungry reaches of the district: greenhouses were blowing up and no one knew why.

"We have to go, NOW!" Daryl was shouting at his impudent teenage daughter. "We do not know why these greenhouses are exploding, and we must get to safety," he intoned more calmly, as Charlie began packing her things.

Charlie emerged from her room feeling mixed emotions. On the one hand, her plan had worked—she was the only person in the Texican Republic who knew what was blowing up the greenhouses. Her kernel had not yet been discovered—they thought it was something wrong with the hardware. Still, Charlie couldn't help but feel a bit of remorse for her deeds when she saw the fear behind the calm face her father was putting so much effort into maintaining.

Once they were on the tram and headed to the Twin City that had sprung from Ciudad Juarez and El Paso to claim its unified identity as the New Capital of the Texican Republic, her father dove into his messages with gusto, seeking to learn more about their situation even as they ventured into what was suddenly the heart of danger. Charlie followed suit, noticing immediately that her stalker had sent her a swarm of messages. She ignored these for the time being, opting instead to move her money around—prices were erratic and volatility in the markets had led to massive opportunities for her anon accounts to profit.

After the trades were executed, Charlie saw a new message icon— this time from Finn. Clicking it, she was shocked to see that Finn had already worked out what had happened. Without replying, she navigated on a hunch to the messages from the anon account that had been following her around since the day before, and sure enough it knew what she had done. And it approved, it had even suggested ways to elevate the pain she was inflicting.

Finn's message now made sense. He was talking about a lockdown that had taken place, which unfortunately for them both, would prevent any non-central Validator from uploading any sort of patch to the network that ran the reactors. As she scrolled through, a sense of dread overtook her and she started to realize what she had done. People had gotten hurt, and the public would not forget the injury it had been dealt. She couldn't just uninstall her kernel and send things back to the way they had been before her attack.

Daryl looked at Charlie for the first time in a few hours.

"Sweetie, are you doing okay? You look like you've seen a ghost!" he exclaimed.

"Dad, I've got a story I need to tell you," Charlie confessed.

4. Panic

Charlie's father didn't react the way she thought he would. This was the first sign that something might be off, with the way she was seeing things. Instead of scolding her, disowning her, or even calling her an asshole, he was *laughing*.

"We played some great pranks back in my day, oh sixty or seventy years ago," he got out through guffaws. "But a kernel level exploit to take down the food and power supply for the whole nation? That's a quarter billion people! I'd have *loved* to pull one off at that scale!"

"Dad, people are going to die, because of what I did."

"Already have, Charlie. But it's okay. You're thirteen. If anything, we should be thanking you. RSA hackers have been attacking nonstop lately, you've discovered and reported a vulnerability they would've *loved* to exploit. And to think, you're so young! You're not even thirty yet. You'll be such a beast when you get a bit older."

He stroked her hair, gave her a hug. And Charlie felt better. The problem hadn't been solved yet, but her father was in a better mood now that he knew the attack hadn't been the first of a series of cleverly planned RSA breaches.

"Dad, one thing still bothers me. The food supply. People are being poisoned, and they don't even know it, everyone!" Charlie said.

"What? Our average life expectancy is over a hundred and fifty years, Charlie. We aren't being poisoned, it's the opposite. What gave you this ridiculous idea?" he demanded, suddenly serious again.

Charlie didn't say anything, glad he was finally over his brief bout of giddy joy at the sudden discovery of his daughter's intellectual superpowers. Instead, she flipped her wrist to activate the HID there and showed her father the articles she had been reading. Maybe she had missed something, but it certainly appeared there were carcinogenic compounds going into the food supply.

Daryl reviewed the articles, then traced attribution, a step Charlie had neglected.

"Look here, Charlie," he said gently. "This account is a known RSA propaganda account. You know what the RSA is, right?" he asked.

"The Republican States of America. They're our enemy, even though we used to share a nation with them. And our government loves to label freethinking Texicans as RSA Terror Agents."

"That's right! Well, mostly the government gets it right when they apply the label. This particular terror cell has been busy. They are going through the toxicology reports, then taking the findings and blowing them out of proportion to make things seem worse than they are. It's an old tactic in their book, I'm surprised you didn't know to trace attribution to analyze the spin.

Still, you're not through secondary school yet. You haven't had a proper education in research techniques so, I can hardly blame you—these fake articles are very convincing."

He scratched his chin for a moment, then gestured to his own HID. Moments later, Finn was on the intercom in the tram.

"Hello Daryl," Finn said dryly. "What seems to be the emergency this time?"

"Well, I have a genius daughter who read a few propaganda articles and played the mother of all pranks on the Texican Republic food supply. Positively brilliant injection attack. We're coming in to apply an emergency patch to the Capital's Validator Node. If not for the lockdown, we'd be able to do it from Post but at least we know it isn't a hardware concern now. And we're already on our way," he trailed off, seeming to get lost in thought.

"What?" Finn's voice was incredulous.

Daryl didn't reply, so Charlie spoke up.

"It's true, Finn. I was convinced we were being poisoned, so I thought of a way to take down the source of the contamination and now our food supply is in jeopardy. I'm sorry." Charlie's face grew hot with embarrassment as she explained.

"Don't worry about it, little girl, just don't do it again. We thought the RSA was getting ready for an attack." Finn's voice was relieved.

"I'm not so sure they aren't," Daryl suddenly broke in.

"Huh?" came Finn's startled reply.

"Well, Charlie here has been reading a very low circulation propaganda magazine that deals in articles about a conspiracy in our food chain. I've explained the issue to her, which allays most of my immediate concerns, especially because the sweet little girl seems repentant," he said, booping Charlie's nose as he spoke. "But there's a problem. Who was funneling these articles to her?"

"I honestly didn't even know she'd been reading them," Finn replied, musing. "I wonder if they intend to stop her from reversing the damage she has done?"

"Hmm. That was my concern as well," Daryl replied. "Well, we should take precautions either way. Can you meet us at the tram station? Maybe bring Bill and Juan? I'll take the boys to the government building, leave the girl with you, and if we're lucky, the RSA spooks will follow me."

"That sounds like a good idea," Finn replied.

Charlie wasn't in the mood for gaming, but she was upset that she had been tricked and wanted to see if she could dig up anything to help her father fix the horrendous mistake she had made. So, she logged in, with about thirty minutes remaining to the Twin Cities, a gleaming glass metropolis that was shining brilliantly even though it was still far off in the distance. All told, the rail commute was about two hours, which was pretty fast considering the distance was over three hundred miles.

Charlie's inbox was now a mess. Anon accounts from all over the Realm had been messaging her various hooks, attempting to get a reply out of her and, she could now easily see, hoping to figure out if she was going to try to undo the damage or not. She adopted a callous approach, refusing to reply to anything except the account that had paid the egregious sum for her in-game item earlier. To that account, she replied.

"I sure am getting tons of spam DMs today. I wanted to say thanks again for doing business with me."

After a few short moments, a reply dinged.

"Hey. All good. We... admire... your work. If you know what I mean."

Charlie felt her face flush. Even though she now knew for a fact that she had been manipulated, she still liked it when people told her how smart she was. She chided herself for being such a tool and thought furiously, trying to determine what to do—she was not surprised in the least that the attacker knew what she had done.

"I was so upset about the poison in our food!" she replied, eager not to say anything to give away the recent change in her plans.

After a pause, she considered. If her frame of mind hadn't changed, she would be withholding the truth from her dad. If the RSA agents wanted to prevent her from modifying the kernel to put it back, which they might do even if she showed no signs outwardly of wanting to restore it, they would let her father walk off and continue following her after the split. She had to seed their expectations, so she composed a new text message.

"Dad got the truth out of me. Is so pissed. Going to fix the error, sticking me with a babysitter when we get to Twin."

No reply came in.

At the station, Finn met Charlie and Daryl, just as planned. Daryl and team left the tall and lanky junior, Finn, to watch Charlie. Then he waved goodbye to her with a stern look on his face and followed Juan and Bill into a new tram that would take them straight to the capitol building. One suspicious-looking man in a cowboy hat followed them, which Charlie noticed. She glanced a few times but managed to avoid staring. He probably still knew he had been made.

Finn led Charlie in a different direction, down an alley on foot. People bustled toward the station from each building they passed, the sun beginning to peek over the horizon. It seemed unlikely that they would be followed if the enemy had taken the bait, but they paused here and there nonetheless, always on the lookout for tails.

Daryl called Charlie, who took the call on her headphones to avoid being overheard. The team was at the Capitol and had been admitted to the war room to explain the new intelligence. The bad news? They had been followed by multiple unknown individuals who were probably RSA Terror

Agents.

Once he was finished with Charlie, Finn's turn came. Daryl's connection passed effortlessly from Charlie to Finn, and Finn received the same briefing in the same manner, but with one additional instruction: keep that girl safe.

Unfortunately for them all, this meant they had to go exactly to where their enemy would be waiting for them, the Capital Validator Node. The mandatory 24-hour lockout window was not yet half past, and already half a dozen fusion reactors had been guided into dangerous territory by their automated systems. One of the greenhouses had exploded, injuring dozens and killing at least three people. Charlie was determined not to let that fate befall anyone else. It was her fault, the least she could do was right the wrong.

"Charlie," Finn said, bending over to get on her level and make direct eye contact with the girl. "I know you want to undo the damage you caused, but our enemy knows that too. And they know where we're headed. The guards will be on full alert, and they will be expecting us, but so will our enemy."

Charlie gulped. She understood, and she was sorry, but the burning thought that shouted loudly in the front of her mind was still the compulsion to undo the damage before anyone else was hurt.

"Charlie, are you listening to me?" Finn asked, gently, bending down a bit to get on her level and speak directly to her. "We may be shot as we approach the building. The good news is that morning traffic will be bringing thousands of commuters in, but the bad news is that men in the crowd working for our enemy will know what we look like and be waiting for us with instructions to shoot. We've given them an advantage, and they know the only way they get to keep that is if they stop us from reaching our goal."

Charlie nodded.

"Good," Finn said. "That's why I've called some backup."

Half a dozen young men greeted them around the next corner, heavily armed and with body armor on. They were Texican Navy Seals, among the best-trained combat troops in the world and certainly the top dogs among Texican military forces. With a declining population and a generally stable social order, the Texican Republic was not widely thought of as a military powerhouse or a particularly militant nation at all, but avoiding war often meant using force to prevent catastrophe.

Finn, at 35, was about the same age as the youngest of the Seals, however, Charlie guessed. Their leader was a bearded man of perhaps ten years more, still a young one in the Texican culture. In twenty or thirty years, these men would have children of their own, she thought. The men had three vehicles, and Finn and Charlie took the back seat in the middle one. Each bore tactical armor that made it bulletproof, and they were fast, but no precaution would be spared. The first and third served as vanguard and rearguard, prioritizing the safety of the occupants of the second vehicle.

Charlie had never seen anything like these transports before. Each had its own wheels, included an automated gun turret mounted top center, and featured manual steering and gunnery controls as well as an automated navigation system and shielded battery packs beneath the floorboard that could keep the vehicle moving even in the case of an EMP attack. The drivers all sounded off and a command came in, instructing them to navigate circuitously toward their destination.

Charlie stared at the nav screen, which was mounted on the dashboard between the driver and gunner. They were only half a dozen miles out, but red markings on the screen denoted hostile emplacements that had been confirmed by Texican Republic Intelligence Operatives.

It was just like being in a movie, she thought. Then Vehicle 1 exploded on the road right in front of them, their driver swerving past the wreckage as the gunner initiated fire at the apartment from which the anti-tank blast had emerged. Vehicle 3 skidded around the wreckage of Vehicle 1, accelerating and taking point. Charlie felt her blood run cold—combat was not a thing she had mentally prepared for. Next to her, Finn had taken an intense, upright posture. He noticed her concern and put a reassuring hand on her shoulder.

Up front, the driver and gunner exchanged a determined glance. Not all of the hostile positions had been cataloged by the TIA. The gunner performed a scan, seeking the next threat. Attacks this bold were uncommon, but not unheard of. The RSA threats were consistent, but the nation was not able to afford full-on assaults very often and had to slake its thirst for blood with psyops and espionage tactics. The result was a hint of danger that permeated urban Texican life, alongside the famous grit that made these people who they were underneath it all.

The next threat did not come from an apartment overlooking the freeway. A civilian transport magnecraft drew up alongside Vehicle 2 and opened fire. The magnecraft was little more than an oblong box with windows that opened. It was a familiar Texican sight, and what made it special was the magnetic levitation effect it was able to achieve by creating an adaptive field just beneath its bottom surface that pushed it ten inches above the ground and could be manipulated to induce the whole thing into motion one direction or the other.

The magnecraft had silently approached, emerging from the ranks of vehicles on the freeway taking people to work with little warning. The occupants of this vehicle must not have realized that their target was bulletproof and more than capable of defending itself, however—the gunner immediately silenced the threat with a blast from the roof-mounted turret.

More vehicles moved to surround the speeding transports in the emergency use lane. Magnecraft were incredibly fast, and as Charlie peered out the window, she got a glimpse of an anti-tank weapon just before the gunner neutralized the hostile with a blast that seemed to pop the advanced hovercraft like a balloon, vaporizing the hostiles inside.

"Code red," the driver noted with a calm that seemed somehow out of place in a combat situation. "Repeat, we have a code red. Hostile vehicles on the freeway, moving to attack. At least a dozen contacts; standard magnecraft, full of well-armed personnel, over."

Vehicle 3 resumed its position behind Vehicle 2, providing some protection from this encircling force. Two police craft pulled out of traffic ahead, forming a phalanx ahead of Charlie and Finn's transport in the emergency lane.

Moments later, the air itself seemed to turn solid *bright* as a brilliant explosion lit up the freeway a mere mile from their destination. The leading police cruisers had been targeted by some sort of high explosive, which Charlie feared could be a tactical suitcase nuke.

What else could the weapon have been? Charlie found herself stunned—the enemy she had previously assumed that she had been imagining was now terrifyingly real. She stopped screaming, suddenly realizing that she was still alive. Finn's hand on her shoulder had clinched tight enough to hurt, but Charlie didn't say anything. Fortunately, the transport's armor had been designed to withstand this sort of blast—the only problem was that the road would now be out.

The magnecraft on the freeway had all collapsed to the ground, forming an impenetrable wall on all sides except the left-hand side. The blast had been caused by a dirty bomb—a small nuclear payload that could devastate an area with a radius of a hundred yards or thereabouts, but whose primary purpose was to emit an electromagnetic pulse that would disable most electronic devices in a much wider range. It was not the first dirty bomb to go off in the Twin City.

Ahead, the suspended bridge over the Rio Grande began to wobble. The driver turned around to face her in the back seat.

"Hold on for dear life," he said, straight-faced.

Charlie nodded, gulped, gripped her seatbelt. Finn released her shoulder to do the same, his dark eyes cold and silent. Charlie redoubled her efforts to stay cold and detached from the situation. Their transport had survived the EMP at critical range, surely the tactical weapon had been the enemy's last resort.

Her thoughts abruptly halted as the driver drove over the edge of the freeway, which resulted in the transport dropping thirty feet into the Rio Grande, eliciting a sick feeling in Charlie's stomach and another scream. Fortunately for its occupants, the transport was undamaged by this rash operation, and the vehicle's ability to spin its tires while floating in water became all- important as it pushed through the water, reaching the bank of the river before the larger chunks of freeway and magnecraft began to rain down behind it.

Navigating into the city's streets, with no support to be seen anywhere, the gunner began slapping the control panel with the radio controls. Since the blast, the radio had gone completely silent—they were now in the most dangerous portion of the journey with no navigation and no radio.

Finn spoke up. "Stop slapping the radio, it got zapped by that tactical nuclear device that vaporized our police escort. How the hell did we live through that?"

"Sir, this vehicle is highly shielded against bioweapons and radiation. Still, if we had been closer to the blast—or if our driver hadn't reacted as he did—we'd be toast just like the rest of them." He gestured to the collapsing freeway fading away back in the distance.

Charlie leaned over, planting her head between her knees. She counted to ten and sat up, feeling that inner coolness return. There was nothing she could do. She had heard about these terror attacks before. Vomiting in the transport wouldn't even the score between her and her enemies, but she wanted no fight. She would avert the famine by restoring the software she had damaged, she silently vowed to herself, staring backward at the ruin and recognizing the thoroughness with which she had been manipulated as well as the danger she was in.

"Ah. Makes sense," Finn replied to the gunner after some moments staring backward with Charlie. "But now how are we supposed to make it to the High-Performance Computing Center?"

"We know the way. It's more a question of whether they think they blew us to smithereens back there. One thing we could try would be to change vehicles, another might be to burn up the Avenue at full speed. It may actually be a good thing that our comms went dark if they were using our frequencies to track us."

The pensive special forces operative who was driving the vehicle sped into a parking garage.

"We have a secret safehouse here. It's shielded from the EMPs." He winked at the apparent shock on Charlie's face. "This ain't our first rodeo. We'll arrange alternative transit and complete our mission using stealth," he announced.

The vehicle came to a stop, and the men exited, beckoning for Charlie and Finn to follow. The group climbed into a family-oriented vehicle with a tall roof and lots of windows, but the windows had been tinted dark. Charlie could see out, but didn't believe others could see in.

Outside, emergency vehicles with their lights and sirens on flew all over the place. Police magnecraft from outside the EMP's effective radius and ambulances and firetrucks all flocked to the detonation site where the freeway's one main bridge had been destroyed, while National Guard vehicles raced to secure major access points and generally harden the Twin Cities against the potential invasion, they had spent over a century preparing for.

The rest of the drive was uneventful, and soon the utilitarian family vehicle had come to rest outside the High-Performance Computing Center. The SEALs jumped out, weapons bristling, covering them, as Charlie and Finn finally entered their destination. Once inside, it took only a few minutes for Charlie's patch to be written and applied. Her computer was dead, apparently a side-effect of that massive dose of radiation, but the concept was so simple it took a standard issue terminal and a small amount of elbow grease to get things situated again. No more greenhouses would explode, and no more blood would stain her young hands.

5. Awakening

On the tram home, Charlie didn't have a moment to herself. She'd been through the scans and the radiation treatment, but now she was discussing her actions and the RSA psyop that had led her to do real damage to her home with political operatives who worked for the President. The President wasn't available, but she was headed home from vacation. Her staff were still assessing the threat posed by actors employed by a foreign nation who had the gall to deploy a tactical nuclear weapon in the middle of her Capital city. These were the sorts of things Charlie reflected as she finally was allowed to pry herself away from the small crowd, that one did well to avoid by living in a place like Post.

Post wasn't her idea of paradise on earth—growing up there was boring, and it was not okay to be stuck inside when the dirt blew. The winters were cold, and the summers bordered on unbearable. And yet, there was a certain allure that the small population offered. You could know people without being overwhelmed by the numbers of them. The bomb had cost a total of around 300 Texican Citizens' lives, mainly commuters on their way to work. Most of these would have been spared if the population was as sparsely distributed as things were in Post.

And there was a quaint methodology to the thoughts people had out here, removed from the more populous coastal regions. Somehow it was easier to get outside the box and come up with something really new if you were removed from the world. Plus, civilization was only an hour or two away by tram.

Ding

The day's newspaper landed in her inbox and Charlie went right to it. The fried primary unit had been carefully placed in her closet as an unrepairable memento, and last year's model was now mounted to Charlie's school clothes. Her eyes widened when the holographic headline flashed in front of her—*The Texican Famine That Didn't Happen: Inside the Secret RSA Plot Foiled in Twin City.*

No mention of her role, just as she'd requested from the reporters. She wouldn't soon forget this day, but she didn't want to become famous for almost devastating her nation.

Daryl would be home in the morning, so Charlie got herself a snack from the kitchen and was asleep soon after without brushing her teeth.

Awake the next morning as if no time had passed, Charlie had one thought on her mind: the monkeys in the greenhouses. She knew the First Greenhouse was in Post because its designer, the only one apparently crazy enough to apply spaceship design techniques to the mundane task of growing crops on earth, was also from Post. What she didn't know was how he had identified a species of monkey well-suited to running the things. Or how he'd bred them.

Daryl burst in a few moments later, all hugs and love and pride in his blossoming teenager. Charlie appreciated this, but she couldn't help taking a moment to reflect on how different this would have been if her mother had still been alive. Her mother's death had been caused by the same people who had manipulated her into the attack she'd mounted. Her father had become both parents, an effort Charlie saw through but did not resent.

"Daddy," Charlie began. "I have a less destructive idea I think I want to try. Earlier, we were learning about the Rhesine monkeys who help us harvest our food, and I was so surprised that they could figure all of that out. There is a game, I did some digging, they have favorite foods. They play by doing chores, which earns them points, and then they get dessert in addition to their base rations. They do *math*, Dad."

Daryl was a bit confused but didn't say anything. He just nodded at Charlie, who took the cue to continue.

"Well, if they're smart enough to do math, they're using language. We don't have a base language to translate our languages into for them, so we mostly speak English to them to give orders or request things."

Daryl nodded.

"Well, you know my game?" Charlie asked.

He did.

"In it, we have gestures we use to chat. They let you make a motion with your hand to type a full word. I want to try to teach one of the monkeys how to use it." Charlie finished, gazing at her father.

Daryl just smiled. "That's a great idea, honey."

"I think today I want to go see Dr. Schwartz. He's old but his boss Leonard Terwiliger built the First Greenhouse almost 200 years ago. He may've tried to teach the monkeys to speak already, but it seems to me that if they're doing work to power our society we should try again. They should have rights and freedoms and things; it isn't right to just make them work all the time."

Daryl yawned. He'd been up all night and, while he was interested in what Charlie was saying, he could only go so many nights in a row without sleeping before the world seemed to glaze over and things stopped making sense. He nodded.

"That sounds good sweetie. I have to get some rest but go ahead and play with those monkeys if you can talk Dr. Schwartz into helping you. I'll buy you pizza every night for a month if you can get one of them to talk." He winked, then gave Charlie a hug and left the room.

Charlie sent a few direct messages, ending with the one to Dr. Schwartz. In no time at all, she was making her way to the garage to get her bike. Dr. Schwartz lived a few blocks away, and Charlie had already created a very rough demo of an application that could teach them to spell English words.

A few weeks later, with no small amount of assistance from her father and Finn, the Rhesines had a basic computer setup that mounted to a little lanyard and went around their necks. A bit under two feet tall, each Rhesine had a different personality, and that information could be studied by watching the projected holographic thought bubble above its head.

One monkey made Charlie laugh and laugh by simply choosing to display exclamation marks there whenever it wasn't having a conversation. She had to go to school, spend time with her dad, and play her games, so there wasn't a lot of time for coding sprints. But Charlie made due, and Dr. Schwartz made sure there was always a live feed for her to peek at if she felt the urge. Something of a family friend, Dr. Schwartz had worked with Daryl for years off and on whenever the older, gray-bearded inventor had a project that required Library assistance.

His eyes enlarged by thick glasses, Dr. Schwartz greeted Charlie at the door to the First Greenhouse. Dressed in his stained lab coat, he ushered her into his kitchen to be sure she had a chance for a snack and some water—he knew it was difficult to get her back out of her laboratory once she had gotten a start.

Charlie had been pushing patch updates to the monkeys' training software for the past few weeks, with no small amount of help from Finn. But today called for her physical presence, and after she turned down the proffered snacks, she made a bee line to a small clearing at the base level of the greenhouse. It was late evening, but Daryl didn't care if she worked at night. The Rhesines were less active, but this could be a good thing.

The Rhesines had seen her coming and recognized her holographic thought bubble—she was using the software she had designed for them. This drew no small amount of attention, and soon the whole squawking tribe had assembled itself in a scattered clump around her, above her. A dozen or so of the fifty-three Rhesines inhabiting the First Greenhouse had been using their text capabilities to communicate with each other, and Charlie was there to try to have a conversation with them.

Charlie swiped her hand to spell "Hi, I'm Charlie."

Her thought bubble refreshed, displaying the new message. Oohs and ahs and squawks filled the air as the Rhesines realized she was trying to communicate with them. They danced around, a few of the younger ones even falling off various higher perches in their excitement. This gave Charlie an idea, and she pulled up the codebase for her app. A quick search of the web later, she had a text-to-speech API hooked into it. The patch was compiled and distributed, and soon the computers' holographic speakers filled the air with all the words that could previously be observed in their thought bubbles.

This led to pure chaos, of course, and Charlie was forced to flee the resultant cacophony. She had a snack and drank some water, Dr. Schwartz practically rolling out a red carpet after observing her in the field.

"You're such a natural..." he kept repeating to her, again and again. "When I heard about the hack, I was shocked, but to see your mind at work is just absolutely fascinating."

Dr. Schwartz was one of the old guard—a centenarian who worked slower and more deliberately. He was also better trained, and hence less likely to have off-the-wall ideas the way Charlie did. Besides, she thought, she hadn't had to do much. A few friends helped in key ways, an AI wrote a few programs, and all of this was so effortless that she was surprised no one else had thought to try to talk to the Rhesines this way before.

She wanted more, though. She wasn't interested in praise, or even really all that interested in Dr. Schwartz for that matter. Charlie's sole goal was to find out what the Rhesines thought of their greenhouse habitat, of their job harvesting and sorting food.

Ding

A new message arrived, this time from Finn. "100% communication" was all it said.

Charlie dashed back out into the greenhouse so quickly that Dr. Schwartz wasn't able to keep up, and the first thing she heard was one of the monkeys speaking to the others, quietly in the semi- darkness a bit off from the grow lights that kept the plants productive even overnight.

"She has given us the gift of speech," its robotic voice said. Charlie wasn't biologically inclined enough to make note of the genders of the monkeys, but this one might have been the oldest male in the colony if she were to guess—all of the other monkeys had silenced their thought bubbles, and they all seemed intently focused on what this one was saying.

"Ah, here she is. What is your name, human?" the monkey asked, its thought bubble transcribing the shockingly fluent sentences even as the robotic voice read them aloud.

"I am Charlie," Charlie said. "Oops. Sorry." Her fingers flew across the projected HID surface, typing I am Charlie and then sending it to her bubble.

"Sorry Charlie?" asked a Rhesine sitting near her in the same robotic voice.

Laughter filled the thought bubbles of the entire tribe and Charlie blushed. What *was* this?

Sensing her chagrin, the chieftain of the tribe paused for a moment and then approached her.

"This gift you have given us, the gift of speech. There are... no words... that could express the gratitude we feel for it. What would you like us to do for you in return?" he asked.

"Well, for starters, what is your name?" Charlie asked.

There was another row, with squawks and general bafflement flooding through the Rhesine community.

"We do not name ourselves," came the eventual reply.

"Oh. That's fine. I can name you if you like," Charlie offered.

"Perhaps another time," said the thought bubble + robot voice of the elder monkey. "We are happy without names."

"Hmm. Okay, well, how are you all so happy?" Charlie asked.

"We are happy because we have all we need. We are safe, we have each other, and we have food. What more could we ask for?" the elder offered.

Charlie's thumb and forefinger found her chin as she thought about this. It seemed too good to be true.

"What's the secret to that?" she asked, genuinely puzzled.

Squawking ensued, and soon it became clear that the monkeys didn't understand why she thought there was a secret here.

"Not secret, never mind. How do you stay so rooted in the present?"

"Take, as your starting point, the idea that everything is as it ought to be. Then think very carefully before you <u>change</u> anything," the elder replied.

Charlie nodded. She wasn't sure what she'd gotten herself into, but something about the shocking violence she had been through weeks previous had awakened a new feeling of contentment in her, too. She was surprised that she was having this conversation with a Rhesine most biology researchers would still have trouble accepting as fully sentient, but perhaps the most bizarre element of the conversation was how deeply the animal's speech resonated—down to her very soul, which felt substantially older now.

Charlie realized she had been taking delight in her prior sources of unhappiness. The world seemed to fit her better, somehow, as if now she knew her place in it. She knelt, putting her arms around the Rhesine leader, embracing the animal in an emotional hug. She spun him around, then put him back down. The other Rhesines laughed and played, and the dawning sun chose that exact moment to peek in through the window. Charlie glanced up at it, feeling the warmth of it on her face and finally identifying the emotion that had awakened in her, replacing the conversation for a moment: it was love, tinged with a bit of awe at the sheer impossibility of everything she was surrounded by.

The future opened before her, wild and beautiful and ageless.

FW 2323

This Isn't Heaven
by Rionna Morgan

"There's been another one, Madam President." Fear and worry cloaked each syllable as the President's assistant spoke.

"Has my granddaughter's plane landed yet?" A quiet voice, a calm voice returned.

"Yes. Security is bringing her now. They are about thirty minutes away."

Mary Margaret Flanagan stood and walked to the doorway of her Dublin home to await her granddaughter's arrival. "Thank you, James." She smiled at the man who had been by her side for what seemed like decades of her life. "For everything."

"I will go now." The man's proud broad shoulders slumped a little as he gathered his coat and hat. "It has been an honor," he whispered as he let himself out and walked down the back steps.

Mary Margaret looked out at the sky, a gold and shimmering midsummer evening. Soaking up the last of the sun's rays, she stood in the open doorway, waiting for Catherine. The breeze from the Irish Sea washed over her face and tossed the tendrils of her graying auburn curls. She brushed her hands along the waist of her trim skirt and straightened the collar of her silk blouse.

She had feared this day, made plans for this day, and accepted that this day would come.

Everything she had resolved, every decision, every sacrifice was for these next several hours. Just now, when James came in, she had tucked the latest and final letter to her granddaughter in the safe built into the wall behind her desk. She had made every preparation she could think of. Now all she had to do was wait.

As soon as the car bringing Catherine pulled in, Mary Margaret hurried to meet it.

She immediately drew Catherine in for a long-overdue hug, relishing the moment with the heart of a grandmother, but also knowing that, with Catherine's arrival, the final piece to her plan was in place.

Mary Margaret and Catherine laughed like teenagers all through dinner, regaling each other of every fun tale and happy memory they'd shared in the last thirty-five years since Catherine's birth.

The hours went by too swiftly. The full moon of that midsummer night rose high in the sky, and it was time to go. Mary Margaret bid Catherine goodnight, much like she had over the years of long summer visits and extended Christmas holidays. She stood just another moment to linger in the doorway of Catherine's bedroom, watching the glowing light of the bedside lamp glimmer at the edges of her face, watched her scribble away in her ever-present journal, said, "I love you, forever" one last time, and shut the door.

Then Mary Margaret slipped out the back of her home, walked down the steps to the waiting car and drove herself to the airport where she tucked herself into the cockpit of a helicopter and flew herself, alone, to the Cliffs of Moher. Upon landing, she turned off the engine, closed the door behind her, and walked toward the rim of the cliffs.

Standing at the edge of the world, her world, Mary Margaret took a deep breath, filling her lungs one last time with the clean fresh air of the North Atlantic. In her heart she knew she was doing the right thing. She knew that this was the only way to protect her country, her people, the ones she loved. A single tear slipped down her cheek, and she let it.

It was okay to grieve, she thought. Okay to let her heart break. She would never again see the bright green valleys and wide tall cliffs of her country, her home. She would never again hear its children laughing as they danced in the mist of the new spring rain. She would never again sit in a warm darkened pub and tap her toe to the lilting music.

Instead, she would protect it.

Mary Margaret walked to the very edge of the cliff, kicked off her shoes and threw aside her cloak. She flicked her fingers toward her feet casting a fire circle around her. The light of it gave a forceful and potent glow to her sky clad form. She called on the power of the moon and vastness of the sky before her. She pulled the tide and summoned the sacred energy of her ancestors from the earth beneath her.

She leaned forward into the night wind, stuck out her arms, hands up, palms out, guarding against any intruder, and uttered, "Grá," in a hushed and final breath.

In less than a blink Mary Margaret Flanagan, a witch, a mother, a grandmother, a sister, a daughter – The President of Ireland – vanished, and all of Ireland fell asleep for three- hundred years.

303 Years in the Future

"Are you sure he's alive?" Catherine asked. Fear and worry cloaked each syllable as she spoke.

"Yes, Madam President. That is the status sent by messenger." The President's assistant responded.

Catherine stood up and walked to the door of her Dublin home. She looked out at the rain drenched gardens. "Bring my car around, James. Please." Catherine gathered her coat and gloves.

As soon as the sleek black car pulled to a stop, Catherine hurried through the misting rain of December and slid into place in the back seat. As soon as her door was closed, she nodded to James to go. On the way to the hospital where the prisoner—stranger, newcomer, intruder—was being held, Catherine Anne Flanagan looked out the window of her car.

She knew she was a rare sight, or rather, her car was. Everyone along the way stopped to look. She made certain to smile and wave so not to alarm anyone. It was raining; it was cold. She needed to go somewhere. It was perfectly understandable that she would have her driver take her so she didn't have to walk or ride in the rain. She sighed and made a mental note to remind her team to brush any concerned questions aside. She was just fine.

The closer they got to the hospital, she made certain to wave more, look happy and healthy, like she was going to visit a friend or maybe a new baby just being born. None of that was out of the ordinary. And all things she did on a regular basis.

But inside, Catherine was terrified. Who was this man? Where did he come from?

How did he get here? How was he alive?

All these questions swirled around in her mind as she exited the car and walked through the automatic double doors of the Mary Margaret Flanagan Medical Hospital. She paused and addressed the doctors and nurses who stopped to greet her as she entered the brightly lit foyer. She made certain to keep her voice light and her mood happy.

Soon she caught James' eye, and he motioned for her to follow him down a long quiet hall. They stopped outside the room where two armed officers stood, guarding, keeping watch, protecting. Catherine took a brief moment, smiled at the two officers, pulled a deep breath into her lungs and let it out, trying to relax, trying to keep the very hard truth at bay. A truth she knew would change everything. She knew that, as soon as she opened the door to this room, her life, her country, her world would never be the same. So, she took another breath and centered her mind, calmed her thoughts, and pulled the handle to open the door.

He ignored the pounding in his head and opened his eyes and squinted against the bright white of the light. *Is this heaven?* He looked at the tall white walls and scanned the rest of the room. He noted the table and chair in the corner and wondered why it would be there. In heaven.

He paused his perusal at the window and just gazed. He could see the sky, a simple gray. The scene looked out onto a crisscrossing path forming a serpentine trench through the span of grass. The trees were tall, skinny, dark, and void of leaves. Their barren branches swayed a bit in what must be a slight wind.

These things were not that remarkable to him, not really. What held his attention was the rain. It was raining. Misty sheets fell from the simple gray sky in among the swaying branches.

It must be a trick. A trick of heaven. He thought serenely, but then abruptly terror clawed at him. *Does that mean... am I dead?* He jerked his hands up to his face. Was it damaged? Did it have skin? Was it real? Did it have form? Was he now just a ghost?

As soon he moved, he felt a sharp pain in his right hand. He looked down at it. There was some sort of tube, small in diameter with a clear liquid in it attached to the top of his hand. It looked like part of it was under the skin. He felt like part of it was under his skin.

He moved to rip it out, when a voice said, "You shouldn't do that."

He jerked his gaze and looked toward the doorway. There he saw the most beautiful woman he'd ever seen; the most beautiful woman *anyone* had ever seen.

She stood tall and proud. Her red hair spilled around her face and shoulders. Her eyes—deep green, steady, strong—looked at him—through him—as if to see his soul.

He scooted up in bed, flinched at the pain in his head, and waited.

Was she his angel? The one who came to announce his fate?

The woman walked the rest of the way into the room. When he grimaced at the pain, her face changed from the near stern look she had to one of compassion and curiosity.

"What will it be then?" He asked. He sat with his back straight, with his head held even, looking forward ready for the final judgment.

"What will what be?"

"My fate?"

"It may come to that," she said as she stepped closer to the edge of his bed.

"What are you here for then?" He reached out and grabbed her hand. His next question lodged in his throat. Compared to his scarred, rough, weather-beaten skin, hers was smooth and warm. He moved his thumb over the palm of her hand. He turned it over and skimmed his fingers along the back of it, marveling at the absence of scars and welts. "Is this heaven?" he whispered, his voice dry, cracked.

The woman pulled her hand from his. Frowned. "No, this isn't heaven." She crossed her arms and stepped back.

As she moved away a stout burly man stepped forward, stomped more like, and scowled at him.

"It's okay." The woman told the man. "What's your name?" the woman asked, looking back at him.

He shrugged. His mind felt foggy, like he knew his name but could not find the way to say it.

"How did you get here?"

He looked around the room again. The only memory he had of this place was from just a few minutes ago when he was watching it rain. He shook his head.

"What do you want?" she asked.

Food, he thought. *I always want food.* He looked up at her face. The stern look was back.

How could he know that he always wanted food but didn't know his own name?

She leaned closer to him, and whispered in a hard, adamant voice, "I want you to tell me who you are, how you got here, and what you want."

"I don't know." He shook his head, trying to clear his thoughts. But it didn't help. The fog stayed. "I don't know. I can't remember," he nearly shouted and winced at the pain in his face. "I'm hungry. That's all I know. That's what I want."

The woman scowled at him and turned on her heel and walked out. The burly man followed.

Catherine walked down the hall away from the man's room. She stopped in a meeting room near the nurse's station, and turned to talk to James, her assistant.

"Thank you for coming and acting as my bodyguard." She smiled at the stout Irishman. "I want to talk to the doctor and find out when he will be well enough to be moved. I don't want him staying here any longer than is medically necessary."

James nodded his head. "Where do you want him to go? Maybe we could set up some extra guards at one of the apartments nearby?"

"I want him to come to the Residence. We have plenty of security there, and I don't want him talking with anyone, not until I know how he got here and who he is. Let's keep that round-the-clock guard outside his door here. I want anything that he had on his person or with him delivered to the Residence this afternoon."

"Yes, Ma'am."

"Please make it clear that I only want the medical professionals assigned to him to go in and out of his room. No one else. Please make sure they don't give him any information about anything outside of what he needs to know for his health, nothing about us, this country, our way of life. Nothing." Catherine knew she sounded harsh, mean even. She normally wasn't so. But she had to be this way now, in this instance. She had to protect her country, her home, her people.

James nodded.

"Oh, and let's get him some food, as much as he'll eat."

Catherine walked down the long hallway, stepped into her waiting car, and went home. Upon arrival, she updated the staff and requested that they prepare a room for their new house guest.

She went to her study intending to re-read the letters from her grandmother again, while she awaited the phone call from the Doctor. Catherine knew each letter by heart and could recall every line and loop of her grandmother's careful, clear text in a moment, but reading them always made her feel closer to her. Especially now, when each of the next few minutes, hours, days seemed so uncertain.

Catherine entered a room that was meant to have a very traditional feel. Deep-red cherry wood ornately graced the room, from the long, tall bookcase along one wall to the sturdy desk with its scrollwork legs and glassy smooth finish. A few chairs with curved legs and wide cushions matched the desk and shelves. A low fire burned traditional peat to ward off the evening chill. Above the fireplace a large coat of arms hung proudly. It was evident that the artisan took special care to craft the inlaid colors and filagree. On the wall behind the desk was a portrait of her grandmother as regal and as queenlike as there ever was.

Catherine pulled the edge of the portrait to reveal a safe tucked into the wall of the room. She lifted the chain from around her neck and used the small, intricate skeleton key to open one of the locks, and she spun the combination dial to open the other. She removed the packet of letters tied in string and left the remaining small wooden box in the back of the safe.

She shut the safe and heard the automatic tumblers of the locks reset. She replaced her grandmother's portrait and set the letters on her desk.

The first letter was on her nightstand when she woke up three years ago. It was that letter that told her about the safe and the other twenty letters, it was that letter that told her that she had not just slept soundly for the span of a single night, but the span of three-hundred years, just like all of Ireland.

Catherine flipped through the envelopes until she found the one marked Protection. She twisted the nob on her desk lamp, and the light spread its golden halo. Catherine fanned out the pages and began to read:

Dear Catherine:

*This letter talks all about protecting our country. I
know you weren't born here, but this place is in your blood,
in your soul. The people here will love you—at first because
you are mine, and I love you, but second, they will love you
because you are you. Your precious loving spirit and fierce
loyalty will win them over in no time.*

*It will be your job to protect Ireland from any and
all threats. On the day you arrived here—that was the last
plane to land at any of our airports. You were the last one
to come home. You thought you were coming for a long visit.
But that's not the entire truth. On the day you landed,
another bomb was detonated in London, obliterating the
city. Your coming was the last piece of the puzzle. Each of
the letters will tell you all the preparations we have all made
for your arrival and what the plans are for the coming
years.*

Catherine stopped reading the letter halfway through. Thinking
about *him* was invading her mind too much. No one had touched her in
three years—or three hundred and three years, if she was going to be
precise. Not like he had. Not because they had wanted to.

Sure, there'd been the gentlemanly gestures of helping in and out
of vehicle, up and down a staircase, or the entering and exiting a building.
But there had been nothing like the way he had touched her, caressed her
hand. She felt treasured, protected in that moment, if that was even
possible. And she couldn't get it out of her mind.

She folded the letter, tucked in with the others, and locked them all
back in the safe.

She would review them again tomorrow. Tonight, she wanted to
talk to the doctor in charge of his care, eat dinner, and be done with details
for the day. She could already feel exhaustion setting in.

She nodded when she heard the phone ring at the edge of desk,
pleased. It seemed like the universe was listening. She picked it up and
listened to the Doctor say that the man could be released from constant care
tomorrow. That, yes, they could easily arrange for a nurse to stay there at
the Residence with him in case he needed medical attention away from the

hospital.

Catherine said goodnight and hung up the phone. She glanced at her calendar. Only three days until Yule. There was still a lot to do. It was the one holiday she insisted the Country of Ireland still celebrate. Today, of all days, she was glad of it. To celebrate the passing of the longest, darkest night of the year seemed extra important with a stranger in their midst, and she still didn't know whether he was going to turn out to be friend or foe.

"James," she called and was not surprised in the least when she heard his deep voice answer.

"Madam, President." He walked into the room.

"Have that man's personal belongings been delivered yet?"

"Yes, Madam, they have been."

"Is there anything in there we should be aware of?"

"There was only a knife and the clothes he was wearing."

"I would like to look at everything tomorrow."

"Yes, Madam."

He spent the first part of the next morning being nothing short of amazed and incredibly grateful. First of all, sometime in the night, amid the sounds of beeping machines and the lights that flashed on the walls of his hospital room, he began to feel glad that he wasn't dead. He still couldn't remember full memories, only snippets of possible memories. He could remember enough or sense enough to realize he was lucky to be alive, not because of the accident he must have been in, but that the place where he landed, the place where he was now didn't have him killed.

They could have. They should have. He felt like, had it been his decision and the roles were reversed, he would have had the stranger killed, no questions asked. He felt like circumstances were dire enough to warrant that where he came from. Wherever that was.

Second, he was glad for the food. He didn't know what he was eating, but it was filling and warm, and there was plenty of it. He had seconds for dinner before they left the hospital, just in case it would be a while before he ate again. Third, he was delivered to the place everyone kept referring to as the Residence and was greeted like an honored guest.

He was set up in a huge room with dark blue walls, a tall wide bed, and shiny floors with flecks of gold in them. He had his own bathroom and sitting room, he heard one of helpers say.

Then finally, *her*.

He got to see her again. Today, he wasn't so groggy and terrified. Today he felt like she'd be less beautiful and smell less good than she had yesterday. Because there was no way anyone could be all that he experienced yesterday. But he was wrong.

"Hi," she said and motioned for him to follow her to her office. He sucked in his breath and his tongue felt too big for his mouth.

"Are you all settled in then." She motioned for him to sit in a wide chair with fat cushions. She walked past him and sat down at her desk, her shoes making soft clicks on the floor.

He nodded and just gazed at her. Around her the dark wood of the room seemed to turn the air into this golden glow. The fire in the fireplace helped, as did the few candles burning on the mantle. Tall cases of books and a few side tables, holding more books and lamps, made the room inviting and welcoming. The great wide desk where she sat made her look small, but only in size. He could tell she was filled with strength and determination.

"Where am I?" He sat up taller and looked directly at her.

"This is my home," she responded. "Have you remembered how you got here? Do you remember who you are?"

He shook his head. "I have not. I know that I've never been anywhere like this before." He remembered the slim streets and tall buildings he saw on the way to the Residence.

"How do you know that?" She asked.

"It's just a feeling I have. I come from a place of war and danger. It feels safe here."

"It is. For the most part." Catherine folded her arms and leaned forward on her desk, edging closer to him. "It is my job to protect us. You may stay as long as you like, if you agree to do the same."

"Yes." He said immediately, recalling all the things he had been grateful for earlier today. "What do I call you?" he asked.

"Madam President," the burly man from yesterday at the hospital walked in. "Oh, I'm sorry, Ma'am," he said when he saw that Catherine was not alone.

"That's alright, James. What is it?"

"I have his things." James nodded toward where he was sitting on the couch.

"Excellent." Catherine held out her hands, motioning toward her desk. "I'll take them."

James set the items on the desk in front of her. "I also had a new set of clothes and personal care items delivered to his room, as requested."

"Thank you," Catherine said as he exited the room.

"You're the President!" he said, not keeping astonishment from his voice. "And you have me here in your home? What if I'm a murderer or something!"

"Are you?" She paused what she was doing and looked at him. She gazed. She looked patient, kind, fierce.

"No. At least, I don't think I am. What do I know?"

"Well, that's good then." She picked up his shirt and pants. "Do you want to keep these?"

The thread was so worn on the shirt, he could nearly see through it. The pants had more stitching than not.

"I don't think so. Your man, James, said I had some different clothes. I don't think I'll need them right now, but shouldn't I keep them, in case? In case someone comes looking for me. I don't exactly look like myself." He tugged on the blue shirt he wore. It still had all its buttons, and the pants he wore didn't have any holes.

"That might be a good idea." She nodded in agreement. "What about this? You won't be needing it."

She held up his knife. The long silver blade gleamed in the lamplight. He frowned. "I would like to keep it."

"Fine. I'll keep them in here." She opened her desk and put them in the bottom drawer. "They will be here if you need them." She tucked them in and closed the drawer. "Now, what do we call you? Do you have any sense of your name?"

"No, Madam, President."

"You may call me Catherine when it's just us."

He nodded and played with the smooth cuff on his shirt.

"Where I come from, whenever we didn't know someone's name, we called them John. Would it be okay if that's what I called you? What we called you?"

"Sure." *John*. He repeated the name in his head. "That sounds okay."

"Good." She stood up. "Now, we have a lot of work to do tomorrow, so go get some rest."

John stood up, said goodnight, and wound his way down the hall to his room.

Catherine hurried with the remaining things she needed to do that night. She made her lists for tomorrow. She wanted everything to be perfect for Yule this year. She washed up and brushed her teeth, grateful for the supplies her grandmother had seen to ensure they had plenty of. Catherine lit the few candles in her room and then taking her lantern, she walked the three flights of stairs up to her tower room. Each flight had thirteen steps, thirteen being lucky and powerful. Tonight, she needed them to offer protection. As she took each step, she breathed in the night air. Even when it was raining, Catherine liked the tower room to have its windows open. She liked the freeing feeling she got from the wind and the misty air.

She closed the door behind her, breathed a quiet spell, and the candles around the room sprung to life, casting a mellow, warm glow into the room. The room itself was wide and long in even lengths. A perfect square of feet measuring thirteen by thirteen. Off to one side, tucked into the wall was a bench filled with all manner of herbs and stones, lined, and labeled with care. There were little pots of lotions and salves. Above the shelf there stood a tall bookshelf that stretched the length of the wall and a ladder just as tall to slide along the rail.

Catherine didn't need books or stones or lotions tonight. She needed the night air and her own power. Every summer of her youth, she spent hours upon hours in this room, learning all her grandmother could teach her.

She loved the tower room. She always felt so powerful and able looking up through the expansive skylights to the shimmer stars above. She remembered what the stars looked like when she was a girl. They were bright, strong, and clear then. Now they were a bit dim. They had to be to ensure the island's survival.

Three hundred and three years ago, Catherine's grandmother cast a spell over the island. This spell put everyone to sleep for three-hundred years. But it also placed a haze between the island's inhabitants and the outside world. Standing here, looking up and out, Catherine could see the stars just enough to know they were there, but she couldn't really see them. There were clouds keeping them from her clear view. Perpetual clouds that never dissipated.

These clouds offered the protection the island needed. In the night that everyone fell to sleep, her grandmother placed this shroud of protection around the island as well.

Part of Catherine's job as President was to ensure that the shroud never got any holes, that no one could ever see in, that no one could ever see out. Once a month she came to the tower room to search the sky, search the clouds for holes and fix them if she found any. And she did come. She came without fail every month. She'd never seen a hole, not even a thinning of the shroud.

But every night since John had washed ashore on the West coast, she'd come up to look. She scanned the sky, quickly, methodically. Nothing. She let out a breath. They were safe tonight as well.

She closed the ritual circle she had cast, put out the candles, and walked the thirty-nine steps back to her room. Tucking herself into bed, she sighed for about the millionth time.

She couldn't quit thinking about her hand in his. She couldn't quit wondering if he was a good man or what intentions he might have. Where he came from. What he wanted. Why he came. But, with him not having his memory, there was no way to know.

She rolled over and pulled her covers up to her chin. Was he a good kisser? She wondered before she could stop herself. "Good grief," she said aloud and pulled the blankets over her head. *There's only one way to find out.* This thought kept repeating itself over and over until she fell asleep. A fitful sleep.

Catherine wasn't the only one experiencing a fitful night. John kept tossing and turning, pulling the blankets, shoving his pillow. Finally, he just got up and got another glass of water.

Sometime during his uncomfortable fidgeting, he decided two

things. One—he'd really like to kiss the President of Wherever-He-Was, and two—the bed was too soft.

Only one of these things could he do anything about. So, there he was—in the middle of the night, rearranging the nicest room he'd ever seen so he could sleep on the floor. He shoved the bed over, moved the nightstands, round table and dressing chairs to the other side of the room. He flipped a single blanket out onto the floor and tossed a single pillow.

He laughed a bit to himself. This is ridiculous. Just as he was about to settle in on the floor, he caught a flash of something at the window.

He instantly wished for his knife. He stilled his breath, clicked off his lamp, and looked out the window. He was careful not to move the curtain or the sheer panel next to the glass.

Out beyond the edge of peaked roof, past the end of his other window, he could see the tower room lit. He was at the wrong angle to see who was in the room, but by the way the light and shadows moved around it, he could tell there was at least one person making wide loops and then smaller loops as they walked.

He wondered what was going on. Who was up there? What were they doing in the middle of the night? He watched and waited. He shifted his weight ever so slightly as he stood, making certain he wouldn't tire. But nothing really happened. After several hours, the figure stopped moving, the light flickered out, and he could tell the person left the room because of the single light travelling from the far end to what must have been the door to the exit. Everything grew dark. He waited a bit more. Listened a bit more to see if he could hear anything else going on in the house. Nothing. He lay down but found that the floor wasn't all that comfortable either.

The next morning Catherine jumped out of bed. She raced through her morning routine, got dressed, zipped to the kitchen for a quick breakfast with her lists tucked inside the pocket of her sweater.

"Good morning," John said from where he stood.

"Good morning," Catherine smiled, surprised to see him up and around so early.

"You look busy already this morning."

"I am." Catherine didn't bother to keep the excitement from her voice.

The dining room was bright with light from the overhead chandelier. Contrasting to it was the cherry red of the dining room table, the twelve matching chairs, and the serving cupboard lining the long wall leading to the kitchen. Around, hanging on the walls, were members of Catherine's family, mother, father, sister. This was the family dining room. Special guests for special dinners were held elsewhere in the residence. This room was one of Catherine's favorites.

She took a moment and added some eggs, sausage, potatoes, and toast to her plate.

She poured herself a cup of coffee, added cream, and one cube of sugar. Her normal breakfast of such a lovely day.

"Did you get enough to eat." She asked as she joined John at the table.

"Yes." He sat up straight and looked at her. "I have had enough for at least two people."

Catherine laughed. "That's good. You're too skinny." She said in a light, teasing voice. "Please feel free to have more if you want later. The cooks here really spoil me."

"Can I ask you something?"

"Sure."

"Where does all this food come from?"

Catherine took a deep breath. "Not today," she answered. "Not today. And not tomorrow, either. I'll try to answer as many of your questions later. But I have other things I want to do today."

"Okay." John took another sip of his hot drink. "Can I ask you something else?"

Catherine looked at him. Hoping he wouldn't keep pressuring her. She simply raised her eyebrows and slighted nodded in agreement.

"What are those?" John pointed to the pile of potatoes on her plate.

"These are potatoes, fixed my favorite way. Cubed with onions and salt and pepper."

"They are delicious. The best thing I've ever eaten."

"Really? You remember then."

John shook his head. "No. I just know that I've never eaten as much as I've eaten here, and I've never had anything that tastes as good as those potatoes."

Catherine laughed. "I'm so glad."

"And this. What is this?" John held up his cup.

"Coffee. I like coffee. It was popular where I came from. Here, they traditionally drink another hot beverage, but I like my coffee. Especially, on cold wet mornings like today."

"Coffee." John took a deep breath, like he was pulling in the scents from heaven, and took another drink.

Catherine laughed again. Then she told him all the things she had planned for the day, and what she expected him to do to help.

The morning of Yule dawned beautifully, gray and misty. The air was lit with magic, a shimmer that spanned the Island. In every home and cottage from cliffs along the ocean shore to the inland rolling hills, the people Ireland paused to celebrate their lives, their home, their country, and each other.

In the Residence the people there did the same. The day began with a hearty breakfast of oatmeal, warm cream, brown sugar, walnuts, and blackcurrants. The cooks began to label everything they served so John would know what he was eating and what he could ask for in the future.

The household staff, Catherine's personal assistants, and the presidential staff all joined in yesterday to decorate and ready the large home for the Yule celebration. They smiled to each other, quietly and quickly when they saw John and Catherine working to hang garland and her favorite fairie lights. They would wink at each other and hurry along with their assigned tasks when Catherine's happy laugh and cheery voice would drift through the house, followed by John's less practiced mirth. It seemed as if the house had been holding its breath for the last three-hundred, three years. Now it could breathe easier, hearing happiness again and not just feeling worry, uncertainty, and occasional fear. This happiness let the house's residents let out the breath they didn't know they had been holding as well.

That afternoon, the whole country, did the same as Catherine, the President of Ireland, addressed its citizens on the radio. She sat beside the fire in her study and told stories of her grandmother, of herself, of the past year. She talked about goals for the future and what she hoped for the coming year. None of this was new to the people of Ireland. The tradition of the yearly Yule talk with the President was one they were used to and looked forward to. However, this year seemed different. The country was feeling a sense of hope, more than they ever had in the past.

Through the radio they could hear the happiness in their President's voice. Not the forced happiness she tried to layer her words with most days, but actual happiness. There was a lot of speculation around dinner tables all over the island that night as to why their leader sounded so happy. Everything from, "Maybe she made a new discovery that she'll tell us about when she visits," or, "Maybe she's excited for winter to be over." None of them thought the happiness in her voice was because of a man, and an unknown stranger of a man at that.

For Catherine it wasn't because of a man, either. The happiness in her voice was not because he was a man, but more that she was able to see things through his eyes. He was a good listener. He was funny. But more so, she got to be someone other than the President of Ireland with him. She could be a little bit of who she remembered she was before she had a country to run and an entire population to protect.

She had been an American. She had grown up in Boston, to parents who were both doctors. She studied art at NYU and loved pizza from Joe's. She liked taking walks in Central Park and calling her grandmother on the weekends. Her friends said she was funny, and she was good at her job—curator for the Museum of Modern Art. She had just met a nice guy who maybe could have been a great boyfriend.

But that all changed when she landed in Ireland to visit her grandmother for a few weeks three hundred and three years ago. That whole first year after the country awakened from its three-hundred-year nap, she spent every day trying to understand and wrap her mind around what had happened. Why she was the one chosen to take her grandmother's place. She'd read every letter at least a hundred times, and she struggled every day to put it all into perspective.

The next year had been easier. It helped that her grandmother had thought of literally everything—every struggle, every could-be issue—and solved it before it had a chance to be a real problem. The third year, lots of things got easier, like the everyday running of the government. Again, she had her grandmother to thank for that. Parliament ran the innerworkings of laws and regulations. Parliament insisted that she live in the President's house, the fancy one a few miles over, but she never felt comfortable there. She had asked instead that it be repurposed as a historical site, to preserve the history of Ireland, to be used for government meetings and gatherings as necessary, and to be lodging for government officials traveling into Dublin from the surrounding areas. She felt much more at home at the Residence anyway. So, she moved into the home she had always shared with her grandmother. Since she was the people's contact and liaison to Parliament, she felt closer to them living there.

But no matter how much time passed or how many people she worked with, she was always treated like their President. John didn't treat her like that. He simply treated her like a person.

Just like tonight as they were sitting by the fire in her study after the Yule radio talk, he'd said, "I made you something." Then he stepped out of the study only to return a little while later with an odd-shaped package, wrapped in what looked like butcher paper and string.

"Here." He placed it in her hands. She looked at him puzzled. "I know you said that we don't give gifts on Yule, but I wanted to."

"Okay." Catherine smiled to herself as she turned the package over. It was heavy and was definitely wrapped in butcher paper and twine from the kitchen.

"Before you open it," John sat down and pulled his bulky, tall-backed chair closer to her, "I didn't have a lot of time. We were so busy yesterday with everything, decorating and getting ready for today." John moved his hand in a circle above his head in a gesturing motion encompassing the whole house and all the decorating they had done. "So, it's not as pretty as it should be."

Catherine smiled. His dark hair was a little unruly even though she could tell he'd spent time combing it. His dark eyes shone bright with excitement, like a little kid with an ice cream cone. A timid smile lit his face.

Catherine pulled the tail of the twine and the paper fell away to reveal a wooden carving. She turned it over and gasped. In her hands she held a fairie with wide wings and a dainty face with a perfectly formed features, with eyes that seemed to really smile up at her.

"I thought of it yesterday, when you told the story of your favorite decoration from when you were a kid." John pointed at the figure. "You said it was a fairie that held a candle."

Catherine traced her fingers along the edges of the wings and down the outstretched arms.

"See there. She can hold a candle."

"How did you do this?"

"I asked the cooks if I could have a chunk of wood and a knife. That I wanted to carve a present for you."

"You made this from a kitchen knife and a piece of firewood?"

"Yes." John's voice faltered. He sounded nervous.

Catherine looked over at him. She shook her head and blinked. "It's unbelievable." She moved the tips of her fingers from the fairie's skirt, along her long slim legs, to the little slippers for shoes. "How did you learn how to do this?"

"I don't know." John shrugged his shoulders and sat back. "I don't know anything, and I don't know if I *want* to know anything." He held out his hands. "Look at my hands. When I got here, they were rough, damaged, and cut. But they're healing. My head is healing." He moved his hand to where the bandage used to be.

"I'm glad." Catherine smiled.

"Well, I don't want to go back to whatever did that to me. I don't want to remember. I want to stay here. Help you decorate for Yule. I can work. I am strong." He crossed his arms and looked into the fire.

Catherine's heart ached. She could hear the fear in his voice. She reached over and took ahold of his hand. He flinched, sat forward, and looked at her. The kid-like excitement from before was gone. His face now looked as if a steel barrier had closed around it, keeping everything out.

"You can stay," Catherine said. "I won't send you away."

John gazed at her. Examined her face. Catherine felt like minutes upon minutes were ticking by, like he was looking to see if she were telling the truth.

"Thank you," he finally said and sat back in his chair again, still holding her hand.

They sat like that, side-by-side, in front of the fire. On the mantle above the fireplace a woven holly branch, dotted with bright red berries, hung in strands of garland. Scattered here and there on every flat surface were candles, burning, bringing light into the space. The entryway, the family dining room, all the guest rooms, even his room shone with the same golden light and had the same drape of garland adorning a mantle, a bookshelf, or doorframe.

Somewhere in the other side of the home, a strong, sweet voice could be heard singing. The scent of cinnamon and vanilla wafted from the kitchen, a promise of a sweet dessert after dinner.

Catherine smiled as she looked again at her fairie, and then she closed her eyes and rested for the first time in three-hundred and three years, feeling safe and happy.

"I'm going to be gone for a few days," Catherine said as she poured her second cup of coffee, the next morning at breakfast.

"Oh yeah?" John set down the book he had grabbed out of the library this morning on his way to the kitchen for a pre-breakfast snack.

"I am going to go to the West coast for a few days. I always do this time of year. Do you want to come along?"

"Sure." John stood up and pushed his chair in. He watched her nod and take a sip of her coffee. Gone was the ponytail from yesterday, the carefree look on her face, and the comfy clothes she wore as they played cards before retiring for the night. Now, her hair was tied in a knot at the base of her neck, no strand out of place. Her face was serious, determined, and she wore dark pants, a no-nonsense top, sturdy walking shoes, and she had her notebook.

"This looks serious," John commented and waited for her to look up.

"It can be. I try to go four times a year, each time visiting a separate part of the country. This trip is business, but it should also be really pleasant. The trip after Yule generally is very nice."

"How far is the West coast?"

"Half a day away." Catherine picked up all the papers she'd been sorting through and put them in her shoulder bag.

John had an uneasy feeling. He couldn't decipher why he was uneasy, maybe it was the half a day away or the fact that Catherine looked different than she had yesterday.

"Can I take my knife?" He asked.

"Why?" Catherine paused what she was doing and looked at him.

"I don't know why." John rubbed his chin. "I guess I don't like being that far away from it."

"You haven't needed it here, and James is coming along with my security team."

"I haven't needed it here, you're right. But I know where it is and could get to it if I needed it. What if I need it there, and I don't have it?"

"Will it help you feel safe if we take it?"

"Yes." John was beginning to feel agitated about the whole ordeal. "I really think it needs to come with us."

"Okay." Catherine finished her coffee and picked up her bag. "You know where it is. I have to check-in with James before we go."

John walked out of the dining room and turned left down the long hallway toward Catherine's study. With each step he felt more uneasy. He told himself it was because they were leaving the Residence, and he wasn't certain what to expect on the trip and that was why he was feeling off. He thought he'd feel better once he had the knife in his hand, so he opened the bottom drawer to Catherine's desk and pulled out the basket that held his belongings.

Instead of feeling better, the uneasiness just grew as he looked at his old things. His clothes looked rancid and hideous. The knife was too heavy in his hand. He pulled it from its sheath, saw the glint of metal in the light. His stomach began to hurt. He wracked his brain for any clue.

What was the matter with him? These were just old, worn-out clothes and a knife. Literally nothing from an old life, he didn't want to go back to.

He put the clothes back in the basket and put them back in the bottom drawer. He sheathed the knife and tucked it behind his back in the waistband of his pants. Then he went to pack and meet Catherine.

Catherine was feeling uneasy too. She wanted John to come. She wanted him to see the country and get to know the place he didn't want to ever leave, the place he had agreed to protect. But she wasn't certain how much to tell him. Should she tell him everything – grandmother was a witch who figured out a way to save all of Ireland from nuclear war, nuclear fallout, and a post-apocalyptic war – or only part of everything? She was torn because she didn't know which part to leave out. By the time she and

John loaded their bags into the car and were underway, with the two other cars in their party following close, she still didn't know what she was going to say.

Luckily, she didn't have to decide because John simply asked, "Are you a witch?"

"What?" Catherine pivoted in her seat beside him to look at him. "A witch?" She repeated.

"Yeah. I read about them in the book I was reading during breakfast. I got it out of the library in your study."

"What makes you think I'm a witch?"

"You love everybody."

Catherine laughed and wondered what book he had been reading.

"Seriously. Everybody. I watch how you are with the people who work for you. Like our driver today: I bet you know his name and the names of his kids and wife, if he has any."

"Kathleen is his wife, and he has three daughters." Catherine nodded.

"See." John nodded. "And you make your home welcoming to everybody too, even a stranger who you probably should have had killed on sight. And not only that; now that stranger is so infatuated with the place—" John tapped his chest with the point of his finger then continued. "—that he never wants to leave. It or you."

She smiled at him, touched that he would come right out and say what he was thinking. Brave, she thought.

"Plus," John went on. "You are very kind and open-minded."

"What do you mean?"

"When we were decorating for Yule, you listened to what the others were thinking, and then you even went so far as incorporating their ideas."

"That's what you think a witch is? Loving, kind, and open-minded?"

"Isn't it?"

"In a way, I suppose. They are loving and protective of everyone, especially those they love. They can be very kind and open-minded, until they aren't." Catherine raised her eyebrow in a mocking, with an edge of serious warning, way. "And some witches are also very powerful. They have powerful gifts. Some can control the seasons and nature. Some can read the minds of others. Some can move things without touching them. Some can see the future." Catherine was careful to watch John's face as she spoke of each gift. Instead of being scared or shocked, he looked like one of her old college professors listening intently to a TED talk.

"What can you do?" he asked.

This was the big deal answer. Should she tell him? Should she not? She believed him when he said he didn't ever want to leave. She hadn't allowed herself to look—to *see*—whether or not he was telling the truth. She only did that the first night at the hospital, to make certain he wasn't lying about his memory being lost, and that the only thing he knew was that he was hungry. It still pained her to feel how hungry he had actually been. Her stomach hurt with hunger pangs for hours after she'd looked.

She knew she could always wipe away his memory of her and the time he spent with her, but she didn't want to do that. Wiping his memory had a downside. Wiping his memory did the same to her. He wouldn't remember her, and she wouldn't remember him either. This knowledge made her sad. She wanted to remember him and the way he made her feel—like just a person somehow.

She looked over at him. He sat patiently, waiting for her answer. His hands were folded in his lap, their fingers laced together in that easy way he had. It was like he knew she was thinking and knew she needed time to decide what to tell him.

She took a deep breath. "I can do all of them."

"I knew it!" He cheered. "You are the most amazing woman I have ever met. The most amazing person I know." He laughed. "I only know like twelve people. But still!"

She laughed and the driver looked back at them, smiling. "That's not what you say when a witch tells you she can do virtually anything!" Catherine stared at him and shook her head.

"Sure, it is." He announced and pulled her to him. "It is when it's my witch." And he kissed her, lingering long enough to wrap his arms around her back and long enough for her sink against him.

Catherine pulled back slowly and squinted between her lashes at him.

"Sorry." He gently slid her back into her original seated position. "I should have asked."

"Yes."

Catherine felt the eyes of her driver focused on her. She mouthed, "I'm okay." To him and looked back at John. He looked sheepish.

"I'm sorry," he said again.

Catherine touched her fingers to her lips. Never in her life had she been kissed like that, strong and sure, but gentle and patient. She thought about the man she met right before she flew to Ireland. He'd kissed her goodnight once after one of their dates, and it was nothing like what had just happened. Did it really take three hundred years for her to meet the man of her dreams?

She almost laughed out loud, but she looked over at John and saw him looking out the window. He looked a little sad with his shoulders slumped, but he also looked like he was seeing the world for the first time the way he leaned against the door of the car. She could feel his happiness at what he was seeing, the wide rolling wintery green hills of Ireland, but also his sadness too.

As the car slowed to the next bend and stopped to let another car go by, she said, "Look." And then pointed to the ground beside the car. There in the cool grass at the edge of a rock wall, a few little purple violets bloomed.

She heard him suck in his breath and reach for her hand.

He looked and looked, until the car moved forward again. He turned his head back and watched until they faded from view.

Then he turned his gaze toward her. "Thank you," he whispered.

She was startled to see tears in his eyes. "You're welcome," she whispered back.

Then she leaned closer, her lips brushed against his ear. "You may kiss me anytime."

"I knew it!" He cheered again. And laughed. Catherine joined him. So did their driver, Frank.

John knew—as much as he could know anything these days with his lost memories—that he'd never been so tired and so happy, ever. On the drive from Dublin to the town of Doolin on the west coast of Ireland, he had learned many things. One of which, he was in the country of Ireland.

He was in the car and motorcade with Catherine, its president, and she was the powerful and amazing granddaughter of Ireland's former president, who had saved the country from certain ruin. Mary Margaret Flannagan had, on a mid-summer night, three hundred and three years ago, cast a wide, strong net of protection over the island making it impossible for outsiders to see the rich, green, lush country it is. She dropped a sleeping spell over the island so the citizens would sleep through the worst of the nuclear fallout in the rest of the world and awaken when the specified time had passed. Awaken, ready to not only live their daily lives like they had done for centuries, but ready to help save and heal the world as well.

For years, Mary Margaret and strategized with the more than thirty county leaders on how best to protect the island and ensure that the people of Ireland would be cared for. They had meetings, and planning sessions, and the entire island voted and agreed.

"'Then the work began,' my grandmother said." Catherine explained. "She made the best plans she could to help the people of Ireland and the world."

"How?" John was amazed at what he was hearing.

"When we get home, we can read the letters she left explaining everything."

"Okay." John nodded watching Catherine intently as she continued.

"She and every county leader agreed and completed a magical contract, binding them and their county for a thousand years."

"A magical contract?"

"It's an agreement stronger than a piece of paper and a signature. It's almost like a blood oath, but my grandmother didn't believe in spilling blood. These contracts are formed when the parties involved exchange a token and a promise with each other."

The world outside the car window grew faint in the dusky light, heading toward evening. The once shimmering light of day drifted away to the edges of the horizon, replaced with a golden hue.

Catherine looked out the car window, took a deep breath, and continued. "My grandmother gave each leader a moonstone, powerful and blessed, to protect them and bind them to their promise of secrecy. Each leader gave a token in return, something that represented their promise and something to bind my grandmother to her promise of protection."

"Do you believe in it?"

"The promises? Yes."

"Spilling blood?"

"Yes, of course I do. I have to believe in it. My country's safety is at stake."

"Do you have to spill blood to kill someone?" John cleared his throat and went on. "I mean with your powers?"

Catherine slowly looked over at him. She wiped the little wisps of hair escaping her bun back from her face. "No." She bent her head and looked down at her entwined fingers in her lap. "I can just stop their heart."

The feeling in the car changed. It seemed heavy to John, like the place and woman he loved had become ominous and scary or rather that they could be ominous and scary. But he could also feel that they were brave and daring, that these people were willing to do whatever had to be done to protect themselves and each other, that she was willing to do whatever had to be done to protect them.

"Have you ever done it?"

"Never." A single tear slipped down Catherine's cheek.

To John it looked like a tear of great sadness, a tear of fear. "Well, let's make sure you never have to." He reached out and pulled her hand into his. He grimaced internally with the chill he felt as he wrapped his hand around hers. "Okay?" In his heart, John made his own vow, that he would do whatever he could to help her protect her people, his people now.

"Yeah." Catherine sniffed.

"Your grandmother was brilliant. What else did she do?" John asked.

"She began making preparations to not only serve and protect Ireland, but to help the world around us. Once she knew Ireland had enough supplies and goods, she implemented her plan to help others who may have survived the bombings. She traded for wine barrels from France, Italy, Portugal, Spain—everywhere." Catherine ticked off the places she said like a list on the tips of her fingers.

"She traded for them, stored them in the caves – in Doolin and the Burren. Filled every barrel with surplus seeds, bags of barley, wheat, oats, and seed potatoes, tea, wool blankets, soap, and medicine. Everything was either imported or repackaged with no identifying markings. Anything that comes from here actually comes from elsewhere. There is no way to trace anything back to us, not even our tea."

Something fuzzy began to surface at the edges of John's brain. The stomachache he had from before was returning. Something wasn't right. But he kept listening, knowing it was important to hear everything Catherine had to say.

"We have enough barrels stored to drop one a week for the next sixty years."

John's head was starting to hurt. His eyes felt bulgy and fat. What was wrong?

"She brought in the best scientists, oceanographers to study the ocean currents and found that the best, strongest currents were on our West coast. That's where we drop one barrel every week—John?"

John swayed back and forth in his seat, like he was sick and needed air.

"Frank! Something's the matter." Catherine hurriedly spoke with her driver.

"We're here now, Madam President," Frank said and pulled into the parking area. "John, let's get out."

With the help of Frank, Catherine pulled John from the car. He took big cleansing breaths and leaned against the hood of the vehicle. He kept seeing flashes of ship riggings and haggard, starving people. He could almost feel the blood from his head would drip into his eyes. Then splash after splash of cold, salty sea water engulfing him. The scene played over and over in his mind, faster and faster.

He ran away from the car, across the span of grass, down the pier and emptied his stomach into the swishing waves. He scrubbed his face clean with his hands and the cuff of his sleeve. Then he walked back to where Catherine, Frank, and about twenty other people stood, waiting to see if he was okay.

"What happened?" Catherine hurried to his side.

"I don't know." John responded. "But I better have my knife."

"Okay."

Catherine nodded to Frank who opened the car, pulled the knife from John's bag, and placed it in his hand. The bile in John's stomach rebelled again. But he forced it down and shoved the knife in the band of his pants behind his back.

Catherine tipped her head questioningly toward John.

"I'm fine." His voice cracked. He cleared it. "Really. I'm fine."

"Okay." Catherine nodded and turned to the waiting group. "Good evening, everyone. Blessed Yule."

Her voice was chipper and happy. The voice John knew was not hers, but the one she used when she needed something to be happy and worry free, but she was still worrying. He could tell. It was the same voice she used when she met him that day in the hospital.

Happy, pleased responses were returned in-kind. Respectful nods and faces with glad smiles looked back, anxious to see what else their President was going to say.

"This is John," she reached for his hand and pulled him up beside her. "You all saved his life, weeks ago now."

The crowd looked at him with a sort of awe and wonder. Many stepped forward to shake his hand and wish him a blessed Yule. John smiled. He felt so welcomed. This was her doing, he thought to himself as a few of the others teased him about puking and clapped him on the back. They began introducing themselves and talking of their families and asking him how his Yule holiday had been.

One tall, fellow stepped forward to stand beside Catherine. His red hair bright in the last rays of the setting sun. "Madam, President," he said. We have the barrel you requested ready to go."

"Thank you, Sean. Let's wheel it over?"

Sean moved to do her bidding and began pulling a hand trolley holding a large wine barrel. The wheels made crunching noises as it moved over the rocks in the path. Hearing this, John looked over and saw Sean and Catherine walking toward the cliffs, leading to the edge of the ocean.

"No!" He yelled. "Don't do it." A ringing ricocheted inside his mind. He ran toward them, holding his head. "Don't do it!" He yelled again, nearly falling.

Catherine and Sean stopped.

"They'll see." John pointed to the wide, tall cliffs and the ocean beyond. "They're waiting!"

Catherine looked at Sean who stepped away and walked back to the join the others. "What are you talking about?" Catherine whispered; her voice sounded scared.

"They're out there waiting to see if this landmass is inhabited. They'll see you drop the barrel. They're watching."

"Who are they?"

"Them. People."

Catherine looked to the ocean. She scanned the horizon. "I don't see anything."

"You won't," he said. "They're waiting for me."

Fear gripped her heart. Fear like she'd never felt. Not ever. She looked over John's shoulder to the small group of people waiting to go have another celebratory Yule dinner with her. She looked beyond them and could see the lights of the nearby village twinkling warmth and welcome.

"What?" Catherine ground the word between her teeth.

"I know who I am. I remembered. I know what they're planning on doing." John spoke in rapid fire.

"Who are you?"

"My name is Michael James. Michael James Hughes. I'm from what used to be the United States, New York."

"Talk faster." Catherine spat out.

"I joined this crew." Michael jutted his hand toward the ocean. "We were going from island to island—everywhere up and down the coastline—looking for any signs of life, any signs of food. One day we ran across one of your barrels, and I swear it saved our lives!"

"What else?" Catherine closed her eyes and imagined the web of protection fastening itself tighter, firmer to the edges of the island. *Please hold. Please hold.* She chanted in the back of her mind as Michael continued.

"We spent six months trying to figure out where it came from, then we found another one. So, we kept looking, sailing in circles. We sailed to Iceland. England. France. We kept sailing past here, ignoring it because it looks like a barren wasteland. No life, no grass, nothing from out there."

"So, how'd you get here then?"

"I volunteered. They gave me this knife, and I jumped overboard. I hit my head on the hull of the ship when I fell. I must have washed up here."

"What were you supposed to do if you found anyone?"

Michael pulled the knife from behind his back. "I was supposed to unscrew the handle here and turn on the signal." He spun the handle.

Around and around until the end fell free in his hand. He tapped out a small remote that had a single button on it. "I was supposed to press that button and call for them."

"Them? How many of them are there?"

"Thousands. On an aircraft carrier."

Catherine fought back tears. How could she be so stupid? She berated herself. Why did she let him on the island. Why did she let him live? What was she supposed to do now? All those people. How was she supposed to help them and protect her people?

"Now what? You're just going to press that button and then here they come?"

"No." Michael responded.

"Whose side are you on?"

"Yours." Michael looked toward where the others were standing. "Theirs." He paused and looked toward the water. "But my sister's out there."

"They can't come here. Nobody can know about us." Catherine held out her hand, and Michael placed the remote on her palm.

"I know."

"I mean it. We don't have an army. We have no way to defend ourselves."

"Except you can kill people with your mind." Michael whispered.

"I'm not going to kill thousands of hungry people!" Catherine whispered back in a stark tone. "And we can't absorb thousands of people here and still be invisible to the world." She walked closer to the edge of the cliff and scanned the horizon for any flash of light or movement in the darkness. "How many ships did you say?"

"Just one." Michael responded as he joined her where she stood. "I might have an idea on how to help them and how to protect us."

"Okay. What do you want me to do?"

"Go tell Sean I need that." She pointed back to where she and Sean had left the first barrel. "And then tell Sean I need four more."

Michael stepped away along the path back toward where the town's folks waited, but tripped in the darkness.

Catherine paused, moved her hand in a sweeping motion like she was tossing a ball. But as she did a low, mellow light lit the walkway for Michael to follow. He looked over and grinned at her. She could feel his pride in her echo back as he walked away.

Pretty quick, the townspeople, James, Sean, and Michael came back with all five barrels she asked for.

"I have to do something I've never done before." Catherine looked at everyone as they waited. Each with hopeful, courageous, faith-filled faces looking back at her. "I don't know if I can do it."

Michael nodded encouragement toward her.

Catherine reached up and pulled the pins loose from her hair and shook the long locks free. She handed the remote to James with her hair pins and her shoes. She dug into the earth with her toes, feeling its power, feeling its warmth. She held her arms out wide, pulling on the fierceness of the wind and the strength of the moon. She turned and looked through the night, out across the miles. She scanned the waters until she found the solitary ship, drifting up and down, up and down in the calm sea. She looked quickly to make sure no one was on deck, then her mind raced back to land.

"I found it." She said a little breathless. "Okay. Let's do it." She dug her feet in more. She called to the goddess. She called to the North, the South, the East, the West. She wrapped each barrel in an invisible shroud and with her mind she transported them to the deck of the ship. All five all at once. Then her mind raced back to land. "I did it!" She laughed. "I did it!"

Her hands shook as she wiped the hair back from her face. She took a deep breath and closed her eyes. "I did it." She sighed and swayed a little against Michael's shoulder. "Now, how will they go away? I don't want them sitting out there forever. Waiting."

"They would have to get a signal from another ship – a distress call or something saying they needed assistance."

"I can do that." Catherine sent the signal, making it come from the direction of Greenland. "That should sound for hours. The invisible barrier on the barrels will disappear and the barrels will be visible on the ship when they are about five hundred miles away from us. Hopefully, they'll think it was just magic."

Catherine turned and looked to Sean, the townspeople, and James who had all circled around her. "Sean?" Catherine spoke.

"Yes, Madam, President." Sean responded and stepped forward.

"Your wife, Aoife, knows a little magic doesn't she?"

"Yes, she does."

"I want to keep dropping these barrels, just like we have always done, but I want them to be invisible when they go into the ocean. Do you think Aoife can make sure that happens when I am not here?"

"Can it last for days?" Michael stepped forward into the circle. "Just to make sure the ocean currents have time to move it away from the Island?"

"I bet so." Sean beamed. "I'll ask her."

"Thank you." Catherine responded and turned to James. She held out her hand for the remote she had given him.

"Now, let's dispose of this." Catherine said to Michael. He nodded his head in agreement.

"Hmm." Catherine said as she thought of what to do.

Then suddenly she walked to the farthest jut of land and waited for Michael to follow.

She crushed the plastic to powder and threw the fine dust high up into the air. It drifted and swirled around them in the soft breeze. Each minuscule piece formed a star in the darkness, casting a soft glow.

Catherine took ahold of Michael's hand and pulled him close to her side. She linked her fingers with his, and together they stood and watched the shimmering lights above them. She let some of the lights fall like shooting stars to land at their feet.

She smiled when she heard Michael's quick gasp of joy when those falling lights turned to small violet flowers carpeting the ground at their feet.

Michael's heart was so full, he felt like it could burst into a billion pieces like the twinkling stars Catherine just tossed up into the sky. He felt as if he was in a constant state of awe. It started when Catherine pulled the pins from her hair and her long red curls blew free in the wind. She figured out a way to protect the people of Ireland, but she also opened her arms, her heart, her soul to save the strangers she'd never meet. Now that he had his memory back, he knew that she was the most amazing woman, person, he'd ever met.

Snippets of their time together flashed through his mind. That first moment when he saw her in his hospital room. Her welcoming him into her home and then her laughing about his asking what a potato was, the soft, far-off grateful look she had when he'd given her the fairie he carved. He thought of the sacrifices she makes every day to be the leader of a country that's not her home by birth. Her strength when she cried when she was scared, but still found a way to save everyone. Even now, when she's destroying something, she still makes it beautiful.

Michael looked at Catherine. She was smiling, the light-in-her-eyes, sheer happiness smiling.

"Are you sure this isn't heaven?" he asked her.

She laughed. "Yes." Then she stood up on her toes and touched her lips to his.

Feels like heaven to me, he thought as he wound his arms around her and pulled her body to his. The glowing flecks of magic curled about them.

Regicide
By E. R. Donaldson

Part I

Jhansi stared out across the accursed lake as the fog cleared. Even before the radiation sensors chirped their pleasant, "All Clear," signal, she knew they'd arrived. They were officially beyond the RSA's borders and within the domain of the Wolverine Isles.

That's where her target lurked: the so-called Immortal Witch Queen of the Isles—CEO of Spartan Aquatics. Jhansi and her team were about to test that fantasy. In the twenty-fourth century, everyone knew there was no such thing as magic—and Jhansi knew, sure as hell, that everyone could die.

Herald, the smuggler contracted by the RSA for this mission, brought his turbocraft around and killed the engines. "This is as far as I go," he growled. "Spartan Drones patrol fifty meters out from the fallout. You're on your own from here."

Tapping the button to seal her suit, Jhansi stepped up to the edge of the craft. She would have said something, but she wasn't in command of this mission.

Derek had that privilege. "Good work," he said, tossing the smuggler a credit chip with his promised fee.

Herald grunted, stowing the chip away in his pocket and then turning right back to his controls. He seemed intent on leaving in the next thirty seconds, regardless of whether the four agents exited the boat or not.

Jhansi, Derek, and their fellow operatives were well-trained. They were off the craft before he could ignite the thrusters. Ice-cold water welcomed Jhansi like the cruel hands of fate. The frigid fluids, one-point-two degrees Celsius to be precise, enveloped Jhansi as she flipped over the edge of the craft. Jhansi spread her arms and began to swim through that icy abyss. Even with the temperature modulation of her body suit, all she could feel was the brutal cold enveloping her.

I've trained for this. I was made for this.

Jhansi was a fish in her element. She pushed past her body's desire to succumb to the chilling temperatures and stroked steadily toward that distant shore she'd had only the briefest glimpse of before diving into the Great Lake.

She emerged soundlessly a few meters offshore. She remained submerged as much as the shallow tides would allow. As if reminding her of the stakes, a Spartan Drone buzzed overhead, flashing its searchlight all around her position. The stealth suits the RSA had provided must have been working because that light never came close to her or her companions..

As a unit, they crawled upon the shore before sprinting into the cover of the treeline. God above, Jhansi had never seen such a forest. It was like something from a fable, something from a long-forgotten myth.

It's just the result of nuclear fallout.

Though no nukes had been used recently, Jhansi had paid attention to her history. Overgrowth of vegetation was a common side-effect of nuclear fallout.

Only when she and her comrades were safely out of sight beneath the great canopy did they pause to rest. Jhansi braced herself against an enormous tree trunk. Her companions took shelter in the small hollow beneath her.

Derek touched the side of his mask, triggering the digital display. "No radiation detected," he reported. "We're clear." He unfastened the back of his hood and removed his mask.

The others followed Derek's lead. Just after removing her mask, Jhansi hesitated. Despite all reports to the contrary, she couldn't imagine how this wasn't a radioactive wasteland.

Her first breath defied her reasoning. In fact, the sensation was so pleasant that she took another, deeper breath. God above. This was the cleanest air she had ever tasted. How could these God-forsaken islands contain such...

This was all because of the Wolverine Isles' unique technology. It was this technology that allowed Spartan Aquatics to become the preeminent technocracy in the modern world. It was this power that the Immortal Witch Queen had leveraged to quietly create her private monarchy within the Maritime Alliance. It was this threat that Jhansi and her companions had been sent here to usurp.

Suddenly, the cleanest, freshest breath of air Jhansi had ever tasted felt stale in her mouth. "Clear," she reported, dropping her helmet.

"Clear," said Jamaal.

"Clear," said Monique.

"All clear," echoed Derek, cracking his neck and stretching his arms above his head.

Jhansi stripped off her dive suit as her companions did the same. Everyone kept their eyes professionally to themselves—at least until they started donning their civilian disguises. Despite technically being clothed, Jhansi felt more naked than she had before she'd pulled on the skin-tight getup. It was a far cry from even the most relaxed renditions of the RSA's modesty standards.

And it wasn't just Jhansi's outfit. All four of them, even the men, now wore disguises that did little to hide their muscular builds. Jhansi found her eyes lingering a bit too long on Derek's muscular back. He must have felt her stare, because, for the briefest instant, he turned and locked eyes with her. Jhansi quickly averted her gaze, heat blossoming in her cheeks. In her peripheral vision, she would have sworn that Derek was a little too slow in shifting his own attention.

Clearing his throat, he spoke to the group. "Ready?"

Jhansi looked at him again to find the same chaste, respectful look he'd given her whenever they worked together. His eyes didn't even seem tempted to wander. Jhansi didn't know whether to feel affirmed or offended.

She shoved that thought aside. Hell, it wasn't anything he hadn't seen before. Modesty had no place in spec ops. Was she really going to start acting like a civvy just because she'd wrapped herself up in something scandalous? She shook away her need for affirmation and stoically replied. "Ready."

Jamaal and Monique reported likewise. Derek nodded. "It's five kilometers to the nearest city. If our implants get us through there, then we're one maglev ride from our destination."

All of this was a repeat of the mission briefing. Everything was going according to plan. Jhansi was glad to hear Derek affirm it regardless.

They buried their dive suits and their packs in a common pit within the hollow of one of the massive tree roots. Though RSA intelligence said the drones did not patrol the forests, the squadron would not be taking any chances.

As they set off toward their destination, Derek wrapped his arms around Jhansi's shoulders. "You ready for this?" he asked. "You seem a bit off."

He wasn't wrong. Jhansi lied all the same. "Just eager to fulfill our mission," she replied, shrugging off the touch that she quietly craved. "Let's get this done."

Part II

The walk through the forest was long and eerie. Jhansi expected some kind of slow transition to the city scarcely two clicks from their landing site. That wasn't the case at all.

The Lansing Gates rose up before them like an impregnable fortress. On the I-96 entrance, there was a massive array of magnecraft lined up seeking entry. The southern entrance on the USC-127 wasn't any better. The M-95 entrance was even worse.

"So," Jamaal began. "Which way? Pick your poison."

Derek scowled as he assessed the options. Jhansi grabbed him by the shoulder. "Look!" She pointed northeast.

There was a concealed access door a short way off the USC-127 gate. It was intentionally dimmed, and the one person Jhansi saw pass through the door swiped an identification card to gain admission.

Monique cut her eyes at Jhansi, shaking her curly hair. "That means we're going to have to strut our stuff."

"You're assuming a certain preference," Jhansi replied. "This isn't the RSA. Those men on guard might be more interested in Derek." God knew she was.

Derek rolled his eyes. "We went over this in the mission briefing. We'll adapt in whatever ways necessary. Barring any other suggestion, I agree with Jhansi's target. Any other opinions?" He paused for a moment, waiting for dissent. There was none. "It's settled then. Let's go."

Despite their ridiculous costumes, the quartet moved silently through the night. The omnipresent drones passing overhead failed to flash a light anywhere near their direction. As they neared the gates, they all assumed a casual walk, marching toward Lansing like any civvy. The lack of foot traffic was the only thing that spoiled this façade.

They approached the black-clad sentry at the checkpoint. Monique took point, tossing her hair flirtatiously. "Hey," she chimed. "We're back from our hike. Are you the same guy I talked to a few hours ago?"

The sentry's expression was implacable under his black mask, "Sorry, miss, this entrance is for city personnel only. I'm going to have to direct you to one of the main ports of entry."

"Ugh." Monique saturated the proclamation with melodrama. "I know. That's why we talked to the other guy on our way out. He promised us we could get back in this way since this is where we came out."

"Shifts changed thirty minutes ago. I'm afraid I wasn't made aware of any changes to protocol."

"Come on." Monique closed the distance between them, drawing close to the sentry. If this had been the RSA, she'd be running the risk of a lewd behavior citation, if not an outright solicitation charge. "It'll just be between us. No one has to know, right?" When the guard didn't shift, she laid a suggestive hand on his black tactical vest. "I can keep a secret if you can."

The guard's momentary hesitation spoke volumes. "I'm going to need your ID," he acquiesced.

"Oh, sure!" Monique produced her fabricated card as she laid her bimbo accent on thick.

Now was the time to test the RSA's intel. The cards they had provided should have given them access to every civilian-level infrastructure in the city.

The guard's device chimed pleasantly in his hand. "Welcome, Ms. Johnson. Please enjoy your stay on the Wolverine Isles."

Hot damn, it worked.

The guard turned to the rest of the party. "I'll need to scan the rest of your IDs, if you'd please."

Despite the guard's politeness, his posture made it clear that he was going to scan their ID cards whether they minded or not. Jamaal went next and the scanner repeated its pleasant chime. Derek followed. Jhansi was last.

Though the device beeped approvingly, the guard eyed Jhansi with unique apprehension. "New to the area, are you?"

Fuck. Jhansi didn't know what kind of backstory had been programmed on her credentials. Why had this bastard singled her out?

She flashed her winningest smile. "Not new. I tend to get around." She gave the guard a playful wink. "You've got my creds right there. Why don't you hit me up after your shift?"

The sentry paused. After a moment he handed her ID back to her. "Just doing my job, miss."

Jhansi had never been so relieved to be turned down. "My loss, I guess." She flipped her hair as she walked past the sentry.

Derek whispered in her ear as the quartet passed through the Lansing Gates. "Any problems?"

Shooting Derek the same smile she'd shone the guard, Jhansi said, "Nothing I couldn't handle." Her eyes went to the surrounding environment. "Holy…"

"…shit." Monique finished. "I'd heard the stories, but I never… I mean... y'all are seeing this too, right?"

They were, and the truth was stranger than fiction.

The forest didn't exactly end at the Lansing Gate. Rather, it took on a new form. Vegetation merged with technology to create something that was simultaneously more glorious and more haunting than anything Jhansi had ever seen. Woody plants slithered across every metallic surface. In some places, it seemed like the walls had been entirely replaced by vegetation.

The surrounding forest could be explained away by nuclear fallout, but this? This was impossible.

Monique put their collective thoughts into words. "This is unbelievable."

Derek set his jaw. "We knew what we were getting into. Come on. We need to make it to the safehouse." He pulled up his phone. "A click and a half away to the east. Let's move. Us gawking like this is going to flag us as tourists."

Tourists? Terrorists, more like it. Let's all be honest with ourselves.

They fell in step behind Derek, moving quietly through the milling throng. Innumerable miracles of civilization unfolded around them. She couldn't help reflecting on how different this was from life in the RSA. That the Witch Queen was evil was obvious, and that the Wolverine Isles was an existential threat to the Great Republic was undoubtable.

But this…? This was something incredible. When the Witch Queen was dead, would the RSA endeavor to recreate such beauty? Was such a recreation even possible?

Stop. This was beyond Jhansi's purview. She had a mission to fulfill. That was where her thoughts needed to be focused now.

Derek guided them through the unsuspecting masses. Their party formed a quiet line along the periphery of the urban expanse. Jhansi couldn't be certain of how long they walked, but it felt like hours. It felt like minutes. It felt like…

God above… what is happening to me?

Jamaal took her by the shoulder. "We're here," he announced in his deep baritone voice.

Jhansi should have known that. She was up in her head, and her colleague had noticed it. "Thank you," she replied simply.

Jamaal nodded. "Bit of friendly advice?"

Damn it, here we go. "Sure," she sighed.

"Put it in the right box," he replied. "Anarchy has done things with civilization that spit in the eyes of God and nature. Remember your training. That's what we're here to fix."

Here to fix, right. She'd heard tales of the moral depravity of the Anarchist states. They lacked the light provided by the RSA's guiding hand. They couldn't help but be what they were. At the same time, Jhansi wasn't expecting anarchy to look so...

Stop it!

Derek provided an irregular knock at the door. After exactly three seconds, he provided another series of irregular knocks. A metallic slit in the door slid open with a sound like a blade being drawn from its sheath.

"Your business?" came a hoarse voice.

Derek didn't hesitate. "Just seeing the sights. Don't see anything like this out east. Heard you can tell us where we can find the good shit."

The slot on the door slammed shut. A half-a-breath later, the lock issued a satisfying click and the door swung open. At the urgings of the dark figure standing in the doorway, Derek and the rest of the party marched inside.

Jhansi had to tighten her jaw to keep it from dropping. She was no stranger to dark ops in foreign territory. She'd been to countless safe houses. This one, however, was as unique as the street outside. The same plant-like constructs that had formed the surreal outlines of the buildings she'd seen upon entering the capital were present in this very room. They formed the rooms, the walls, even the very desk at which a technician worked on a distinctively RSA terminal.

The dark figure removed his hood. The massive guardian had a complexion that seemed forsaken by the sun. "Glad you've arrived," he said with a placid smile. "We've been waiting for the RSA to send reinforcements. What is the order?"

"Termination," Derek replied. "Your intel has provided us with no other option."

The figure's smile dissolved into a look of determination. "Understood," he said. "I'm John. The guy at the terminal is Paul. As far as we know, we're the only active RSA assets in the Wolverine Isles. We are at your service."

Jhansi turned her attention to the computer operator. Paul had skin as dark as onyx and a frame that was emaciated to the point of suggesting chronic disease. "I'm glad you made it," he said with a soft tone that betrayed his young age. "I couldn't help but overhear; are we really under a Termination order?"

"That is correct," Derek said. "And we were told that you have planned for this contingency. Is that true?"

"Yeah, sure. I… I'll just pull it up. Give me a sec."

Though Paul entered his command on a retro laptop, the diagram he accessed triggered the modern technology in the room. Projectors in the four corners of the chamber projected lasers to produce hard-light construct in the center of the room.

"This is the Central Tower," he said. "Right in the heart of the Capitol District. It's accessible only by maglev, and all occupants on the rail are scanned at regular five-minute intervals."

"Do we need to be concerned about those scans?" Jamaal asked.

"No," Paul replied, perhaps a bit too quickly. "Since your credentials got you through the gates, they'll get you into the Tower. Lower levels are for public commerce. Anyone in the city is allowed to be in there."

"Then what's with the scans?" Monique asked.

"Capitol Security keeps active tags on everyone's movements throughout the district. You'll be scanned every time you enter or leave a given area within the tower. They feed all that data back into their security AI for cataloguing. It expedites investigations for suspicious and illegal activity."

"Perfect," Jhansi quipped. "Good thing we're not here to do anything suspicious or illegal."

Paul stammered, flustered by Jhansi's outburst and seemingly uncertain as to whether he should respond.

"Focus, people," Derek barked. "Paul, I take it there's a route to the top of the tower that doesn't scan us on our way to the target."

"Yes." Paul highlighted a service elevator on the Tower's northern edge. "This will get you up to the eighty-sixth floor. That's as close as I can get you."

"Then it's run-and-gun the rest of the way to the Witch Queen's lair," Jamaal noted. He planted his hands and leaned over the table, giving the impression that he might actually be looking forward to that part.

"We can sneak supplies for that phase of the mission into the service platform at the base of the elevator," said John. "Military grade gear goes through there all the time. There's a staging area for Capitol Security below the Tower, so it won't get flagged. Means you're going to have to use W.I. kits though. Anything from the RSA would immediately trigger a lockdown."

"We've trained with their gear," said Derek. "Alright then. Let's go over the known defenses at the top of the tower. If we're going in guns-blazing, I'd like to know what we're shooting at."

Part III

They worked on planning the operation throughout the remainder of the night and well into the next day. When Derek was satisfied they had something workable, they broke for food and rest. At 16:00 local time the following day, they booked their tickets on the maglev and boarded the train.

Though the station had been built with the same fairy-tale mix of nature and technology that composed the rest of the city, the maglev was just a maglev: all smooth technological efficiency. It was comfortable, but crowded, necessitating that the team press in close to each other.

Normally Jhansi wouldn't have minded, but they were back in their scandalous civvy gear. She blamed this for the way that she noticed the firm swells of Derek's muscular torso when she was forced to invade his personal space.

When they hadn't been working out the details of the operation, Jhansi had taken the time to think over this strange and sudden attraction she experienced toward her team lead. This unexpected development was not only a professional taboo, it was dangerous. Operators were encouraged to bond with their teams, but romantic entanglements were strictly prohibited. Romantic entanglements among spec ops teams led to errors in judgment in the field—errors that might cost lives. Professional conduct was non-negotiable.

If Jhansi had become aware of her feelings before the operation, she could have requested a transfer. Since they were in the field, however, that option was off the table. Instead, she just had to muster whatever semblance of professionalism she still had and do her damn job.

It's just the clothes. Stop overthinking it.

Derek's hand went to her shoulder, and she nearly jumped out of her skin. "You're wound tight," he noted. "You all good?"

At that point she did what any self-respecting operator would do: she deflected her awkwardness with banter. She leaned into him, her lips grazing his jawline as she tilted her face toward his. "I'm good if you are, cowboy."

She felt him tense, and she wondered for a moment if she wasn't the only one suffering from this strange, inappropriate attraction. He worked his lips. He swallowed hard. "Good. Just checking on you."

The lights on the upward section of the train car cascaded back toward them. As that stream of lights flashed overhead, Jhansi felt a tingle under her skin.

They must have just scanned us.

She held her breath for a hard second. Nothing happened. No evidence that the scan had gone awry. She exhaled sharply. "Looks like we're good," she whispered.

Derek cleared his throat. "Yeah. Looks like it."

They suffered through two subsequent scans. Each time Jhansi felt the same subcutaneous tingle.

How do people get used to shit like this? Before she had the answer to her question, they'd arrived at the Tower.

The station on level two of the Tower was any capitalist's fantasy. Holographic billboards assaulted everyone who stepped off the maglev, pleading for their attention. Scantily clad men and women writhed against each other in virtual promises that this procedure or that gadget would dramatically increase sex appeal. Panoramas of landscapes completely alien to the local area promised an escape, a simple break from the horrors of the anarcho-capitalist movement.

They all assaulted Jhansi like dust in a windstorm. She turned to her three companions. "Ready?" Each one nodded in turn; even Derek, from whom she'd stolen the privilege of asserting command. Truthfully, Derek seemed just as enraptured by the holographic seduction of the Wolverine Isles as any tourist. On Jhansi's prompting, however, he was quick to remedy his condition.

"Okay," he agreed. "Let's go."

From here, they had agreed to split up, venturing to the far corners of the civilian market before meeting up on the sublevel below. That wouldn't be for another two hours, however; enough time to allow for their shipment of gear to arrive and be checked through security. That meant Jhansi was left exploring the southeastern quadrant of the building for an uncomfortably long time.

She tried to make the most of it, however. She visited a pharmacy, making casual note of the medications on the shelves and marveling at how many controlled substances were available for purchase without a prescription. She visited a digital assets retailer, browsing their catalogue of images, books, music, and videos. This storefront felt largely similar to anything she could have found in the RSA; her native crypto wallets were even compatible, though she didn't dare connect them.

Eventually, she found herself in a café. She sampled the local fare and found it bland. That made sense, of course; the Wolverine Isles were famous for their wild game—genuine, self-replicating, natural animal protein—not their baked goods. Though she had to admit the fudge was rather tasty.

To kill the rest of the time, she browsed through the newsfeeds and found herself overwhelmed. Without her connecting her digital ID to the feeds, curation was nonexistent. Censorship appeared to be a distant memory. Whatever AI they used to filter and cater content to customers seemed highly dependent on consumer information to achieve relevancy.

Still… that she was able to browse the feeds without a formal check-in was a nuance unto itself. No way in hell that the RSA would allow such access to anyone who would not identify themselves and give full consent for security tracking of their activity.

Seconds ticked by. Minutes. Eventually, long hours. Jhansi was fatigued by the time her watch indicated it was time to rendezvous with her companions.

She made one last stop on the floor just above where she would sneak into the shipping docks. It was a menagerie of sorts, hosting woodcraft that was enviable even in this land of plant-laced technology. She pretended to peruse an assortment of wines and beers completely foreign to the government-sanctioned concoctions she'd enjoyed. There were animals, too—some kept in cages, others left to roam about the establishment.

What a strange and alien place this is.

Jhansi lingered only long enough to make sure she was clear to slip through the door marked, 'Authorized Personnel Only.' Once inside, she found the access hatch she was looking for and used the authorization code supplied to her by Paul back at the safehouse. The hatch popped open with a cheerful beep, and Jhansi slipped inside, closing the portal behind her.

She descended the ladder two levels and opened the door she found there. On exiting, she found that she was the last to arrive.

Monique and Derek stood over a trio of security personnel. Jamaal was already cracking into a black shipment crate a few meters away. "Damn," said Jhansi. "Seems like I missed the party."

"We got bored," Jamaal said, not turning his attention from the crate.

Jhansice glanced at her watch. She was only a minute overdue. Maybe less. "I take it the security measures have been taken care of."

"Of course," Derek replied, removing his shirt. Though Jhansi knew better, the move seemed strangely provocative. He wasn't coming onto her, was he?

Get a hold of yourself.

"Sounds good," she said, stepping over toward Jamaal and pointedly keeping her eyes off Derek. "Got something for me?"

Jamaal tossed her an assault rifle. Jhansi caught it expertly and examined the readout. *Damn, Spartan BR-47. That's the good shit.* "Armor?" she asked, suppressing the smile on her lips.

"Already laid out," Jamaal replied, nodding over his shoulder. "Get suited up. It's go time."

Part IV

They called the elevator to the bottom floor and locked it into place. The lift was surely monitored, and the lock wouldn't last forever, but it would hopefully last long enough with Paul running interference back at the safehouse. It was a simple matter to cut open the emergency access panel at the top of the elevator car and enter the shaft above.

The shaft was utterly dark save for blue safety lights that ran up each corner of the passage. These were expected. The roots that threaded through the walls of the darkened chamber were not. "Those damned plants penetrate even in here?" asked Monique. "How does that not screw with the elevator?"

"Not our problem," Derek spat as he strapped himself to one of the safety cables extending from the elevator car. "Strap in. It's a long way to the top, and we're short on time."

Jhansi approached the cable at the corner opposite Derek, clipping onto the cord and affixing the motor at her belt. When everything was secure, she gave the all-clear sign. Derek waited for Jamaal and Monique to do the same. When they had, he gave the order. "Engage."

The ascension motor jerked Jhansi violently upward. She engaged her core to stabilize herself but kept only the most tenuous touch on the cable that carried her upward. Floor after floor rushed by at alarming speed. She kept her eyes at the top, attempting to sight the point where she would need to engage the brake.

"Shit!" Monique shouted.

Jhansi slammed on the brake upon hearing the curse. Her body jerked painfully to a halt. She turned to see what had happened.

Monique was two floors below, clinging by one hand to a vine-shrouded ledge. The cable she'd been attached to swung listlessly above her, severed and dangling.

"Status," called Derek from her left.

"It just snapped!" Monique protested. "Everything was fine and then…" she trailed off for a span of heartbeats. "Team? Are you seeing this?"

Jhansi and the others followed her gaze. At the edge where Monique's cable had been severed, something crawled in the darkness. A thick woody tendril slithered down from the severed line, reaching toward where Monique clung to the wall. Something had damaged it—perhaps the cable itself when the tension suddenly snapped. A wide gash split the end of the tendril in two.

From that tear in the object, sparks of light glistened. Not a plant at all. A machine.

And it wasn't the only one. The shaft was suddenly alive as the pseudo-plants wriggled anxiously.

"Jamaal, Jhansi," Derek barked. "We're made. Exit the shaft on this floor. A quick surge should override the locks and get the door open. Monique, I'm coming for you. Hold tight."

No one questioned. No one acknowledged. Everyone did exactly as their leader ordered. Jhansi shot a grappling cable from her wrist, aiming at the door between her and Jamaal. She released her clip on the elevator's safety cable and dove toward the exit. Her cable pulled her forward, reducing its pull at the last instant to keep her from colliding with the still-sealed door.

Jamaal was right behind her, already with a charge in his hand. He placed the silver disk against the metal door. The object flared briefly with blue light, and the door slid open. Both agents slipped inside.

Neither looked back to see how Derek and Monique fared. They trusted their teammates to take care of themselves. They also had plenty to worry about on their own.

Though Jhansi hadn't had a chance to check her map to figure out where they'd ended up, this floor definitely wasn't a public access level. Every figure in the long hall wore the same black tactical gear she and Jamaal were wearing. Every one of them bore a rifle.

The surprise of their sudden emergence was all that kept Jhansi and Jamaal from being shot immediately. Their training kicked in, and Jamaal had his weapon in hand in an instant, quickly downing two security personnel. Jhansi's hands went to her belt. She seized a grenade with each hand and tossed them in either direction.

A blinding flash. Torrents of smoke. Jhansi triggered her visor before reaching for the automatic pistols at her waist. Normal vision was compromised, but red outlines appeared around each hostile still standing. The wire-frame ghosts were all scrambling to react.

They were too slow. Jhansi and Jamaal tore into them, eliminating each with extreme prejudice.

"Best way up?" Jamaal asked.

Jhansi pulled up the holographic display on her wrist terminal. "Twenty floors. Damn, that's quite the trip. There's an elevator bank on the western face and an emergency stairwell in the central pillar."

"Recommendation?"

"After this display, it's safe to say they know we're here. They can kill power to an elevator. Worst they can do is flood a stairwell with security. The stairs have my vote."

Jamaal nodded. "Left or right from here?"

"Right, then right again at the third hallway. From there, it's a straight shot."

They pressed forward. Even after the smoke dissipated, no security personnel crossed their path. They encountered no one. No alarms, no shouts, no sign that anyone had been on the entire floor aside from the score of guards they'd slaughtered outside the elevator.

"Assessment?" Jamaal asked.

Read: You see something wrong too, right? "I don't know what they're planning," Jhansi replied. "But yeah, this op has gone to hell. We haven't heard from Derek or Monique, so they must be jamming our comms. Any other op, I'd immediately abort. Your thoughts?"

The big man hesitated, continuing to stare down the sights of his rifle as if they might reveal the answer he longed for. "There's no turning back," he said. "So, where do you think they'll ambush us?"

"Stairwell is still my best bet."

"Going in hot then?"

"Affirmative." Jhansi couldn't help but ask. "Do you think they're alright?"

She didn't have to clarify who she was referring to. Jamaal chose not to provide a straight answer. "We stick to the mission. That's all that matters."

Part V

It was like the ambush in the stairwell never happened. Jhansi and Jamaal marched up twenty flights of stairs to the highest public access level. On exiting the stairwell, they found the floor completely empty—no people, no windows. There wasn't even the omnipresent plant growth that enshrouded the rest of the city. Just a pure white expanse of floor, ceiling and wall around them.

"What the hell is this?" Jamaal asked, lowering his weapon.

"I... I don't know," Jhansi admitted, pulling up her holographic map once more. "It... It's not supposed to look like this."

"Intel is flawed then?"

"Got to be."

"Perfect," Jamaal heaved a sigh. "Mission still stands, though. We need to find a way up."

As if that isn't obvious.

"Scan the walls. There's got to be some kind of control mechanism somewhere." Unless this was all one big trap. But to what end?

The thought didn't even begin to make sense. So what if the Witch Queen managed to ensnare a cohort of RSA agents? It wasn't like the International Confederation was unaware of the RSA's attempts to expand their territory and influence. Why go through all the effort to plant faulty intelligence? If the Wolverine Isles knew of the RSA's intentions, it would have been more efficient to stop the plan in its tracks by eliminating the team quickly and quietly.

Jhansi scanned the blank floors, walls, and ceiling in the northeastern quadrant. Wasn't the elevator supposed to stop here? That meant there had to be an access point. She pulled up the map and moved to roughly where the elevator should have been.

There was no shaft, but a scan of the floor revealed an invisible seam in the sea of white. A similar seam appeared directly above it in the ceiling. There must be some code to make the elevator bypass this level, Jhansi realized.

This floor is just a catch-all, an extra layer of security before reaching the top two floors. But why is it empty? Shouldn't there be a squadron of soldiers waiting here?

It didn't matter. They'd already established they were in a trap. Now it was do-or-die; or do-and-die, as the case might be. "Jamaal," she said. "I found a way up."

Jamaal approached looking at the upward expanse skeptically. "You're sure?"

"Positive. I need a boost. Help me out?"

He knelt and cupped his hands. She stepped into his grip, and he hefted her toward the ceiling. She felt along the seam.

There was nothing to distinguish the target area from the rest of the featureless ceiling. "Pass me a charge. I want to see if I can force it open."

Jamaal grunted, shifting his grip to hold her with one hand while he reached for his belt. "You're expecting a lot of my strength right now."

"Asking too much of you, big guy?"

"I didn't say that." He passed her the charge. "Just make this work, okay?"

Jhansi placed the charge against the surface of the ceiling, pressing down on the button at its center. The device flared to life, sending a blue pulse radiating out from where it rested. That pulse illuminated the hidden door perfectly. With an affirming beep, the device fell from the door as false ceiling slid open to reveal a darkened opening.

Wasting no time, Jhansi reached up and pulled herself over the metal lip before reaching back down to offer Jamaal a hand. The big man jumped, using Jhansi's arm as the last bit of leverage he needed to secure his grip on the edge. He pulled his body upward. Jhansi leaned back to help pull him over the ledge.

The door snapped shut. Jhansi fell backward. There was the spray of something warm and wet. Someone wailed in the distance.

"Jamaal?" Jhansi asked. Then, realizing she still grasped the big man's hand—now suddenly absent the rest of his weight—she shrieked. "Jamaal!"

She thought she could hear him, but his cries were distant. The only proof that Jamaal had ever been with her was the rictus grip by which his severed forearm still grasped hers. Jhansi tore free of the limb and cast it aside.

Everything around her was dark. All she could make out in any direction was pure and utter blackness as blinding as the whiteness of the floor below them. Jhansi stumbled, noting another significant difference from the lower level. Thick, sinuous threads coated every inch of the floor, rendering it as uneven and treacherous as a roiling sea. She tried to recover her balance. Tripped again. Fell to the floor.

The pseudo-vegetation, that monstrous facsimile of life, slithered beneath her. She jerked and attempted to push herself up, afraid that these cybernetic abominations would seize hold of her.

They did not. Instead, they flattened, creating a space where she could regain her footing. Still not trusting the autonomous landscape, Jhansi regained her stance and drew her pistols.

Light appeared, running along the million vines and wooden tendrils that shrouded every surface of the chamber. Unlike the wide open expanse of the level below, Jhansi found herself in a narrow corridor, illuminated only by the strange mechanical false-life that strangled it.

The hallway stretched on into infinity, fading to darkness at the edge of Jhansi's sight. She tried to scan it but found her equipment nonresponsive. She had only her senses to take in the nightmare chamber. She removed her helmet and tossed it aside.

Though her eyes served her only as far as the lights of the robotic vines, her ears detected something else. The voice was as dark as the chamber, as beautiful as the serene violet glow of the surrounding vegetation. It spoke a single word—not a request, but a command:

"Come."

Part VI

The light moved with Jhansi as she marched into the labyrinth. The vines before her parted, revealing a path ever onward into the dark. The vegetation closed ranks behind her, ensuring that she could not venture back. Around progressive twists and turns, ramps and stairways, ups and downs, Jhansi continued. Paths branched off at several points, but the light always indicated which direction she should progress. Several times she got the impression that she had backtracked, circled around, or returned to the same intersection.

Not that it mattered. She was trapped in this maze, a victim without agency. Had the powers behind these strange machines wished it, the vines could have reached up and snuffed her out—just as they had with the rest of her team. Survival was now a distant fantasy that Jhansi refused to entertain. What minor spark of hope she still harbored burned so that, despite all odds, she might somehow still complete her mission.

Maybe then—just maybe—she could meet her God with the knowledge that the deaths of her squad mates had not been in vain.

At long last, the series of passageways terminated in a dark, open area. The vines and roots curled away around an open portal to reveal a stretch of glistening black tile extending into the darkness. Jhansi stepped out onto the hard flooring; pistols raised in front of her. When she was free from the vine-laden hallway, the cybernetic vegetation knitted together, blocking her way back.

With the exit closed, distant lights began to burn away the darkness. They appeared at the far end of the room, revealing a chamber more massive than any arena or stadium Jhansi had ever seen. Those shining beacons seemed to replicate, cascading toward her like a rising tide.

The illumination soon revealed a gargantuan machine in the center of the chamber. Nothing but a silhouette at first, the shadow took on dimension and shape as more lights glistened in the surrounding expanse. Its core was a massive cylinder, partially translucent and reinforced by a steel exoskeleton. Wires thicker than Jhansi's waist wrapped around this central structure like some infernal nest. Metallic protrusions with functions unknown thrust out at irregular intervals all around the twisted contraption.

Directly in front of her, half-submerged in a network of supports and wiring, rested a human form. Even before the light revealed the full extent of the being's features, Jhansi knew the truth.

This was the Immortal Witch Queen of the Wolverine Isles.

"Hello, Jhansi." Though the Witch Queen's lips moved as she spoke, the voice came from the entire room. "I hear you have been looking for me. Welcome to Spartan Aquatics, the beating heart of the Wolverine Isles. Is it everything that you hoped it would be?"

Jhansi realized that she had both pistols trained on the Witch Queen's center mass, but lacked the will to pull the triggers. All she could do was stand there, rigid and enraptured by the woman's presence.

She was beautiful but alien. Her flesh glistened silver but without the metallic firmness of her mechanical trappings. Machinery and wiring was all that she wore, the mechanism which served as her throne and holding chamber completely enveloping her at her hip bones. Luscious dark hair cascaded onto the toned flesh of her shoulders. Her arms were slightly elevated from her sides, thick cables holding them aloft in a gesture somewhere between a welcome embrace and crucifixion. Her eyes were pure silver orbs that looked everywhere and nowhere at all.

Jhansi was enthralled and terrified, enraptured and despaired. While she was certain magic did not exist, she knew unearthly power when she saw it. This creature was anything but human.

"What are you?" Jhansi asked, voice trembling.

The Queen smiled. "Only what this world made me. Your RSA had a heavy hand in my creation. Resorting to tactics frowned upon by everyone on the world stage—and on their own people, no less. It was disgusting really, but they have my thanks. If not for the desperation they fostered, I may never have come to be."

"You didn't answer my question."

"No, I did not. Perhaps that is due to the spirit in which it was asked." The Witch Queen's smile never faltered, though she did shake her head. "I am the ruler of this sovereign nation, a ruler that you and your companions were sent here to assassinate. Under the laws of the International Confederation of Nations, I am authorized to not only execute you, but to sue for the removal of the RSA from the security council. Still, I don't think that answers your real question."

Hydraulics hissed and the Witch Queen was propelled closer to Jhansi. Her trappings of metal and wire moved with her like some perverse train on a technological gown. She stopped less than three meters from Jhansi, her chest placed directly before the barrels of the RSA agent's automatic weapons. Still, Jhansi did not fire.

"I am change, Jhansi Ramgarhia. I am the fusion of mankind and its creations. I am the incarnation of humanity and technology that fools like Longmunsk can only pretend at being. I am the future, Jhansi—and I do believe that you were sent here to find me."

"I was sent here to kill you."

"So you believe. If you were one of the others, you might have tried to do so already. But you aren't them, Jhansi. I've been watching you. There is a reason you are here and they are not. You have potential. I thought, perhaps, that we might talk."

Objections welled up in Jhansi's heart but did not reach her throat. Her hands and arms seemed frozen, unable to retract, unable to execute their purpose. She willed her fingers to tighten about the triggers. Instead, she only trembled.

"Go on, then," she whispered. "You wanted to talk? Let's talk."

The Witch Queen's smile broadened. "Good girl. Tell me, why is it that you were sent to assassinate me?"

A voice in the back of her mind screamed at Jhansi not to answer. At worst, it begged that she lie. Instead, she spoke the truth. "You will not share your life-saving technologies with the RSA. You leave us as victims to sins committed a hundred years ago, and you profit off our suffering."

"Is that what they told you?"

"Is it false?"

"Categorically. I did not refuse to trade with the RSA or any other nation-state. Did they tell you what I asked for in return?" the Queen paused for a long moment. "Silly question, of course they didn't. Refusal to meet demands is not a refusal to partake in an exchange. Your country is the same as it was a century ago. Do not doubt it."

Jhansi frowned. "You lie."

"Do I? Why would I bother? If I was as closed off as your superiors say, why bother to speak with you at all?"

The Queen had a point, but Jhansi willed herself not to see it.

This is all just some sick game. I don't know why she's playing me, but she is. God damn it, why can't I pull the trigger?

The Witch Queen let out a soft chuckle. "I think the time has come for a gesture of goodwill. I do apologize for what became of your companions. Automated security protocols are vicious. Jamaal is in my care, and he will pull through. Monique, I'm afraid, will not be so lucky.

She threw herself from the ledge rather than let herself be captured. There was not much for me to save when she hit the bottom."

Jamaal? Monique? She'd tried to save them? But what of...?

The Queen drew back with another mechanical hiss. A hole opened in the floor beneath where she'd been resting, and a figure bound to an obsidian post rose from its depths. Derek's head lolled to the side, his body held vertical only by the black cords that bound him to the post.

Derek had been stripped to the waist, and his torso showed several deep bruises and bloodied gashes. Still, his muscular chest heaved with the intake of breath. He was alive.

"You are pleased?" the Queen asked.

Jhansi holstered her pistols and rushed to him. "Derek? Derek, speak to me. Are you alright?"

Derek groaned. The Witch Queen chuckled. "I thought you would be. I saw the way you looked at him on the beach. I saw the way he looked at you. I observed you both on the maglev on your way to my tower. You care for him. You desire him."

Derek opened bleary eyes. "Jhansi?"

Jhansi looked to the Witch Queen. "Release him. If you mean what you say, release him. Give him back to me."

"As you desire."

The cords that bound Derek to the post retracted, and he fell into Jhansi's arms. He was heavy, but adrenaline and forbidden affection gave her the strength to steady him.

"Jhansi," he repeated. "The Witch, she..."

"I know," she replied. "Don't, Derek. The mission is over."

Her team lead stiffened at the pronouncement. "What?"

"We can't do what we came here to do, but maybe we can still do some good." She raised a hand to brush back a lock of hair from his forehead. "She wants to talk, Derek. I think... I think we may have been lied to."

Derek fell silent for a long moment. A hint of strength began to return to his limbs. He pulled back, looking Jhansi in the eyes. "Perhaps," he agreed. "But ours is not to ask why."

With a sudden burst of speed, he drew Jhansi's pistol from its holster. He pushed her back, turned to face the Witch Queen, and fired.

The muzzle flashed. The roar of gunfire echoed across the chamber. Light flared in front of the Witch Queen.

Despite the proximity, not a single bullet hit its mark. Lightning arced from the forcefield, flashing back from the point of impact and lancing straight into Derek. With a thunderous boom, his body was thrown across the chamber.

Jhansi screamed. "Derek!" She rushed to his side, hefting him in her arms. His eyes stared sightlessly into the darkness above them. Jhansi could not find a pulse.

"I am sorry," said the Witch Queen. "Automated defenses. I had no control over this. He sealed his own fate."

No, no, no, no, no...

This couldn't be happening. Not him. Not Derek. Not when they were so close to reaching an accord. "Save him," Jhansi cried.

"He is dead, child. What is it that you are asking me to do?"

Jhansi jerked her head back around to stare the Witch in the eye. "Aren't you as powerful as they say? Do something! You can fix this. I know it."

The Witch Queen took on a contemplative look. The corner of her mouth curled up in the hint of that same mysterious smile. "I can do as you ask. He will not be the same, though. There will be... consequences."

"I... I don't care." Tears flowed freely down Jhansi's cheeks. "I can't... I can't lose him. Not now." Not after she'd crossed that forbidden line. Not after she'd let her feelings interfere with their relationship.

"As you wish."

The plants—those wicked cybernetic imitations of an entire kingdom of wildlife—began to stir. They snaked out from the wall, encircling Jhansi as she held Derek's body. Barbed edges emerged from the tips of the woody tendrils. Like biting vipers, they plunged into his skin.

The vines glowed, and Derek's eyes resonated with the same violet light. He drew in a sharp breath. His heart started beating anew.

"Derek?" Jhansi pulled him close to her, the vines stretching with the motion and remaining firmly implanted in his flesh. "Derek, are you okay?"

"J... Jhansi. I... I feel... strange." He looked confused but relaxed. His eyes searched blankly before settling on her face. Fear flashed in his expression before giving way to something new: relief.

"It will not be a seamless transition," the Queen cautioned. "It will take time, but he will live—much as I live now. Perhaps both of you, in time, will come to know this new life. That, however, is a conversation for another evening." She drew back. The lights began to dim, and her machine-clad figure disappeared into the darkness. "Soon, though, we will talk. For now, I leave you unto yourselves."

When it was all finished, the light of the encircling vines was all that illuminated them. "Jhansi," Derek whispered, reaching up to touch her face. "What just happened?"

"I don't know," she sobbed. "But we live to fight another day. Maybe tomorrow, we'll find out the truth."

"The truth." His brow furrowed. "How will we know the truth? What if it's just more lies?"

More lies. Derek hadn't conceded that the RSA had lied to them in the first place. Was this him? It sounded like him, yet he sounded different. Was this a byproduct of what the Witch Queen had done to him?

Did it matter?

"I don't know," Jhansi conceded. "But we will find out together."

Derek's gaze locked with hers. His eyes were not the same as they were before, but there was enough of him in there to light Jhansi's heart aflame. Like the fruit of the fabled garden, his lips promised fateful knowledge—both good and evil. Jhansi leaned forward and pulled him close. Together, they took a taste.

The Midnight Warrior of Ishavkara
Aparna Merchant (Quanta)

To you who shrink in pain yet shatter not.
To you who've lost your world and are hopeless not.
To you who feel like wasted rot.
The thought that you have nothing more to lose than yourself.
And yet yourself, you auction not.
Never.
To you I dedicate this work in all humility and reverence.
This work also honors those who have succumbed.

Dear Reader,

You are about to connect with the Ikshavakra tribe in the pages that follow. Here are some mentions that could enhance your experience. As you interact with the narrative, some words may slow you down. While you do get a semblance of what they are when you're in the flow, a glossary at the tail end of this book will explain all to you.

You might also like to peruse a quick recount of the lands and its people, and a chronology of the events in the concluding pages. This story is a dialogue by its various actors—the narrator is credited at the beginning of every chapter.

This is where I leave you. The Ikshavakrus welcome you into their world.

- Aparna Merchant (Quanta)

Prologue

What is given is replenished. What is taken is returned. The void will seek compensation. This is Dharoma'kshama, the law of balance.

Dharoma'kshama is the principle of all creation. It is the way of the Ikshavakrus.

Aummm.

I thank thee, o' resplendent Rahoul, for your blazing light that nourishes. I thank thee, o' luminous Karpura, creator of my life's mooncycles.

I thank thee, o' mighty Vayuka, carrier of my messages. I thank thee, o' stunning Kaali, keeper of my time.

I thank thee, o' merciful Abja, for your waters that quench. I thank thee, o' nurturing Maati, for your soil that holds my tread.

And I thank thee, o' supreme Suvaasi, my life force, for inhabiting my flesh. In humble prostration, I offer thou my existence in servitude.

Aummm.

- Khenpo

The Midnight Warrior

Aucthumbar (October) 16, 2335
Khenpo Rudham

The giant Kelushi range of icy peaks and silver-gray slopes has always fostered us as her own, sheltering us in the folds of her bosom, offering her waters and native life-forms for our nourishment. We had metaported here from Saiyon, ancient Ceylon, over fifty nights ago.

The mountains of the north always feel like home to me. They stand imposing, stark naked in their greys. If they love you, they are unabashed about it. If they don't, then too.

I am at her water stream, my spearhead stuck into a large genuja fish. I had just offered grace to the genuja, running my fingers gently over its motionless body when I caught a shadow from the corner of my eye

"Khenpo. Siama is compromised." Ishka's speech is rapid and excited. She is also panting from running the uphill distance. "King Vibhasta is martyred, and the new Ruskian regime has exhumed the particle project. If this residue is exposed, th—"

"I know," I interrupted her. "Take this genuja to Palina. She cooks it well. I will be there soon."

Ishka stares, hesitates, and leaves reluctantly. I sit motionless on the sopping rocks.

Ishka is our commanding general. Things rarely rile her. That is how she leads us into battle: emotionless, focused, and determinedly clear. Her excitement today, therefore, agitates me. Yet, it is not unwarranted.

We had visited Siama on several occasions, at times as a quick stop-over. It is a forward-thinking nation with a friendly disposition, content and flourishing within its borders. I have admired its leader King Vibhasta for his ethics of governance. Compared to the other members of the Indian Ocean Mutual Nations, Siama is a tiny landmass, but Vibhasta built its repute as a power to reckon with. Still, the man did have his eccentricities; in particular, his obsession with astral sciences.

The Particle Simulator was the king's pet project of eleven years. It was most audacious, yet I acknowledge his bold intent. The purpose was to restore energy imbalances in nature's ecosystems. King Vibhasta had invested in three research centers enclosed within high security confines, each completely dedicated to this mission. Our visits to Siama had been solely in answer to his requests for guidance.

Three years ago, I was adamant the experiment be put down completely with all its remnants. The project had reached some point of fruition—the beta tests were celebratory. We were at Siama for the final test run, and some of us Ikshavakrus witnessed the particle generator infiltrate the encapsulated air with simulations of energy at the precise preset level. But that level was leaking pressurized residue into the generator's inner chamber. I saw the king stare at the inner capsule aghast—there was disappointment and weakness in his demeanor, his eyes questioned me. I took over.

"This residue holds an energy thrust of incomprehensible volatility," I expounded on the possible disaster. "Do not underestimate its potency and magnitude. You make your land vulnerable. You must abandon this, o' wise King, and work on containing it."

And so, it came to be enclosed within several layers of impenetrable seranium boxes—a material developed in the Siaman labs that could withhold controlled nuclear fission. It was buried deep underground, beneath the foundations of the main research center.

And now Vibhasta was no more.

"We accept failure with dignity when it is to protect what must be protected." His words and the history come forth as I sit acutely silent in the sacred lotus posture, palms upturned on my knees, Kelushi's waters giggle by my side, unconcerned. I consciously draw my breath into my karawe till it starts breathing of its own accord. I surrender to its will and lose semblance of all sensations. An abused and violated Siama materializes into my vision. Its plea for divine help hangs heavy while the Siamans gallantly accede to their fate. Armies from Jakotri, Nepaula, and

Prutharv are in the fray with Siama, storming in hysterical rage, without King Vibhasta. A petite Prutharva is leading the entire alliance against the Ruskians. They are failing…

"We need to leave. Now." I am at our make-shift settlement, commanding urgency. Ishka hadn't awaited my instructions and had already readied the tribe. The genuja lies on the ground with flowers placed around it.

"Dharomi chattari'aym sva karashute," five of us chant, undoing our protective shield. We offer our gratitude and obeisance to Mother Kelushi and port right beside the allied camp. The night sky is approaching this part of the world.

"O' valiant warriors of Ikshavakra, we are of immense gratitude that you should be with us," says the petite Prutharva, commander-in-chief princess Sathr'yi. The allied army bows in response to her salutation to us.

"It is our honor to defend the purpose and join you."

I acknowledge with a low bow. The Ikshavakrus follow my lead. "Is the particle generator safe?" My anxiety betrays me.

Princess Sathr'yi nods to a Siaman warrior. "Ruskian attempts to penetrate the seranium safe boxes have been unsuccessful so far. But a crate arrived this afternoon, tightly guarded," shares the warrior.

This was worrisome. "And your people?" I ask.

"We have lost many. We could extract the wounded and the shaken to the fields beyond here. They are not without hope, great Khenpo Rudham."

I turn my gaze to the fields. There are makeshift pyres exhaling ashen fumes. The one closest to us has disheveled people, some supported by others, laying leaves and withered flowers on it.

"King Vibhasta lays there. It is the best we could do." His head hangs low. He moves his tear- stricken gaze away from me.

"We must go in now," I declare.

"Now? But we cannot attack at this hour," protests princess Sathr'yi. "Dusk hastens. It's a violent dishonor of the warrior code."

"We accept the dishonor, brave Princess. For we shall forever rot in remorse should the particle residue be released," replied Ishka, out of turn. I placed my hand on her shoulder. Her sutras were turning a shade brighter.

"So be it. We offer ourselves to the cause. Guide us, great warrior

Khenpo."

"Ahauma. Ahauma. Ahauma."

Victory. Victory. Victory.

"Bhumartha. Aasakartha. Manusaartha."

For the land. For the skies. For its people.

I feel a faint foreboding in my entire being. Tcha. Probably my nerves.

Ishka has slipped into the enemy base within the kingdom with a portion of the allied troops. Ashafa, the Siaman warrior, is leading them to the research center.

The rest of us confront an astonished army head-on, brazenly, with no stealth. We, Ikshavakrus, are on foot. The princess leads the Jakotrians, Nepaulas and Prutharvas. Most are in pods—some flying, some terrestrial; the rest are on foot with us.

"Ahauma. Ahauma. Ahauma."

"Arraa'eka Ruskia. Hom. Hom. Hom." The Ruskians react immediately.

"Dharomi chattari'aym sva." We, Ikshavakrus, summon an energy shield from the spirit of ether, Vayuka, enclosing the entire allied force in an invisible bubble, and cross enemy lines.

The Ruskians rain fire on our protective cover. These slide off the insulating skin. This works against us too. We cannot retaliate without violating our protection. This was intended, and we're succeeding. Ishka and her unit should have reached the research base now. Where is her signal?

"Princess, when do we hit headquarters?"

"*Now.*"

We disengage our shields.

"Glory be to the Creator. Glory be to the Created. Glory be to King Vibhasta."

"*Raaaaaaghh.*"

I storm into the enemy core with Hukara'an and Dyarah, and Jakotri's Goyyir. Princess Sathr'yi and the others are holding off the Ruskians outside. I hear raucous calls to arms, and aggravated explosions behind me. I entrust their fate to the almighty Ishraha.

Three figures in iridescent boiler suits are crowded around a familiar eight-inch capsule holding the 125 ml of putrid black sebaceous jelly. The figures jerk up. We stare at each other.

I see raw savagery in the pair of eyes on the right. Everything seems to happen at once.

My body reacts to the barbaric stare and somewhere Ishka shrieks for me, "Khenpo." My karawe stings me. I am spreading my arms out forcing my companions behind me. My head hung low, chin touching my chest, I expose the nape of my neck to the perpetrators.

My karawe is sucking in hellfire, lapping it.

Mercy Ishraha. Mercy.

I am writhing within, but I swear I will not move. I feel the contamination grease the hollow of my spine, and now into my sutras. I feel wretched and violated.

O' life-giving Suvaasi, give me courage.

Every pore has an icy needle prick into it. My eyes are pierced with them too, they don't open. My insides feel arid. I can't breathe.

Stay with me, merciful Suvaasi. My chest is wrung out. *Suvaasi, stay with... me... stay... Suvaasi... st...*

Grief

Aucthumbar (October) 17, 2335
Sathr'yi

    Guide my nerves o' Mother.
    I cannot control the tremble in my fingers as I pinch open his jaw as slight as need be to pour the concoction in. It falls in drops from the pital leaf I have crumpled into a spoon. *Thank you, Mother Earth, for your forests that heal. I prostrate before you.* The Sakhi forests bordering the eastern Siaman parameter would've been scorched to cinders—as would have all the land, and all the skies, all of us that stand here—had it not been for this debilitated soul that lays lifeless before us. Raha'rya and I had scoured the forest for the herbs. Mother Sakhi had a tiny shrubbery of medicinal Ayuresha for us. One of her stalwart giant pital trees had fallen on the tiny plants. It was the only bit of shiny green in the dullness that surrounded it.
    "Devo sanjivaniyam cha'haara tvam. Devo amrutayam cha'haara tvam. Devo rakshayam cha'haara tvam. Devo... " I whisper scriptural words of healing in continuous repetition, praying that the aura and wisdom of ancient texts penetrate into his comatose awareness.
    Ishka has smoothed a small rock on a stone and is etching markings and symbols on the ground with it beside the fallen Khenpo.
    For the first time in the last ten hours, I take in the grandeur of this being they call Khenpo. My kingdom had heard of the valiant Khenpo Rudham and his virtuous people, the Ikshavakrus. We know stories of their highly evolved intellect. Their reputation for honor and integrity, and unsurpassed gallantry precedes them. Yesterday, we encountered it all.

Before yesterday, Khenpo Rudham was an overdramatized phenomenon for me, someone worthy of a teenage crush. Now as I sit beside his limp form…

Ishka has placed the rounded piece of stone on Khenpo's forehead, between his brows. She is staring at his face fixedly. Her eyes seem cold, almost frigid. But I sense reverence, fear, and guilt sucked into their dark depths. She is now tracing out ancient Aryan alphabets in the mud with a stick. Her lips, barely parted, are uttering something inaudible.

I put some more drops of muddy green into the benumbed mouth.

His skin is singed, every part of it is charred black, and it still exudes a majestic aura. There is a smear of heavenly gold from the nape of his neck to his crown. *O' Deva. This is thou incarnate. Will not thou save thyself?*

Khenpo's skin was a rich sacred violet when his tribe and he appeared at our campsite. He was attired in humble garbs with clustered ropes of Raudak seeds draped around his neck. Roughly beaten gold rings adorned his ear lobes. His forehead was imprinted with a mark of ash. Every Ikshavakru had a smudge of ash branding them. It was their homage to the spirit of the Creator and the Created, before the start of their day. Khenpo wore a thick strap of animal skin across his body which held a dagger with an outline of a large teecha tooth impressed in its hilt.

When we came to after that savage explosion, we saw Khenpo sprawled unconscious, his body was convulsing violently- the radiation still coursing through him. We saw his magnificent purple tarnish to its deeper shade and then to midnight. It was both horrific and spellbinding at the same time. His clothes were brutally ripped off, scorched in the demonic fire. He was almost naked, save for whatever was stuck to his skin. The dagger lay unharmed a few feet away.

We humans could not touch him as his body still carried ripples of nuclear emissions. Ishka and some of the Ikshavakrus shoved us out of the scene. It was way too crowded. They also foresaw the risk of our contamination at the site. I hung back stubbornly. The Ikshavakrus invoked the Water spirit to quieten the rage within their leader. Each one focused on a specific part of Khenpo's body – every part of the face, feet, legs, hands, chest, abdomen, neck, lungs, spine, and every sutra marking. Ishka connected each one of their conjured forces into a ball and thrust it into his skull between his brows. The seizures stopped immediately. The midnight skin cooled to an ashen charcoal. Only his throat retained its glorious purple. It surprised me. They lifted the impressive body and the dagger, and carried it out to the grounds.

Now we are awaiting his resurrection. We are praying, calling upon every universal force to grant his awakening.

This man funneled the nuclear inferno into his being, swallowing it to fulfill and honor his purpose of protecting All That Is Created.

O' Deva.

It is daybreak, and nothing suggests Khenpo is waking. The gentle rise and descent of his chest is our only beacon of hope.

The Ikshavakrus get up and head towards the Sakhi forests to pay salutations to the rising Sun spirit, Rahoul. The Jakotrians, Nepaulas and my Prutharva people join them, walking to the east of the battleground. A battle-worn tall figure who I later know to be Nayoma, is leading the ritual. I sit alone with Khenpo, for here lies my Sun spirit. He is my Black Sun God. I kneel and touch my forehead to his feet. I feel a faint pulse in his soles.

I open his mouth slightly and squeeze more herbal juice into it. "Devo sanjivaniyam cha'haara tvam. Devo amrutayam cha'haara tvam. Devo rakshayam cha'haara tvam. Devo…"

Ishka's stick lies abandoned as she has joined the others in prayer. Strange. The stone she had placed on Khenpo's forehead seems to be getting smaller.

The troops are exhausted and famished, and save for the Ikshavakrus, they have taken refuge in the Sakhi forests. They will head home once the noon sun starts journeying westwards. The Siamans have joined the retirees before they begin the arduous task of picking up their pieces.

Nayoma has taken over Ishka's rough scratching on the ground, though Ishka still sits beside her chief. She flips the stone on his forehead. It is burnt. She gasps. I see a flicker of triumph in her eyes. She looks away, conscious of the embarrassing display of excitement. She is smoothing another stone, murmuring syllables in sync with Nayoma whose writings seem steadier and more refined than those of the previous etcher.

The shadows on the ground are stretching out; it is getting cooler. The troops have returned and have encircled us at a distance. They do not want to leave. They can't bring themselves to.

I feed more Ayuresha drops to the motionless figure. "Devo sanjivaniyam cha'haara tvam. Devo amrutayam cha'haara tvam. Devo rakshayam cha'haara tvam." The circle of devotees are reciting with me. The air vibrates. Every particle in the air echoes the sounds. My spine prickles.

Nayoma is drawing a different ancient text now and mouthing the chant in chorus. Ishka has placed the newly buffed rock on Khenpo's forehead.

Somebody yells. "The arm twitched! The Protector's arm twitched!"

Huh? My heart whoops a beat. But I see nothing.

"Hush. We need to wait until Rahoul's first rays," reprimands Nayoma.

But the deepest recesses of our hearts tell us the darkest hour has passed.

Reborn

Aucthumbar (October) 17, 2335)
Khenpo Rudham

"Khenpo. Mighty Khenpo. Khenpo Rudham."

The sounds are barely audible, so far away are they, but their desperation echoes loud within me.

"No, no, no. Khenpo."

I can feel a frenzied crowd of footsteps running towards where I lay. Am I laying down? I feel no ground, no sky. My body is ablaze. *What is this fire, o' Rahoul?* It freezes me and numbs me. O' *Ishraha.*

Somebody has pried my mouth open, and drops of liquid wet my tongue and throat. It tastes of rich dirt. A sweet scent mixed with sweat is vaguely familiar. So is this almost inaudible chanting. So close. I feel the words brush my face

"Devo sanjivaniyam cha'haara tvam. Devo amrutayam cha'haara tvam. Devo rakshayam cha'haara tvam. Devo…" There is some scratching on the ground beside my ear. More liquid soil in my mouth, and something smooth and warm is placed between my brows.

More sounds of scraping. They are clearer now. "Devo sanjivaniyam cha'haara tvam. Devo…" The chant is turning into a heightened rhythmic chorus. My body is sweating profusely. I feel the coarse wet hardness that I lie upon.

"The arm twitched. The Protector's arm twitched."

"Hush. He is not out of it yet. We need to wait until Rahoul's first rays."

"DEVO SANJIVANIYAM. DEVO AMRUTAYAM."

The incantation is deafening, but its reverberations comfort. The smooth weight placed between my brows presses through my skull. *Ah*. I am drowning, sinking into someplace somewhere of a somewhat. My karawe at the base of my skull is excited. I sense its anxious tingle. I feel it bleed into my sutras. O' *Ishraha. Lord of supreme wisdom and judgement. O' Creator of Creators, Mother Ishawi. What hast thou blessed this flesh with?* The viscous secretion feels luminous. It flows thick and slow, seemingly coating every cell of every sutra in my body. I surrender myself wholly to the process, aware that the fluid is now engulfing the very last cell of my cerebral sutra.

Slap. Aach. Gasp. Air. My nostrils are in pain, tormented as I inhale in my surroundings. There is a faint accent of that warm fragrance again.

"Khenpo. Khenpo. Our Savior returns. Our warrior returns. Khenpo. Sweet mighty Khenpo. You did not abandon us." Some hands have clutched my feet, their emotions wetting my soles.

A different chant vibrates around me, and my lips part of their own bidding to mouth the words. "I thank thee, o' resplendent Rahoul. I thank thee, o' luminous Karpura. I thank thee, o' supreme Suvaasi. In humble prostration, I offer thou my existence in servitude. Aummm."

My eyes are the first to awaken, followed by my spine that sits me up erect. Everything drops dead quiet. So quiet, I hear every pair of eyes bore into me. They are carrying hope and joy and tears. I am aware, yet I feel no desire to reach out to my people. The first light of the glorious Rahoul is calling out to me. It penetrates my pupils. The shaft is soft and gentle. My eyes water from the strain, but they don't dare blink.

Ah. What is this I see? What is this trickery? I see waves, rapidly vibrating waves creating shimmering outlines of the scene in front of me.

Where is the bloodied land? Where are the fallen trees and my people?

O' *Ishraha.* My eyelids close of their own accord.

"Khenpo. Khenpo Rudham. Do you hear us? Can you see us?"

Yes. Yes, I can. I see the desecrated land now and the martyred trees. I see my people, the valiant Ikshavakrus, and I see the courageous Prutharvas.

"I thank thee, oh brave Maati. You besmirched yourself and sacrificed your forests to uphold us. May we be of service to you, as you have been to us." I smear some soil on my forehead.

"I thank thee, oh gallant warriors for the blood you have shed to honor our purpose. I offer myself in service to you." With my head bowed low, I run my forefinger from my chin to my chest marking my commitment from words to my soul.

Somebody has brought me water in a bowl that seems hewn hastily from a fallen bark. It is that sweetish oily scent again. *Sathr'yi*. She is staring into my eyes, bewildered. I swallow the joy that's lumped tight in my throat. *Ow*. This was painful.

"I thank thee for thy waters, O' forgiving Abja." In obeisance, I touch the bowl to my forehead, lowering it to my mouth to sip in the first drop. A piercing pair of black onyx socketed in a blackened head stares at me from within the bowl. *Ishraha*. This is my own face, aghast and disbelieving, looking up at me from the waters. My chest is thudding uncontrollably against my battered ribs.

A warm palm encircles my wrist. The grasp is firm and assuring. I look into Sathr'yi's cool black irises. They nod. I raise the bowl to my mouth and allow the waters to purge my palette of its parched and putrid state.

I push myself off the hard rock, and with the benevolence of the supreme Suvaasi, I stand mountainous with my feet rooted solid on the ground. Everything and everyone halted, suspended in mid-motion. Their unspoken expectations unnerve me.

Give me strength supreme Mother.

I raise my hands and bless them all. From the rock solid wall of brave soldiers in front of me, to those that have fallen; from the microscopic amoeba, to the forgiving Maati who upholds us.

"AH'M THATHA'ASHI TVAAM. I bless you."

The uproar is terrific. "Ahauma. Ahauma. Ahauma. The Midnight Warrior."

Matrimony

Aucthumbar (October) 17, 2335
Sathr'yi

I'm getting impatient about those first rays. We all are. Not because we are fatigued, but because we have been hanging by a very fragile string of hope for over twenty-four hours.

As the first virgin light of the morning sun is breaking through, the Ikshavakra chief awakens. The revival plays out like a well-staged drama; the timing so perfect, it exaggerates the theatrics. Never had I consciously witnessed the universe synchronize its intentions.

The impressive but frail form of Khenpo Rudham stands upright and raises his hands to bless us all. The call of victory bellows from every soul standing there, hearts wrought in reverence. I can feel the ground shudder. The heavens must have heard it too. "Ahauma. Ahauma. Ahauma. The Midnight Warrior."

Midnight Warrior, wilt thou be mine?

The armies are preparing for their return to their native lands. We thank each other for the alliance and seek forgiveness for unintended trespasses. This is the way of righteous warriors. The Ikshavakrus will camp at the Sakhi forests for another day with their leader. Yes, he would need to heal and recenter. I bow my head low in deep veneration to Khenpo. He acknowledges and bows down to me in gratitude. o' *Deva.* My heart is breathless, and my feet are numbed. I look up into his eyes, and I know I have betrayed my guarded emotions. I walk away clumsily towards Ishka and Nayoma, and I convey my greetings to the nomadic tribe. Why do I feel our acquaintance is not so recent?

We are home by nightfall. But there is no evidence of dark skies. So bright are the streets of Prutharv lit for our homecoming. We fly lower, over our water and land, and we see every child and elder out of their homes shining bhasus or flares from their torches that bear the Prutharv insignia, their kamishas. Our yellow gold flag bearing the celestial disc Chayara looks even more resplendent. Maybe I imagine it so. Fatigue and relief are possessing me.

Home for me is an expansive structure of Sange, a virgin white sandstone from the Sangemar range that is native to Prutharv. In fact, every home and commercial center, and every public installation is made of this glorious white stone and adorned with gilded gold or brightly colored mosaics. Royals and distinguished luminaries from other lands have wooed us with exorbitant amounts in exchange for the rock. A day before leaving for Siama, I had courteously refused one such vulgar offer from the Republican States of America (RSA) in the far west.

The king and the queen are at the airstrip. We offer our customary salutations and convey our allegiance and greetings to our land and to our king and queen. "Askaya Prutharv vibhova. Askaya tvam vibhova." May the Supreme bless Prutharv with prosperity. May the Supreme bless you with prosperity.

"Askaya Prutharv vibhova. Askaya tvam vibhova." Their voices are firm with pride, their eyes moist – our appearances probably tell them tales of our little adventure. "You bring prestige and dignity to the Prutharv clan and to your land oh valiant ones. May the supreme Achyutayam, Bearer of the Chayara, reward you for your selfless service. You shall be knighted as Rakhavi, protector of the exploited. May you forever uphold the honor. There will be a yagusa ceremony at dawn to honor the gallant lives that have perished."

Our reverence for our King Ramakien now comes from a deep admiration for this virtuous justice. The yagusa is an intense rite ordained for purification and coronation ceremonies.

Back home in my bed, sleep evades me. *Dear father, King Ramakien, how shall I share this with you? Your daughter has bequeathed her heart to a wandering nomad who isn't even all human.*

Aucthumbar (October) 21, 2335

There's a gentle knock at my door.

"Mum. Dad."

"Oh, my child, my brave child. How fearlessly you wear your scars. I am a proud mother." She is tearing up.

"Mum …" I hug her. Father isn't saying anything, but I hear his unspoken words. The three of us stand in silence, the queen has my palms clenched in hers. There is much that is said, although not verbally.

Two days have passed since our celebrated return. The war keeps replaying itself, not just in our heads. I am not alone in this. What singles me out is my stubborn devotion to the magnificent Ikshavakra chief. It torments me. Raha'rya, the others, and I have resumed our combat training sessions. The adrenaline seems healthy for us; it distracts, gives us some semblance of peace.

"Princess Sathr'yi." Sumakya is yelling from a distance, running towards me. "Princess." I had just strapped on my gear and Raha'rya has brought my thenuka, my light beam spear, to me. "Princess." Sumakya is flailing her hands animatedly. I stare at the panting face.

"The Ikshavakrus…"

"What about them?" I grip her arms tight.

"They are here… with their chief… with the king… in the court."

I tear towards the palace grounds and brace myself as I turn around a pillar. The entire Ikshavakra tribe is outside the room. We nod to greet each other. Ishka is beaming, and I run to hug her before I enter the assembly chamber.

Khenpo has his back to me, standing majestic in a more vibrant and deeper shade of charcoal, the gold stripe on his scalp is dazzling in the rays filtering through the skylights.

"…and I ask for your daughter's hand in marriage."

Goodbye

Aucthumbar (October) 21, 2335
King Ramakien

The imposing figure startles me. Everything about him does: his stature, his demeanor, and yes, his skin instinctively elicits awe and respect. His behavior is courteous and seems genuinely respectful, but there is something raw and naive about it.

This man is the sole reason Siama is free today. No matter how pompously I gloat over our recent victory, there is only one man responsible for the turn of events. And he is in front of me.

"Please accept our deepest gratitude, o' mighty Khenpo Rudham. Prutharv owes its life to you. It is our honor that you and the Ikshavakrus should be upon our land."

"Greetings, o' righteous one." Khenpo reciprocates with a bow. "Prutharv owes me nothing. Nor does Siama. Neither do Jakotri and Nepaula. My actions were prompted by my destined commitment to serve. Please understand, you are not indebted to my actions nor to me. Please bear this in mind when I convey the purpose of our visit here."

The magnitude of his service hits me. I am uneasy about what shall to follow.

"King Ramakien, I stand before you with the consent of all my people and ask for your daughter's hand in marriage."

My head and heart pass out for a few seconds. My eyes see the princess standing in the doorway, her face in utter shock, just as mine probably is. But look at the exhilaration in her eyes. O' *Deva. What is happening here?*

Sathr'yi enters and stands beside the towering Ikshavakra chief, implying she accepts. Her head coyly hangs low. She is absentmindedly playing with her fingers.

"I need some time to assimilate this great Khenpo. Meanwhile, please allow us to be of service to you and your people."

"We are honored to receive your hospitality," replies the leader with a polite bow. He steals a glimpse at Sathr'yi and strides out of the hall.

I look at Sathr'yi and she at me. Her gaze questions me. I say nothing. I have nothing to say. I walk past her out to the manicured lawns announcing my desire to be left alone. I do not need distractions, especially emotional ones.

There is no warrior greater than this valiant leader of the Ikshavakrus, but he is not even human. He has been divinely ordained, endowed with the wisdom of higher realms. But he is unpolished. And unpretentious about it; you get what you see. I know there is truth in his adoration for Sathr'yi. And with his life, he will deliver on his commitment to protect her.

And yet...

He is charred charcoal while his people have skins of blues and greens and amber. Their physical evolution has created strange patterns they call sutras, on their skins. It is quite unappealing. They have no permanent abode. They are a wandering tribe that live in forests and in the mountains.

"Can they even procreate?" The queen has joined me, I realize. I am quiet for a long while, the ripples are calming down.

"My dear Thary'ni." I speak this more to myself than to the queen. "When Prutharv entrusted itself to Sathr'yi as its commander-in-chief, its people invested their faith in her impassive judgement and wisdom. Why do we distrust Sathr'yi's instincts now? You are anxious, for she will have no gold bedecking her. But she will still be queen. Our daughter will have no secure home to call her own, yet no greater protector will she ever find. She will not be amongst humans like us, but she will find family with the Ikshavakrus. They already love her as their own.

"Let us bless the couple with all the love we have ever known, mother of Sathr'yi. Let your heart ache not in angst for her, but in the sadness that will tug at you when you fondly bid her farewell."

Bloodline

Nalumbar (November) 07, 2335
Khenpo Rudham

Being a groom is exhausting and uselessly indulgent. I would rather duel a Yakashvi, a mountain demon. We beings are habituated to over-dramatize our reasons for feeling joy, so few have they become. This kind of joy is transitory. Balance makes it eternal.

Our wedding day was predestined by the stars to occur on Aucthumbar 25, when Rahoul and Karpura had aligned themselves along the same cosmic path—sun and moon, fire and water, male and female—celestial symbols of opposing energies yielding to each other.

Prutharv had decked its streets and skies, resplendent and loud in color, sounds and scents, proclaiming to the heavens that I had welcomed Sathr'yi into my life as she had welcomed me into hers.

Ten days later, we returned to the Kelushi mountains. I desired that Mother Kelushi welcome Sathr'yi into her ecosystem, just as she has always loved and welcomed me and all the Ikshavakrus. It took over a week to prepare Sathr'yi to metaport. Her first few attempts at metatravel were clownish and clumsy. They got her in splits. They also got her dizzy, and she vomited a few times. Sathr'yi was a good student, determined and very patient about it. And Ishka was a good teacher. When she was confident to leave, Sathr'yi and I walked to the palace from the Sangemar mountains that edged Prutharv and sought blessings of her parents.

I am sitting now on my usual flattened rock atop one of Mount Kelushi's peaks, staring at the expanse before me. Rahoul's beams flash on a few splotches of snow illuminating Sathr'yi and the others that are playing in the patches.

"You've got a lousy aim, Khwari," taunts Abouja, and Sathr'yi pelts her with snow bombs, squealing.

Sathr'yi is now Khwari—one that is divinely bonded to a Khenpo. She is the first human Ikshavakru in eons, and she is a Khwari. That is tremendous weight to shoulder, and there is little I can do to help, other than stand by her rock solid. *Does she know this?*

Yesterday, Sathr'yi was officially absorbed into the Ikshavakra lineage at the yagusa ceremony we held for her by the Kelushi stream. This rite was never observed before. No foreigner had ever been inducted into the Ikshavakra clan. Ishka and Abouja fussed over Sathr'yi childishly, dolling her up for the initiation. I was deeply moved and equally amused. They had smeared her entire body with Dharati—a composite of every soil, forest, mountain and desert that Ikshavakrus have ever walked upon.

It carries memories and blessings of ancient lands. Abouja threaded strings of white kori shells that had fallen off the Kamaru tree and draped them around her neck. Ishka dotted my bride's arms, feet, and forehead with an ashen paste ground out of Kelushi's grey rocks.

Just before dawn cracked, they brought her by the Kelushi stream, and sat her on a long rock. Some of the tribe had decorated the makeshift throne with small pebbles and leaves. Every Ikshavakru was at the riverside, dressed and ornamented, encircling Sathr'yi and the yagusa fire that flickered from a dug-out pit. I included. Then each Ikshavakru stepped forward, dropped an offering of a pebble or dried wood or fallen flower into the purification fire, took a pinch of Dharati and marked Sathr'yi's forehead with it.

"Ah'm purasthu Ikshavakra tvam." *I am honored to accept you into the Ikshavakra bloodline.*

Sathr'yi took a pinch of Dharati and reciprocated the same. "Ah'm bhodu chaha'arastu Ikshavakra tvam." *I am deeply honored to be included in the Ikshavakra bloodline.*

I was the last to mark her with Dharati. "Ah'm purasthu Ikshavakra tvam."

Her eyes were shy and ecstatic. "Ah'm bhodu chaha'arastu Ikshavakra tvam." She held my palms in hers, tight, silently declaring she meant every word she recited.

After the initiation, I was made to sit beside her on the rock throne.

Nayoma painted my spine with symbols from our ancient text and dotted my forehead skin in patterns that matched Sathr'yi's. He knotted one of my Raudak strings with Sathr'yi's Kori threads and held the knot in his palm while incanting sacred words to call upon celestial blessings. Ishka placed crowns, actually rings, of rolled up tambacu leaves on our heads. When Nayoma let go of his release on the knot, the two cords fused together and streams of iridescent light had materialized from the knot, weaving themselves into our crowns, and back to the knot, completing the circle.

"I thank thee, o' resplendent Rahoul, for your blazing light that nourishes. I thank thee, o' luminous Karpura, creator of my life's cycles. I thank thee, o' mighty Vayuka, carrier..." Our tribe was singing the Ikshavakra prayer repeatedly, synchronizing the chant with the flow of the bands of light. The sounds reverberated in deep bass and their repetition had turned hypnotic.

Sathr'yi and I concluded in chorus, as the threads faded into our crowns. "In humble prostration, I offer thou my existence in servitude. Aummm."

The light streams had proclaimed her Khwari.

Sathr'yi did not become Ikshavakru by wedding me, nor by these ceremonial rituals. The Ikshavakru way of Dharoma'kshama was a part of her even before we met. The Heavenly Spirits knew of it. Did they also know she would be sworn into our lineage? The tribe had perceived it during that brief but tumultuous meeting during the Siaman war. Which is why they had ecstatically approved of our wedding.

Ikshavakra is not a nation or kingdom, and Ikshavakru is not a nationality. Ikshavakrus *are* Ikshavakra.

Ikshavakra

Nalumbar (November) 07, 2335
Khenpo Rudham

I am a shaman warrior. It is not because of what I do. It is who I am. Just as I am an Ikshavakru.

Ikshavakrus were all human a few centuries ago, before the wise Jova took over as Khenpo in 2153. We are the only shaman warriors that ever were, and we still are. Which is why her predecessor Khenpo Nada'yn desired the Ikshavakra progeny have evolved into beings with amplified sensory abilities. Therefore, we may never fail to serve All-that-is-Created.

We are a wandering tribe. Every land that beckons us is home. But Mount Kelushi comforts me as only a mother would. Our human ancestors were from the ancient island land of Kaysankha. They were content wanderers roaming between tiny kingdoms in the island mass. In 2058, Kaysankha joined the nations of the Indian Ocean like Harappa, Jakotri, Madhugha, Nepaula, Prutharv, Saiyon, Tey'chi and other island nations to collectively form the Indian Mutual Nations (IMN).

In the latter quarter of the twenty-first century, the affluent nation of Sahudaria—formerly Sauda Arabia—was liberally investing its national reserves in experiments to crack open the core atomic structure of All-that-is-Created. The crowned prince Mahoud was not much different from King Vibhasta in his gutsy ambition. The prince had been playing with quarks to alter the atomic structures of ore. We are told he was wildly ecstatic when Khenpo Nada'yn requested Sahudaria for its modified quark seeds to transform a human tribe.

No human can change the core life structure of another human. A shaman can—a highly elevated shaman like Khenpo Nada'yn.

Five Ikshavakra pregnant wombs offered to carry the quark seeds in them. We are told stories of these mothers' courage. My grandmother was one of them. Every one of us can trace our ancestry back to one of these five wombs.

Ikshavakrus metamorphosed into cyboid shamans.

Khenpo Nada'yn had not perceived the extent of our developed abilities. The new breed of Ikshavakra shamans could call upon the subtlest elements of existence unknown to the human race. We do not have natural deaths. We pass over at will, or when we are so damaged that our life spirit Suvaasi begs to leave our body. Our physical forms stop aging before they reach fifty human years.

I have lived 117 so far, and I will go on as long as the supreme Ishraha commands me to serve. The day my servitude ends, I do too.

It is absurd that humans should crave immortality. When they do not know how to live the moments given, what differently would they do if they had eternity to go through? It is difficult.

We eat, sleep, walk, talk, excrete, sweat, bleed just as humans do. We procreate as naturally too. But our needs come from a necessity to add numbers to the tribe. As there are few that move on, we do not beget as often as humans do.

Most humans are intimidated by our appearance, so acute is our connection with the elemental forces. It is glaringly blatant in how we look. And fortunately, tales of our appearance are so widely talked about that humans rarely keel over in shock. Still, they are uncomfortable. We are accustomed to their innocent rudeness.

Every one of us belongs to an energy lineage which marks us with our skin color. This is not about genetics. The spirit of the energy chooses by virtue. Seven primary energies: soil, fire, water, sky, cellular, time, and mind; and seven skin tones: red, amber, blue, iridescence, green, white, and grey.

Ishka is descended from the spirit of soil. She is a deep earthy red and carries energy traits of being hard grounded. Abouja is a dull white, bearing time energies within her. Her lineage is mathematically inclined, her kind know of the geometric precision of the universe. Time is the common denominator of its construction. The spirit of fire symbolizes creation and fortification. My father was an Agnosha, a fire descendant.

His skin was stained a rich ochre. My mother was azure. The water spirit is partial to the female species. Phases of the moon affect the intensity of their blue. Nayoma is pigmented in an oily lustrous grey by the mind spirit. He carries highly potent energies of knowledge, wisdom and mind-connection. Nayoma can manipulate mind-stuff.

I was the only Ikshavakru who did not fit in this seven-color spectrum. Now there are two of us. I am looking at the other sitting with Abouja far below. Sathr'yi looks up and smiles.

My skin was violet, the only Ikshavakru to have worn a purple skin tone before that nuclear blaze at Siama had charred me. That shade in particular holds all seven elemental energies and carries the spiritual essence of the supreme Ishraha and Ishawi within its hue. By blessing me such, I am sworn to forever serve and protect everything that ever exists. Their faith in me is overwhelming, and I wear It as a crown.

Yet, I have wished things were otherwise. I have wished I was not... special.

I am stark charcoal now, except for my palms and soles which are an ashen grey, and the patch of my throat which retains its original violet. My eyes have turned onyx entirely, they have no white. They startled me when I first saw them reflected in a water bowl. They have pupils that glow ultraviolet. The color seeps like ice cracks into my black irises.

A smear of gold runs from my karawe at the nape of my skull up to the crown—Ishawi's mark of protection when I lay incapacitated on Siaman soil. Getting scorched there aroused the energies I was endowed with. They are more sensitive now. They get excited when my mind twitches. I am a ticking mass of ripe energy.

Our younglings are born translucent. A Khenpo initiates a new life into the Ikshavakra way, within the hour it is born. This first hour is crucial. The newborn receptors are virgin and naked, intuitively sensitive to the energies that will mark them. They start sealing up as soon as they are out of the womb.

If only Mandha'ar had made it in the first hour...

I have performed a few Karipa initiation ceremonies. The experience is breathtaking, witnessing raw energy surge from its spirit source and infiltrate receptacles that draw it into the being. As it pervades the bloodstream, the energy dyes the skin in its color. Infant Ikshavakrus are pale shades of energy colors. The colors deepen with age. Ishka's shade of red borders on a thick brown. She is over two hundred.

The Karipa ceremony is actually about the imprinting of the karawe. A karawe is our plug-in to the subtlest universal energies in the higher realms of creation. Whilst the spirit energy is still coursing through every cell of a newly born life, I offer the child to the Universe and unite the three of us—the universe, the infant, and me—into a single source of life. My thumb is guided by the Source to imprint a mark on the body. This roundish depression is a karawe. This isn't painful; it is gentle and soothing, and it shimmers, turning black when the hour passes. The karawe is embedded with the seed of wisdom from Ishraha. It is the source of our intuition from the subtle higher realms. The Supreme Energy speaks to us from that birthmark.

Garay'an has joined Sathr'yi and Abouja. He looks excited as he talks with arms flapping about, dramatizing what he is saying. I think this is the first time he has shared a conversation with his Khwari. Sathr'yi is tracing her fingers over Abouja's outstretched arm. They are following the corded sutra patterns on Abouja's forearm.

Humans find our skin and sutras disturbing. Our skin is patterned with cord-like impressions that begin at the spine and radiate into our arms and back thighs. The patterns are unique to every Ikshavakru, like fingerprints. An offspring carries patterns of both parents that weave into each other making a new set of intersecting and concentric lines and shapes. Our sutras hold our genetic story. They light our intuitive abilities and survival instincts in this material realm.

Sathr'yi is sitting by herself now, looking at Rahoul sink into Kelushi's outstretched embrace. I roll up a tambacu leaf and strike some pebbles to light it. I take a long drag, drowning deeper into my reveries.

Sathr'yi is the first Khwari who is not marked with a karawe. She has no sutras that guide her or carry the history of her DNA. Her skin tone is tinted an earthy brown from its human energies. Yet, she is blessed and accepted by heaven and tribe as Ikshavakra Khwari.

Mandha'ar wasn't.

Rahoul's dimming light is tinting everything orange. My dagger blade winks at the last rays. The teecha tooth impression on its hilt grows dark in the blade's shadow.

Sathr'yi is walking uphill towards me, beaming and panting. I tuck the dagger into the strap, take a last drag and walk towards her.

Family

Nalumbar (November) 07, 2335
Khwari Sathr'yi

"You do know that I love you all," I said, looking at Abouja's pale face. It was more an assertion than a doubt that needed clarification.

"Yes, we do. We all do, and we love you too, Khwari." She squeezes my fist in assurance. Abouja hasn't left my side today. I am so grateful for her affection, and her perception that I would need support from the tribe to ease into their family.

I am forever indebted to fate for planting me here. I feel I have returned to my people. I turn to look at Rudham, sun rays blinding my eyes. He is at his favorite perch up at Mount Kelushi's peak, looking at something straight ahead.

"I am the only one carrying Kaali's energies of time, since Khenpo Jova. She was ivory too." Abouja explains. We are sitting on a flat stretch of barren grey rock, wet from our snow fights.

I am curious. "What happened? Why did she move on?"

"She had to port herself to a future time. We don't know why or when. We lost her." Abouja lowers her eyes, scratches the hard rock with her forefinger. She says nothing for some time, and I allow her silence to prevail. "Khenpo Jova was my makhasha, my guru."

I clasp her palm, and we stare at the terrain in front of us, not taking in anything.

"Abouja, have you ever time tr—"

I am interrupted by Garay'an's salutations. "Amo Khwari. Amo Abouja."

"Amo Garay'an."

Garay'an is a supercharged battery, always excited. His iridescent skin glows aggressively to announce his passionate moods. He is a darling.

"Khwari, did you know that I am Abouja's shikasha? Her pupil? There is no greater mentor than she. I owe my learnings of the Ikshavakra way to her. I was her favorite student, and still am, aren't I makhasha?" Garay'an expresses with hand movements, as though words cannot speak by themselves.

"O Deva. How did I get that wrong?" Abouja laments playfully. Garay'an twists his face in pretended offense, and I savor this moment of light banter.

"These are sutras, Khwari," Abouja's voice turns intense now. She lets me touch the raised patterns on her forearm.

Garay'an is beaming. "Aren't they cool? Look at this shape on my shoulder. It looks like a trident drawn with concentric lines. I carry my parents' sutra patterns in mine. You will find something of dad's and mum's here. See this fish-like thing? Mum has it on her arm." Garay'an is proud of his sutras, and I see no reason why he should not be. His body is etched with the most detailed patterns of all the tribe.

"We must get dinner before sundown Garay'an. Do you want to join us, Khwari?" offers Abouja. "We are going to the stream,"

"I want to sit here a bit longer and bathe in Rahoul's cooling rays. I will join you for food picking tomorrow."

Abouja's face gets serious. "Rahoul is beautiful when he sinks into Maati. He turns all that he touches into gold. He intoxicates all. But do not bathe in his descending energies, Khwari. We will see you later at the square."

"Abouja." I call out. She turns around. "Thank you." The ivory face beams her warmest smile.

I look up at Rudham. He seems frozen in meditation. His posture hasn't budged the slightest since morning. Sometimes he drifts to a space far deep within him. I feel it must be dark in there, because it gnaws at him silently. *Will you trust me with your invisible demons Rudham? Do you believe I am strong enough?*

Despite Abouja's foreboding, I surrender myself to Rahoul's intoxicating warmth, letting it permeate my senses.

Rudham's parents passed on at the turn of this century, before

Rudham became Khenpo. They had willingly surrendered their life force. I wonder why?

Although they had lived many years longer than any human lifespan, surrendering their Ikshavakra existence needed a strong purpose. Rudham's mother Yasiyaka was from the water lineage, her emotional energies were stormy, the currents had coursed wild within her. I am told she trained her children to look beyond rigid protocols and follow their karawe, even if they were shamed, or worse, ostracized from the tribe. She was stronger willed than her husband. She was also 18 years older than him.

Rudham's father Aruva'ya was chosen by the fire spirit. Those who shared his lineage revered him as master. Aruva'ya purged all that did not align with the natural order of the Universe. His blazing energies would rip through the defiled, absolving them of their impurities. His squad restored the sanity of several warring leaders. Unfortunately, Aruva'ya could not redeem Mandha'ar, his rebel son. Perhaps being a father diluted his intentions.

Why do I feel Rudham's suppressed anguish has something to do with Mandha'ar?

Mandha'ar is Rudham's twin brother. Nobody knows anything about him anymore. He is branded as Ikshavakra's failure. It was deemed so by Rudham's predecessor Khenpo Oharam and is still dropped in passing conversations. Khenpo Oharam was embarrassed about the stain on Ikshavakra's chaste repute. So, he brazenly exhibited it, with the intent of publicly disowning the stigma. Aruva'ya and Yasiyaka carried their child's weighted disgrace. So did Rudham. And Mandha'ar?

Khenpo Oharam could never ostracize this family. Because while Mandha'ar was an ugly stain, Rudham was the tribe's sacred purple child. Khenpo Oharam knew better than to barter that.

Rudham was born a half hour before Mandha'ar. When the purple tint started seeping into his skin at the Karipa ceremony, Khenpo Oharam could not let go of the phenomenon in his arms. Mandha'ar was not initiated within his hour. So Mandha'ar was destined to remain translucent. And he was destined to not be blessed with his karawe.

Was it his destiny? Do one's actions turn into another's destiny? Is this the Ikshavakra way? Is this the way of the Universe?

Dear Mandha'ar. I am so sorry.

I turn around. Rudham is also staring at Rahoul now. I can see wisps of smoke floating around his face. He looks breathtaking. Rahoul's rays outline his form with a mystical glow.

Were the two siblings so disparate that nothing could prove they were twins? Or that they were even related by blood? I cannot bring myself to believe so. Nothing can tug that cord free. If you are destined to be birth siblings, you are destined to be tied together.

"Ah'm pareyanam tvam Rahoul." I offer my salutations to Rahoul and walk towards Rudham. He is looking at me. *O' Deva.*

My heart is hammering so hard. Will I make it to Kelushi's peak? Rudham is striding down the slope, gazing intently at me, his eyes don't waver. *O' Mother Kelushi, support my feet.*

Rogue Warrior

Diyasabaar (December) 15, 2335
Abouja

Khwari and Ishka are sweating profusely, beaming with adrenaline as they walk up to where Khenpo Rudham, Nayoma, and I stand. The spectators are still cheering and whistling raucously as the two challengers turn around and raise their hands in acknowledgement. Khwari and Ishka have just had another high, frenzied impromptu duel—Khwari with her phantom lasso, and Ishka with her light spear. Oftentimes, our combat training sessions get so intense, they provoke the two commanders to challenge each other.

And we provoke them further. "Did anybody bet on you two?" Khenpo jests. He squeezes Khwari's hand, and she looks up at him, swelling up in his confidence.

"Did you win or lose chief?" Ishka chuckles. She loves taking a dig at our leader.

"She got you this time Khenpo," Nayoma quips.

Khenpo feigns hurt. "Never the next," he challenges. He walks away with Nayoma leaving the three of us to savor his defeat.

We sit down on the stoney stretch, sipping tea of rhoma flower extracts, sharing the bowl between us. The other trainees do the same, scattered in groups around us. I raise our bowl to acknowledge them.

"That was some rush Khwari and Ishka." Gara'yan yells from afar, raising his drink. Palina has brewed this for us, she is best at her infusions. She says it replenishes our salts. She would know. She carries cellular spirit energies within her emerald skin.

Khwari has been emotionally distracted the last few days.

"Are you missing home Khwari?" Ishka enquires, concerned, hoping Khwari opens up.

Khwari is lost again. "Hunh? Not at all Ishka. Whatever gave you that idea?" They share a hug. I join in too.

"He is not his whole self," Khwari shares her distress after a while. "A part of him wanders off to a memory I am not familiar with. How can I help him?"

"I do not have the audacity to present my assumptions to you Khwari, and that is what they are. Assumptions. I will never forgive myself if I lured you on to something based on my suppositions. Khenpo Rudham has entrusted himself to you, you need to believe that. Give him time," says Ishka. "Abouja?"

I nod and look intently into Khwari's eyes. They looked comforted. "I want some more of this delicious tea," she says. "I hope Palina has a big batch prepared. Coming?"

Ishka and Khwari walk towards the square promising to bring some back for me. I doubt they can.

Khwari's anxiety comes from not knowing what to do about something she knows nothing about. It is warranted, she isn't playing dramatics, over sensitizing her concern. Has Khenpo been revisiting his guilt? Poor Khwari. She has an arduous task of replacing his guilt into a cherished love for his twin brother.

No pair of twins could be so diametrically opposite as Khenpo Rudham and Mandha'ar are. I don't believe it would have been so, had circumstances been otherwise. But then, circumstances are destined. The contrast was not genetically ordained.

Where is Mandha'ar? Does he look the same? Has he found a tribe family? Because nobody could befriend him. His walls were unscalable. After a point, we all stopped trying. But Khenpo was obsessed with getting through, through to his core buried alive under layers and layers of rejection, all packed tight beneath his skin.

Until his teens, Mandha'ar's translucent skin would camouflage itself to reflect his temperaments. He had grown conscious of this nakedness, of his mind bearing itself to all through his skin. He struggled to screen himself, to disconnect emotions from his sensory organs. It was his own burden. He had no mentor. As he transitioned, nobody knew

Mandha'ar anymore.

His facade turned fake. His love was frosty. His compassion felt heartless. Self-preservation made him adapt himself to and manipulate situations, seeking advantageous propositions. Aruva'ya and Yasiyaka never did discriminate between their two boys, not consciously at least. Their parenting just got interpreted two very different ways. Often, they unloaded their unease onto young Rudham, that one day Mandha'ar would go too far.

The parents' fears silently built over the guilt that had already germinated in the purple boy's conscience ever since he realized his skin had pronounced him special. As a child, Khenpo often asked me the toughest questions, questions about the fairness of it all, to which I never had any answers and still don't. Why did he draw in his brother's share of energies? Why should Khenpo Oharam's failure be touted as Mandha'ar's?

"Every life is destined for the energy it does and does not receive." This is how Aruva'ya and Yasiyaka pacified an angry and guilt-ridden young Rudham. Even though he knew the words spoke the Universal Truth, he would brush them off as mollycoddles. His hatred for Khenpo Oharam was a dormant volcano.

Then Mandha'ar disappeared. We weren't surprised. I had felt it would do him better, separating himself from the torment for a few years. Staying away from a situation gives a broader view.

Mandha'ar has not yet returned.

Khenpo Oharam had publicized his sympathies to the distraught family, lauding Mandha'ar's courageous decision to ostracize himself from the tribe. This had aroused Rudham's dormant rage—it exploded with extreme profanities mixed with vehement accusations. Mandha'ar would never forgo his brother, his family or his tribe, never. He would have announced his decision to walk out. How can he walk out in shame when he never felt any? Khenpo Oharam was standing at the community center silently, observing, taunting Rudham with his condescending smirk.

Rudham may have butchered him to death. It had taken five of us to drag Rudham away.

Rudham had pushed us away as he walked deep into the enclosed forests. He returned with his anger and guilt concealed in the deepest trenches of his conscience.

As time went by, Mandhaar was forgotten by us all. And Rudham allowed weeds to grow over his buried monsters. They are alive, hibernating since decades before, but alive.

My dear Khwari, this will not be easy for you.

"Where is Khwari?" Khenpo Rudham asks, waking me out of my recollections. "Are you alright, Abouja? Did Palina's brew get to you?" He smiles.

"Right behind you, Khenpo." I point out Khwari's arrival. She seems lightheaded. It amuses him.

It's a good day. All seems well.

Crowned

Diyasabaar (December) 15, 2335
Khenpo Rudham

"We do bear the sin of slaughter, don't we? We were destined to be warriors, destined to shed other blood on battlefields, and so, involuntarily destined to sin." Sathr'yi is speaking from a subtler state of mind. She has overdosed on Palina's potion. "The price is exorbitant. A single life is not payment enough. How do you balance that equation? What does Dharoma'kshama say?"

"Go ahead, Nayoma," I requested.

Nayoma grins. "This is not involuntary, Khwari. Have you ever been restless when you weren't at war or training for it?"

Sathr'yi is quiet, eyes focused on something far away. What she saw must have corroborated what Nayoma said. "I *want* to kill?"

"No, Khwari," Nayoma clarifies. "You want to bring justice. It calls for bloodshed. The origin of sin lies in your intent. If there were a way to restore justice and truth without the bloodshed, would you opt for it?"

Sathr'yi's eyes widen.

Nayoma continues. "You carry the sin of a kill when your intent is generated from the dark fires of revenge and hate. This is why, before every battle, Ikshavakrus seek forgiveness and offer gratitude to those who would be sacrificing themselves to the call of greater good, our enemies included. This does not mean we do not pay. Dharoma'kshama *will* wend its way through our lifespans and call for something in return from us; it will find some way to restore balance. But we do not pay for sin. There is no sin here; this is our duty. Our ultimate call to duty. Shying away from it incurs sin. Rudham taking over as our Khenpo is the best way to understand this."

Sathr'yi looks at me. Nayoma and Abouja too. I say nothing. I pretend to be distracted by rolling up a tambacu leaf. The silence is very awkward. It's hounding me to say something.

"Garay'an has seen something. Look, he is beckoning us. We'll be back." Abouja fakes excitement and yanks Nayoma away with her.

"May I?" Sathr'yi requests to share my rolled up bedhi. We savor the quietude and the bedhi together.

"I murdered Khenpo Oharam."

There is no judgement in Sathry'i's eyes, although they question me to know more.

"No matter what you may have heard Sathr'yi, Oharam was exceptionally intellectual and wise. His knowledge of the ways of the universe was unsurpassable, except probably by Nayoma. We revered him for his mental prowess, he could perceive and foresee probabilities naturally. This is how he mastered manipulating situations and beings in his favor."

I realize my personal conflicts are not influencing this conversation today. I feel grateful.

"His obsession for greatness was his downfall. He pined for Ikshavakra's glory, to see his tribe on the highest pedestal, hailed and feared by every land beyond. He hoarded affluence for us and himself. We were displayed as an unblemished righteous super tribe decorated with gold and jewels. The tribe had grown uncomfortable with that superficial weight. We were paying for that glory with our integrity."

There's some hatred in my mouth now as I speak. I spit out some dry saliva and light up another rolled leaf. Sathr'yi is quiet and patient.

"Sahudaria never abandoned its pursuit for the final core of an atom, even though prince Mahoud was long gone. Perhaps because they had already bled their reserves dry. They were intent on replenishing them, or they were actually getting closer to the beginning of an atom. So they believed."

Sathr'yi frowns in question.

"They never will, Sathr'yi," I say. "Nobody will. An atom has no beginning. Its core has another core embedded into it which has another. Its origin goes deeper than the subtlest states of materialization."

She takes a drag, inhaling my words with it.

"Twelve years ago, Sahudaria's experiments generated genodium, a highly volatile energy born of quark fission."

"The quark?" Sathr'yi asks.

"Yes, it's supreme Ishraha's lousiest scheme. Our evolved state originated from Sahudaria's experiments with a quark seed. Genodium was created by splitting the quark, the quark of quasiatoms of Sahudarian oil ores and—" *How do I say this?* "—Sange."

No response from Sathr'yi, neither verbal nor physical.

"Ikshavakrus are sensitive to Universal Intelligence—and it to us—because our cells vibrate at the same frequency of Avom, the first sound of Aum. The energy in the genodium pulsates the same. Since we all share the same frequency—"

Sathr'yi does not let me finish. "—the genodium can affect Ikshavakrus and the Universal Energy." She looks aghast.

"Yes, my dear. Humans are intrinsically hunters. In their pursuit to know more about the Universal Intelligence, they carry hidden their darkest desire to conquer and tame the Source."

"Khenpo Oharam desired this?" Sathr'yi does not disguise her disgust.

"You must realize, Sathr'yi, we owe our existence to Sahudaria. Twelve years ago, Sheikhafa Saladuan invited Khenpo Oharam to Sahudaria. He played up the debt-and-honor game with Khenpo Oharam when he requested we deliver his kingdom's energy experiment to the Republican States of America, the RSA, in the far-out west. Khenpo Oharam repaid Ikshavakra's debt when he accepted the invitation, but implementing the request did not come under the requisite of the debt we owed."

"Why is that?"

"No universal law, or debt, or binding commitment can ever justify the use of genodium. Genodium by itself is an energy state, extremely volatile, but significantly placid when not provoked. Its energy thrust can destroy all in its path within a 200-mile radius. The destruction is as violent as a natural hurricane or quake that lands have known. But to turn into an inferno, genodium needs a catalyst. Twelve years ago, a broadcasting technology developed in the west carried that potential. It was the brainchild of the mediacratic Bear and Salmon Republic.

"The BSR is a mostly honorable federation of states. It is

everything the RSA is not. The RSA is a totalitarian system of leadership where political heads act under a dubious veil of democracy. Ikshavakrus never ventured as far west earlier. Winds always brought us news of their ill and well. Khenpo Oharam was the first."

"You mean… "

"Khenpo Oharam had covertly bartered his services for gold."

Adrenaline fuels my forehead nerves. I half close my eyes to soothe the heat in them.

"At dusk that evening, I killed Khenpo Oharam." My eyes are still half closed, the wave has calmed. "He did not resist the final verdict and virtuously requested Suvaasi to leave his being. He said he knew this to be so, and that, 'It was only a matter of when'. Nayoma had conducted his last rites, being descended from the same lineage. The chants purified energies around the ceremony, the departing was peaceful and serene. We watched a silver shimmer disappear into nothingness before us.

"I cannot forget that scene, Sathr'yi. The entire tribe was staring at me after the passing rites, the expectations in their eyes as they crowned me Khenpo. Even today, those eyes remind me of my purpose."

Abouja returns.

"Where is the genodium now? Was it destroyed?" Sathr'yi sounds desperate.

"No, Khwari, it is indestructible," Abouja declares.

"It lies with the RSA in a small canister, pressurized into an inert state. They have no use for it without an agitator. Those within the BSR who recognize the dangers have safeguarded their transmission technology from the perpetrators," I explain.

"So far," interjects Abouja, implying the possibility of doom.

Khwari is upset. "You are not going to do anything about it?"

I did. I did something about it. Twelve years ago. I look at Abouja knowingly. She nods.

I should roll up another bedhi. This is going to take a while.

Time Travel

Ahôut (August) 11, 2323
Twelve years ago
Abouja

We believed Rudham would eventually lead us one day, but like this?

Rudham knelt before Khenpo Oharam, who lays sprawled on the ground, a dagger with a familiar teecha tooth hilt lying next to them, shining, newly wet with blood.

No. We didn't make it in time.

Five minutes ago, Sahaki had rudely interrupted our evening get-together with news of Khenpo Oharam and genodium, an energy experiment. We barely registered Rudham get up and run towards Khenpo Oharam's quarters before Sahaki finished saying "…is back."

Ishka, Nayoma, Sahaki and I are watching the scene, stunned. The victim whispering something to his killer, the killer chanting, offering gratitude and seeking forgiveness from his victim. After a while, silence gags the air around us. Ishka steps forward and closes the dead man's eyes. She is tying his toes together with twine. Nayoma has gone to fetch some Dharati.

"Rudham." I reach out to the kneeling man and help him to his feet. He is very unsteady, so I let him flop down on the ground again.

"This was inevitable Abouja. If not today, then on a tomorrow." His voice is composed and steady. "I questioned him. He was gloating over the Ikshavakra debt. Look at what he has brought with him. This tiny bead has a single molecule of genodium in it. *Ishraha.* What possessed his intellect? We can't keep this here." Rudham is hysterical.

Suddenly, he is up on his feet, driven insane with a purpose. "Send me back, Abouja. I will stop him before he hands over the genodium to the RSA. Send me back. *Send. Me. Back.*" Rudham is shaking me hard, forcing my acquiescence.

"Rudham." I had to slap him. The others are as upset as I am. Nayoma is standing in the doorway with his mouth agape.

"Give me a minute to tell you why not, Rudham. This is not metaporting." I shriek. "First, you are not permitted to change a damn thing about what has occurred. You can advise, and suggest, you cannot relay the future to them. Second, I have never attempted a timeport. Khenpo Jova did, and she never returned. We cannot lose you, dammit!"

Ishka supports me. "She is correct, Rudham. She knows."

"Do you not comprehend what has happened, or will happen?" Rudham pleads. "The Universal Intelligence is now accessible to monkey men to manipulate and to play with. Does this not frighten you? The cosmos will be governed and guided by human intellect—a regressive, arrogant, ignorant human intellect. I don't even bring Ikshavakra into the equation here, even though unleashing genodium will unplug our karawe. This will not affect humans or other living species immediately. But gradually, within the first century…

"They won't even realize the cosmos is disintegrating. Their destruction will be slow, but they *will* succumb to it. Why are we wasting time? Abouja. Send me back. *Now.*"

The truth behind his madness provokes me. "Alright. I will come with you, Rudham. You need to get back here too, don't you?" I smile, trying to lighten things up.

Khenpo Oharam's skin has started fading its grey and turning translucent. Nayoma stops applying Dharati onto the cold forehead and looks at us.

I prepare for our departure. *O' Mother Kaali, I need you more than ever now. Guide me. Take over my intellect so that my weak judgement does not override yours.* I draw a circle five feet wide with my forefinger and scribble our ancient scriptures of protection and time within. My hands are shaking.

"Let me help you," Nayoma offers, getting up from his position next to the body. While he writes the scripts of our other six energies, Ishka conjures luminous cords between them and the ones I had scribbled.

"*Tavema Kaali rakhashavi, ahema punyasvi, tavema Kaali rakhashavi, ahema punyasvi, tavema Kaali rakhashavi, ahema punyasvi,*" Sahaki begins the chants. They need to be repeated 1100 times. The three of us join in the chorus, drawing symbols at the same time.

I take some soil and go over the circular outline with it, enclosing the scripts within it. "Rudham?"

Rudham has gouged out the teecha tooth from his dagger's hilt. It now dangles from the gold chain around his neck—his father's parting token to his son. Rudham has embedded the tiny genodium bead into the tooth next to its two lapis blue stone eyes. The bead glistens black, like an evil eye. I frown in question.

"We cannot leave this here," he says.

I take some soil, smear it on Rudham's feet and mine, and we step into the circle. "Rudham, do you remember what I mentioned earlier? We cannot stop the Oharam of the past." He nods. "You need to focus on where we need to be."

He nods again.

"Are you ready?"

Another nod.

Am I ready? Mother Kaali. O' Mother Kaali, carry us and bring us home safe.

"Ishka, you will have to connect our soil-smeared feet to the soil on the circle. When we leave, you need to make sure that connection exists. Don't let it shift, and definitely don't let it break. We need to be back here at this exact moment. Good luck."

Ishka tenses. "No sweat." She forces a laugh.

"*Tavema Kaali rakhashavi, ahema punyasvi.*" I invoke cords to connect my karawe with Rudham's.

Hurgh. The force of his energy is jabbing at me, hard. I am sucked into oblivion. Every part of my insides are pulled into my chest. I cannot breath. I feel sharp stabs hacking at my core. *Mother Kaali.*

I hit the ground and drop on all fours, gasping, shivering, drenched in sweat. My limbs are palpitating uncontrollably. I turn my head instinctively and see Rudham crumpled on the floor. "Rudham?"

There is no movement.

O Mother Kaali. "Rudham!"

He stirs, struggling to lift his head off the floor. "That was some ride eh, Abouja?"

"Damn you, Rudham." We laugh nervously, applauding our insanity. *O' Kaali. Thank you, Mother of Time. A million times, I prostrate before you.*

Rudham and I are in our sub-space manifestations, unseen by naked human eyes. We are a set of molecules moving about in the physical realm. I force my protesting body off the pristine polished floor. I can see my molecular-self reflected in it. "Where are we, Rudham?"

There is an overwhelming sea of humans around us, dressed in immaculate fineries and uniforms. The crowd exudes confusing, complicated energies. It is affecting me. This is not good.

"Where are we, Rudham?" I repeat with rude impatience.

He pulls me to a far corner of the elaborate room, and we scan the scene in front of us. All I see is sophistication dripping all over the rotunda room, the glossed floor, and the high-domed glass ceiling.

I ask a different question. "What are we searching for?"

"I'm looking for somebody who can recognize our frequencies, Abouja." Rudham explains.

"Do we have that kind of time?"

"Come," he says, pulling me across the stately space and out the exit. The wind is frigid here, hitting our faces, everything is drowned in white with dabs of mucky greys scattered as footprints. We walk further towards a lake. "This is a good place, we are alone. She will be here soon."

He didn't need to complete that last bit—two female figures in overcoats are walking towards us.

"I will step out," Rudham declares, already slipping out of his molecular state, and materializing into his physical self.

"Your frequencies are going to kick into hyperdrive with you stepping into your physical state Rudham. you need to make this very quick."

"You're telling me this now?" He is completely out of his invisible vibratory shell.

The women are taken aback by Rudham's form. The one on the left instinctively reaches for her coat pocket, when other grabs her arm, "Stand down, Butters, it's alright." The calmer one looks like an android, which explains how she could discern our frequency waves.

"I am Rudham of the Ikshavakra tribe." The android and Butters do not respond. It seems like they are still recovering or are suspicious of Rudham. He gives them a few seconds and continues, "I come to you with a forewarning and a plea for your assistance. There is an imminent threat of devastation that must never materialize. The frequencies of this place make it impossible for us to intervene." The women relax their shoulders, but their eyes look more nervous than they already were.

I move forward to Rudham. Why did he not take us to the RSA where the genodium is? What is he doing?

"The RSA has come into possession of a highly volatile energy substance known as genodium. We should never have let this happen." Rudham pauses. "But the past is immutable. The genodium is currently compressed into its inert state and contained in a canister. To activate it, your BSR's broadcasting technology is required as its catalyst. As long as the two do not come near each other, the genodium remains dormant. If the fission energy should get triggered, the entire structure of the universe—macro and microcosm, and all included in it—will cave in."

Rudham takes a quick glance at the android before continuing. "It will drastically affect you. And us. We know we are asking much of you without you knowing us or our mission. I bring you this so you can learn more of us and see the truth of my words."

Rudham plucks the teecha tooth from his neck chain. He punctures a hole in his forearm with his dagger, and lets his sutra flow a bit of its intelligence into the tooth. He holds it out. The one called Butters accepts it politely.

"Encoded in the tooth is our history, and that black bead lodged in it contains a molecule of genodium. I give it to you so that you may know of the danger it poses." Butters, gasps. "Don't worry, the molecule is locked in its inert state. But please, beware. It should not be removed from its casing.

"The future of all relies upon you. I wish I could explain more, but my time here is through." Rudham bows his head, taking leave of the two people in front of him. Their expressions are visibly strained.

The women still haven't said anything, nor have they introduced themselves. All we know is that they are from the BSR, and that is enough.

Rudham is dematerializing as he turns to me. "Abouja, I am ready."

As am I, Rudham. As am I.

I feel my nerves shiver again. *Mother Kaali, lead us. I have entrusted our journey to you, yet my hands tremble so. Take us home, Mother.*

I entwine our karawe together while Rudham joins me in the chant. *"Tavema Kaali rakhashavi, ahema punyasvi, tavema Kaali rakhashavi, ahema punyasvi, tavema..."*

"Mandha'ar."

Rudham calls out just as our karawe fuse together and I get whipped with his energy again. I barely get a look at him flinging his gold chain before we get dunked senseless into the void.

We fall hard on the ground. I smell the familiar anxiety and sweat of my family. Ishka has fallen back with the force of our arrival. Nayoma is applying Dharati on Khenpo Oharam's forehead. Sahaki is chanting as she had been before we left. Not a second has passed between our departure and arrival. All is as it was.

I fall prostrate on the ground. "Mother, you have saved us all. Take from me as you will."

I cannot stop weeping. They all let me be. Ishka picks me up. She is beaming and crying. We hug each other. Sahaki has completed the chant. She screams and falls on me. Nayoma looks overjoyed. I invite him to join in the huddle.

I look at Rudham and he at me. We both know what we have shared, and we both know what he saw when we were leaving. There are no words that can speak these things. It is just a knowing, a feeling. We hug, acknowledging the experience.

Then I bow to this madman proclaiming him Khenpo.

Leaving Impressions

"I am never happy leaving you, Mother, and this time I feel it intensely. O' Mother." Resting on her slab of grey stone, my palm can feel Mount Kelushi reciprocate. It seems like she is sucking my palm into her rock, pulling me in, trying to hold me back. She has never been possessive before, which makes me worry for her.

I am habituated to sitting on the mountain's outcrop of ashen grey that protrudes out conspicuously like a throne near her crest. The tribe assumes it's my perch, and I leave it at that. I sit here for hours on end. The quietude arouses the Universal Energy within me to connect with the energies of my surroundings, sometimes when the silence percolates deep into my skin I hear the cosmos speak.

Mother Kelushi is unlike herself today. We have left her abode often and returned to her embrace. Never before has she been sensitive to our leaving.

I get a semblance of Kelushi's expanse stretching just a bit short of the horizon. She is breathtaking. Dotted in her stretch are Nayoma the teacher and Sathr'yi the student. His hands are moving in the air making invisible scribbles.

Sathr'yi and Ikshavakra are one. Ten lunar cycles ago she had pledged herself to the tribe, and we to her. It is impossible to not know her as Ikshavakru, the tribe has also imbibed her values as its own. And yet, neither of us expected the other to comply. The threads are interlacing of their own accord.

Sathr'yi and Ishka share an affection for each other that only commanding warriors know of. They have exchanged and imbued one another's warrior ethics and techniques and imparted them to Ikshavakrus. Sathr'yi is still sloppy at catching a genuja, but she prepares it well. There is an aroma of soil in her roasting it.

Nayoma has introduced our scriptures to Sathr'yi. I particularly remember that month when she wouldn't leave sight of Nayoma, nagging him as a pesky child would. He had been expounding our texts on sub space and quantum energies to her. Sathr'yi respects the Ikshavakra code of Dharoma'kshama as we honor Karmashti—Prutharv's highest law of duty. These are not opposing ways, and they *will* integrate into one another. That time, however, is not now.

Kelushi has adopted Sathr'yi as her own and Sathr'yi has made a home of this grey wilderness. Is this why I hesitate to leave the mountain's abode?

Three days ago, Abouja suggested we, "…move to the plains for a while before the winds turn icy here." She is intuitive about Sathr'yi. "She misses the warmth and green of her land," she had said. I hadn't seen that. We should be moving anyways. We never stay as long. We may return, but we don't root ourselves anywhere. The attachment binds us.

At the end of Karpura's waning cycle, we will leave for the Shindai forests that lay at the tip of the island nation of Tey'chi.

Sathr'yi has completed her class for the day. She bows to Nayoma. She is walking towards me. Nayoma turns and looks at me, waving his hand.

"I have a strange feeling about leaving Mother Kelushi, Rudham," Sathr'yi says taking deep breaths in between. She is sitting next to me on the rocky slab after walking up that slope.

I clasp her palm. "I feel the same, Sathr'yi. I don't know why. Let the winds guide us." We sit here together for a long while, silently sharing the same foreboding as we watch Rahoul disappear into the horizon's belly.

We get up to join the others and I see an imprint of my palm on Kelushi's rock. Sathr'yi looks at me, and we walk down together, lost in our minds, saying nothing.

Change of Plans

Aucthumbar (October) 02, 2336
Khenpo Rudham

"*Dharomi chattari'aym sva karashute, dharomi chattari'aym sva karashute, dharomi...*" I can hear them chant below. The tribe is undoing our protective energy shields, preparing for us to leave Kelushi.

"Mother, what are you not telling me?" Even though my consciousness is in the subspace, alert to every breath of every stone and whisper of moving air, I hear the recitations echo within Kelushi's folds. But Mother is quiet, as are the grains of rock and the molecules in the air. So eerily quiet, like a sign before a storm.

No, there is something. I hear something. My karawe is tingling. *I hear you o' Vayuka. Carry me on your wings, O' Carrier of the Winds.*

I see it all. In the void between my skull and my eyes, I can see it all. Two figures in white thobes are handing over a metal container to Sheikhafa Saladuan. There are a few humans in lab coats behind the Sheikhafa.

"*Khenpo.*"

They are talking about taking their...

"*Khenpo.*"

The Sheikhafa mentions a date and they are lowering the container into a thick-walled box. They look triumphant.

"*Khenpo Rudham. Khenpo.*"

I have heard and seen enough. I descend back to material reality. The appalling revelation gets me unstable. I grip the edge of the rock tight, feeling the pressure in my knuckles. What is happening at Sahudaria was inevitable. It always was.

"Khenpo."

How foolish of me to assume otherwise.

"Khenpo."

Ishka is walking towards me.

"We are ready to leave, Khenpo?" A pause. Ishka's voice changes from annoyance to suspicion. "Khenpo?"

"We will not be leaving just yet." I pause to quieten my nervous trepidation. Ishka frowns. I continue. "Sahudaria has finally succeeded in building an agitator for the—"

Ishka cuts me off. *"No.* Why?"

"Sahudaria has finally established itself as a technocracy. Sahudarians are obsessed with success. This agitator took them thirteen years to build. A successful experiment needed to materialize. Consequences be damned. Such is the influence of their leader Sheikhafa Saladuan. He is not King Vibhasta."

Ishka's eyes tense up. There is panic in them.

"Sahudaria is waiting for the auspicious seventh hour of the sixth day of Karpura's cycle. Four days from now. We have one sunrise to work up a strategy."

Some of the Ikshavakrus are walking towards us.

I return my attention to Ishka and continue. "If there is to be war, I foresee a repetition of the Siaman bloodbath, only more savage. Sahudaria will stop at nothing. It is important to understand their fanatic madness, Ishka. I will meet with the Sheikhafa, but the probability of him acquiescing looks very thin."

The others have joined us.

I look back to Ishka. "I entrust Sathr'yi and you with preparing us for Armageddon."

Familiar Faces

Aucthumbar (October) 04, 2336
Khwari Sathr'yi

Life has weird mood swings. It thinks it is having fun with us, but the players experience it otherwise. I laugh at its flitting fancies, and sometimes I resist them. The latter is more painful and exhausting. It will eventually consume me.

"I entrust Sathr'yi and you with preparing us for Armageddon." Those were Rudham's words two days ago, minutes before we were to leave Mother Kelushi for the forests of Shindai. The five of us had stood stunned in front of him, each one of us processing the gravity of his words in our own way. Life had played its cards.

We needed help. I visited Prutharv as Ikshvakra's commanding warrior seeking assistance from its king. It felt unnatural, separating myself from the familiarity of my land and my people. I am holding on tight to the hug I received from its king and queen when I embraced them as a daughter and not as an army leader. I wish my visit would have been one of happy tidings.

King Ramakien offered his Omakshi dagger to me. It is an heirloom handed down Prutharv's royal lineage. Its ivory hilt bears the celestial disk Chayara, Prutharv's crest. The dagger bears the spirit of the supreme Achyutayam, the All Pervading and All Knowing. It is forbidden to be used in situations that do not call for it desperately. The blade only responds to those it deems as worthy.

"Try it," the king had said when I protested. The blade had materialized from its hilt when I called it forth. I saw a knowing pride in my father's eyes. I ported with his blessings and a tight knot in my chest. I can recall the weight of his palm on my head.

No matter how and what we strategize for the battle, it's the instinct that plays out in that nano second on the field. That moment is when years of training guide our actions intuitively.

We are camped in the Kuwasa (previous Kuwait) deserts that border Sahudaria's southern edge. Kuwasa has extended its assistance by offering its land where we have set up base. The Prutharvas are here with us. So are the armies from Siama, Harappa, Jakotri, Nepaula, Saiyon and Tey'chi. We offer our salutations to each other, acknowledging with gratitude the other's presence for this virtuous war.

We are awaiting Rudham and Ishka's return from the Sheikhafa's headquarters.

"Pacing will tense us up too, Khwari. Why don't you sit down?" Nayoma suggests.

"They have been gone for way too long." I complain before sitting down cross-legged beside Raha'rya. It is comforting to be with my childhood soul-sister even if circumstances are such, especially when circumstances are such.

"I miss you, Princess." The joy in her amber pupils reflects the elation in my heart.

"I miss you too Raha'rya. Sometimes, I see you in Abouja. Come. I want you to meet her." I pull her with me. "Abouja, this is my childhood friend Rahar."

"They're back." somebody cries out.

We swarm around the two Ikshavakrus that have returned from their meeting with Sheikhafa Saladuan. I am hoping against the inevitable, I know we all are. But those two beaten faces crush every iota of hope we carry.

Ishka shakes her head. "It would have surprised me should the conflict have settled amicably," she says. "Sheikhafa Saladuan has quite an unusual approach, doesn't he Khenpo? He questioned us, 'What is the point of any creation if not to serve the purpose it is created for? Everything in this universe has materialized to serve; you, me, four-legged creatures, even a single grain of sand. You seek to suppress it, let it wither away. You go against the laws of universal creation, my sentient friends.'"

Somebody whistles their breath out.

Rudham is frowning. "Yes, their philosophy is completely deranged. It is distorted. I was thrown aback by his argument. Still, it was imperative to propose an open discussion. To declare war, the law calls for every probability that can be exploited to prevent the bloody aftermath."

"My righteous brother," somebody taunts from behind us. "As always."

Rudham whips his head around violently. I am startled too.

No singular word comes to me that can aptly describe the emotion on Rudham's face. His eyes look stunned and watery. His mouth is agape, even as it seeks to smile. His forehead frowns as though it carries weighted questions and memories. His cheeks have wet tracks, and he is unable to voice his words.

He simply hugs his brother. They hold on to each other, letting the years gone by melt in the embrace.

"Ikshavakrus got one thing right when they made you Khenpo," Mandha'ar grins, and nods to Rudham in acknowledgement. "There is somebody else here with me," he discloses.

He fetches an Ikshavakru from the crowd. Nobody noticed her presence earlier. Abouja shrieks, her nails digging into her cheeks, "Khenpo Jova." Abouja runs and almost throws Khenpo Jova off balance with her affection.

"You *do* know how to make a dramatic entrance, brother-in-law." I jest.

"Khenpo Jova, Mandha'ar, this is my wife, Sathr'yi," Rudham introduces me to the two Ikshavakrus who, many decades ago, had vanished untraceably.

I bow and offer my salutations. "Amo Khenpo Jova. Amo brother Mandha'ar. I am honored to meet you." They reciprocate the same.

Khenpo Jova pulls me to her and hugs me. "There is only one Khenpo, and he is standing here before you. I am merely Jova. May every Ikshavakru acknowledge that," she announces, looking at Abouja as she completes her sentence.

Abouja smiles in approval. "Ahauma. Ahauma. Ahauma." The crowd is jubilant.

Our camp is getting chaotic, exhilaration pouring in all at once. "Where were you, Jova? Where were you Mandha'ar? How did you two meet?" Naturally, everyone assembled wants a glimpse of this never-could-be-perceived-of scene.

Jova speaks. "I am going to cut this really short. My appearance has distracted all of you. Where and how of what was, has little bearing on what is to come, and what we are here for." The crowd quiets.

She continues, "The day before I had apparently disappeared, I was guided to a future vision of Khenpo Oharam presenting the genodium canister to the RSA. I traveled forward to the time of that disastrous occurrence." Rudham let out a gasp. "Yes, Khenpo Rudham. I traveled over a hundred years into the future. This is where I met Mandha'ar. I saw you and Abouja too. You made me proud that day, Abouja. Traveling through time is precarious enough for a solo traveler, and you brought Khenpo with you. You took a bold risk, girl. It was wise of you both to talk to Maria and Butters of the BSR. Unbeknownst to the RSA, Mandha'ar and I have watched over that tube of genodium over the last decade, manipulating situations to prevent it from being removed from its place of custody. I was unable to intervene when the Sahudarians collected the canister. Mandha'ar could, but it would have been unwise to reveal ourselves."

"We have a war to fight people." Mandha'ar abruptly arouses the warriors.

"Ahauma. Ahauma. Ahauma," we respond to him.

"We battle to protect all Creation. We battle for Righteousness." He is provoking us.

"Ahauma. Ahauma. Ahauma," we retaliate.

"This is the Righteous War. May the Heavens protect us as we battle to protect them." Mandha'ar is pushing us off the edge now.

"Ahauma. Ahauma. *Ahauma*." We are screaming wildly.

"Khenpo Rudham. Lead us to our divine fate."

"*Yaaaarhh.*" My feet feel the ground vibrate with the deafening chorus.

Rudham raises his arms to quieten the agitated warriors. He smiles. "We will move in the time before Rahoul awakens. Ishka and Sathr'yi will lead…"

There is a warm feeling in my heart. I know the Grand Universe has predestined our victory. Why else would it have sent unexpected goodness along our way?

The Final War

Aucthumbar (October) 05, 2336
Khenpo Rudham

We meet the Sahudarians at Jeyasha, a sprawling barren land of rock with a thick layer of sand, that lay between our Kuwasa base and Sahudaria's capital city Raizah. The sand will impede our movements and slow us down. Sahudaria will score here.

As soon as Rahoul leaked its first light, we awakened the skies with our war cries, both sides ruthlessly bellowing chants of victory and righteousness. Ironically, it is the differing interpretation of the latter that has seeded this war.

"*Ahauma. Ahauma. Ahauma.*" Victory. Victory. Victory.

"*Sathya'artha asate.*" I call out. *May the righteous truth prevail.*

"*Ahauma. Ahauma. Ahauma.*"

"*Dharoma asate.*" Jova and Ishka incite the troops with their frenzied cry. *For the supreme law of Creation.*

"*Ahauma. Ahauma. Ahauma.*"

"*Karmasa asate.*" Sathr'yi roars. *For the call of supreme duty.*

"*Ahauma. Ahauma. Ahauma.*"

"*Bhumartha. Aasakartha. Manusaartha.*" For the land. For the skies. For its people.

"*Ahauma. Ahauma. Ahauma.*"

The Sahudarians are bellowing their call with maddening intent. They are instigating us and we are falling prey. "*Yaaaaarrrhhh.*"

Our battle strategy is to tear them apart. Their core heavyweight team numbers as many as the entire Ikshavakra troop. Together, their pressure can be tremendously brutal and fatal. Our advantage is, we have three core teams with peculiar battle strengths innate to each of the three. We will dilute the central Sahudarian structure by luring their attention to all three simultaneously. *O' Ishraha, you must make this work.*

Sathr'yi is heading the Prutharvas in their aerial and terrestrial pods. Jova and Ishka lead the Ikshavakrus and the Siamans on foot. Mandha'ar and I are on foot too, commanding our allies. When there is sufficient engagement and chaos, I will lead a small unit of Ikshavakra warriors to the Sheikhafa's headquarters. We must seize that deathly capsule. *Ishraha. Watch our backs. This war is for you.*

This foot deep sand is crippling our movements. We are losing precious time and ground.

"Garay'an. We need foothold. *Now.*" I hear Jova shriek her command. There is a terrific storm of sand dust arising, lethal tornadoes caused by iridescent hands are sucking tons of grains into their belly. We are all blinded, Sahudarians too. There are random movements of assault and now nothing. The Mother of Time, Kaali, has slowed down.

There is faint visibility now. "*Hraaaaagh.*" Mandha'ar thrusts ahead, half blind, slashing all that lay in his path. I clear the dust cover for our unit of allied troops, and we plunge ahead with Mandha'ar. The Tey'chiyans are indomitable tracers, master practitioners of parkour. They overtake us with graceful agility and plunge their laser spears into their victims, deftly escaping any injury to themselves, not unlike ruthless blood sucking insects that cannot be swatted. The Harappans are spitting fire with their armors and weaponry conceived in their labs. They materialize when called upon. Nepaula has borne the most skilled archers. Their phaser arrows are programmed to connect with the intended target.

The sand cover has finally lifted, and we are storming on hard ground. The field is overcharged with vulgar aggression. I can hear Ishka's taunts for victory. The Ikshavakrus have moved ahead of us. The skies are exploding with sharp light beams webbing into each other, hitting and missing their intended targets. The Prutharvas are retaliating with fury. I look up for a split second. Sathr'yi is standing on her airborne pod, using her phantom lariat to lasso the opponents in.

Shit. She must've run out of ammunition. *Vayuka. Steady her vehicle with your winds.* I cannot linger on her safety any longer. I must entrust it to the Prutharvas. I refocus.

I feel a whoop inside me. We have ripped apart and maimed our opponent's unified strength. The Sahudarians are flapping wildly to stay afloat. I slip back heading towards the Ikshavakra team, ready to stealthily infiltrate the headquarters.

"Ishka. Where are the retrievers? We have to go." I'm getting a little hysterical.

"They left with Khwari, Khenpo." Ishka replies frantically, comprehending what has just happened.

"Who is with her, Ishka?"

"All seven, just as it was decided. Nayoma, Abouja, Garay'an, Hukara'an, Sahaki, Agna'hashi and Para."

"She won't be able to do this. What is she thinking?"

"Khenpo, Khwari was blabbering something about Sange—" Ishka is still speaking as I port myself to the Sahudarian headquarters. *Please Deva. It can't be what I heard.*

There she is, in that patch of brilliant green. "Get out of there, Sathr'yi. What are you doing?" I scream, pleading helplessly with every ounce of strength in my lungs and gut.

Sathr'yi has the canister in her lap. She looks at me with pride, her eyes are streaming. And as a wounded lion she roars, *"Karmasa asate."* She plunges a dagger from her cummerbund into the heart of the capsule and doubles up over it.

Sathr'yi. This can't be happening. *Sathr'yi. No, no, no. What did you do.* Her body is writhing. *Ishraha.* I think I see a flash of a hand in the flames. *Sathr'yi.* I put my own hands into the blaze. Maybe I can pull her out. I can't feel her.

"I can't feel her Abouja." There are just freezing flames licking my hands.

Somebody's hands remove mine from the fire.

"We cannot douse it, Khenpo," somebody says. "It has to cool down of its own accord."

I withdraw, numb and senseless. I feel myself crumple into nothingness. I sit here by the toxic flames, with my Sathr'yi.

Even righteous wars cannot be forgiven.

Karmashti

Aucthumbar (October) 05, 2336
Khwari Sathr'yi

The Prutharvas are holding up valiantly without me, now is when I should get to the genodium capsule. There will never be another time, not for me. And it is only I who can annihilate it.

Sange, the pristine white sandstone from my motherland of Prutharv has borne the genodium. Only the hand that carries Prutharv soil in its blood can extinguish the demonic energy with a weapon hewn by Prutharv's lineage. Prutharv has to repay the debt. This is Dharoma'kshama. And I have been placed here to repay it. This is my Karmashti, my sacred call of Supreme Duty.

I need that Ikshavakra team of seven energy bearers with me. They need to contain the explosion if there be any, and should it get uncontrollable.

I tear through the pandemonium to the Ikshavakra troops, pushing everybody, I don't care who, out of my way. I have to speak with Ishka. She is in the front line of her battalion.

"Where is the squad assigned for the genodium?"

Ishka is occupied with the action in front of her. "Huh? Oh. Khwari? They are at the very end of this unit, awaiting Rudham's signal."

"I am taking them with me."

"But Khenpo was..." She looks at me trying hard to shift her attention. "Why are you taking them?"

"It has to be me, Ishka. I am bound to it by Sange. Tell Rudham." I doubt she comprehends what I just said, and it matters not.

The seven Ikshavakrus bearing seven energies are reluctant to accompany me. Nayoma protests, "Khwari, we don't doubt your aggression, but dealing with the vicious vial should be left to Khenpo Rudham."

"I don't have time to explain. Understand what I'm saying and trust me. Only a Prutharva can completely destroy it. All Khenpo Rudham can do is suppress it, prolonging its life. Wars like this will replay themselves over and over again." I give them a second to let it sink in. "Are you all with me?"

"Lead the way Khwari," they acquiesce unanimously.

"We need to dismantle the security guarding the vial. The Sheikhafa and his aides will obviously be an active part of the protective cover. In fact, it is imperative to bring the crown prince down. They would not expect us to make an appearance this way, but we never know. I will get to the capsule. All good?" Seven nods.

We port right into enemy base.

The Sahudarians are completely unprepared for our arrival, but their reflexes are intuitively sharp. They retaliate mercilessly.

Stealth and timing are vital for us. I have to slip out of the melee. It wasn't difficult to locate the energy capsule. It sits unprotected now— encased in glass, heinously displayed like a museum exhibit—but I can't get at it. *Damn this.* It isn't glass.

"Hukara'an. I could use your help here."

He places both palms on the cube, and it shatters after ten breaths. "Good luck Khwari." He wishes me and disappears back to the warring group.

I step outside the building structure and sit with the canister in my lap. I touch manicured grass around me and evoke my purpose for strength.

O' Deva Achyutayam, Bearer of the Chayara. Hold thy child in thy embrace. I fear the pain. Carry me through. Dear Prutharv, you are redeemed of your sin. May you prosper."

Rudham appears at a distance to my right. He is running wildly towards me, his hand is outstretched pleading with me to give up.

This Sathr'yi has been made complete by you, Rudham. I look at him. I draw out the Omakshi dagger throttling my rising hesitation and draw out every tiny ounce of resolve within me, "*Karmasa asate.*" I stab the canister.

I bend over it instinctively, assuming my body will contain the detonation. I feel no pain, just a sweet sleep that engulfs me. I am drifting through light beams in transcendental hues. A tune drones in the background, dulling my senses. I want to surrender to this peace.

I let go.

Ackch. I am gasping. Something has yanked me out of my holy state. I can't breathe. I need air. I need to breathe. I am sucked tight into a vortex. *Let go of me.* I collapse on hard ground and vomit.

I see familiar eyes, but they are fading.

No. Stay with me.

I feel excruciating pain, but I am comforted.

I am sinking into the ground.

I surrender.

The Close

Aucthumbar (October) 05, 2336
Khenpo Rudham

The flames have cooled, leaving black and gray smoldering residue. My heart yearns for Mother Kelushi. Her terrain was tinted similar, but it carried Sathr'yi's laughter. A warm wind wafts by gently scattering the ashen dust around and over me. Rahoul is also leaving me for the day, but not before emblazoning everything in rich coppery tones. He had often blessed Sathr'yi and me before His descent down Kelushi's horizon.

There is a badly charred hilt in the debris with a faint circle etched on it. There are shards of glass, but I cannot see Sathr'yi anywhere.

The retriever troops had laid to death the inhabitants of the Sahudarian base, including the Sheikhafa. The genodium was destroyed. War has ended.

The small unit stayed with me till embers started cooling. Ishka, Jova, Rahar'ya and some others were here too, and then returned to join the troops. I rummage through the remnants searching for Sathr'yi. There must be something. *Why didn't you leave me anything?*

Dusk falls. I don't intend to return to camp anytime soon. I know why she did this. Why didn't you tell me? We could have brought this down together. You would still have been here.

But these are presumptions I make, assuming what could be by denying what is. I respect and honor you, my love. I worship your sacrifice.

I stretch myself on the rubble, prostrating before the site of her last presence.

I see it. Barely a twinkle reflecting the moonlight.

Sathr'yi's lapis pendant, once a glorious blue, lies scorched black in the soft ashes. The tear-drop jewel cracked down its center, and a tiny bit has been chewed off. I clench it in my palm, gently, lest it should crumble away. I will not besmirch your valor with my weakness, o' valiant Sathr'yi.

I press the blackened stone between my brows. It feels painfully cold as it sinks into my skin. Its rough surface is part of my forehead now, making a tear-drop mark.

I port back to the troops waiting at the battlefield.

These scents of soiled blood and ash are not new, but every battle scars a distinct impression. There have not been many fatalities at our end, but there is deadened gloom hanging overhead. Those proficient at Araveca healing are tending to the injured with make-shift resources. The Sahudarians will pick up their own pieces.

I walk up to a small cluster of Ikshavakrus sitting in a circle. Mandha'ar is the first to look at me. They halt their talk abruptly as soon as they realize my presence. I feel awkward.

"Jova, I entrust the tribe to you," I say. "You will now be Khenpo."

"What?" Jova and several others stand up.

"I have to restructure my entire being. I lost myself in that pyre with Sathr'yi." I pause, taking control of my emotions. "I will return. Where else would I be? But for now, I take leave of you."

I look at Mandha'ar. "I hope you will be with the tribe?"

He looks at me and nods. "After all, 'where else would I be?'" he jests. "And brother—" He tugs at the gold string around his neck. "—thank you for this." He pulls me into his embrace.

I walk to every warrior here on the battlefield, conveying my salutations and gratitude to them. They had fearlessly offered themselves to this holy battle.

Rahoul is awakening, hinting at my departure. I can never truly leave, not yet. Not until the day my servitude ends.

Not until the supreme Ishraha blesses me so.

Appendix

Lands, Tribes and People
- *Ikshavakra*
- Abouja
- Aruva'ya: *Rudham's father*
- Dyarah Garay'an Hukara'an
- Ishka: *commanding general Khenpo* Jova

- Mandha'ar: Khenpo Rudham's twin brother
- *Khenpo* Nada'yn Nayoma
- *Khenpo* Oharam
- *Khenpo* Rudham
- *Khwari* Sathr'yi: *wife to Khenpo Rudham and Prutharv's princess*
- Sahaki
- Yasiyaka: *Rudham's mother*
- *Jakotri:*
- Goyyir
- *Nepaula*
- *Prutharv:*
- Raha'rya
- *King* Ramakien: *princess Sathr'yi's father*
- Sumakya
- *Princess* Sathr'yi
- *Queen* Thary'ni: *princess Sathr'yi's mother*
- *Ruskia*
- *Siama:*
- *King* Vibhasta Ashafa
- *Sahudaria:*
- Sheikhafa Saladuan
- *Tey'chi*
- *RSA:* Republican States of America
- *BSR:* Bear and Salmon Republic

Gods of Ikshavakra

- **Ishraha:** *supreme Source or God of all universes.*
- **Ishawi:** *supreme Energy that runs through all that is created—living and inanimate.*
- **Rahoul:** *spirit of the sun.*
- **Karpura:** *spirit of the moon.*
- **Vayuka:** *spirit of ether, wind and air.*
- **Abja:** *spirit of water.*
- **Kaali:** *deity of time.*
- **Maati:** *spirit of soil.*

- **Suvaasi:** *breath spirit, life energy.*

Gods of Prutharv
- **Achyutayam:** *supreme Creator of all universes, equates to Ishraha of the Ikshavakrus.*
- **Deva:** *God.*

Terminology
- **Ahauma:** *a call to victory.*
- **Amo:** *a greeting or hello.*
- **Araveca:** *a science of healing with medicinal herbs.*
- **Bedhi:** *a raw, natural cigarette.*
- **Chayara:** *the royal crest of Prutharv.*
- **Dharati:** *a mixture of various soils from lands Ikshavakrus have ever walked on. It carries memories of those lands and thereby also ancient energies and blessings.*
- **Dharoma'kshama:** *the Ikshavakra law of balance. (See prologue)*
- **Genuja: a** *large fish.*
- **Ikshavakra:** *a nomadic tribe of cyboid (cyborg +humanoid) shamans. It is a warrior tribe whose human ancestors hailed from the olden island of Kaysankha in early southern Asia.*
- **Ikshavakru:** *a member of the Ikshavakra tribe.*
- **Karmashti:** *Prutharv's law of highest duty, a soul's highest purpose.*
- **Karawe:** *a roundish, black birthmark on every Ikshvakru. It is imprinted on a newborn at a Karipa ceremony. A karawe connects an Ikshavakru to the singular Source of universal energy.*
- **Khenpo:** *(m or f or n) leader of Ikshavakra tribe.*
- **Khwari:** *a wife to Khenpo.*
- **Khwara:** *a husband to Khenpo.*
- **Makhasha:** *a guru or mentor.*
- **Metaport or metatravel:** *the act of traveling from one place to another through subspace.*
- **Particle Simulator:** *a seven meter long tunnel of seranium*

metal coated with a magnetic field. Artificial energy is condensed and fed into it to simulate natural energy sources. Created in the Siaman labs, its purpose is to replenish depleted natural energy in the environment.

- **Sange:** *a white sandstone indigenous to the land of Prutharv. The rock is coveted by every land, for its rare physical and chemical characteristics.*
- **Shikasha:** *a student.*
- **Subspace:** *a dimension above the physical realm where travel is faster than the speed of light.*
- **Sutras:** *raised cord-like concentric patterns on every Ikshavakru's skin. Like fingerprints, sutras are unique to every Ikshavakru. They carry genetic memory.*
- **Tambacu:** *tobacco.*
- **Teecha:** *a saber tooth.*
- **Yagusa:** *an extensive purification and coronation ceremony- one of the highest rites performed.*

The Bear and Salmon Republic
by CD Damitio

Chapter 1

Charles Actor, a rancher from Presidio, Texas, was on a spaceship with a yeti, an android, and a bunch of surfer dude Space Marines. To say that it was a scenario he never would have imagined was an understatement. Sure, the surfer dudes didn't call themselves that. They were BSR Marines, but their intonation, their shoulder length hair, and their repeated use of the word, "Duuuuuuude..." made it impossible for Charles to label them as anything else. Surfer dude Space Marines were the most believable part of all of this when it came down to it. That alone said something.

Charles looked around the recreational lounge they were all traveling in on the long slow journey to Big Bear Lake, California political capital of the Bear and Salmon Republic.

It was a great step up from air travel of his time. Gone were the rows of sardine can seats, shoulder belts for crash theater, and cattle car dynamics of cramming as many people into the craft as possible. Yes, this was a military craft, but it was striking that it more resembled a hotel lobby than anything else. Comfy couches, desks and workspaces, even a central kitchen. The Marines (Charles was trying really hard to train himself to call them such) lounged around like college students in a commons. Several of them were playing boardgames with no concern that the pieces might be scattered by turbulence. A few of them were working out in the gym section of the lounge. With them was Frank, the yeti. Frank was lifting immense amounts of weight while the gathered Marines placed bets as to whether he could, how long he might hold it, or how many reps he could do. It had almost reached the point where none would bet against him, mainly because there probably weren't enough weights on the ship to actually strain him. Frank fit right in with the Marines and a listener would have easily mistaken him for one of them as he quickly adopted "dude-speak" and even some of the BSR slang and intonations. But of course, as soon as the listener saw him, that illusion would be shattered. Frank was over ten feet tall and covered in long shaggy white fur.

The Yeti were one of the many surprises Charles had encountered after he had been unexplainably transported to this world three hundred years in his future. He had landed in the Texican Nation, pursued by the authorities, and with the help of new friends had escaped into the heart of "the Blizzard" a centuries long perpetual storm in the Rocky Mountains. There he had been captured by the Yeti. Then, with the help of his girlfriend Maria (it was amazing how quickly he'd started to think of her that way), he had managed to escape, liberate the Yeti from their overlord/creator, and was now on a mission to build diplomatic ties between the Texican Nation, Yeti Mountain, and the Bear and Salmon Republic: the BSR.

Charles looked to where Maria was sprawled out on a couch watching an episode of *Friends*, her favorite entertainment from all of time. He shook his head, smiling amusedly. Maria was actually an acronym. M.A.R.I.A stood for *Marveloso Androida Rapido Investigación Asistante,* but he couldn't even force himself to think of her as an acronym. It was hard enough to think of her as an android. She was the womanliest woman he had ever met, and so much more. As Maria sat there laughing at Phoebe's rendition of "Smelly Cat," she looked like anything but an android built by the same evil cyborg that had created the yeti. She was Maria to him and to everyone else who came to know her. That was that.

At one point in their brief but action-packed relationship, he'd confessed to her that he didn't know the difference between an android and a cyborg. She'd begun to explain things in technical jargon that had quickly gone over his head. Knowing about her love of *Friends* he had stopped her and said, "Explain it like you are explaining it to Phoebe…"

Maria laughed. "Phoebe is a lot smarter than people give her credit for but I get you. Okay, androids and cyborgs. So, an android is like a robot that is built to look and act like a human. They're like, super-advanced machines that can do all sorts of human-like things. But a cyborg is different. A cyborg is like a real live human being, but with some robotic parts. Ya know? It's like they're part human, part robot. Kind of like how Ross is part nerd, part cool guy.

"An android, for example, would be like Data from Star Trek, an artificial being designed to look and act like a human, while a cyborg would be like Robocop, it's a human being with robotic enhancements. So, you could say that an android is a robot trying to be human, while a cyborg is a human that's trying to be a robot. It's like the difference between Rachel trying to make the perfect pastry, and Joey trying to make a sandwich, they are both trying to do something but with a different approach."

Charles looked at her closely. There were times it was so hard to believe that she was the most advanced person to ever exist. She was so good at everything she did, even dumbing herself down and downplaying her abilities.

"Are you trying to be human?" he asked her. The idea was disturbing to him for reasons that he couldn't quite understand.

She laughed merrily. "Oh, no way. I said that to illustrate the difference. I'm super-happy not being human. Don't get me wrong. You guys are really unique, and I'm glad that I'm a part of you and you are a part of me, but I'd never want to be one of you."

She scooted in closer to him. Her body was the perfect temperature, the perfect softness, the perfect human. Again, Charles couldn't think of her as anything other than a woman; the woman he'd fallen in love with.

She looked up into his eyes. "All I ever wanted was to fall in love, and now I have you. I think I've managed to perfectly dose the right compounds into my neo-cortex via my proto-enzyme production cells to show me just how wonderful love really is."

"You must say that to all the humans," Charles joked.

For a split-second Maria looked confused but then she got the joke. She cracked a quirky half- smile "Promise me you'll never call me a cyborg," she said to him "I don't think I could bear to be thrown into the same category as that fucker E. Longmunsk. He was so... messy."

E. Longmunsk, the cyborg who had created the Yeti and Maria's more-or-less eternal batteries, had been packaged in light and sent on a long, long journey in a photon packet. His ambition of making himself into a God had been foiled by Maria, the Yeti, and Charles. E. Longmunsk had taken over the body, mind, and life of his creator, the billionaire Elon Musk from Charles' time. They were fairly certain that he had engineered the events that had jumped Charles and other time travelers from the past to this present. What they didn't understand was why. Charles couldn't help feeling at least a moment of gratitude to E. Longmunsk, but the memory of him filling the sky with light as he announced his ascendency to godhood was still too recent to not invoke a feeling of combined nausea and horror.

Charles was still trying to get his head around this world and the events that had brought it into being. It was a completely new world for him, and things didn't work at all in the ways that his world had. North America was divided into several nations that didn't really equate to the North America of his time, but the correlation of North American countries was helpful in his mind.

The USA of his time had evolved into a theological dictatorship called the Republican States of America (RSA). Made up of the middle and southern states of the former USA along with the middle of Canada. It sounded like a nasty place, but of course, that might all be propaganda. He was new here and still trying to work out the details. Stretching from Florida north to New Jersey before veering up across the plains states and all the way through Ontario and Alberta. It extended west all the way to the Canadian Rockies, the Cascade Mountains, and the Sierra Nevada.

The Mexico of his time had been replaced with the Texican Nation which had absorbed Texas, Oklahoma and most of the 'southwest' states as well as Mexico and Central America. The Texican Nation was where he had "landed" when he was somehow pulled through time. He would have liked to have explored it further, but unfortunately, he had been forced to flee when the authorities learned of his existence.

The eastern part of twenty-first century Canada had been replaced with the Maritime Alliance. Made up of the New England parts of the US combined with the regions around the northeastern parts of the Great Lakes and Maritime provinces of Canada. He'd heard about a rebellious region called the Wolverine Isles but hadn't yet had the chance to delve into it in any detail.

Right now, Charles was en route to the place that most fascinated him: The Bear and Salmon Republic. The BSR was a powerful nation that stretched from Alaska all the way down the West Coast of North America. It encompassed several hundred miles inland from the Pacific Ocean, including the former states and territories of Alaska, British Columbia, Washington, Oregon, California, and the entire Baja California peninsula.

It was a golden nation in every sense that one could think of such things. Rich in resources, entertainment, agriculture, access, aerospace, technology, and much more. As he looked at Maria still mindlessly (but not really) watching Friends—he was reminded that the BSR was still an entertainment complex as well. He was looking forward to discovering how entertainment had changed—something he had not yet had a chance to do.

Further west in the Pacific, the Mutual Nation of Hawaii, and the Pacific Mutual Nations were fairly mysterious to him so far, but having formerly been an American who never went to Hawaii—was he still an American now that his nation didn't exist?—his main interest had been in what had happened to the mainland portion of his former country. Given a choice, he wasn't sure where he would have gone—most likely into the RSA since it was where most of his family had lived—but then, the RSA sounded like a sort of hell on earth—so maybe not. The situation he'd fallen into had been chaotic, but now wasn't an unpleasant one. He was traveling to California on a comfortable spaceship with his android girlfriend and his yeti friend.

He corrected himself. Technically it wasn't a spaceship but a futuristic troop transport named the *Coho*. The captain of the ship, Commander Jane Smiley had repeatedly corrected him on this front while they prepped for the journey at Yeti Mountain. She was one of those hard-as-nails officers that woke up and did a hundred pushups before starting her workout. She and Charles had become friendly right away. Smiley didn't have a bit of femininity about her and despite her name, it was likely she hadn't actually smiled in her entire life. Her brittle looking parchment skin carried wrinkles like battle scars. There was no way to even start to guess how old she was—but there was no doubt that she had lived harder, longer, and faster than anyone who met her.

Whip smart and no nonsense. She was the kind of person that would have made a great Texas neighbor. Steady, dependable, predictable, and wouldn't need a fence between properties because she knew right where the line ran and wouldn't cross it unless she was invited to—or let you.

Smiley had lectured him about calling the *Coho* a spaceship—but he couldn't help it. It looked like a spaceship, and Charles freely admitted to himself, "traveling on a spaceship with his android girlfriend and a yeti," was a description he enjoyed repeating, even if it wasn't completely accurate.

If the ship hadn't been damaged, the trip from Yeti Mountain to the BSR would have taken less than an hour. The fuel that made that sort of speed possible had evaporated with a laser strike during the battle of Yeti Mountain. That was the reason the ship and her occupants had been forced to stay behind when everyone else left. Despite the abundant resources and technical knowledge available at Yeti Mountain, Commander Smiley wouldn't share any details about the fuel, so they were left with a "spaceship" that moved slower than a farm tractor. They could have driven to the BSR faster, but since there were no roads from Yeti Mountain, that wasn't an option. Plus, Smiley wasn't going to leave her ship in the hands of the Yeti. Things could have been much worse because while the trip was slow, it was comfortable.

There were other things Smiley was tight-lipped about. She was an old school officer that believed in the adage of "loose lips sink ships" and she was a fierce BSR patriot. She had become as friendly with Charles as people like her were likely to get, but she wasn't going to give him anything that might resemble intel capable of weakening her nation's position in any way.

Her voice boomed through the intercom system, "We have successfully traversed over the Sin City freezone and are back in BSR controlled territory. Command has ordered us to proceed to Big Bear Field for repairs and upgrades to the *Coho*. ETA is one hour and forty-five minutes."

Charles decided to spend at least some of that time watching *Friends* with Maria. He put his arm around her. She snuggled into him as if she had been waiting. How had he gotten this lucky?

Chapter 2

As the *Coho* descended to a perfect landing, Charles marveled at the landscape around him. He'd never heard of Big Bear, but it looked like a futuristic utopia. Huge mountains with glacial tops surrounding a flat valley dominated by a sapphire blue lake. It looked more like Switzerland than California, but then you saw the tall, rounded skyscrapers of the city and the giant igloo like domes that contained perfect climate controlled apartment complexes.

"Is Big Bear a new city?" he asked Maria. She had been designed to be the perfect research assistant, but of course had become much more, largely through researching and experimenting to improve herself. As such, she never minded his streams of questions. Actually, she enjoyed them.

"Big Bear is the political capital of the Bear and Salmon Republic. It is a large city in the San Bernardino Mountains of the California province. It was founded by a gold hunter named William Holcomb around 1860 and went through the boom and bust of the gold period before settling in to become a four-season resort during the twentieth and twenty-first centuries. When California and the other states seceded from the USA in 2031, Big Bear grew in importance. It's ring of high mountains and dense ore and basalt geologic structure were ideal for placement of a protected capital and operations base for the BSR's high-tech defensive capabilities."

Charles interrupted her. "Like NORAD?"

"Yes," Maria continued. "While the details have been largely kept secret, the Texican intelligence service has thought that there are deep underground complexes mined beneath the city of Big Bear. In addition, there are generally thought to be impenetrable laser air defense systems on the surrounding mountains. Big Bear is a fortress, but still retains much of the charm of the twentieth century resort. There are strict entry and exit protocols, but it is still a place where the rich and famous like to be seen playing."

Commander Smiley approached them now. As usual, she wasn't smiling, but her demeanor was friendly none-the-less.

"I wanted to brief your team on a few things before we disembark," she said. Charles motioned to Frank, and the yeti came over to where they were seated. He threw a crisp salute at Commander Smiley, and Charles would almost have sworn that he saw the corners of her mouth twitch as if they wanted to smile before she regained her stern demeanor. Frank's big toothy grin wasn't contained at all. Charles once again noted that the yeti had all the love appeal of big friendly dogs.

This wasn't belittling to them. They were strong, smart, and loyal. They were so good-natured and friendly that it seemed impossible they had been created by E. Longmunsk.

"Reporting for duty, Commander," Frank said.

"As you were—" Commander Smiley had almost called him "marine" but corrected herself on the fly. "—Ambassador." It was what he was: an ambassador from a new nation and a new species. The first ambassador from the Yeti people.

Frank threw himself on a huge sofa, completely filling it, but somehow looking like a happy teenager joining friends in their living room.

"There are some issues in the BSR that we generally don't like to share," Smiley started. "First of all, I want you to understand that everything is recorded. All of your private conversations, your time in the bathroom, everything. It has been the same on this ship. Nothing is private in the BSR, especially in Big Bear."

Charles realized that they had said things they definitely should not have. Nothing overtly dangerous, but little things like the fact that Maria had access to all data from the Texican Intelligence agencies—at least, everything until a few weeks ago. Smiley must have seen the alarm on his face.

"I don't want you to worry. Somehow, all of the recordings and data from this ship will be mysteriously erased about two minutes after we have this conversation."

Charles had suspected she was a friend, but now he knew it.

"The thing is," Smiley said to them, "that's all I can control. Once this conversation is done, you are on your own in terms of privacy. I recommend that you take some precautions. The other thing you need to know is that there are factions within the BSR that have very different agendas. The military is generally neutral in these things, but there have been some indications that things are changing in that regard."

"Can you give us more details?" Charles asked.

"Not much, but here is a general run-down. Van-Wood—that's Vancouver and Hollywood—are big power players in the BSR. They represent the needs of our entertainment-control-complex. The BSR has mastered using entertainment as a control system that drives economic and policy decisions. Van-Wood is where many of the top decisions are made about the future of our economy and the way that we interact with the other nations of the world. The important thing to know is that this faction of our government wants to restore ties with the RSA because the RSA markets have been largely untapped by modern entertainment. They see a huge potential for profits and economic expansion."

"That doesn't sound terrible," Charles said.

Smiley nodded. "On the surface it isn't, but the cost to our way of life is more than I think we should pay. A big part of such an agreement happening would be normalizing relations with the RSA—something that will only happen if we agree to not dispute their revisionist history—allow them access to our citizenry through their own entertainment and programming, and share some of our entertainment tech—the control system stuff—with them. Such a situation is unthinkable. The RSA would be far more empowered by such a deal than we would, but the monetary rewards are so big that Vancouver and Hollywood are leaning heavily in favor of it.

"Okay, that does sound bad," Charles said, noting that she had very effectively shown how much the negative outweighed the positive.

"A big part of the issue is that our focus on off-world and in-world development has ended up being far more expensive than anyone anticipated. San Francisco and Seattle—SF&S—have gone way over budget with defensive off-world and in-world projects. So, there really is a good argument to expand our entertainment markets, but not when the cost is so high."

"What is in-world development?" Maria asked. Charles had assumed it was on-world, but her question made him realize they were very different things

"It's a good thing our recordings are going to be deleted," Smiley said. "I didn't mean to mention that. One of the most closely guarded secrets in the BSR is that we've been excavating the planet on a scale the world has never known. It started with an idea to dig down to the continental plates to relieve the pressure on fault lines like the San Andreas, but what we realized was that there is a whole world down there. We've been creating the infrastructure for colonization deep under the surface for nearly fifty years and it's gotten expensive."

"So, this is a budget issue," Charles said. "One side wants to continue work that doesn't pay for itself, and the other side wants to make a bad alliance to pay for it?"

"Sort of," Smiley replied with a bigger grimace. "The suspicion in military intelligence circles is that the RSA has already infiltrated the power structure of Van-Wood. SF&S, which is much more closely aligned with the military, is operating on this assumption. So, there already exists a schism in our government with one side demanding we move full speed ahead to align with the RSA in order to cover our expenses, and the other side urging caution and claiming that in-world farming and off-world mining will repay the deficits they are now incurring in less than a decade."

"Where does Big Bear stand? It's the political capitol, right?" It was Frank that asked this. It was sometimes hard to remember that he was a very intelligent being in a friendly shaggy dog yeti body.

"The government still stands with SF&S, but there have been signs that is changing. I hope you believe me when I tell you that if that changes, it will be a huge disaster for everyone. Not just the BSR, but the entire world. The RSA stands to gain far more than anyone can understand, and if the off-world and in-world initiatives stop, we all stand to lose a lot."

"Who should we trust? Are there people you know you can count on?" Maria asked the question this time.

Smiley shook her head. "Even in the time we were gone, the situation has probably evolved so much that I can't say for certain that anyone is one-hundred-percent reliable. I'll put some feelers out and will let you know what I can, but for the moment, I just wanted you to know that you should tread very carefully and don't assume that anyone is really who they represent themselves as. "

It was not an ideal way to start a diplomatic mission.

"I've got to go deal with the bureaucracy of returning home with a ship that was presumed lost and a very complicated passenger manifest," Smiley said. "I'll reach out when I can."

Frank jumped to his feet when she stood up and threw another smart salute at her. Charles wondered if she knew he was a time traveler and Maria was an android. It wasn't something they had advertised, but her comment about surveillance made him think it was likely. Though she might have been referring to Frank; that was enough complication.

"You really should have been a Marine," Commander Smiley said, returning the salute before she walked away. It really looked like her face wanted to smile but simply wasn't able to.

Frank's grin was even bigger than it normally was.

Chapter 3

In hindsight, Charles realized that it had been foolish to think that their arrival in the BSR would be quiet or understated in any way. Somehow, he had allowed himself to think that they would be met by a dignified delegation of politicians and then led away to quiet talks with the leaders before being offered the chance to enjoy a mini vacation in California. What he'd forgotten was that the BSR was the world's first "mediacracy," where at least half of the representative power of the government was carried by those who entertained.

Thankfully, Commander Smiley understood her country better than he did. The BSR Marines, now in smart uniforms and looking far less dude-ish than they had before, jumped to their assigned duties. A full detail had been assigned to Frank. Their job was to guide him through the maze of press and paparazzi between the *Coho's* mooring spot on the tarmac and the hotel where he was staying. As the head of a diplomatic mission from a new species and a new nation, Frank was a big, big deal. There would be thousands of cameras trained on him when he stepped off the ship and anywhere else that wasn't strictly controlled.

Two of the Marines separated from Frank's complement. A male and a female. The female Marines had been no less "dude" than the males during the flight and their time at Yeti Mountain, but there were fewer of them. As with all the dudes though, when it was time for work, they were spit and polish with nothing but formal protocol.

"Ma'am," the female Marine said to Maria. "I'm Lieutenant Butters. Commander Smiley has assigned me to be your attaché during your time in the BSR. My colleague, Chief Warrant Officer Ming, has been assigned to Mr. Actor."

Lt. Butters was a tall, thin woman, about the same height as Charles, with bright red hair. Her freckle complected face was serious, but the laugh wrinkles around her eyes gave a better judgment of her character. Both she and CWO Ming appeared to be in their early thirties. Butters was slightly taller than Ming and appeared to be the one in charge.

Ming took a tiny but crisp step forward and gave Charles a salute that snapped into place at a perfect 45-degree triangle in the space between his bicep, forearm, and the side of his head. Ming's body was rigid with musculature, the tendons of his neck looked ready to burst from under his skin. Charles certainly wouldn't have wanted to have a physical altercation with the man. Ming was around five and a half feet, Charles reckoned; a little taller than Maria, but a good six inches shorter than Charles or Lt. Butters.

"At ease." Charles wasn't real sure what to say to military people. He'd seen movies and had friends and family who had served, but he never had. "I'm not sure we need to have attachés…"

Ming stepped back and relaxed a little. Lt. Butters now spoke. "Ma'am, Sir, permission to speak freely?" She seemed to be the one in charge here.

Charles nodded, but Lt. Butters was looking at Maria who, Charles realized, was also pretty obviously the one in charge of their party. That was a relief to him, although it did send another alarm bell. Butters knew more than they had told her. Charles only hoped that his impression of her was correct, and she was indeed a friend.,

Maria had no problem at all jumping into military protocol and jargon. "Permission to speak freely, granted, Lieutenant. Carry on."

Butters relaxed significantly. "Dude," she exclaimed. "Smiley fully briefed me and the Mingster on you two. We know that you are a part of the diplomatic delegation for the very righteous Frank en Baum the Yeti. We know that you are both more than you seem, and we've been instructed to help you in every way possible and to keep you safe. Also, Commander Smiley thought it might be cool to keep you both off the entertainment screens for as long as possible."

Frank looked at Maria to see what she thought of all this. She met his eyes and gave a tiny nod. If she was good with it, he was good with it. He was inclined to feel like they were among allies now, and honestly, having Ming and Butters to help guide them through any blunders they might make was a big positive.

Butters continued. "The Commander thought it best that we take the crew exit and go straight to your quarters via the undergrounds. This is going to raise suspicion among those who will be expecting to see Frank's delegation with him, but ultimately, she thought it best that every Tom, Dick, and Harriet in the BSR doesn't instantly recognize you when you meet them."

Charles was grateful for this consideration. His brief time in the Texican Nation had been marred by footage revealing that he wasn't a normie and as a result, he would be glad to avoid anything like having his face plastered on screens again.

That reminded him. "Hey, in the Texican Nation I was all over the screens being accused of working with the RSA. Did those images and alerts get seen here too?"

Butters shook her head. "Dude, as far as we know, there are only three people in the BSR who know where you really came from. The Mingster here is smarter than his muscles might lead you to believe, and he knows a lot about your time period. He's, like, published books about it." She nudged him but Ming didn't break face at all. "Smiley ordered us to keep your origins and your persons secure. The security services have seen you on the Texican feeds, so there's no need to pretend that they don't know there is something up with you. But your face hasn't been shown on our feeds, so you don't have to worry about public recognition. Okay, so, we good? On with the mission?"

"To your orders, Marines," Maria barked out—a little more harshly than Charles thought necessary. Butters re-stiffened, and Ming, somehow also got more rigid in his standing.

"Grab your small things and follow us," Butters said. "Your baggage and other personals will be delivered to you later. Oh, by the way, don't leave anything personal in them. They'll definitely be searched and sniffed." There was nothing in their baggage that they needed to worry about, but it was definitely good to know that everything in the BSR wasn't as free and easy as Charles had hoped it would be.

They threw their rucksacks on and followed the Marines into the bowels of the *Coho.*

They left through a small hatch connected to the bottom of one of the landing pods. The pods connected to the tunnels underneath through a unique locking mechanism that kept them in place on the tarmac and allowed crew and maintenance full access to the craft without having to deal with any weather or other issues. In this case it allowed Charles, Maria, and the two Marines to leave the ship without being seen. Charles wondered if this feature had been built into the docking on purpose. Looking up he noticed a red light attached to what he was pretty sure was a security camera. Remembering Smiley's words, he reminded himself that in the BSR, apparently, there was no such thing as not being seen—but he supposed that it did matter who was doing the looking. In this case, at least, they seemed to have dodged the press but not all the cameras.

The tunnels had a natural light that seemed to come from the walls. He couldn't see a source for the light. It simply existed.

"Lieutenant Butters," he asked, "what's the source of the light?"

"Call me Butters," she said to him. "The lights are pretty cool, right? Fiber optic strands are run down at quarter mile intervals. The walls are painted with light diffusion paint that allows the light to spread naturally and evenly. It doesn't work at night, of course, but when the lights come on you know the workday is done."

Ming grunted. Butters laughed and gestured to him as they all moved at a pretty fast pace through the tunnel system. "The workday is never done when you're serving your country though, right Ming?"

Charles wanted to ask more questions, but the urgency of their pace dissuaded him. Maria was taking it all in and any questions he might have, he would certainly be able to ask her about later. He wondered if she had access to an "online" system here, or whether she was connected to the Texican or Yeti Mountain "internets" for that matter. He'd never thought to ask her if she carried all her information with her or was somehow wired in.

"Where are we being taken?" she asked. Her face was relaxed, and her body moved with a grace and ease that told Charles there was nothing to worry about.

"We're taking you to the same place Ambassador Frank is staying. Don't worry, you won't have to keep dodging the press. They wanted to catch his arrival, and the paparazzi agreements give the press the rights to certain kinds of footage and access, but those same accords are very strict about privacy for media personalities, officials, and private citizens. The arrival was a biggie, but after that it will all be press-conferences and staged events. You should be able to dodge the press-cameras pretty easily."

They came into a hangar bay where a dozen enclosed golf cart style vehicles were parked. Ming examined a couple and then indicated they should all get in one. Charles had no idea what the difference between them was, but he was happy Ming had found one he liked. Once inside, Ming drove them up a ramp and back into the outside world—the "upside" world, actually. The change in the light was almost imperceptible and there was no need to squint or adjust as Charles would have expected when emerging from underground tunnels into the open air.

It was a fifteen-minute drive to the hotel. The beauty of this place was astounding. High majestic mountains covered with pine trees and snow. The blue of the sky was magnified by the crispness of the high-altitude air. The hotel sat on a raised peninsula that jutted into the iced-over expanse of the lake. It was a magnificent building. Marble columns, tiled rooftops, and delicate looking porticos all surrounding bright yellow plaster walls. The sides of the building were lined with windows and gabled patios. The entire thing looked like a Mediterranean palace that the gods had transported and dropped into place. Somehow, it fit the surroundings and made them even more beautiful.

Just as Charles was wondering if they would need to go through some sort of check-in process, Ming turned and zipped them down another ramp. Instantly they were back on the downside, but only for a few moments before Ming parked the vehicle in another parking bay.

"Ming will go get the access cards," Butters explained as Ming walked away. "I'll take you up to our apartment."

"Our apartment," caught Charles by surprise.

"We're staying in your home?" he asked. Butters looked confused for a moment before laughing.

"No way man," she told him. "We don't live here. That would be nice though. We'll be sharing quarters with you while you are here, though. Don't worry, we won't get in your way or invade your privacy. They've assigned you to a three-bedroom suite. Our assumption was that the two of you would share a room?"

"That's a good assumption," Maria said.

Butters nodded. "Good. If you each wanted your own, Ming and I could share. But honestly, he snores, so I'm happy to not do that. The suite has two living areas, and the master room has its own bathroom. You won't see us unless you want to. The idea is that we are close enough to assist or protect you if needed without being a bother."

"Do we need to be protected?" Charles asked. They'd gotten in an elevator now and were moving upwards judging by the floor indicator, but Charles couldn't detect any motion.

Butters looked up meaningfully at the camera in the corner of the elevator car. "Of course not. The BSR is the safest nation in the world, and we have a harmonious unified government that provides us with everything we need. There is no crime or violence here. We are lucky. So, you have nothing to worry about. It's just protocol."

Her message was clear. Charles would need to keep the surveillance in mind. He wondered if that was the reason that Maria was communicating so little. It made sense. Her normally bubbly persona had been fully contained since their arrival. At one point he asked her if she was alright. She had smiled and squeezed his hand warmly in response, which put him at ease on one level, but didn't answer his question.

Leaving the elevator, Butters led them down a red stucco hallway with beautiful creamy white enamel doors highlighted with gold leaf paint. The sound of their footsteps on the marble tiles were crisp, but strangely didn't echo through the hallway. It was disconcerting, but he attributed it to some sort of sound dampening in the architecture or materials. Ming was already waiting at the door to their suite.

"Is Frank already here?" Maria asked.

Butters laughed out loud. "No way. He's still at the arrival press conference. I don't imagine he'll be here any sooner than a few hours. Don't worry though, he'll be fine. Actually, I think he'd be fine in any situation. He's a really remarkable person. I got to know him a little bit on the ship."

Charles agreed. He wasn't worried about Frank, but he wasn't entirely happy about having been separated from him as soon as they arrived. He understood and appreciated the reasoning behind it, but it created a sense of unease.

"Your luggage should get here before too long," Butters told them as she led them into the suite. It was as impressive as the building itself.

Truly they had been dropped into palatial luxury. The rooms were as Butters had told them but much bigger and laid out in a sort of Medici luxury that told Charles that they were being given the royal treatment.

After showing them the two sitting rooms, the kitchen, the rooms where Ming and she would be staying along with the "guest" bathroom, Butters led them to their master suite. Big windows, a perfect view of the mountains and the lake, two desks, a spa-like bathroom—it was a billionaire's quarters. Charles wondered if it was the most luxurious suite in the hotel. How could something exceed this?

"I'll get out of your hair and give you guys some privacy now," Butters told them. "We'll let you know when your luggage gets here and, in an hour or so, we'll do a little briefing about what you are going to see, who you will meet, and all that stuff. By the way, thank you for letting us dispense with a bit of the protocol. We'll keep to it in public, but it's nice to be able to chill and hang with you while still doing our jobs." Ming was behind her as she said this. He nodded curtly in agreement. "Oh, and I probably don't need to say this, but if you have a bath make sure you don't have anything in your pockets."

That last bit was strange enough to be meaningful. Butters closed the door of the bedroom, and they were alone. Just Charles and Maria in a palatial wonderland.

Instantly, Maria relaxed and became herself again. "Would you look at this place?" She threw herself on the huge fluffy bed and began making snow angels in the thick snow white down comforter. Charles stood looking down at her with a goofy smile on his face. An overwhelming feeling of love and desire to protect her and keep her safe washed over him. He knew now that what he had once thought of as love had been something else. It had been desire, amiability, friendliness, and a different thing than what he felt now. The feelings that he had for Maria made those "loves" into trivial things.

He'd thought he loved his ex-wife for most of their thirty-plus year marriage, but now he realized why their marriage had failed; why he and she had felt incomplete and unfulfilled. The tidal wave of emotion his inner self experienced each time he looked at or thought of Maria was made up of his totality.

The funny part was that his desire to protect her was probably the most useless part. Maria was stronger, faster, smarter, and more capable of protecting herself than any woman in the world, any person in the world. Yet, that didn't bother him, and he still felt that maybe his knowledge of the past—his human experience, his flawed imperfections, and all the things that Maria didn't have—might help or protect her.

She noticed him looking down at her and her smile broadened even as her eyes narrowed. He couldn't begin to imagine her thoughts or feelings, but it didn't matter. She reached up to him, and he fell into her arms.

Later, when they were both refreshed. They stood side by side, looking into the large mirror in the master suite bathroom. Charles was straightening his clothes while Maria brushed her silky black hair. Just because she was an android didn't mean that her hair didn't get messy, and her makeup didn't need to be adjusted now and then. She was a woman in every sense, and so much more.

"Don't forget to check your pockets," she said to him. Charles was still getting used to the one-piece utility suits that seemed to be the future's main item of clothing. They were almost like the old fashioned long-johns he'd worn as a kid, complete with a barn door over his bum that was released from the belt line over his bum. They came in an endless variety of styles from onesies to matching top and bottom to what he thought of as track suits. No buttons on the barn door or the front. Instead, they had an invisible strip that seemed something like microscopic Velcro. You couldn't see it, but it was the same concept. It created invisible seams that could be opened and closed but without sound and tactile feeling as Velcro.

"Huh?" Charles looked at her, not understanding. It took a moment before he remembered Butters' strange comment. Maria saw his face register. She walked to the bath and began running water into it. Charles reached into his front pockets, which had been empty before.

In them he found a folded piece of paper. Opening it, he saw that it was stationery from the *Coho*. Looking at the bottom, he saw it was signed by Commander Smiley.

> *The fact you are reading this means you have settled in, and things are going well so far. You can trust Butters and Ming as if they are me. They and the marines from the* Coho *have all been personally vetted by me. Please don't assume that you can trust all marines*

though. Stick with the ones you know. These two are some of the best of the best.

We've managed to remove the cameras from your bathroom, which is fairly normal protocol for most people, but we had to leave the audio bugs in place since they are built into the room itself. If you have to speak, the best practice is to whisper with the water running. It works for most situations unless they are using the most advanced surveillance tech, which your hotel and most places are not.

Butters will brief you on the people you will meet this afternoon, but here are a few names that will be worth knowing. We have two prime ministers and a president.

Prime Minister Duwali is a BSR patriot and former fighter pilot. He rose to power after his retirement from the BSR forces. His passion and loyalty are laser focused on developing off-world habitations and space colonies. He has seen combat with the BSR and is one-hundred-percent working towards the same interests we hold. That doesn't mean you should trust him, because he is still a politician and will quickly trade or sacrifice you for something that will carry his agenda forward.

Prime Minister Jones is a very different story. His family made their fortune in entertainment. He is charming, charismatic, and slippery as an eel. He was a daytime drama star for several years before being nominated to run for office. We don't have any hard evidence, but our suspicion has been that he is working with the RSA. He is in it for power, not duty.

President Weissman is the wild card. Her political abilities and loyalties are a complete unknown. She has managed to create equitable and successful dealings with both sides. Part of the reason she has retained power for so long is because of her ability to craft agreements that give both sides just enough of what they want while still keeping the balance of power from tipping one way or another. She has met and entertained leaders from both sides. She has had friendly public meetings with the RSA ambassadors, but not more so than she has done with ambassadors from other nations.

The way our system works is that a measure or bill requires the signatures of both Prime Ministers or the President. The Prime Ministers can jointly veto presidential actions (which is probably an impossibility given the polarity of the current two), but if that doesn't occur, it is her signature that turns ideas into reality.

While the PMs are popular with their power bases, and hated by the power base of the other, President Weissman is widely popular on both sides and the middle. Bottom line: we're pretty sure Duwali is with us and Jones is against us, but we have no idea where Weissman stands or will throw her weight. She's been a big supporter of in-world development but has recently made some comments that lead us to believe her commitment to it may be wavering.

One more important thing to note. As an ambassador, Frank has been assigned two attaché and a security detail. We managed to get Sergeant Palido, one of our Marines from the Coho, *in his detail, but were unable to vet or place any of his other personnel. Until we can find out who they are, Sergeant Palido is the only person attached to Frank that you should trust.*

If we need to communicate, we'll keep doing so through your pockets. Flush this after reading.

Charles looked at the paper in the light to make sure there was no hidden watermark and then handed it to Maria. His assumption was that she did a more thorough check before dropping it into the toilet, closing the clear lid, and watching it be incinerated the same way urine and feces were. There was still a small amount of water in the toilets, probably to catch and hold the majority of the odor. When the lid was closed a super-high temperature flame burned and evaporated the water and whatever was in it.

The leftover powder, dust, and ash was then liquified with a high-pressure explosion of water. All of this happened quickly and then when the lid was lifted, the toilet bowl with a little bit of water in it was sitting there looking for all the world just like a toilet from his time. Charles was a fan of this innovation in plumbing but would hate for something to have gone wrong. It looked to him like there was a lot that could go wrong with it.

"I can't figure out why the water stays clear and why there is no smell," he said to Maria. "Wouldn't the rehydration of the ash powder bring all of that back?"

Maria never seemed to mind his non-linear dives into non-related topics. It was one more reason to love her. He was free to be himself without having to adjust anything to fit with her view of the world.

"The temperature of the flames consumes the molecules that would provide color or odor," she told him. "Over time though, the amount of particulate matter in the water becomes greater than the carrying capacity of the water molecules. At that point—the matter dense liquid—which weighs slightly more than pure water of the same volume is diverted to the matter generators where it is made into a variety of synthetic fabric and cloth."

"They make defecation into cloth? What do they do with the cloth?"

"It's what your clothes are made out of," Maria said. Her grin told him that she understood exactly how this revelation would make him feel. Suddenly, he felt a little less comfortable in his utility suit. But, as a rancher who had needed to sometimes shove his arm up a cow's ass, he figured he could deal with clothes that were made out of the world's shit.

Chapter 4

The briefing from Butters covered the information about the President and PMs but without the inside information. It also introduced a number of other key political figures they were likely to meet, several corporations and the people who ran them, and an overview of the BSR's history, economy, and political structure. Charles assumed that all of this information had been vetted as safe to allow all sides to know they were being told. It was a very neutral presentation, but still interesting in terms of demonstrating the ways things had changed and how they had remained the same.

The BSR had a dual parliamentary system with a legislative body that carried out the main executive functions of government from that which was put forward by the parliaments. The 3D parliament was focused on defense, development, and data management. The ELF parliament was focused on Entertainment, Life, and Fiduciary. The 3D members were nominated by the military, industry, and tech sectors. ELF members were nominated by the public, the entertainment complex, and the financial institutions. It was an interesting system, and learning about it cleared up why PM Jones and PM Duwali were so different. PMs were appointed by the two parliaments. The president was elected to six-year terms by a general election. Charles appreciated the function and complexity of the system, but like the incinerator toilets, he could see a lot of potential for things to go wrong in it.

Over the coming days they would join Frank at dinners, meet and greet events, and a conference. All of this was taking place in Big Bear. In three days, they would all board the *Coho* again and be taken on a whirlwind tour of the BSR. With the *Coho* repaired and refueled they would visit the San Francisco Stock Exchange, Hollywood, the Seattle Space Port, and the Vancouver Studio Complex. Four days later they would be back in Big Bear for President Weissman's State of the Republic address. Frank was the guest of honor. Maria and Charles were designated as advisors to Frank, and Charles looked forward to reuniting with their Yeti friend to share notes and intel.

The dinner at the Capitol Rotunda that evening was a black-tie event welcoming Frank and Yeti Mountain into the BSR family of diplomatic allies. There would be representatives from the Mutual Nation of Hawai'i, the Texican and Maritime ambassadors, a company rep from the Wolverine Isles, as well as dignitaries from big BSR companies along with some well-known sports and entertainment stars. The unofficial ambassador from the RSA, Bryce Hilliard, would also be there. Since there was no official diplomatic relationship with the RSA, he was in the BSR as a private citizen and a businessman, yet presumably with more than a citizen's normal clout and bargaining power. This was evidenced by his attendance at this dinner.

Maria wore a dark blue gown. She would have looked gorgeous in anything, but the gown accentuated the feminine while giving her an air of sophistication. Charles was provided with a tuxedo. Some things would never change, and the tux seemed to be one of them. They met up with Frank and his retinue in the lobby of the hotel, and the entire delegation was transported by bus-limousine to the rotunda. Frank was in good spirits. There was no opportunity to talk of anything important, since most of Franks assigned detail was of uncertain loyalty, but the Yeti Ambassador seemed to be having a good time and making friends.

"I wondered if they were going to put you in one of these monkey suits," Charles joked to the yeti. Frank looked momentarily confused but Charles motioning to his own clothing cleared things up.

"I didn't realize they were called monkey suits," Frank said. "They brought me one, but we yeti have never worn clothes. Our fur provides us with all the protection of the elements. And, as to the sexual and defecation parts, our creator made them in such a way that they are discreet and hidden unless we are using them."

Charles had never thought about this, and he was afraid now he might not be able to stop thinking about it. Luckily, he could ask Maria for details later and thus satisfy the unpleasant curiosity he now felt. It was true though; Frank wore nothing, but none of his private parts were exposed.

"Are they treating you okay so far? Any problems we should know about," he wanted Frank to know that they were being watched carefully, but he knew that the yeti would hold his tongue about sensitive subjects. He hoped that Frank had somehow been briefed on their situation.

"It's all good. I've heard that we'll be having salmon tonight. It will be my first time, and I'm looking forward to it." Frank gave him a wink. Charles wasn't sure what to do with that but decided it was best to let it go.

Charles had never lived a fancy life of balls and receptions, but he had watched enough films and television shows to know that the pre-dinner reception was fairly standard. Cocktails, waiters with trays of hors-devours, and plenty of small talk. Frank was the center of attention. He was already immensely popular and told jokes and stories that elicited oohs, ahs, and peals of laughter from the assembled lords and ladies. They weren't really lords and ladies, but that was how Charles thought of them.

Unlike the US-style capitals of earlier eras, the capitol city of the BSR showed little to no overt influence from Greek or Roman architecture. The dome of the Bear and Salmon Republic's capitol was made of clear glass that allowed the twinkling light of the stars above to shine down on the attendees of the gala event. It was a full moon, and while the light of the event itself prevented a full appreciation of the heavens above, the high altitude and some technological innovations created the illusion that the party was taking place in the open air but with full climate control. At over seven thousand feet in altitude, it was cold in Big Bear during the winter.

Maria and Charles moved about the event, largely ignored. They weren't anyone of particular importance, and as such, didn't have the social climbers jockeying for position or the sycophants looking for a new host to attach to. It was ideal in almost every sense. Frank knew not to draw attention to them, and Butters and Ming had blended into the sea of escorts, bodyguards, attaché, and other attendants that filled the edges of the event without actually being there. Charles had never been one for small talk, but he was grateful for it now. It was easy to deflect questions with references to the weather, pop culture, or news of the day. Butters had provided them with a handful of topics for exactly that reason.

"Where do you come from in the Texican Nation?" a person might ask to which they might reply, "Oh, our country is so boring, we don't have any celebrity royalty like Hudson Brigadoon or Felicia Silvers. Did you hear about their affair?" or, "What I'm most excited about is being able to see one of your surf ball matches. Bob Hariman has to be the best water receiver in the world," or even a historical conspiracy reference like, "Maybe you can clear this up: in my country, there are rumors that the pulse was a lie told in order to ban dangerous technology. Do you think it ever really existed?"

The last one was his own contribution to the list. Charles was fascinated by "the pulse," a global EMP that made a connected high-tech civilization impossible until just a decade before. It had ended jet travel across oceans, anything like a global information super-highway, and also erased the majority of history and knowledge of his time from all electronic databases. Maria told him that the reason he didn't see handheld computers, laptops, smart watches, and cell phones was because the pulse had made the use of such devices impossible for nearly two centuries.

A beam weapon had sat in high orbit and blanketed the planet in an electro-magnetic pulse every day for hundreds of years. Life and technology had found ways to overcome it, of course, but the civilization of handheld silicon and chip-based computers had vanished along with the wireless connectivity that had powered his time. Cars had become useless, screens had gone black, connections that weren't wired had evaporated. Organic cellular-based computing and technology had eventually replaced much of what twenty-first century high-tech had provided. But, in the meantime, the world had developed in ways that it otherwise would not have.

Maria, the woman he was in love with, was a product of all of this. She was pulse proof, as was most of the tech that had been developed until a decade ago. It was around that time that scientists noticed the pulse had stopped. No one knew why, or at least, no one was telling.

Since then, twenty-first century style technology had been creeping back into people's lives. It was cheap and easy to produce, but vulnerable if the pulse should it ever start up again. Smart phones and pocket computers were banned in the BSR and most other countries. Charles wasn't exactly sure why, but he thought it was generally a good idea.

Finding himself trapped in a conversation with an aging narcissist actor and the head of a mining consortium, Charles felt pretty safe. The actor turned every topic to his own career, and the mining executive didn't have much to say at all. A part of Charles felt like he was a cowboy James Bond on a secret mission, but the truth was that there really wasn't any mission beyond the vague and disturbing details that Commander Smiley had given them. He and Maria were on a holiday in a new country, and he supposed they were looking for a home, though it was still very early days in their relationship. Despite that, Charles already couldn't imagine life without her.

Since neither of them could go back to the Texican Nation, the BSR was the best candidate for a place to hang their hats. That was the mission, not the secret agent stuff. Although, he had to admit it was fun to pretend.

The actor asked an outward directed question of the executive. "Your company is the one that has those asteroid mining commercials, right? I love the jingle; you should put me in one of them. Can you just imagine me in one of those space suits?" *And of course*. He'd managed to turn it back to his favorite topic.

The executive ignored the second question. "Yes, we're excited about the possibilities inherent. It's been centuries since humans have stepped off-world, but we think the time is right and the resources that can be extracted will be useful in our post-pulse era." While this would have been a good point to throw into his small talking point into the mix, Charles decided to hold back. It was an interesting topic.

The actor was nodding enthusiastically. "I was in a movie about a post-pulse world many years ago. Maybe you saw it: *The Barnacle*. It was a horror film. The whole thing was a dream sequence, and when the dream ends, the protagonist wakes up and there I am—her loving father bringing her breakfast in a world where the pulse and her nightmare never happened." Charles was figuring out what kind of an actor this guy was: a bit-part player. And yet, for some reason, he was here. There must have been something important about him.

"I'm going to go find the washroom," Maria said to him. It was their code for her wanting to move on. Charles was becoming interested in the conversation, though. The asteroid mining part and the pulse part, at least.

"I'll be right here," he said. "If you get lost on the way back, I'll come find you."

She stood on tiptoes and kissed his cheek. "My knight in shining armor." She walked away, and he realized that he had never been this happy. Somehow, she had brought a total fulfillment to him at a time when he thought he already understood what life was all about. The uncertainty and chaos of being dropped three hundred years into the future was a small price to pay for these feelings. He wasn't one to lie to himself though; he was enjoying the uncertainty and chaos of it all too.

As Maria walked away, another man joined them. He was tall, standing an inch or two higher than Charles. His stiff blond hair was plastered to his head in a style reminiscent of 1980s televangelists. His bangs stiffened into a permanent wave. He had deep pockmarks on his face that the big owlish glasses he wore barely distracted from. He wore a dark red bow tie and cumber bun that was dark enough in color to get him in the door but distinct enough to set him apart.

"Did someone say, '*The Barnacle?*' I loved that film. It played in Savannah for almost a year." Charles had already identified the man as Bryce Hilliard, the unofficial RSA ambassador. He was distinct enough to stand out, but mentioning the capital of the RSA was an easy way to tell who he was just in case someone didn't know.

The actor brightened and held out his hand. "I'm Rory Jones." Hilliard took it and held it for a few moments too long.

"Bryce Hilliard," he said looking at the executive and then at Charles before letting go of Rory Jones hand.

The executive looked distinctly uncomfortable. He didn't offer his own hand to Hilliard but instead looked at his drink before mumbling, "If you gentlemen will excuse me, I need to go find my wife." With that he turned and walked away. Hilliard didn't seem bothered by it and held his hand out to Charles.

Charles shook it, wondering if he was making a mistake. "Charles Actor," he said and forced the handshake to end before it went on too long. Hilliard didn't force it for which Charles was grateful.

"So, here I am with two famous actors from two different nations," Hilliard said in a joking tone. Rory Jones now looked at Charles with a different expression, completely missing that Hilliard was making a joke of Charles name. He also missed the implied knowledge in the quip, but Charles heard it loud and clear.

"What shows have you done?" Jones now asked Charles.

Hilliard didn't give him a chance to respond. "Oh, he's quite famous in the Texican Nation. My favorite was the show where he played an agent of my government on the run from the Federales. It was an amazing performance, but there was one thing I never really understood about that film, Chuck." Charles was not a fan of the nickname and was sorry to hear it had survived from his time. Hilliard went on. "Your character definitely wasn't an RSA agent, but it was never clear exactly why the authorities were after him. What was the inciting incident? I hope you don't mind my asking."

The evening had just turned from pleasant to terrible. Charles wasn't an actor, and the film Hilliard was describing wasn't a film. The truth was that, after arriving in the future, the Texican authorities had identified him as a time traveler and had manufactured the story of him being an RSA agent in order to start a nationwide manhunt from which he had fled into the Blizzard with Maria and other friends. Bryce Hilliard obviously knew about the manhunt, but he wasn't coming out and saying it, so maybe things weren't as bad as they might have been.

"It's Charles, but I'm honored that you've seen my work," he said. "It was never really a big hit like Rory's films."

"Oh, you are too modest Chuck," Hilliard said. "Everyone in the Texican Nation saw it and in certain circles of the RSA, your film has been studied exhaustively. Some of our research institutions have written extensively about it. Still, I won't force you to talk about it now. Did you know that Rory here is the oldest brother of Prime Minister Jones?"

Charles hadn't known that. He found himself grateful for the change of subject.

"In the RSA we're working hard to create the kind of top-tier entertainment that the BSR seems to make so effortlessly—I don't want to spill the tea, of course I'm happy to be able to, but please keep it between the three of us. Rory is going to be offered an opportunity to become the studio head at one of our big entertainment hubs in Branson. It's all pending approval from the government here of course...but I feel confident it will all fall into place."

Jones seemed shocked by the news and by the fact that the man he had been telling about his acting career seemed to be a more famous actor than he was—even though he actually wasn't. "Well, I'd be foolish to not take that opportunity if it came," he said to Hilliard and then turning to Charles "Are you planning to act in anything out here, Chuck?"

Charles hated Hilliard instantly for sharing the nickname and Jones for using it. "It looks like I need to go find my companion as well—nice meeting the both of you." He turned and walked in the direction that Maria had gone. The night no longer felt so magical as it had before.

Chapter 5

None of them got to try the salmon that evening.

The alarms ended any further conversation and in a matter of moments, special forces and bodyguards were ushering their people out the doors into the cold night air. Ming appeared from nowhere and grabbed Charles by the elbow, leading him to the exit through the confused crowd. Charles looked around to see if he could spot Frank or Maria. Frank and his delegation were easy to spot, but he didn't see Maria.

He turned to Ming ready to break free and go back to find her, but Ming had an answer ready. "She's with Butters," Ming's voice was surprisingly deep and resonant. He could have been a radio announcer. "They'll be fine, but we have to get out of this building right now."

Charles didn't argue, in truth Maria didn't need his help. There was very little he could do to help her in a situation like this beyond getting himself out of the building. His male sense of pride and responsibility wanted him to make a gesture, but he was aware enough of Maria's capabilities and inner workings that he understood it would be an empty one.

It was below freezing outside, and no one had been able to get their coats. There was more than a little bit of grumbling as the disorganized horde of dignitaries and guests were herded away from the capitol building. The grounds surrounding it were large and though there were several smaller structures, no one was able to open them up for the party attendees in the short time they had been outside.

All thoughts of the cold, salmon dinners, or anything else were wiped away when a massive explosion shook the ground and filled the glass dome of the clear capitol rotunda with flames and destruction. It was deafening but surprisingly clean. The capitol building stood complete even as the flames and debris from the inside were completely contained within the building. He would learn later that the building had been constructed to be bomb-proof.

From the outside. The structure of the building was all but indestructible, but no one had expected a bomb to be placed inside it.

The attendees were seemingly all okay. They were loaded into buses and taken to their hotels or residences. No one was given any explanation for what had happened, probably because no one knew. On the one hand Charles was surprised they weren't all questioned about the bombing and whether they had seen anything strange, but then he remembered Commander Smiley's warning that everything was recorded and realized that in such a society, there would be very little need for eyewitness accounts. Besides which, the guests were all known, recorded, and available to be questioned at a later time.

Ming, having finally spoken, didn't loosen the tap on his words. Back at the hotel there was still no sign of Butters or Maria. Charles felt the beginning of panic. The last he had seen of Maria she was heading to the ladies' room. What if she had still been in the building? What if she were dead?

He raised these concerns to Ming, but the Marine seemed nonplussed. "She's with Butters. They'll be fine. Trust me. I'll go see what I can find out. Stay here and wait."

Charles was left alone in the room. It was the first time he had truly been alone since arriving in the future. He didn't like the feeling at all. He turned on one of the entertainment screens and using the voice controls directed it to find a news channel where a female anchor was detailing what was known.

"… reports have been filtering in about what might have caused the explosion, but we have been told that all attendees were successfully evacuated and there were no casualties. This was a literal trial by fire of the indestructible glass developed by Off-World Industries. The material science company released a statement from their CEO."

A grey-haired, dark-skinned man in a white shirt and tie appeared on the screen with a company logo green screened behind him.

"While we are shocked and horrified at this outrageous tragedy, we are pleased that Forever Glass lived up to the standards we had set for it.

Had the capitol building been constructed of any other material it is likely that the destruction would have been widespread and the death toll in the hundreds. Forever Glass kept the explosion contained and allowed firefighters to seal the building and smother the fire by pulling out all the oxygen. Like everyone, we are saddened and upset about this event, but we couldn't be happier that our Forever Glass functioned as intended and likely saved lives and property."

The news footage showed the explosion happening from every possible angle. The view from the top was the most striking, showing a massive orange fireball that began to push outward and was stopped by the glass walls of the building. Within minutes the fires inside were smothered. Forever Glass really had saved the day. On a different channel, commentators were already speculating that the stock was going to go parabolic the next day.

Ming returned about twenty minutes later. He was alone. Still no sign of Maria or Butters.

"Nobody has seen them. I haven't been able to see the interior footage yet, they've got it locked down. They aren't the only ones missing, but one thing I was able to find out was that the body sensors in the building showed that no one was inside when the explosion happened, so we know they got out, but we just don't know where they went."

It was a relief. "Who else is missing? Maybe that will help us determine where they are? Would they have evacuated into tunnels or from another exit?"

Ming shook his head and his jaw tightened. It was clear he didn't like what he was about to say. "There doesn't seem to be anything random about the other missing guests. President Weissman, Prime Minister Duwali, and Bryce Hilliard, the RSA man you met. None of their security details are missing. Aside from Maria and Butters, everyone else that was at the event has been accounted for."

"Hilliard," Charles said, more to himself than Ming. "That son of a bitch did this."

"That's our assumption, Sir. Unfortunately, until we know more, that's all it is."

As much as he wanted to do something, there was nothing Charles could actually do. He spent most of a sleepless night reconstructing the evening, looking for clues in his memory, and even attempted to return to the crime scene or go out and find witnesses to interrogate. He wasn't a policeman though, he didn't have any sort of investigative credentials, and when he wanted to leave the suite, Ming informed him that everyone was on lockdown until the following day.

Prime Minister Jones had declared the lockdown within minutes of the explosion.

The following morning, there was a knock on the door and a courier delivered a message. It was from Frank. "I need you to come join us," was all it said. This sounded like music to Charles' ears. The big empty space of his own rooms was becoming difficult to bear.

Franks apartment/office was a hive of activity. Where Charles and Maria had been mostly ignored, Frank was the recipient of care packages, fan mail, sponsorship offerings, and then all the actual political stuff. Charles felt a little guilty about not having been there to help Frank navigate through it all but reminded himself that just like he wasn't a policeman, he wasn't a politician. He was a rancher who had been dropped three hundred years into the future, and while he was a pretty intelligent guy, that didn't really qualify him for much. His guilt lingered however, over the fact that Frank had been left to navigate everything alone, and aside from being everything else he was, Charles was Franks's friend.

Frank had an actual office with a giant desk for him to work at. In a different moment, Charles would have been amused or amazed or both at seeing the yeti sitting in a power pose behind the big mahogany surface of his desk, fingers steepled together as he sat in deep thought. He smiled when Charles and Ming walked in.

"Everyone out," Frank said. He motioned to Ming and asked Charles "Do you want him to stay?" Charles nodded. Ming sat in a chair to the side and Charles took the seat opposite Frank.

With the last of his staff out, Frank started to speak.

Charles interrupted. "You know this room is probably filled with microphones and cameras, right?" Frank looked surprised but then his features showed that he understood. He looked as if he were deciding whether to speak, but then with a determined look barreled into it.

"That makes sense, given where we are. I've learned a lot about the BSR in the short time we've been here. The people here are always looking for an angle, a way to profit, a way to turn every situation to their advantage. What at first seems like sincere overtures of friendship, pretty quickly becomes obvious as mercenary. Then, if it benefits them, they will smile while they stab you or if there seems to be a better profit motive in crying while they prop you up—they will do that. Does that sound accurate to you?" Frank was talking to Ming when he asked this.

Ming nodded. "Most of the people in the capitols are there to find an advantage. It's different when you get to the small coasts. Military are generally small coast men and women, so there isn't much of that in our ranks. At least, not until you get to the higher ranks. Commander Smiley is a small coaster who managed to rise high, but she is a rare bird. Butters will probably follow the same course."

"What's a small coast?" Charles asked.

Ming explained. "Big coasts are the major cities where position and power get established Hollywood, SF, Seattle, Vancouver—even some of the regionals are generally considered big coasts. Small coasts are everything else. TSD, that's Tijuana San Diego, is a military run city so it's different and the ports generally have a different mentality running them. But other than that, you have it right. My grandfather in Oakland used to say, 'a soldier will kill for his country, a small coaster will kill for their family, but a big coaster will kill for their profit'."

Charles liked the more talkative Ming. "Why were you so quiet before?"

Ming actually looked a little embarrassed. "Butters is a lot smarter than I am, but we've learned that while she is talking, I can learn a lot by watching closely how people react. I'm not worried about her, by the way. I have no doubt that she is getting control of whatever situation she is in."

Charles would have preferred to not have had that bit of information fed to whatever bugs were listening. He pointed up and around, indicating the hidden mics and cameras. "Frank, is there a bathroom in this office?"

Frank laughed. "I don't know how you do things where you come from, but no, we don't have a bathroom in the office, but there is one attached." He pointed to a door on his left. Charles hoped that the cameras had also been removed from Frank's bathroom. He stood up and motioned that the other two should follow him.

Once inside, Charles turned on all the taps and the shower. It was a big bathroom with four sinks and two showers. There was plenty of room for the three of them to stand and speak. Charles moved close to Frank and began to whisper.

"Everything here is bugged; this might be the only way that we can communicate. There are cameras everywhere. I believe that the RSA man, Hilliard, is behind the bombing and somehow took the PM and President hostage. I'm not sure how Maria and Butters are involved, but it seems like maybe this is a power play by PM Jones and the RSA. That's everything I know. Oh, and also: you can trust Sergeant Palido. Commander Smiley had him put on your team, but as far as everyone else, we have no idea."

Frank smiled "That's good news, I like the gunny but wasn't sure I could trust him." His whisper was surprisingly quiet. Charles had thought it might be a booming whisper and was relieved that it wasn't. "We have some news. I was visited by some sort of detective who asked me questions about Maria and Butters. He wanted to know why they left the gala before the bombing took place. I didn't know anything about that, so I was able to honestly answer. He asked a lot of questions about you and Maria that I didn't give him answers to. Apparently, they know that you were running from the Texican government. I told him that both of you are considered Citizens of Yeti Mountain and are to be afforded complete diplomatic immunity. He wasn't happy about that. I think he had intended to arrest you."

Charles had wondered if anyone besides Hilliard had seen the footage from the Texican's Most Wanted piece. It would have been foolish to think they had not, but he had hoped.

Ming moved close "Don't forget to check your pockets." Charles didn't know how Ming knew about that but was glad of the reminder. Reaching into his pocket he found a note. He wished he had found it earlier but in the trauma of the night hadn't even considered looking. The note was short but sweet to his soul.

> *Something is going on. I'm going to step out to investigate, I'm sure Butters will come with me.*
> *The actor is a lot more than he is pretending to be. Don't trust his act. I love you.*
> *~Maria*

Relief washed over him and was quickly followed by confusion. Where had she gone? Rory Jones was more than he appeared? How the hell had she put this note in his pocket? When had she written it, and how had she placed it?

He was grateful for it. It gave him hope that Maria and Butters were still alive and also out there somewhere on the offensive. It gave them a starting point for figuring out what was going on.

"See if you can set up a meeting with Rory Jones," he said to Frank while allowing him to read the note. Then, despite a sentimental desire to fold up the note and save it, he tore it into pieces and flushed most of them. He simply couldn't let go of the piece that said, "I love you" and slipped it into his other pocket.

"I have a meeting with PM Jones later today," Frank said. "It's why I wanted you to come down, I want you to be there. They also requested you attend."

This was a surprise. It might work in their favor. "PM Jones' older brother is an actor named Rory Jones. I think you should set up a meeting with him too…but wait until after we talk with the PM. Did he give a reason for the meeting?"

Frank nodded. "He wants to start the process of a defensive pact with a mutual technology treaty."

Jesus, these guys moved quickly. Charles would have thought finding the missing President and other PM would have been the only priority, but in light of the suspicion being thrown on Rory Jones by Maria, and now this strangely urgent diplomatic meeting, Charles began to think that there were much bigger things going on than an RSA terrorism event.

Chapter 6

The meeting with PM Jones took place at the presidential residence, which was not where the Prime Minister usually worked. As an ambassador, Frank had diplomatic liberty to move where he wanted despite the lockdown. Even without that, having a meeting with the PM was probably a reason that it could be ignored. The presidential residence was less of a palace and more of a big Bavarian chateau. PM Jones sat behind the president's desk. It was obvious that he had been going through paperwork and desk drawers. The dark bags under his eyes made it clear that he had not slept.

"Pardon me bringing you here for this," PM Jones said as they were escorted into the room. He was a very handsome man. Sandy brown hair, a light beard, and sharp angular features that all sat under a perfect California tan even though it was winter. He wore a light blue cardigan sweater over a pair of faded blue jeans.

The PM smiled abashedly "No one knows how this happened or why. We don't have anyone claiming responsibility. What I'm saying to you now is not to leave this room, which we've searched and cleared of all recording devices. We found Prime Minister Duwali. His body, anyway. He was bound and decapitated. Again, there is no one claiming responsibility, and we don't have a motive. He and I have gone head-to-head many times over the years, but I respected him and enjoyed much of the time we spent together when we weren't engaged in arguments over governance."

Jones had tears in his eyes. "We have to assume that President Weissman has also been executed, but we are hoping that isn't the case. The footage that should have shown us what happened was erased by a device of a type we've never seen before. We thought that much of our technology was pulse proof, but it seems that we got lazy inside the capitol because the building itself was impregnable and protected from the outside.

"I'm sharing all of this because I know that some suspicion has been cast on your missing companion and her attaché. That suspicion will remain until we know more about everything that has happened. Personally, I am sure that your names will be cleared." Charles didn't like the way this was heading. "As a diplomatic party, you have certain rights, but these are extraordinary times. As such, nothing is as it was. I've declared martial law until we discover what has happened. I've drafted special emergency powers that allow me to assume the title of Prime President, a combined role and powers of our two prime ministers and the president."

So, this was a coup.

"Yeti Mountain has the unique opportunity to be the first nation to align with the new Bear and Salmon Republic. I've taken the liberty of drafting the agreement which will allow us to share our entertainment and surveillance control systems with your young nation and grant us access to some of the technology we suspect you have. Normally this wouldn't be a priority, but I believe the celebrity status you have achieved will help pave the way for our population to accept the new order of things. Also, since we expect things to be chaotic here at the capital for some time, you would be free to head to the Seattle spaceport and begin training right away."

It was a lot to take in. Charles looked at Frank, hoping the yeti would ask for some time or consult with him before making a decision. It was immediately clear that wasn't going to happen.

"You must think we are a bunch of stupid animals," Frank said from behind a clenched jaw. "We are not going to be used for some PR stunt that will enable you to seize power from the nation that we came here to form an alliance with, and we're not going anywhere until we find our friend."

"I do hope that you will reconsider that," PM Jones said to them "Maybe you can talk some sense to him." He was looking at Charles as he said that. "It's no way to start a diplomatic friendship with incarceration."

Charles knew Frank well enough to know that even if he wanted to, there was no way to change his mind once it was made up. Frank had definitely made up his mind. "You run the risk of starting a war with Yeti

Mountain. Trust me, Prime Minister, you do not want to be on the receiving end of the technology we have at our disposal."

The PM laughed. "You are a bunch of hounds that have taken control of your master's kennel. There is nothing you can do to us. Yeti Mountain is an abomination, and you and all your abominable snowman friends will soon be wiped away from the planet. Thank you for making my decisions easier. Guards. Take them away. Every member of their party. I want them all locked up and never heard from again."

"You can't do this," Charles said. It was a silly thing to say, and he knew it when he said it but sometimes melodramatic lines force themselves on the unwilling.

"Of course I can," PM Jones said. "If you had agreed to my offer, that would have been helpful. Yet, it is more helpful to be able to blame this entire thing on Yeti Mountain. Thank you, and we'll be seeing each other again—on execution day."

Charles looked at Ming wondering if they should fight. Ming, recognizing the question shook his head. There were too many soldiers and policemen around them. They quickly moved in and cuffed them all with plastic straps. Frank had an old-fashioned leg iron snapped onto his ankle and a metal collar snapped around his neck. They were marched out of the Weissman's office, but where the house and driveway had been empty before, now there were dozens of reporters, cameras, and microphones.

"Did you kill President Weissman?" a reporter shouted.

"Is it true that the Yeti ripped off PM Duwali's head?" another demanded of Charles as he walked by.

Another reporter was giving an on-air monologue with them walking by in the background "...the unprecedented attack on the capital by Yeti Mountain is an act of war. Spokesmen from the RSA and the Texican Nation have both condemned the act of terrorism and offered their full support to acting Prime President Jones as he navigates our nation's biggest crisis in over a century. We are expecting a statement from P.P. Jones in just a few minutes."

Despite the gravity of the situation and the unexpected circumstances which had led to Charles once again being escorted to a prison cell in the future. He couldn't help laughing as he heard the reporter give Jones his new designation. This had obviously not been vetted.

Charles decided to at least use the moment to sew doubt and

mockery even as he struggled to keep a smile from reaching his lips "Peepee Jones is a liar and a criminal. He is stealing your—"

Everything went black as a policeman tasered Charles unconscious.

Chapter 7

Maria had never been happier. Until recently, the idea of a happy android was something that probably would have sounded silly even to her, and she was an android. Technically, she did have some biological parts but only in the broadest sense of the word biological. There were parts of her that had been and continued to grow in an organic manner, but which had actually been created using the same processes that her non-organic parts worked with. Her cells constantly reproduced themselves, just like those in humans and other animals, but in a slower and much more organized manner. All of her cellular reproduction was driven by smart nanites that she could consciously control and organize, because unlike other sentient lifeforms on Earth, her data processing capability was a part of her awareness.

A human, for example, had large parts of their brain, their nervous system, and their other bodily functions that even the most conscious among them were only thirty to forty percent aware of. Maria's brain, being organized as a series of quantum processors that were spread throughout her entire body, was fully aware and participating in every bit of her functioning. Her "biology" was conscious of itself and thus a part of her self-awareness.

That was the reason she would have thought a "happy" android was an impossibility. She would have explained that since she was fully in control of her neurochemical limbic system and the release of dopamine-like substances that cause happiness, that actual happiness was not a thing that might be considered. She could make herself laugh, she could make herself feel good, she could watch centuries old episodes of *Friends* or *I Love Lucy* and allow herself to feel that unexpected moment of mirthful surprise that caused laughter, but only if she intentionally closed off portions of her processing. She liked laughing, she enjoyed the sensations of created moments of positivity, but none of that was happiness. Happiness was an unsolicited and unexpected satisfaction with one's state of being. A feeling of, "this is all I want and it's good enough to stop tweaking it and simply be present with it," and that feeling seemed to require a spontaneous reaction where the conscious met the unconscious. Maria was a fully conscious being.

Or so she had believed, until she met Charles. When she had first seen him sitting there looking lost in Dr. Rodriguez's Texican laboratory, she had felt a tiny thrill run through her processors that had seemed to come from nowhere. When she ran a diagnostic on herself, it appeared to have been a spontaneously born electrical charge that caused a chain reaction of events in her limbic systems. It had caused her to blush. It was a new and strange sensation.

If that had been the only time it happened, it would have just been a malfunction or anomaly, but it kept happening whenever she interacted with him. She found herself wanting to impress him with her abilities, her personality, her whatever. She just really wanted him to like her.

And he did. She had thought that would be the end of it but oddly, she discovered that she found everything about him to be... wonderful.

She loved the way he smelled. He had a different scent than other humans. She liked the way he walked and talked, and she found herself in awe of the way he adapted to situations and the way he thought about them.

He wasn't perfect. There were things about him that were very sub-optimized, but she found those easy to live with by virtue of all the things about him that activated her. When he saw her lose her temper—the first time it had happened—she had expected him to change the way he treated her, but he had smiled and treated her with respect. She had thought that when she clearly demonstrated how non-human she was, he would start to treat her as a machine or a pet as others had done.

But he didn't. In turn, instead of losing respect for him, hers grew as he demonstrated who he was. The fact that he liked her, loved her, made her value him even more.

She was in love with Charles. If she had been a human, she might have taken years to journal, think, obsess, ponder, and explore what all of this meant.

But she was an android. There was no need for her to go through the entire teenage first crush experience. She realized within a few days that there was some other force acting on her, and she was not in control of it. It was a feeling that went against everything she had thought she knew about herself and about humans. If there was a force acting on her and causing her to produce chemicals and sensations in an unconscious way, it was very likely that many of her previous explanations of how and why humans did what they did were wrong. Her conclusion was that love was something that existed outside of the known forces of the universe. She was fascinated by it and dedicated as many of her subroutines to tracking it down as she could, but with no luck.

Meeting Frank and the other Yeti had confirmed her conclusion without getting her any closer to solving where love came from. The Yeti were created biological creatures who also experienced the sensation of love. It had not been built into them; it had appeared spontaneously. Love, anger, hatred, and happiness—they were not as easily explained as she had thought, but she knew one thing for sure: she was happy and had never been happier.

She was there, at the ball with the man she loved, enjoying a moment of pure bliss when she caught sight of something that should not have been there. An in-and-out fading of electrical energy that separated the air molecules and moved towards the back of the rotunda ballroom.

"I'm going to find the washroom," she said to Charles as she slid a note in his pocket which she had instantly generated from sloughed off skin cells that she needed to recycle anyway. She was bored with the other humans Charles was talking with, though the actor, Rory Jones had given off more biological "lying signals" than she had ever encountered in a human. It was a stark contrast to Charles who didn't have a single lie in him or if he did, was somehow able to hide them from her. She had never doubted her ability to read human signals before him. It was something else that drew her to him. He created an uncertainty in her that had never existed before.

She hated leaving him with the liar, but the unnatural collection of molecules was moving away from her and there was no way to explain things to him without giving away more than she was willing to the other guests. So, the washroom was the easiest exit. She followed the molecular glitch through the ballroom to the exit. She knew cameras were following her every movement and was aware that Butters was discreetly tailing her. She liked Butters. Butters was far more optimized than most of her human counterparts but pretended to be less optimized to give herself a strategic advantage—sort of like Phoebe from *Friends*. She motioned for Butters to join her before they went outside.

The security detail at the door asked if they wanted their coats. She declined, but he insisted and sent a runner to get them.

"We just need a moment of fresh air," she said. Honestly, it was probably better because Butters would have frozen without her coat. The glitch waited just beyond the building's steps. She was sure of it.

With their coats on, they went down the steps. "Do you see how beautiful the night is?" Maria asked Butters, motioning towards the glitch. She could sense that Butters knew something was happening, and now she confirmed that Butters could not see the glitch. Once again, she was impressed by the woman's ability to hold her tongue and not ask what was happening. The glitch followed a winding path out to the lakefront and onto one of the pontoon docks. The lights in the area flickered for a moment before going out. Maria could see the glitch materializing.

The glitch formed into a human male. The normally stoic Butters gasped and was ready to go defensive, but Maria grabbed her arm and steadied her. "Stand down, it's all right."

She suspected it to be true, and even if it weren't there was probably nothing Butters could do.

The male figure stepped forward.

"I am Khenpo of the Ikshavakra," he said. His voice was human but not human. "There is an imminent danger that must be stopped. The frequencies of this place make it impossible for us to intervene, so we come to you with a warning and a plea for your assistance."

"The RSA has come into possession of a pressurized energy substance known as genodium. We should never have let this happen, but the past is immutable. Genodium, when combined with the broadcasting technology which the Bear and Salmon Republic holds, will end free will among humanity. We are working to recover the genodium, but it is essential that the broadcast control systems of the BSR not be shared especially with the RSA."

"You must keep any alliance from happening between them. We know that we are asking much without your knowing us or our mission, but it is essential that you do this, or all is lost. I bring you this so you can learn more of us and see the truth of my words."

Khenpo held out a thick gold chain from which dangled a large tooth set with gemstones. Maria accepted it.

"Encoded in the gems is our history and within the tooth is a molecule of genodium so that you may see the danger it poses. The molecule is locked in an inert state and will incinerate itself if removed from the encasing. The future of all relies upon you. I wish I could explain more, but my time here is through."

Khenpo winked out of existence. In that same moment, the pandemonium of the explosion within the capitol began.

"We are not going back in there," Butters said.

"But Charles…" Maria could have thrown Butters aside but knew she was right.

"Ming will take care of him and besides, he seems more than capable of taking care of himself. We have to go. *Now*." Butters ran down the dock towards land, and Maria followed. There was nothing they could do now but find someplace secure to lay low.

"Where are we going?" Maria asked.

"We're going back to the *Coho*. As soon as we are able, we will get Charles, Ming, and Frank there too."

Chapter 8

Getting to the *Coho* wasn't as hard as Maria might have imagined it would be. The chaos of the bombing had all eyes focused on the capitol building, and the electrical surges had disrupted a lot of the surveillance systems. Butters was able to get them underground, in a cart, and to the hangar in less than twenty minutes. By the time Charles got back to his hotel room, Maria and Butters were boarding the *Coho*. Maria could have gotten there without Butter's assistance, but she innately knew that allowing humans to "help" her made her more human in their eyes and while it was illogical, that was something that she desperately wanted: to be treated the same as any other person.

Commander Smiley was waiting for them. Agitated energy crackled from her skin, and although it seemed impossible, her eyes and mouth were more severe than usual. There was no tearful reunion between Butters and Smiley. There was not so much as a hello. All three women understood it was unnecessary and only stood in the way of their individual missions.

The Commander looked at them both and said, "Good, you're here. Report."

Butters snapped to attention and threw a crisp salute. "Ma'am. I suggest we move to the security of your ready room." Smiley's eyes widened just a bit, Maria could tell she was surprised by the side-stepping of her command, but she nodded and turned heel. Maria and Butters followed.

Once in the ready room, Butters didn't hold back. "I think there is a coup underway and that you should recall all trusted personnel from shore leave ASAP, Ma'am. We encountered a foreign, possibly alien agent who informed us that the RSA is making moves that endanger the free will of everyone. It is my opinion that the bombing at the capitol is only the beginning."

Smiley now turned towards Maria. Maria had no duty or connection to Commander Smiley in a military sense because she was a Texican citizen as well as a citizen and representative from Yeti Mountain, but it was clear to her that Commander Smiley was an ally. Charles liked and trusted Smiley, and that was enough for her.

"We don't know the status of Frank, Charles, Ming or any of the guests at the ball," Maria said. "My recommendation based on our interaction with the foreign alien is that we operate on a basis of unknown unknowns and carefully consider who to listen to, who to ally with, and who to be careful of. I have verified that the foreign alien, Khenpo, was telling us the truth."

During the trip to the *Coho*, her sensors and processors had opened the data archive inside the jewels of the tooth Khenpo had given her. Somehow, he had known she would have the ability to do this. She had analyzed the properties of the genodium molecule, and while unable to detail all that it might do, in theory, she could see that what Khenpo had told them was true.

Commander Smiley nodded. "I'm glad you're with us, Maria, I'd like to give you a special field commission of Colonel based on your unique abilities and skills. I will need you and *Captain* Butters—" She emphasized the rank to make sure that both of them understood that Butters' promotion. "—to carry out some unorthodox duties since we are going to have to depart without clearance. It will be helpful for you to have rank. Do you have a last name Maria?"

She didn't have a last name. She decided to take Frank's.

"Actor," she said.

Smiley's eyebrows shot up. "You two are married? The world will never cease to surprise me. I'll draw up the paperwork and issue the electro-tagged insignia for your commission. I assume that's a yes on entering my command. Captain Butters, recall all the Marines from shore duty. Colonel Actor—I'm just going to keep calling you Maria, actually—come with me. I'll brief you on what you need to know and swear you in as an officer of the BSR. You will be seeing some unique aspects of the *Coho* that will require an oath to the BSR."

Maria felt a strange thrill coursing through her. She had been forced to manually suppress a blush response when Smiley said they were married. They weren't, of course, but the idea of it sent a thrill through her body. She had no idea why but didn't spend too much processing time analyzing it.

By the time morning came, most of the necessary tasks had been completed. With the exception of Ming and Sergeant Pallido, all of the Marines had been recalled and were onboard. The hotel where Frank and Charles were housed was on a severe surveillance lockdown. There were unusual levels of security in place that didn't allow the usual access that Smiley and her network should have had. The surveillance camera system had been secured against the military accessing it, and the capitol police who were more loyal to the entertainment faction than the military faction had key control of all urban areas.

From the *Coho,* still parked in the hangar, they watched the broadcast news with the rest of the world. The speculation about Yeti Mountain being behind the bombing, the angry drumming of the hawkish media heads, and finally they saw their friends being led out of the presidential residence as prisoners.

"They can't do that," Butters said. "What about diplomatic immunity?"

"It seems to me they don't care about anything but seizing power at this point," Commander Smiley said. "We need to take off, right now." They watched as Charles was tazed into unconsciousness.

"I'm going to rip that policeman's head off," Maria said. She had never felt this kind of anger before. It burned white hot.

"Holy shit," Butters had backed up against the wall.

"Colonel," Commander Smiley barked out "Stand down and get control of yourself at once."

Smiley's order brought Maria back to her senses. Only then could Maria see that the room was filled with electric blue light pouring from the tooth necklace. Maria checked and the molecule was still contained and inert within, the light faded as she regained control of her consciousness. Her processors told her that the reaction had started at her positronic core and then somehow had focused into the jewels of the tooth where the emotional energy had been converted into light.

"Want to tell us what that was?" Smiley said.

"I'm not sure at the moment," Maria said. "Thank you for bringing me back, now that I'm aware of it, I should be able to control it, but that was a completely unexpected phenomenon."

Moving from the wall, Butter's asked "Do you think it was a trap of some sort from Khenpo?"

Maria shook her head no. "There's no way they could have known that would happen. I think this is a happy accident."

"Why happy?" Commander Smiley asked.

"No one here is dead yet," Maria said as if it was the clearest and simplest thing in the world.

Smiley turned to the intercom. "Prepare for emergency takeoff," she said into the mic. A computer voice took over and began the countdown and preparation. The *Coho* shook as the engines powered up. Smiley switched to the fleet control channel. "Attention all BSR personnel. The security situation in the Capitol has gone code red. It is not clear what the events of the last twelve hours mean. It is recommended that all military personnel, vehicles, and armor be withdrawn from Big Bear until the situation is clarified. It is my recommendation that the military leadership convene a martial withdrawal from civilian control until matters are operationally clear."

"What did you just do, Ma'am? What does that mean?" Butters wouldn't normally have asked but this was completely unprecedented.

"I don't know if it will work, but essentially, I just took military control away from Jones. In a situation like this, the military can elect to divorce from civilian chains of command until the validity of the chains have been verified."

"Does that leave the BSR defenseless?" Maria asked.

"Absolutely not," Smiley said. "We will keep doing our jobs but without civilian oversight. Though, I think it is likely that some units and personnel will choose to disregard the code red directive. If enough of the top brass sides with Jones, then it is already over. I don't think he has that level of support yet though."

"It sounds like civil war," Maria observed.

"Yes, it does," Commander Smiley turned to the console as the ship began to lift off.

Chapter 9

The view-screens on the console erupted in activity as police ran into the hangar pointing weapons at the *Coho*. Maria wasn't sure what Commander Smiley's reaction would be but looking at her face, it almost appeared she was grinning. It was a horrifying sight.

"These fracking ground pounders don't seem to know anything about Marine landing craft," she chuckled. "While it would be sort of fun to flame them, technically they are on the same team as we are. So, let's just disable them for a few days with a sonic burst."

A visible shockwave of ultra-sonic sound pulsed outwards from the *Coho*, knocking the shouting policemen and women from their feet and turning their shouting faces into painful grimaces before the solace of unconsciousness hit them.

"It's non-lethal?" Maria asked.

Smiley was definitely enjoying herself. "Yes, and while we haven't ever used it on this scale before, it should cause non-permanent damage to their inner ears which will make it impossible for them to stand up for about seventy-two hours."

Maria could see that some of the hardier police were still conscious and attempting to stand up without success. They were left with no mechanism to balance. It didn't stop them from pointing their weapons and shooting though.

"Butters, zap those bastards that are still awake."

Butters used a targeting matrix to send bolts of lightning out to those who were still conscious.

"Also non-lethal?" Maria asked.

"Barely," Smiley said. "If they have heart problems it might end them."

They were airborne now. The *Coho* was fully fueled, repaired, and functional. The directed EMP that Maria had used to knock it out of the sky at Yeti Mountain had been one of the only vulnerabilities the ship had.

"We're fully protected from pulse weapons now," Smiley said to her. "Thank you for pointing out that vulnerability."

"There are always weak points," Maria cautioned.

"Well, there are a lot less of them here than there were previously," Commander Smiley said.

"Colonel," she said to Maria "Do you have any sort of tracking device attached to your husband."

Maria felt that inner thrill again as Smiley referred to Charles as her husband. What in the world was that?

"Yes, Ma'am. I can share that information on the screen now." The note she'd placed in his pocket was made from her cells and effectively worked as a tracker.

"It looks like they are on the way to 'the Zoo,'" Commander Smiley said. "My guess is they will be given a kangaroo court trial, found guilty, and executed within the hour. We don't have time to wait. This is going to be messy."

"What is 'the Zoo'?" Maria asked. There was no record of it in her notes. According to her notes there had once been a small zoo in Big Bear, but it had been closed more than a century before. It had been located in a small flat valley called Moon Ridge.

"The Zoo is where we keep the animals," Smiley explained. "It's our federal lockup and penitentiary. Technically there are no prisons in the BSR, but sometimes people are too important to kill and too dangerous to allow to be free. The Zoo is like a halfway house where prisoners are kept for short term before they are either executed or expelled from the BSR. With the way things have been going, I don't think they are going to risk sending Frank back to Yeti Mountain or allowing Charles to go free."

"How long will it take to get there?" Maria asked. She didn't know everything, even though sometimes she was treated as if she did.

"We're here," Smiley said. "We're about to commit treason. And, unfortunately, if we are breaking some animals out of the Zoo, we have to break all of them out. These are the eggs that get broken to make the omelet."

The screens showed a star shaped building made of thick weathered concrete. It was surrounded by massive ponderosa pines that created an ad hoc fence inside of which armored vehicles moved.

"Why don't they see you?" Maria asked.

"We're in subspace mode," Commander Smiley said. "Right now, the *Coho* technically doesn't exist. We are phased between molecules of the present and the past."

"I didn't know this kind of technology existed," Maria said.

"As of right now you are one of a dozen people who are aware of it. President Weissman, some top brass, the scientists who developed it, and I are the only ones. If you weren't already an officer in the BSR, it would be a secret you would have to die for knowing."

"Ma'am," Butters interrupted. "They are arriving in approximately 45 seconds."

"Well, let's welcome them with a surprise," Smiley answered. "As soon as we phase out of subspace, hit the entire motorcade with a directed electro-magnetic pulse. At the same time, blast the gates of the zoo open. I don't know what kind of animals they have in there currently but keeping them secure should be their priority. Our priority is Colonel Actor's husband and the Yeti Ambassador. Deploy with six Marines in battle suits and extract our people. If we do this right, there should be no casualties."

"What do you want me to do, Ma'am?" Maria asked.

"I need you to figure out how we escape from Big Bear without getting blown out of the sky. I don't have any idea how we are going to do that, but if anyone can compute it, I'm sure that person is you. Take my console and get to work."

Maria moved to the console. She was immediately able to see that Commander Smiley was correct. There was no possible way they were going to be able to fly out.

They were trapped.

Chapter 10

Charles wasn't feeling good about the situation. He was usually stoic in the face of long odds, but this felt worse than usual. He had no idea where Maria was, let alone how he would rescue her. He desperately wanted to be her knight in shining armor, but here he was, a prisoner once again.

"This reminds me of the time I took you prisoner," Frank said to him cheerily. "This is the first time for me. I wondered what it might feel like. Do you think their torture chamber will be worse than the one at Yeti Mountain?"

Charles instantly felt better. The memory of the Yeti Mountain torture chamber even brought a smile to his face. It had looked like a hotel gym. He was sure there must have been some terrible stuff in it, but thankfully it had never come to that. Frank, as usual, looked upbeat.

"I liked the Yeti guards a lot better than these guys," Charles motioned with his thumb to the unsmiling police in body armor. He had tried to converse with them, but they were stone faced and silent. They knew they were participating in a coup, and they hoped they had picked the right side.

"That's enough chatter," one of the guards barked at them. Charles wondered if he was offended at being liked less than the Yeti.

Charles didn't have any gambits to play. They were loaded into an armored bus and sent on their way. "Take them to Moon Ridge," a guard said to him. It sounded like a lovely place. Charles liked the naming conventions he'd heard so far in the BSR. Most of the names were nouns with a descriptive noun attached. Moon Ridge. Boulder Bay. Bear Lake. Barton Flat. Maybe it was that they were in English rather than Spanish, but he found the names both rustic and endearing.

Moon Ridge in particular didn't sound like a terrible place to be sent to. The paddy wagon they were loaded in didn't have windows for him to look out.

The hum of the vehicle was the only indication they were moving. In a way, Charles missed the roll, pitch, and bumps of being in a vehicle from his time. It gave some indication of where you were going or at least that you were going. The hum of the vehicle stopped suddenly. There was a loud explosion and the sound of debris hitting the vehicle.

"What the...?" One of their captors was trying to use his comm device. "I'm going to see what's happening," he said to the other guards. He reached for the door handle and just as he grabbed it, he was ripped from the vehicle along with the door itself. Charles saw a giant robot looking down at him.

"The Marines are here," Ming said. Charles was relieved. Frank, who had been cramped up inside the bus—he was simply too large for most human vehicles—immediately moved out. The robot, actually a Marine in a battle suit, cut the plastic cuffs from Franks hands and motioned to Ming, Charles, and the others to come forward to do the same.

The police didn't attempt to fight. They either ran or held their hands up in surrender. They were police, not soldiers. They weren't mentally or physically equipped to engage with a half dozen Marines in battle suits. Most of them were running towards a large concrete building that had been blasted open. The giant robot reached up and raised the armored visor so they could see her face. It was Butters.

"Is Maria with you?" Charles asked. He was overwhelmed with relief.

"She's fine," Butters said to him. "You guys get to the *Coho*. Ming, Palido, go suit up. I could use you both here in the field. There's something odd going on at the Zoo and Commander Smiley wants us to make sure we don't release any baddies that we shouldn't. We probably didn't need to blast it open, but since we did...let's have a look."

The battlefield was dead quiet. Since the police had chosen to run away or surrender, and all the vehicles and electronics had been fried. There was an immense silence. The loudest noise was the crunch of the snow as they ran towards the *Coho*. Nonetheless, the feeling of fleeing captivity came with a dread at being shot from behind. It wasn't far, but the time it took them to get to the open hatch felt like forever.

Frank's entire entourage were with them as they stepped into the receiving bay of the *Coho*. Commander Smiley was there to meet them.

"I'm glad to see that you've all made it. You Marines under my command are clear to suit up and engage," she motioned to Ming and Palido. "Frank, Charles, welcome home. You are clear to head up onto the ship. As for the rest of you, my apologies, but until you are properly vetted by my people, you will be quartered in the brig. Times are too uncertain, and since I don't know you, you won't get the run of my ship."

Charles was once again impressed by Smiley's preparedness.

"It's good to see you Commander," he held out his hand to her. She took it and shook it firmly.

"Likewise. Now get up to my bridge, your wife has been worried sick about you."

His wife? That was an unpleasant bump in his reality. He'd thought he left her three hundred years in the past on the day he was supposed to deliver the divorce papers. He'd never thought of Maria as his wife, though he was deeply in love with her and wanted to spend the rest of his life with her, so it didn't occur to him that it was Maria who Smiley was referring to. There was no time to question the commander however, so Charles went straight to the bridge.

"Can I go join the fight?" Frank asked Commander Smiley.

"Absolutely not. I know that you Yeti have great battle skills, but you are a diplomatic foreign national and now that you are secure. This is an internal BSR matter. Your safety is of the utmost importance right now. Head to the lounge and wait for me to connect you with the proper authorities so we can assure Yeti Mountain that you are safe."

On the way to the bridge, it finally dawned on Charles that the commander must have been talking about Maria. Where had she gotten the idea that they were married though?

Reaching the bridge, he found Maria immersed in data collection and analysis. She looked up at him, beaming. "I'm sorry I couldn't meet you when you came on board, but the commander gave me an impossible task. It's taking everything I have to find a way out of it."

"Maybe I can help," Charles said moving towards her. She met him halfway across the room, and they were in each other's arms. Reunited, relieved, happy. "She called you my wife."

Maria pulled away from him and stiffened. She looked at the

ground, abashed. "I'm sorry. I should have corrected her, but I liked it when she called you my husband."

"I'd like to be your husband," Charles said, pulling her to him and kissing her. "Will you marry me?"

Maria screamed like a girl seeing her rock star dream crush on a stage in front of her. It was a little over the top but it came from the heart. "Of course I will. You are all I want."

Their joy was ecstatic, but it was cut short as the *Coho* lost all power and everything went dark.

Chapter 11

It was less than thirty-seconds before the lights and the familiar hum of the *Coho's* systems powering up returned. As with all such things, it felt like an eternity as they waited for whatever was coming next, but nothing did. Unless you counted Frank bursting onto the bridge and shouting, "We've got the president."

"The actual president or Peepee Jones?" Charles asked.

"President Weissman. Come on, you guys need to see this."

"I've got to figure out how to get us out of here," Maria said, "or we're all going to be dead soon."

Frank's enthusiasm didn't wane. "No, you're fine. It's over. The military refused to support Peepee. Hundreds of battleships appeared, and the police forces surrendered. All of them. Weren't you watching the screens?" Frank motioned to the screens where they would have seen the entire thing unfold, but of course, they had been caught up in each other. They had missed the surrender as they surrendered to each other—in love.

Frank was too excited to pursue why they had missed it though. "Come on. It's amazing."

He led them to the deployment hatch where most of the Marines and personnel still on the ship had gathered. Overhead, the sky was filled with a blanket of ships. Commander Smiley stepped forward.

"Looks like we didn't need that impossible exit after all, Colonel Actor." Charles did a double-take before realizing Smiley was talking to Maria.

When had she been commissioned? It was going to take some getting used to, sharing his name with her, but he was happy to have the opportunity.

"I'm glad we didn't need it, but it wasn't impossible. I found a way. We could still take it if we need to."

Commander Smiley's jaw dropped. "You've got to be kidding me. You found a way? Explain it to me, briefly."

"By modifying the *Coho's* subspace drive, we could travel in-world, even if there aren't tunnels big enough—just as long as there is something. I'm assuming you have maps."

Smiley's eyes widened. "You are all ordered to forget you heard that. Colonel Actor, Mr. Actor, you will brief me on all of this later. Until that time, I order you to keep this information to yourself. For our security and the future, it is essential that no one else hears of this. You've done a great thing here, Colonel."

"Thank you, Ma'am," Maria said.

"So, that's it?" Charles asked, motioning to what had been the battlefield a few minutes earlier. What happened to the power on the *Coho*? Why did it go dark?"

Commander Smiley stood just a little taller. "I realized after our misadventure at Yeti Mountain that the *Coho* was vulnerable to pulse weapons, but there was an easy way to bypass that. Pulse weapons have a pre-telltale—split seconds before they are used, they convert huge amounts of air trapped hydrogen into hydrozone. I programmed the *Coho's* operating system to look for hydrozone spikes and if they were found to reset all vulnerable systems while also shielding with a nano-driven Farraday cage. The combination of actions, actually preserves systems and keeps them from getting fried, but it also creates a vulnerability."

Charles immediately understood the vulnerability part. "If you are in the air, you lose flight systems. I'm glad we were on the ground."

"There's an odd detail though," Commander Smiley said. "First, we didn't register any pulse weapons being used."

Overhead the BSR ships were making a statement by filling the sky of the capital with firepower that could not be matched. The ships moved in a coordinated dance that was both beautiful and oppressive.

"Where is President Weissman?" Charles asked. "What happened to the Jones brothers? Was Bryce Hilliard, the RSA agent found?" There was so much they needed to know.

"How did you know about the brother?" Commander Smiley asked. "That detail hasn't been released."

"We met him at the gala," Charles said. "He seemed to be hiding something."

"President Weissman was being held in the zoo. She should be joining us soon. Butters has her. The Marines are sweeping through the facility looking for other illegally held captives and making sure that the dangerous ones are still secure.

"As for the Jones brothers and Hilliard, they are gone without a trace. We've been watching Rory Jones for some time now. He may not seem like it, but we suspect that the older Jones actually orchestrated this whole thing. Not only did he guide and direct his younger brother, Prime Minister Jones, throughout his entire career, but we are fairly certain that he has been working with the RSA for decades now. Their father was a well-known RSA sympathizer, but it was thought that those connections died with him. Now, it appears not to have been the case."

"So, that's it? Everything is resolved now and tied up with a big bow?" It seemed very unlikely that was possible, but from Charles perspective, it looked like the good guys had won.

"Not even close," Commander Smiley grimaced. "We think the Jones brothers may have delivered exactly what we didn't want the RSA to get. It looks like Hilliard's mission was a success snatched from the jaws of defeat. We'll be lucky if all of this doesn't flash into a hot war. But, even if that is the case, make no mistake: we are at war with the RSA now. The moves they've made will have to be met. It's going to take every bit of influence I have to keep the hot heads on our side from launching an invasion or full-on assault, but I feel confident that would only end up working in the RSA's favor. No, this isn't over by a long shot."

Captain Butters and President Weissman now approached. Butters was wearing her battle armor, and the President was cradled in her arms like a child being protected by a giant robot parent after suffering some trauma. Butters set the President down gently on her feet. Weissman looked ragged and angry as hell.

"Thank you for the extraction, Commander Smiley. What the hell took you so long?" Weissman wasted no time on pleasantries. She looked at Maria, Frank, and Charles appraisingly. "I've heard of you three. Nice to meet you, and if you had a part in this, thank you."

"Colonel Actor was instrumental in making this work," Commander Smiley said.

"Colonel?" Weissman said looking at Charles. Smiley grabbed Weissman's shoulders and turned her towards Maria.

"This one, Ma'am. I swore her in with a battlefield commission. She's one of us now."

"Good." Weissman said. "You've all earned citizenship in the Bear and Salmon Republic if you want it. Now, get me to the capitol; right away."

"Yes Ma'am," Smiley said. "By your leave, I'm going to get there a bit slower than we have to and that will give you a chance to clean up in a stateroom." Weissman reached up to her hair, it was a disheveled mess and the dirt and smudges on her face made her look more tragic than heroic.

"Good idea, Commander. As always, I'm glad to have you on my side."

"This way Ma'am," Butters led the President away.

"What now?" Frank asked looking at the group questioningly.

"Now we have the hard job of cleaning up our house," Commander Smiley said. "Then we're going to need all of your help to resolve this. At some point, don't be surprised if we need you to go to the RSA."

Frank, Maria, and Charles all looked at each other.

"We'll do what we have to," Frank said.

"You'll need to stay here, Mr. Ambassador," Commander Smiley said "As for you two—"

"We've got a wedding to plan," Maria said stubbornly. "I'm not going anywhere before that is done."

A light of recognition flashed across Smiley's face.

"Congratulations to you both," she said. "I hope I'll be invited."

"You're going to officiate," Maria said.

It wasn't a question, and—despite Commander Smiley being her superior officer—she wasn't about to argue with an android in love.

Postscript: The Android's Wedding

Maria was going to explode if the flower arrangements weren't made on time. Not literally, although she could have if she so chose, but figuratively. The most frustrating thing about being a sentient super-being wasn't dealing with her own limitations, because those were a known quantity that she could always account for. Actually, it was dealing with the lack of humanity's ability to judge their own abilities accurately. It had taken her the equivalent of two hundred years processing time to realize that when most humans said they could do something, they were actually only thirty-five percent capable of delivering that. Not seventy-five, not even fifty, but thirty-five percent. She'd gotten used to it and generally made her adjustments accordingly, but they were down to the wire now.

The wedding was going to happen in three-hours with or without the flowers, but she wanted the flowers, dammit. Technically, she was only eleven-years old when measured in terms of sol- years but when measured in terms of processor-years she was closer to two-hundred-and-ten, but that didn't make it any easier to deal with a flowerless wedding. She had built multiple redundancies into the delivery. She had ordered from three different florists, she had set the delivery time for sixty-five percent earlier than necessary, and she had confirmed delivery the previous night and this morning.

All to no avail. The flowers still were not here.

She wished she could have complained about it to Charles, her husband-to-be, but Maria was sticking with all of the many bizarre and largely meaningless traditions she had read about from his time. The bride would not see the groom before the wedding and afterward she would smash a piece of pastry in his face. Charles had told her that none of that mattered, that all he cared about was her being happy. That had been yesterday and every day before yesterday since he had proposed. When he said it yesterday, she had responded to him the same as she had every other time.

"Don't you understand yet? This is what will make me happy," she griped. "I want a dream wedding."

"In that case," he told her "We should probably go to sleep."

She couldn't see if he was smiling when he said it, because he had rolled over on his side and gone to sleep. Was he making a clever pun or referring to the need to be well rested? She didn't need to rest. Her sleep was essentially a powered-down body with resources that would otherwise be controlling her movement and action being used to increase her ability to solve complex problems. She used a huge amount overnight as she ran subroutines to determine if Charles had meant she would be able to dream about a wedding or whether he was saying a dream wedding deserved good rest. Ultimately, she settled on a ninety-nine percent probability that he was making a pun.

There was a one hundred percent probability that she loved him—puns and all. Part of that was that he was so inscrutable. He was far harder to predict than others. She usually failed at it.

The florists arrived. All three of them. She asked Commander Jane Smiley, who would be conducting the marriage, to deal with the florists. While technically her commanding officer, Commander Smiley was happy to be given a task that involved dressing someone down. All of the florists would be paid—this was a state sponsored wedding, after all—but the florists were about to learn the true cost of overpromising and late-delivering: their dignity.

Maria had been battle commissioned during the troubles in the Bear and Salmon Republic's capitol six months earlier. In gratitude for her assistance in rescuing the President of the BSR, both she and Charles were given BSR citizenship and when Commander Smiley learned they were to be married, she had petitioned for the state to pay for everything. Maria did not waste this blank check.

The wedding was being held at the BSR Presidential Residence. The biggest names in BSR entertainment, politics, military, and sports were attending. Charles had suggested that it might be a good idea to stay off the radar and not become media personalities, but in analyzing the data, Maria had determined that the best protection they could have was to be famous—despite all the downsides it brought with it.

Charles didn't want to be famous. He was an accidental time-traveler from the twenty-first century. A small-hold Texas rancher who unexpectedly found himself three-hundred years in his future where he was caught up in international intrigue and unexpected emotional romance with a girl he never could have imagined existed. Maria laid out the benefits versus the costs and convinced him this was the better way.

Commander Smiley and the top brass in the BSR agreed. Having Maria and Charles become public figures not only would give them protection, but it would also create opportunities for sensitive trips to be easily explained as PR. Smiley still used her rank as designation despite having been raised to the position of co-Prime Minister. Her counterpart co-PM was a semi- conservative former late night talk show host named Sarah Black. Ms. Black was also at the wedding, though without an official part to play in it.

The wedding would be a spectacle, which was for certain. Charles' best-man was actually not a man at all. Frank was the ambassador from Yeti Mountain, a new nation that had recently formed in the depths of the perpetual blizzard that sat between the BSR and the Texican Nation. The bride and groom had also been granted citizenship to Yeti Mountain for the part they had played in the young country's birth. So far, there was no indication that there would be anything but harmony between the two nations, even though it had seemed possible while the chaos of the BSR president's abduction had taken place.

The public was not aware that Charles was a time-traveler, nor that Maria was an android. As far as they knew—Charles and Maria were Texican nationals who had helped liberate Yeti Mountain and come to the BSR to aid the Yeti Ambassador in his mission of building alliances with the friendly nations of the world. They had been vaulted into the spotlight by the abduction, and the BSR viewing public had fallen in love with them. A tabloid show had called them the Romeo and Juliet of Yeti Mountain and that was it. The public's imagination had taken off. There were those who said they were secretly part of a royal lineage that controlled Yeti Mountain, which was ridiculous because they weren't even yeti. The truth though, plays very little role in tabloid journalism.

And here they were.

Maria's bridesmaids were President Weissman, Klee, the ambassador from the Mutual Nation of Hawai'i, and Maria's friend Captain Butters of the BSR Marines. Frank's co-groomsmen were Benito Mussolini Rodriguez who was Charles' and Maria's friend from the Texican Nation, and also Chief Warrant Officer Ming, another BSR Marine.

Klee and Maria had become friends within moments of meeting one another. They were both "girly-girls" while not being girls at all really. Klee was eighty-five years old, though she didn't look a day over thirty-five and Maria...

Well, she was an android.

They both spent a considerable amount of time acting as if they had less going on upstairs than they really did. Klee explained her reason thus, "If they think you are smarter than them, people clam up like a pohaku," which was the Hawaiian word for a rock. Maria agreed. Klee was a surgeon, a diplomat, and a singer. That last one being the one that people made all their assumptions upon. It was an intentional dumbing down by design, plus, she really was a talented voice. She would be performing after the wedding at the reception.

Charles and Maria would not be attending. It was something for the guests, not for them.

With the flowers in place, the seating arranged, and the final preparations made, it was almost time for Maria to walk down the aisle. She didn't have a father or brother to "give her away." So instead, she decided to change this tradition up by dancing down the aisle. Charles hadn't thought this was a great idea, but Klee loved it.

After the two of them argued the case for it, he agreed, but only after Maria told him what song would be playing. Maria would dance down the aisle to the theme song of *Friends* the three-hundred-year-old sitcom which she had become enamored with when she was still living in a lab and trying to learn passable human behavior. Charles laughed when she told him her song choice.

"I don't know how I could disapprove of that," he smiled.

It was a catchy tune that somehow encouraged free form dancing. The wedding started with, "Here Comes the Bride," but after the first stanza segued into the *Friends* theme. The audience was prompted from overhead screens to "stand up and dance."

At first, they didn't but when they looked to the pulpit and saw the groom, Frank the Yeti, and a bunch of uniformed Marines busting a groove, they couldn't not dance. Maria sprang down the aisle in her beautiful designer gown doing cartwheels, tango, and freestyle moves the entire way. By the time she reached the pulpit, everyone in attendance or watching at home was smiling. This was not a tearful wedding.

Commander Smiley began "We are gathered here today to see two heroic figures, our friends, our comrades joined in wedded bliss for as long as they should choose to be. As their friend and commanding officer, I can tell you that these are two very special people—but you already know this. Their selfless dedication to the people of the Bear and Salmon Republic, Yeti Mountain, and each other has been an inspiration to me—to all of us. I know that I don't need to ask if anyone objects to this union. I only need to ask, 'Do you Maria and you Charles agree to love, honor, and respect one another from now until you should decide to part'?"

The last part of this was standard BSR wedding jargon. Most marriages in the BSR only lasted five to ten years. There were those people who chose to stay together longer, mostly small coasters but in the big coast cities of Vancouver, Seatac, Portland, SF, Los Hollywood, and Diegojuana marriage was a temporary state of being that people joined into for child-rearing or expense sharing partnerships. It was slightly more romantic than a business partnership, but generally, an utterly practical arrangement. People lived far longer lives and parenting had become a far less nuclear-family job than it had ever been. Grandparents took a larger role as they moved from the youth of their 20s-60s and became more available to act as teachers and caregivers. Short marriages weren't always the norm though, some marriages lasted until death, but this was far less likely than people simply deciding it was time to part.

Charles had no intention of ever leaving Maria. She was the most infinitely fascinating person he had ever encountered.

"I do," Charles said.

"I do too," Maria said with no gap.

Commander Smiley motioned for Frank to step forward. He held out a big furry hand and opened it to reveal two beautiful platinum rings. Charles and Maria took them and placed them upon one another's fingers. Their eyes met. Both of them burst into laughter and smiled at one another as the rest of the room faded from their reality.

The guests and officiates were, it must be admitted, somewhat shocked as the bride and groom burst into uncontrollable fits of laughter. Then Frank began to laugh, his booming peals of laughter filled the chamber and truth be told were contagious. Soon the bridesmaids and the guests were all laughing as well. This was the most bizarre wedding any of them would ever attend, there would be stories told about it and since this was the BSR, the whole thing was recorded and broadcast live to those who enjoyed watching such things. The laughter scene was memeified and shared endlessly. It wasn't long before other weddings began to copy some of the oddities including using the ancient theme song of 'Friends' and having the bride and groom burst into laughter at the altar. There were many attempts at recreating this moment, but in truth, the unexpected nature of it, the presence of Frank, and the first-time quality of it would never be matched.

After several happy minutes, the one person not laughing, Commander Jane Smiley, the officiate cleared her throat. It was all she had to do. The laughter subsided, but the smiles did not. Smiley's mouth was still unsmiling, but her eyes were filled with mirth.

"I now pronounce you spoused to one another," she said. "You may now demonstrate your attraction to one another by engaging in a public display of affection."

Charles knew that things had changed but this was too much. "If you don't mind," he said. "Would you just say 'I pronounce you husband and wife," and, "You may kiss the bride?'"

Smiley looked at Maria to see if she approved and got a quick nod yes. "I now pronounce you husband and wife," she said. "You may kiss the bride."

Charles stepped forward and wrapped his arms around Maria. She fell into his embrace. The moment their lips met, cheers erupted from the gathered guests. They were both strangers in a strange land, but now, in this moment, their lives became the property of the people of the BSR and the BSR became their family.

Maria threw the stunning bouquet of brightly colored flowers over her shoulder where it almost smashed into Klee, who somehow didn't see it coming. Luckily Chief Warrant Officer Ming was able to dive forward, snatch the flowers before they impacted, tumble onto the ground doing a somersault, and somehow end up back on his feet before turning and presenting the flowers to her. Klee accepted with a smile that made Ming blush.

There were many adventures ahead of them, but for now they walked hand-in-hand back down the aisle and left the Presidential residence. They climbed into a limodrone and disappeared from the screens as they flew south toward their honeymoon in Baja.

"I think we've found our home," Charles said to Maria as she piloted the craft towards the golden Pacific sunset.

"You are my home," she told him. "I just need to figure out how to increase your lifespan."

About the Authors

C. D. Damitio is an author, adventurer, and storyteller currently residing in Otaru, Japan. Hailing from California and Hawaii, Damitio's work draws inspiration from his global experiences. He blends humor, insight, and curiosity in his books. He regularly posts about his philosophy, travels, and the future at indgnified.substack.com. His books, including *The Keys to the Riad* and many others, are available on Amazon, Barnes & Noble, and everywhere books are sold. Active on social media and YouTube, he shares insights into his philosophy, travels, thoughts on the future, and creative projects.

Rionna Morgan is an internationally published, best-selling mystery suspense novelist. She was *Vagobond Magazine's* final Editor in Chief and is the author and creator of *The 7 Love Stories*. Her passion for the written word and the voices of those who write is powerful. She is a leading creator, speaker, and educator. Rionna has been a presenter at NFTNYC, The Academic Web3 Conference, and has been featured on Fortune.com and in *Celtic Life International*. She is always creating something new.

E. R. Donaldson began writing in earnest in 2017. He published his first novel, *Star Spire*, in December 2020 through Mythic North Press LLC. In 2022 he edited and published the anthology *Mythic Winter* with the goal of creating a paid venue for lesser-known authors. Since then, Donaldson has published a number of short works and serials on blockchain and other experimental digital mediums. His upcoming novel, *To Seize the Stars*, was shortlisted as a finalist for renown editor Tang Feng's SciFidea Dyson Sphere writing competition. When he's not writing, Donaldson spends his time with his wife and three children at their home in central Michigan.

Ameera Rashid, born and raised in the city of Lucknow, is currently

pursuing her master's degree in English Literature. A lifelong passion for reading sparked her fascination with storytelling from an early age. During the Covid lockdown, she finally found the opportunity to pick up the pen. What began as a distraction during challenging times soon became much more than a hobby. Over time, she honed her craft by participating in and winning multiple international writing contests. Her science fiction story, "Stranded," has been published in the *Mythic Winter*, available on from Mythic North Press.

T. Dylan Daniel is an author, philosopher, and scientist in Lubbock, Texas. A lifelong learner, Daniel has attended six different institutions of higher learning and has taught philosophy at two of them. Daniel is currently studying for his Ph.D in Cognition & Cognitive Neuroscience at Texas Tech University. His books include *Formal Dialectics* (2018) and *INEVITABLE: Distributed Cognition & Network Superintelligence* (2024). For more of his work, head to epicdylan.com.

Aparna Merchant (Quanta) is a bespoke fashion creator, fashion writer, and storyteller. The two disparate disciplines, for her, draw on each other - 'every piece of fashion ever authentically crafted must carry a story within it'. Her story and other creative writings are influenced by human life, and lean towards a metaphorical narration. Some of her short fictional works and verse can be read on t2.world. She has published NFT storytelling projects: S.Q.U.A.D. , Skullies, and Pixels For Christmas, on objkt.com. Seeking solutions for her own industry experience, she reports on the use of technology for a responsible fashion industry in her newsletter, Dress Me Digital, on substack.com. When not designing or writing, Merchant slow travels in search of her human existence.

Time Travelers

As with all art, it only truly comes to fruition when it finds its audience. This wouldn't have been possible without our generous backers on Kickstarter. Thank you to everyone who chipped in to make this anthology possible.

Alp Saldamli
Amber Eckert
Asakunotomohiro
Bill Kohn
Bryan Altaker
Captain Dan MT
Carolyn Roath
Chesscommands
Colleeen Feeney
Conrad Wade III
Denw Wade
Duane
Dylan Merz
Ed Keyes
Edward Carpenter
Fawn
Grace Lovart
Greg R. Fishbone
Ian C
José Antonio Muñiz Borrero
Juliet Delta Romeo

Keric
Kristen Deppe
Mark Findlater
Mark Kelsey
Marsha J. Obrien
OddWritings
Patrick Hay
Quanta
Quinine
Rionna Morgan
Rob in AUS
Shalvah & Zerah
Sophia Damitio
Steven Tomlinson
Surgarkaa (aka Jasper)
Thomas Bull
Wednaud J. Ronelus
Zack Fissel

www.ingramcontent.com/pod-product-compliance
Lightning Source LLC
Chambersburg PA
CBHW070839260626
47170CB00007B/2430